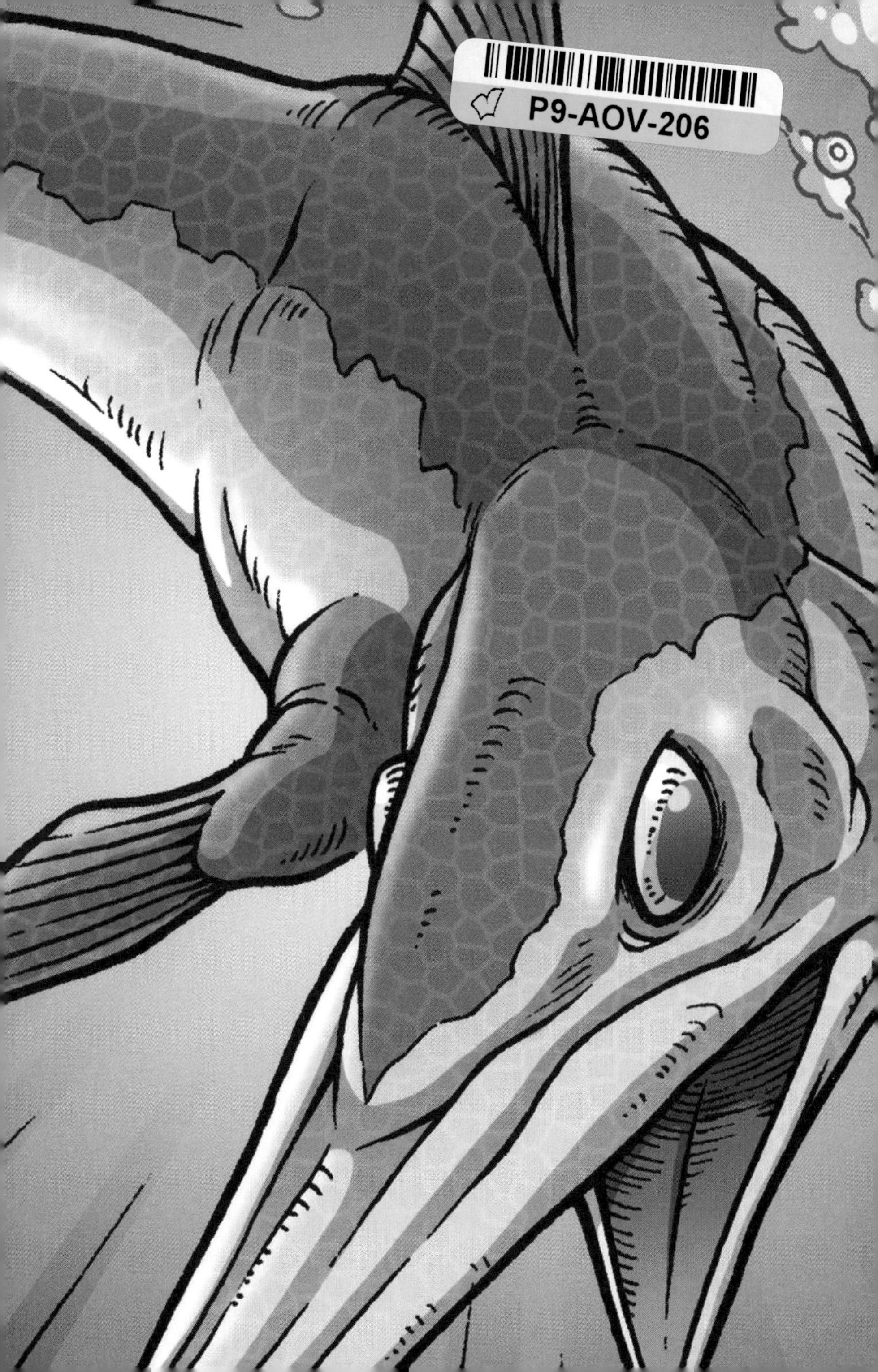

X-VENTURE XPLORERS™

KINGDOM OF ANIMALS

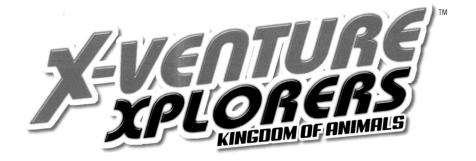

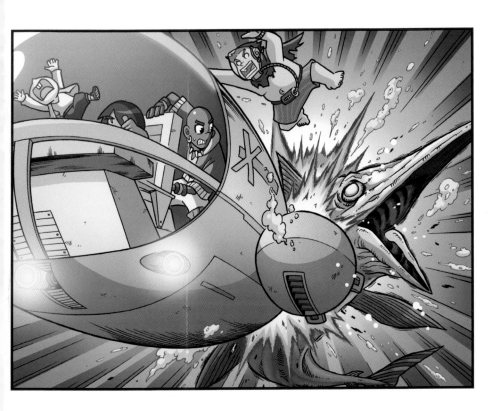

PAPERCUTZ™

#3 FISH OF FURY

© 2012 KADOKAWA GEMPAK STARZ.
All rights reserved.
Original Chinese edition published in 2012 by
KADOKAWA GEMPAK STARZ SDN. BHD., Malaysia.
English translation rights in
the United States arranged with
KADOKAWA GEMPAK STARZ SDN. BHD., Malaysia.
www.gempakstarz.com

All other editorial material © 2021 by Papercutz.
All rights reserved.

SLAIUM / MENG — Story
BLACK INK TEAM — Art
BLACK INK TEAM — Cover Illustration
BLACK INK TEAM / SANTA FUNG / PUPPETEER — Illustrators
SIEW / EVA / FUN FUN / MAX / HO — Coloring
KIAT — Translator

KENNY CHUA — Creative Director
KIAONG — Art Director
BEAN — Original Graphic & Layout
NIUH JIT ENG / ROSS BAUER — Original Editors

MARK McNABB — Editor & Production
JEFF WHITMAN — Managing Editor
JIM SALICRUP
Editor-in-Chief

Papercutz books may be purchased for business or promotional use.
For information on bulk purchase please contact Macmillan
Corporate and Premium Sales Department at (800) 221-7945 x5442.

ISBN HC: 978-1-5458-0697-5
ISBN PB: 978-1-5458-0698-2

Printed in Malaysia by Ultimate Print Sdn. Bhd.
June 2021

Distributed by Macmillan
First Papercutz Printing

In this volume of X-VENTURE XPLORERS, there is animated violence and gore that is a representation of natural and man-made occurrences that currently happen. Reader discretion is advised.

X-VENTURE XPLORERS™
KINGDOM OF ANIMALS

#3 FISH OF FURY

SLAIUM & MENG
Writers

BLACK INK TEAM
Art

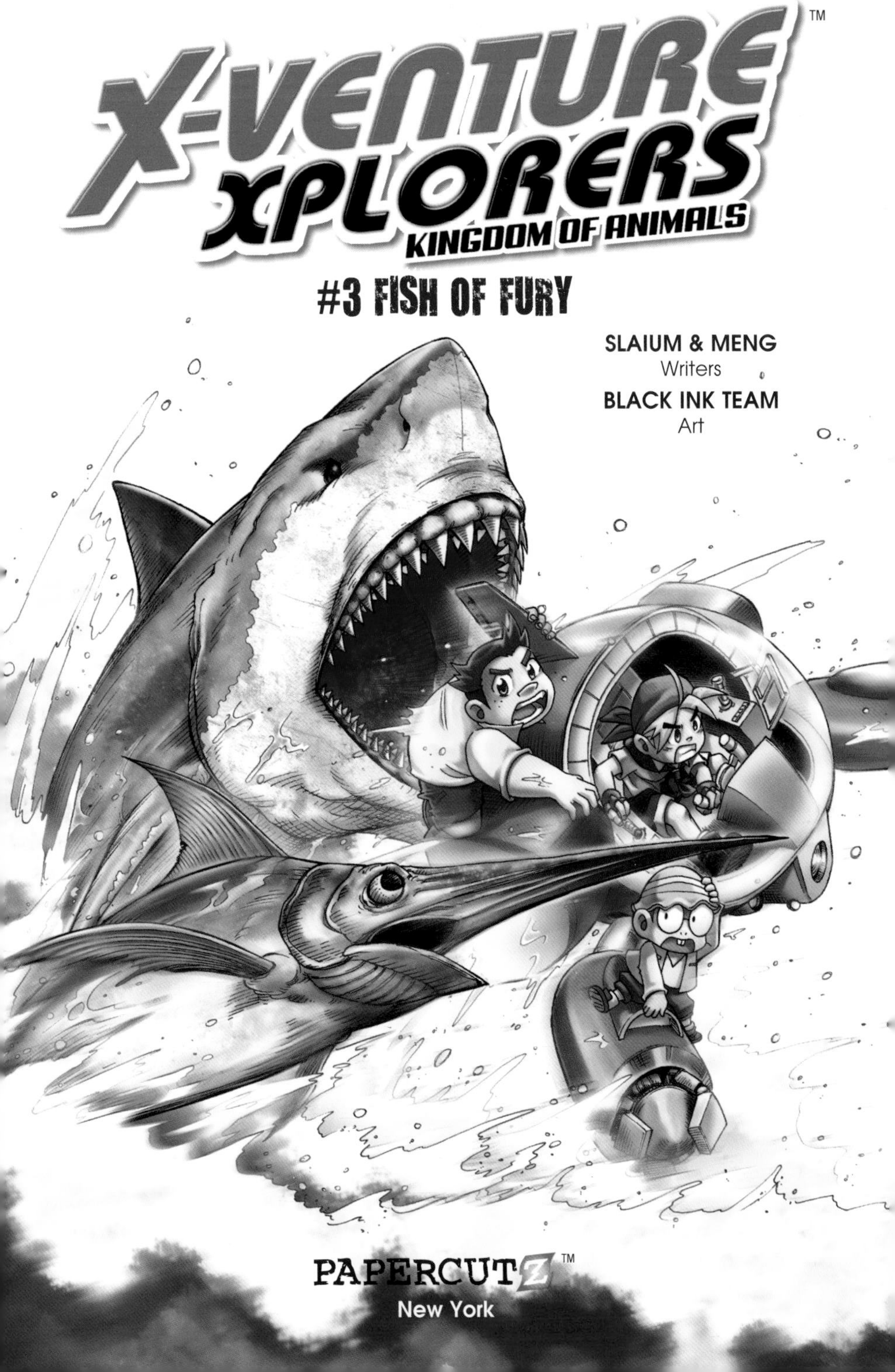

PAPERCUTZ™
New York

FOREWORD

As a result of the publication of numerous educational comics in recent years, the perception of comics as frivolous and fantastical fiction has slowly been changed. For students, the partnership of words and pictures has been observed to enhance information retention, and consequently comics are having an increasingly important role as part of the learning process. Educational comics have become one of the sources of extra-curricular knowledge; harnessing young learner's enthusiasm for well-visualized and creative stories which simultaneously convey comprehensible information.

X-VENTURE XPLORERS pits animal antagonists against each other. Battles between beasts of similar strength such as Lion Vs. Tiger, Elephant Vs. Rhinoceros, Boa Vs. Crocodile, and so forth not only offer young learners the joy of reading, but also a starting point to enjoy learning about the natural world.

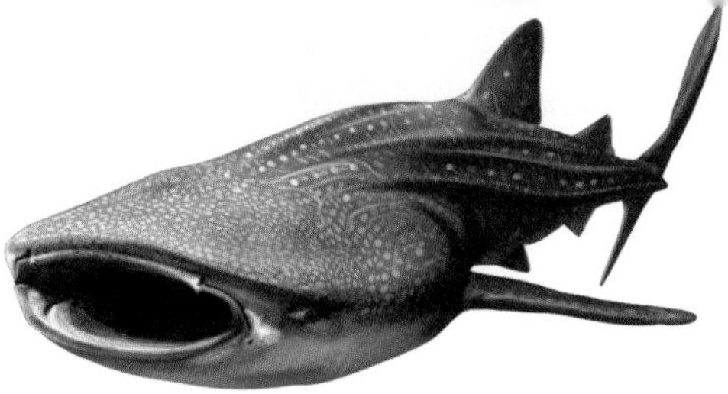

Upholding the principle of interesting scientific knowledge central to any X-VENTURE XPLORERS comic series, we provide young minds the space for imagination and help them explore the wonders of natural science. As an educational comic, this series prioritizes the moral values of love and friendship, courage and the joy of learning so as to help nurture the right values in our readers.

Incisive information alongside vivid visuals, interspersing the chapters of the story provide readers with ample and accessible knowledge of wildlife and their world. Additionally, to gauge what you have learned, you can test your wits by answering a short quiz presented after the story. With equal emphasis on entertainment and education, it ought to be clear that X-VENTURE XPLORERS represents value, fun, and furnishes a fruitful factual future for our formative friends!

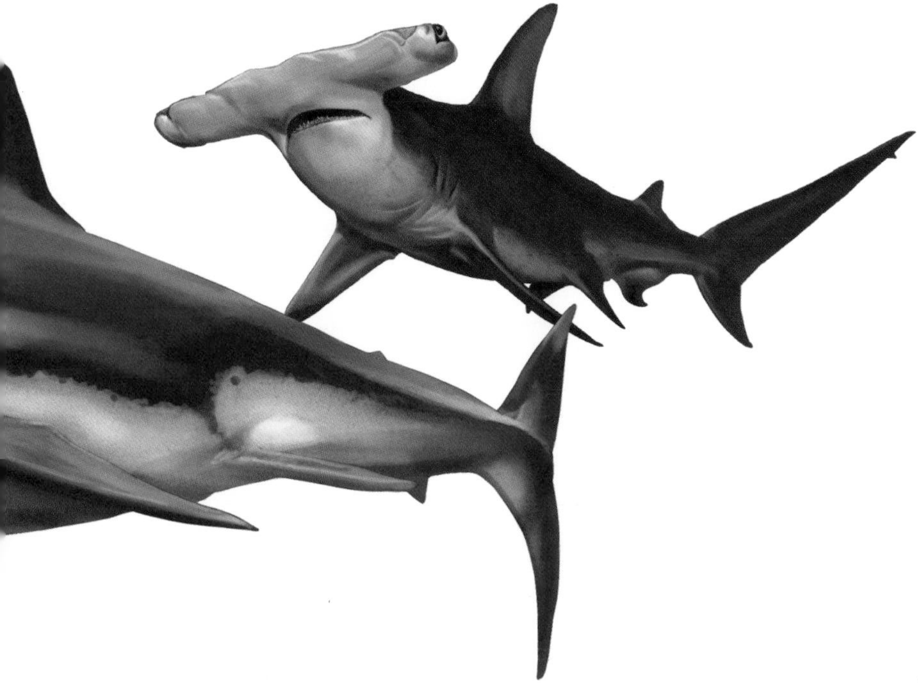

CAST

SHERRY

Hardworking and a keen learner, she wishes to become a veterinarian. She assumes the role of peacemaker, especially between Jake and Louis who argue constantly.

JAKE

Brave and passionate, he enjoys the company of animals and is proud of being a boy scout. He is often careless, however, causing trouble for himself and his friends.

TAZEN

A little native with a huge appetite who grew up in the Sumatran rainforest, raised by orangutans. Has the ability to communicate with animals, but finds humans a harder prospect.

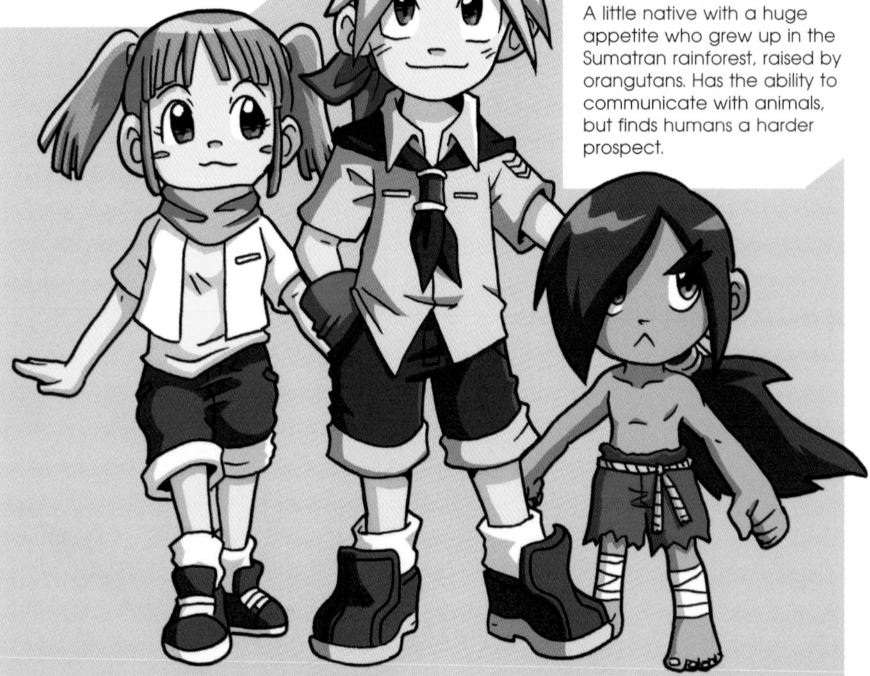

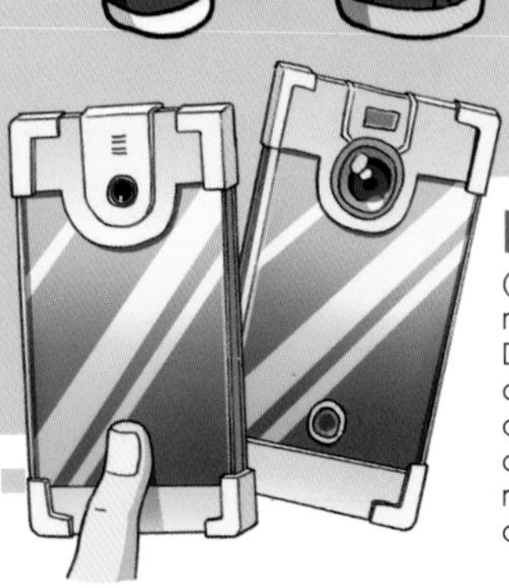

NLIZR

(Natural Life Zoographic Resource, more commonly known as "the analyzer") Dr. Darwin's e-evolution in evidence; able to record, analyze, extrapolate details pertaining to localized ecology, climate, lifeform identification, and much more via an instant uplink to the lab database.

LOUIS

Despite being loud, lazy, and constantly antagonizing Jake, he never accepts failure and is a very reliable partner during a crisis.

KWAME

A member of the Bushmen tribe of South Africa, he knows the wild like the back of his hand, constantly on the alert for potential threats, both animal and otherwise.

BEAN

Shy and quiet, and short in stature, makes up in extraordinary wealth of knowledge what he lacks in physical size.

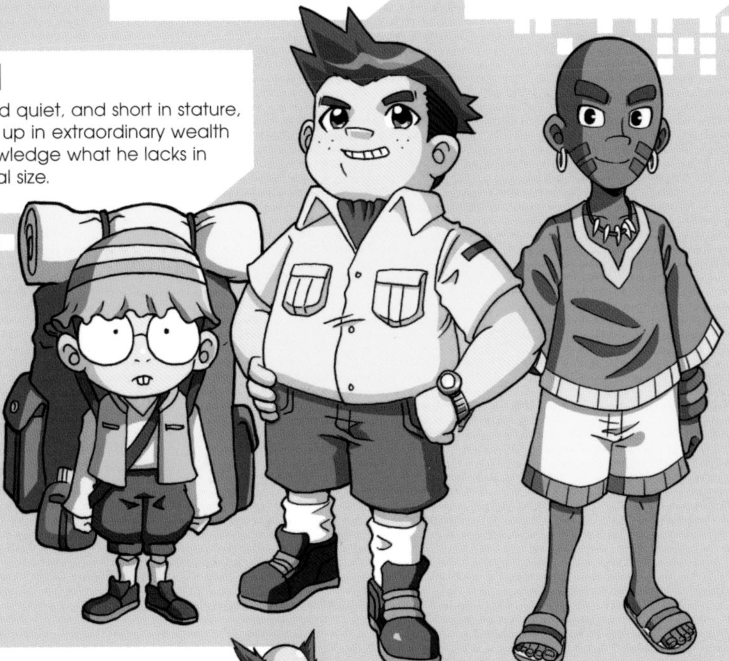

DR. DARWIN

A renowned authority in the fields of biology and zoology, who remains in impeccable physical shape, despite his age, with a flair for the dramatic. Harsh but generous, he demands focus and discipline from the X-Venture team at all times, or else!

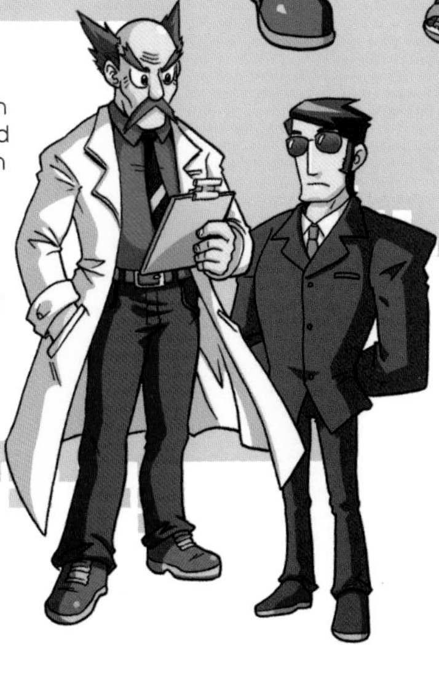

SMITH

Dr. Darwin's faithful assistant's dedicated diligence to his duties does him no favors when facing the ripping rages of his buff boss!

CONTENTS

*Some animal sizes have been altered to make the comics as visually dramatic and exciting as possible.

CHAPTER 1

JAWS OF DEATH

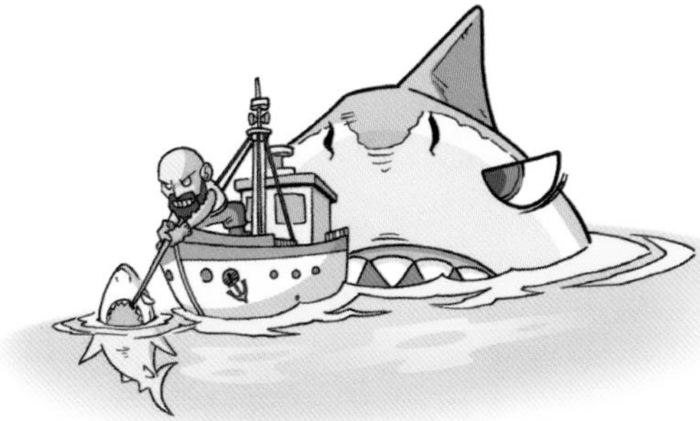

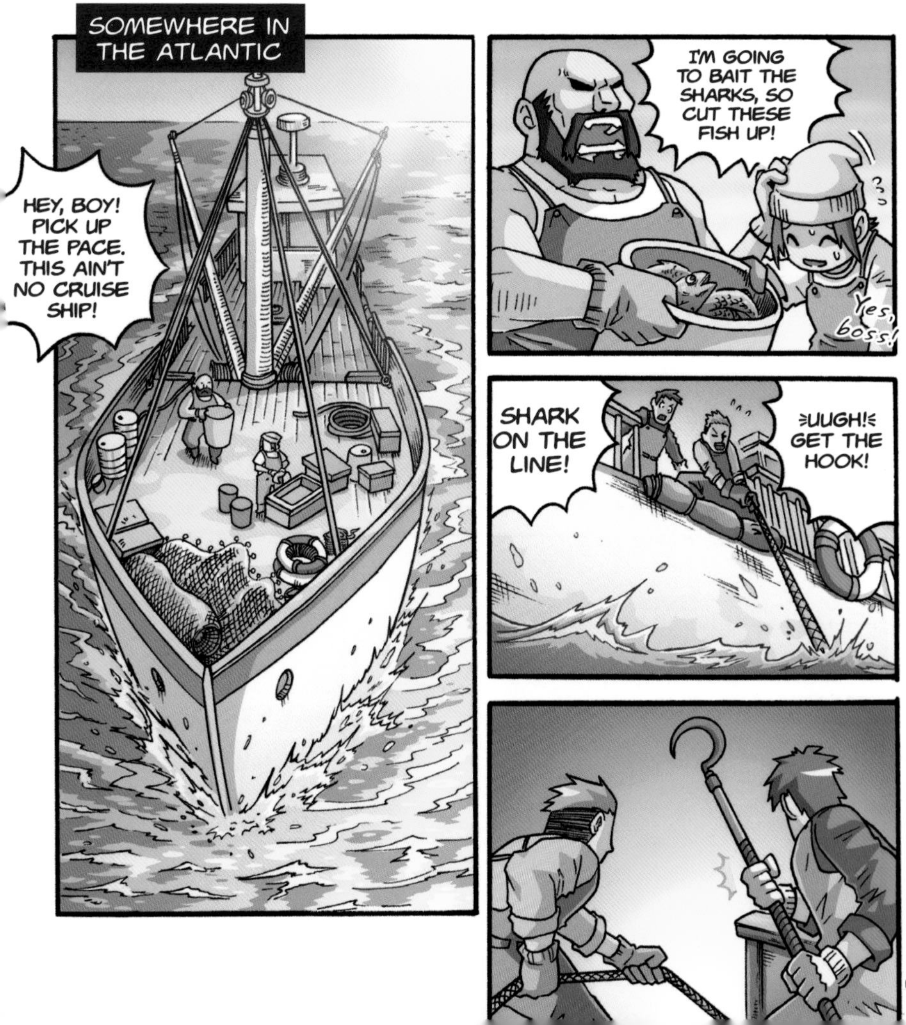
SOMEWHERE IN THE ATLANTIC
HEY, BOY! PICK UP THE PACE. THIS AIN'T NO CRUISE SHIP!
I'M GOING TO BAIT THE SHARKS, SO CUT THESE FISH UP!
Yes, boss!
SHARK ON THE LINE!
UUGH! GET THE HOOK!

BLUE SHARK

NOW, CUT THE FINS!

WELL? WHAT ARE YOU WAITING FOR? CUT THEM, ALREADY!

ERR...

MOVE!

USELESS! IF YOU CAN'T HACK IT, YOU DON'T BELONG HERE, KID!

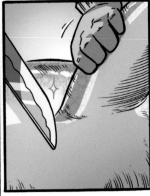

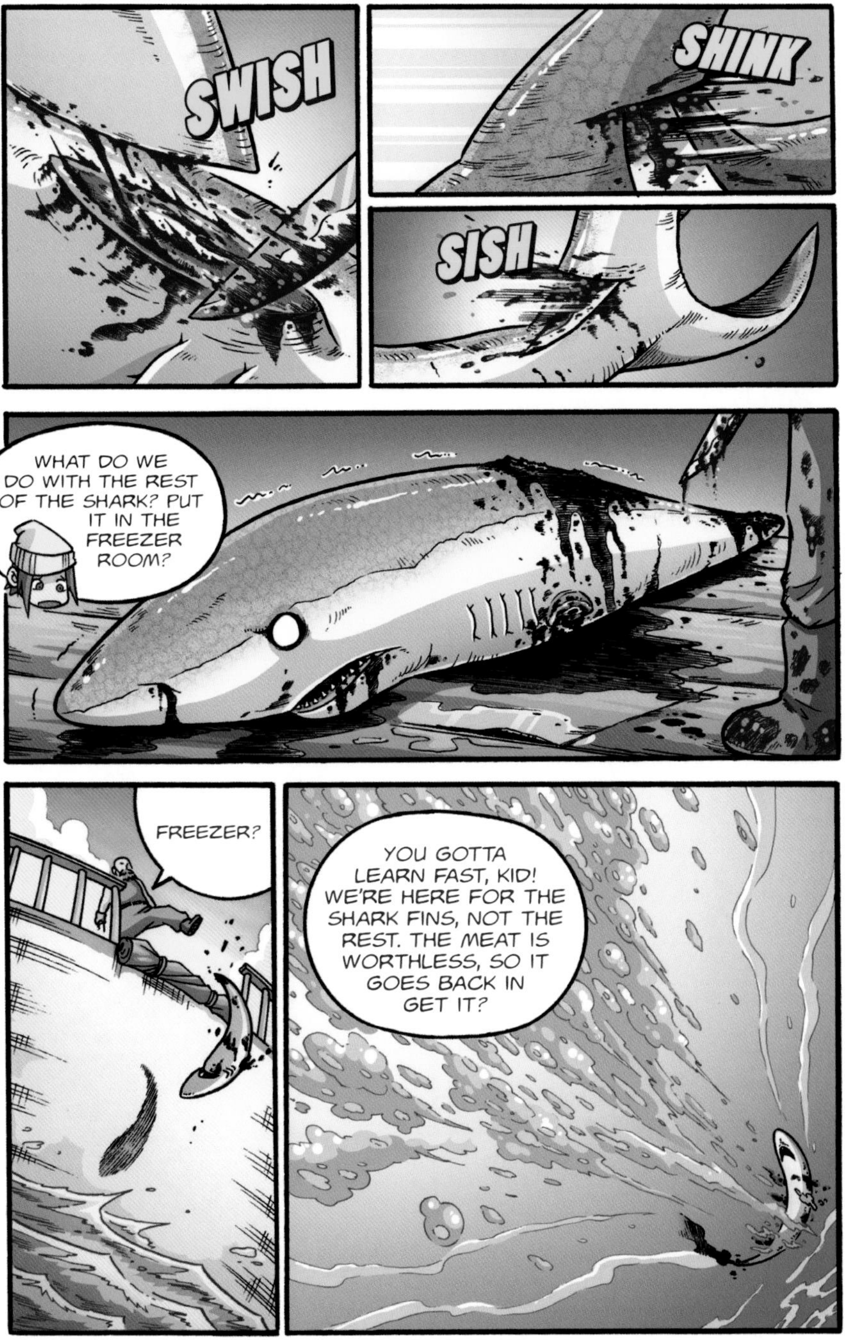
SWISH
SHINK
SISH
WHAT DO WE DO WITH THE REST OF THE SHARK? PUT IT IN THE FREEZER ROOM?
FREEZER?
YOU GOTTA LEARN FAST, KID! WE'RE HERE FOR THE SHARK FINS, NOT THE REST. THE MEAT IS WORTHLESS, SO IT GOES BACK IN GET IT?

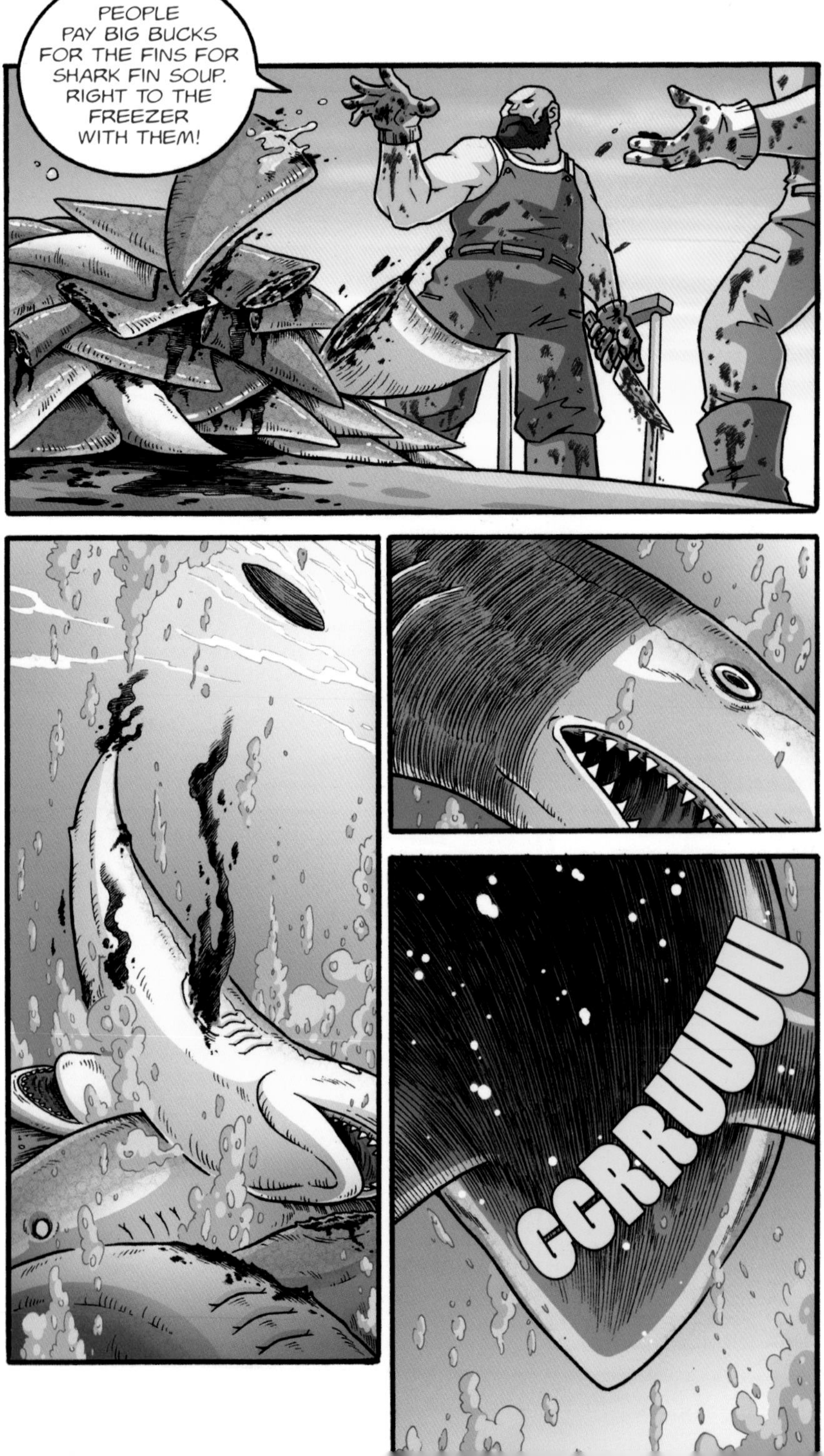
PEOPLE PAY BIG BUCKS FOR THE FINS FOR SHARK FIN SOUP. RIGHT TO THE FREEZER WITH THEM!
CGRUUUU

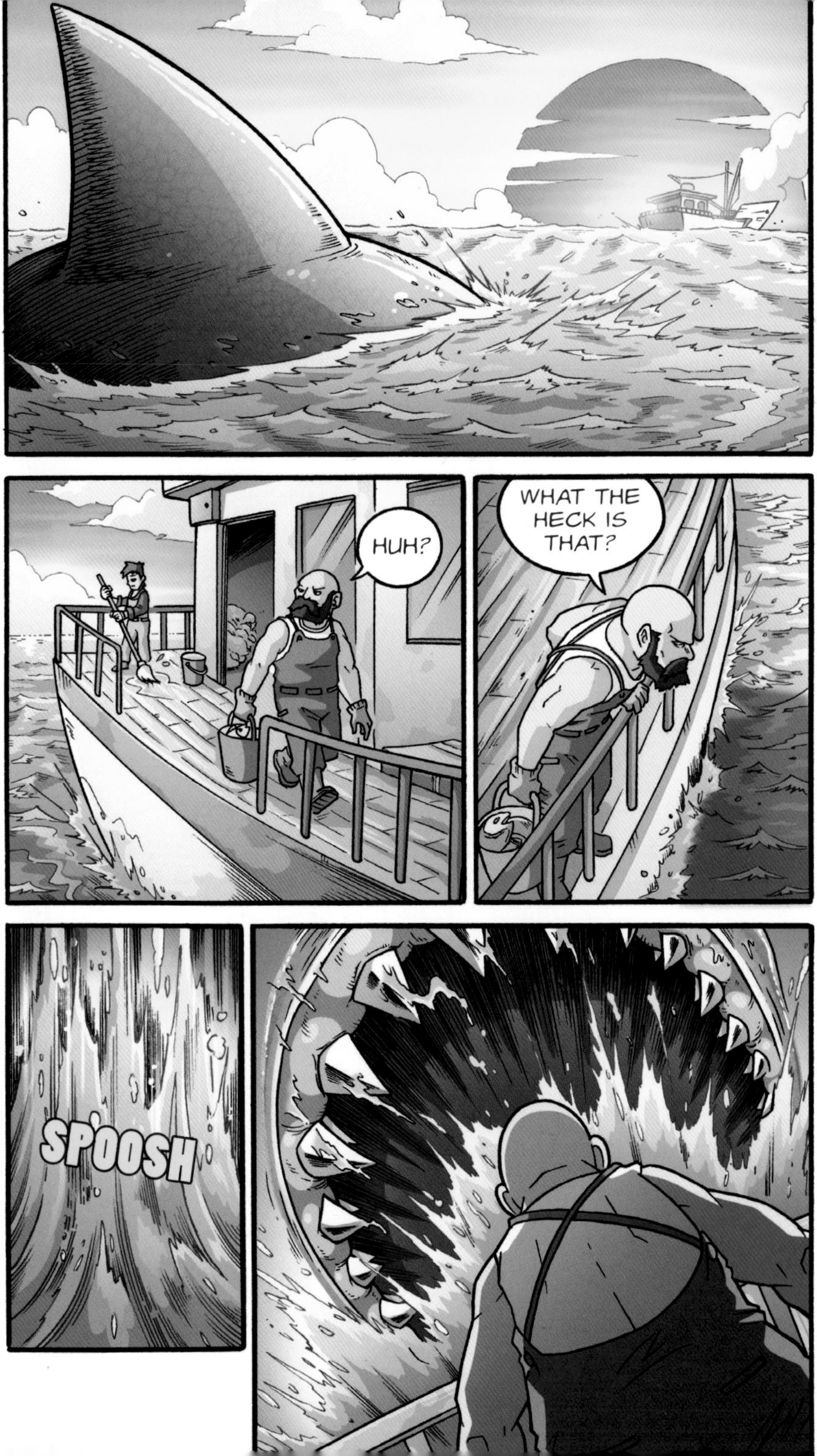
HUH?
WHAT THE HECK IS THAT?
SPOOSH

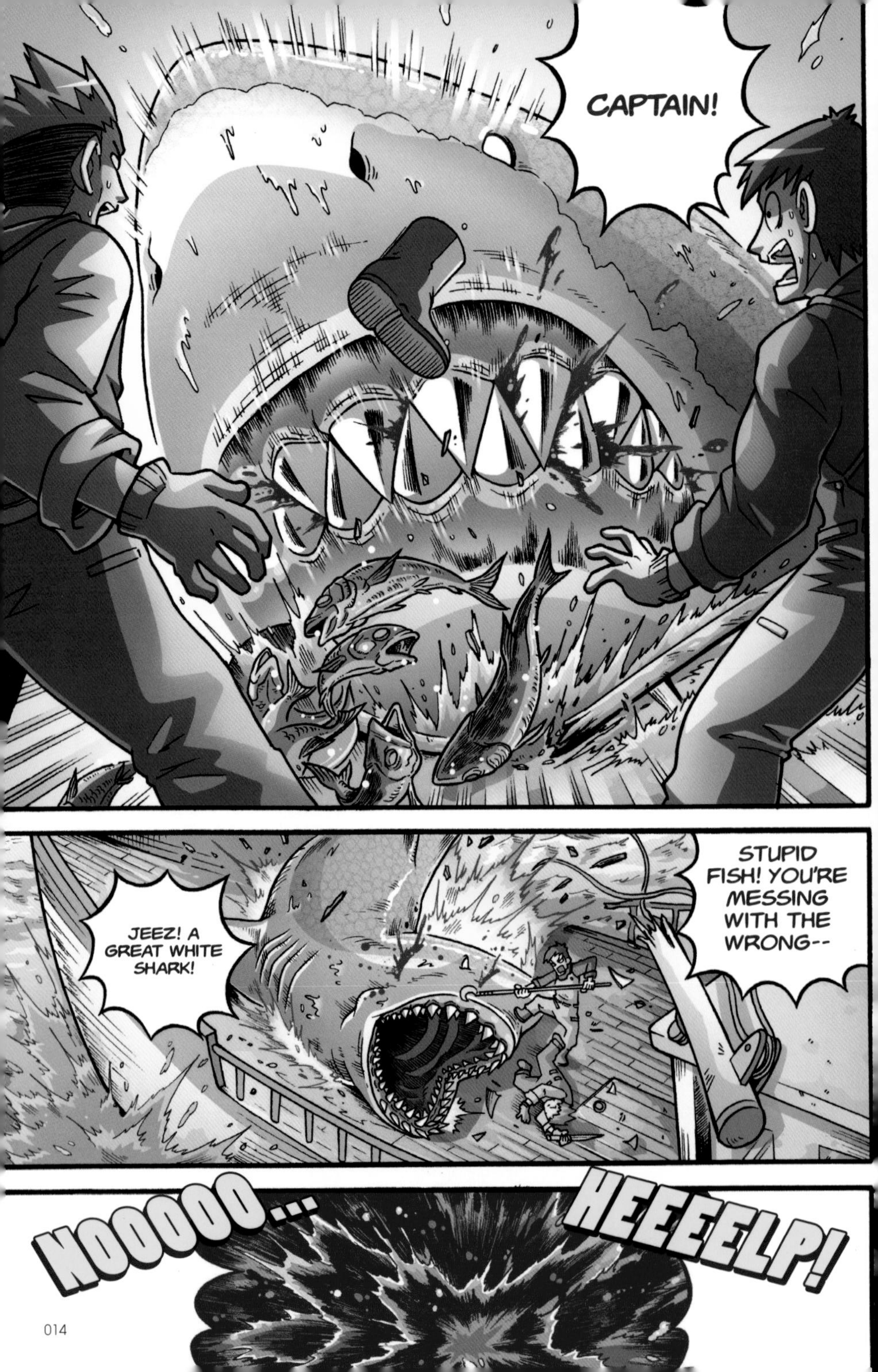
CAPTAIN!
STUPID FISH! YOU'RE MESSING WITH THE WRONG--
JEEZ! A GREAT WHITE SHARK!
NOOOOO...
HEEEELP!

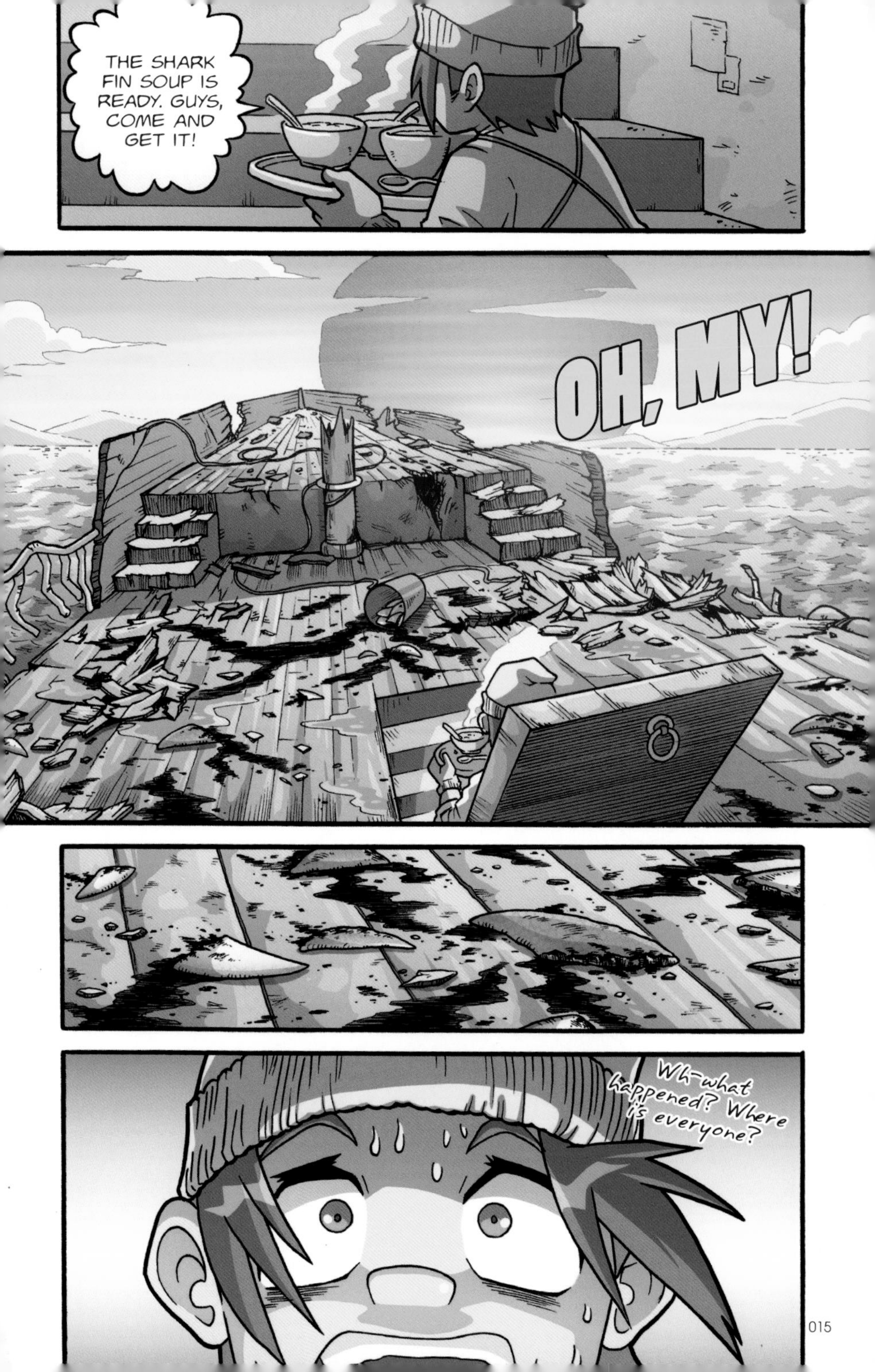
THE SHARK FIN SOUP IS READY. GUYS, COME AND GET IT!
OH, MY!
Wh-what happened? Where is everyone?

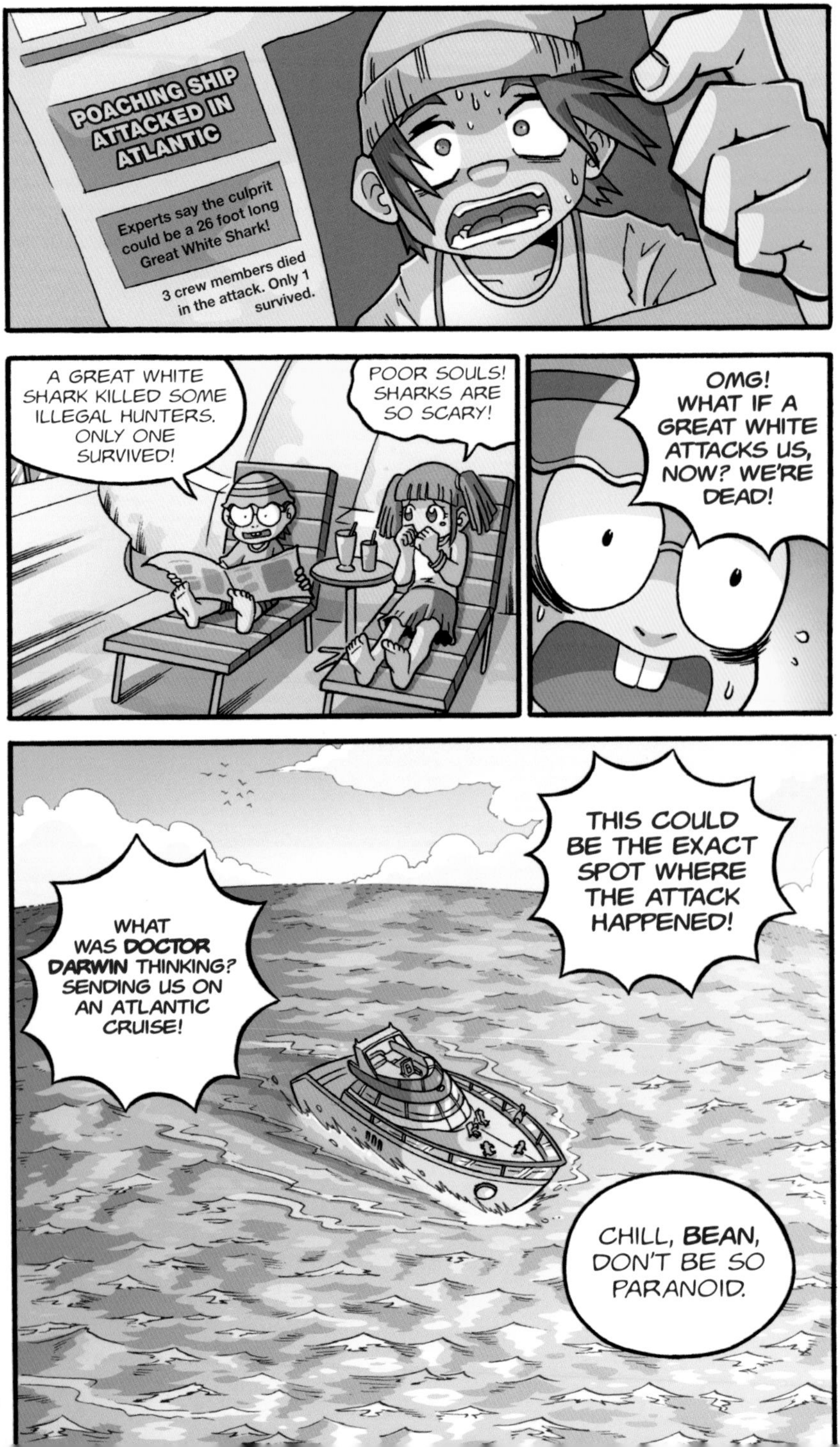

POACHING SHIP ATTACKED IN ATLANTIC
Experts say the culprit could be a 26 foot long Great White Shark!
3 crew members died in the attack. Only 1 survived.
A GREAT WHITE SHARK KILLED SOME ILLEGAL HUNTERS. ONLY ONE SURVIVED!
POOR SOULS! SHARKS ARE SO SCARY!
OMG! WHAT IF A GREAT WHITE ATTACKS US, NOW? WE'RE DEAD!
THIS COULD BE THE EXACT SPOT WHERE THE ATTACK HAPPENED!
WHAT WAS **DOCTOR DARWIN** THINKING? SENDING US ON AN ATLANTIC CRUISE!
CHILL, **BEAN**, DON'T BE SO PARANOID.

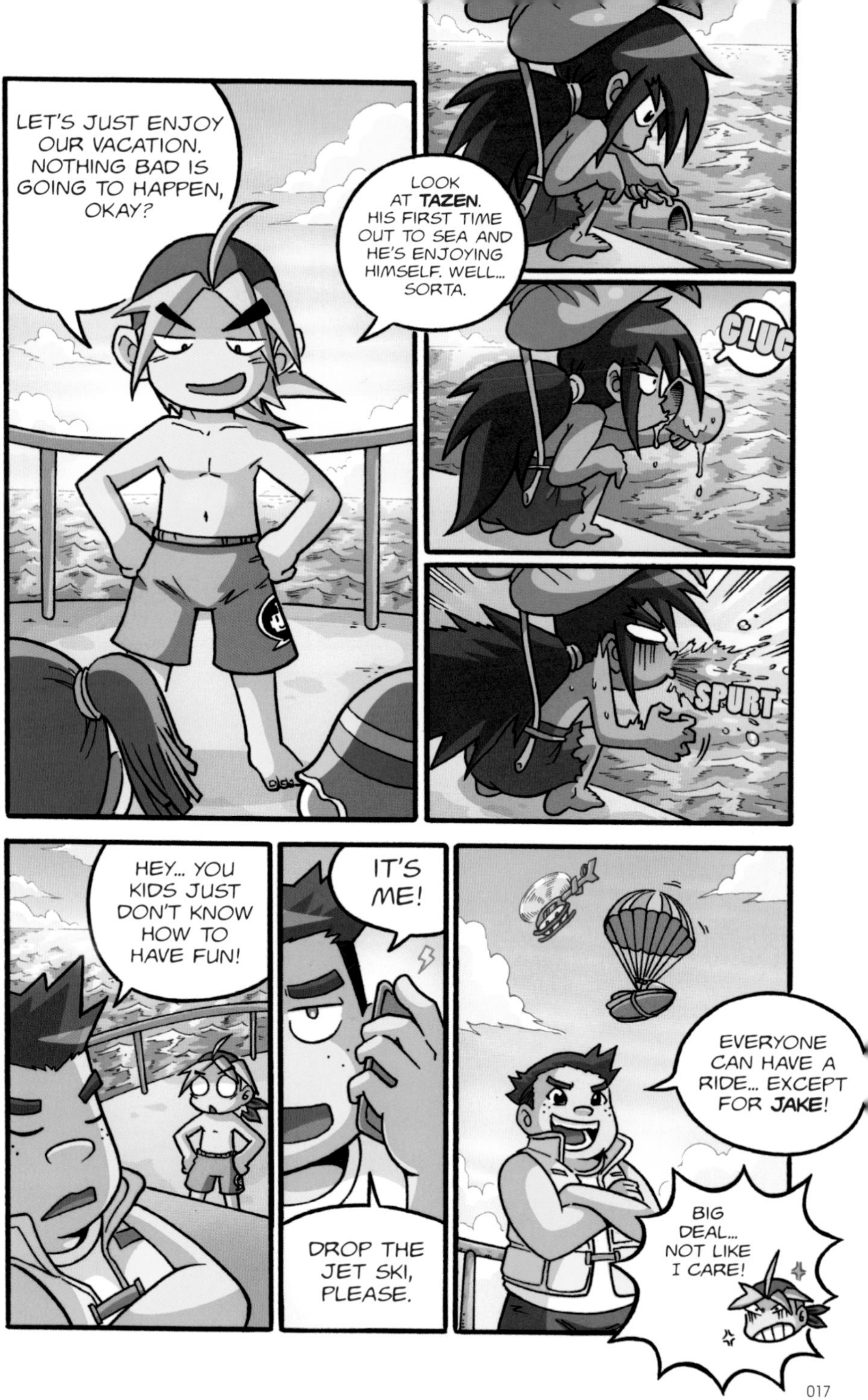
LET'S JUST ENJOY OUR VACATION. NOTHING BAD IS GOING TO HAPPEN, OKAY?
LOOK AT **TAZEN**. HIS FIRST TIME OUT TO SEA AND HE'S ENJOYING HIMSELF. WELL... SORTA.
CLUC
SPURT
HEY... YOU KIDS JUST DON'T KNOW HOW TO HAVE FUN!
IT'S ME!
DROP THE JET SKI, PLEASE.
EVERYONE CAN HAVE A RIDE... EXCEPT FOR **JAKE**!
BIG DEAL... NOT LIKE I CARE!

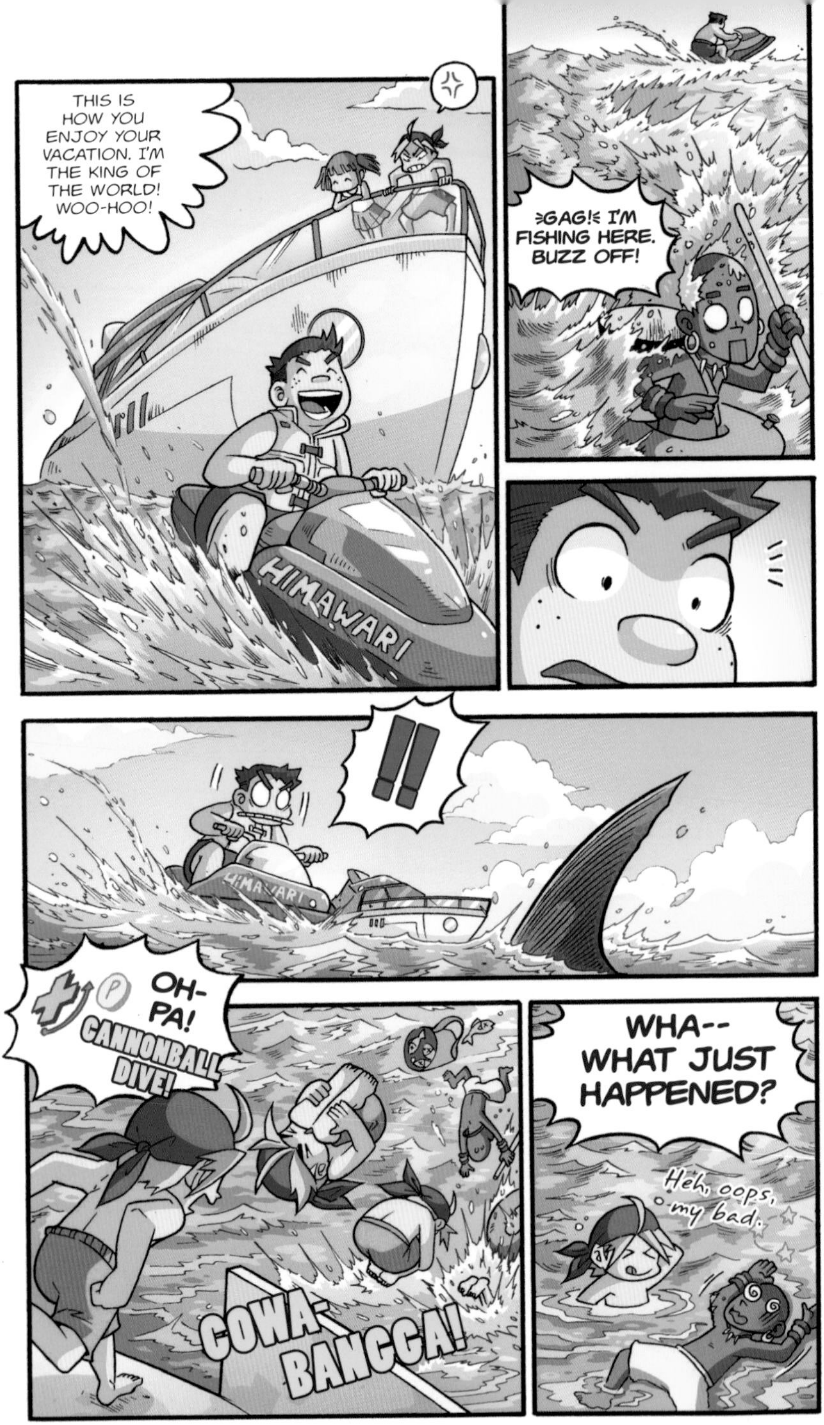
THIS IS HOW YOU ENJOY YOUR VACATION. I'M THE KING OF THE WORLD! WOO-HOO!
HIMAWARI
GAG! I'M FISHING HERE. BUZZ OFF!
!!
HIMAWARI
OH-PA!
CANNONBALL DIVE!
COWA-BANGCA!
WHA-- WHAT JUST HAPPENED?
Heh, oops, my bad.

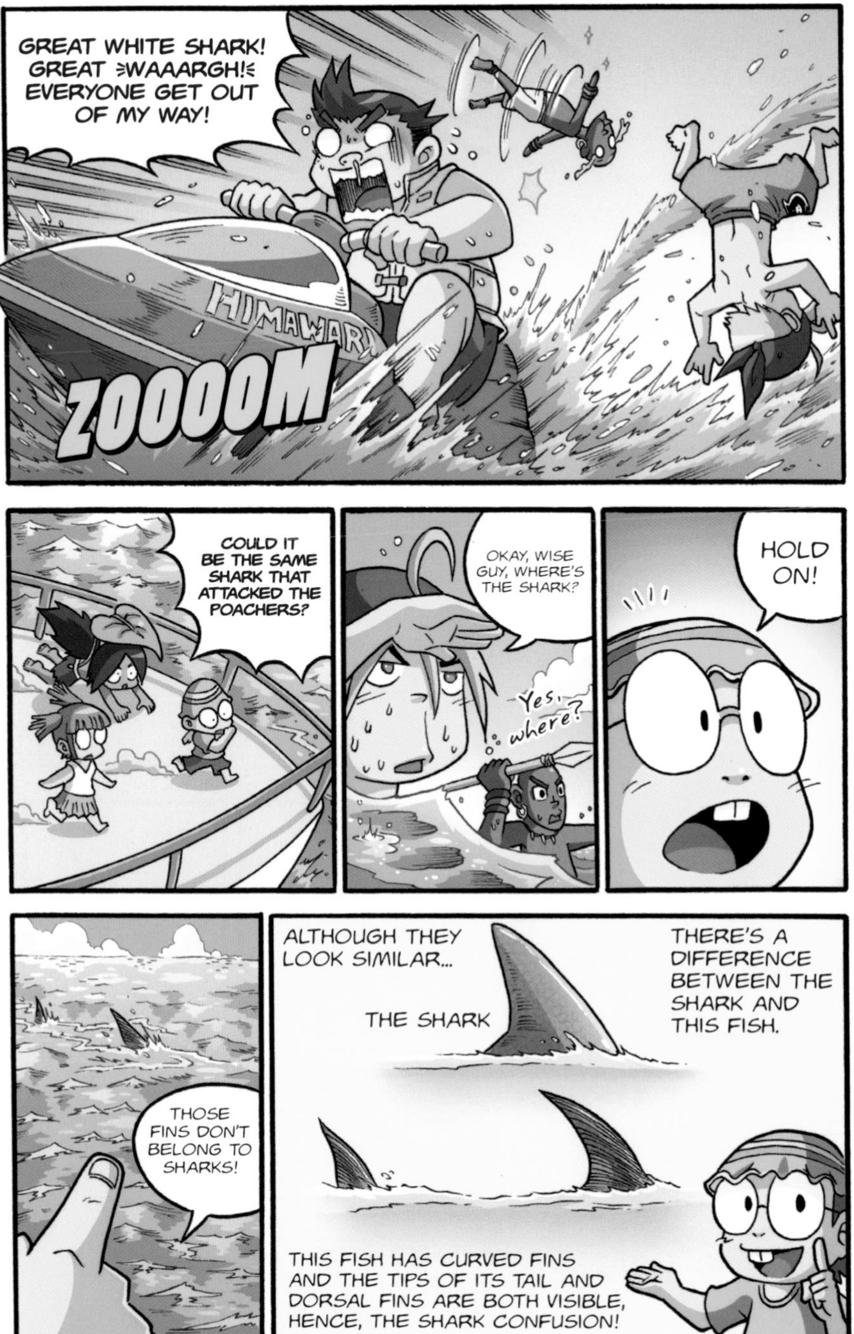
GREAT WHITE SHARK! GREAT ⩺WAAARGH!⩹ EVERYONE GET OUT OF MY WAY!
HIMAWARI
ZOOOOM
COULD IT BE THE SAME SHARK THAT ATTACKED THE POACHERS?
OKAY, WISE GUY, WHERE'S THE SHARK?
Yes, where?
HOLD ON!
THOSE FINS DON'T BELONG TO SHARKS!
ALTHOUGH THEY LOOK SIMILAR...
THERE'S A DIFFERENCE BETWEEN THE SHARK AND THIS FISH.
THE SHARK
THIS FISH HAS CURVED FINS AND THE TIPS OF ITS TAIL AND DORSAL FINS ARE BOTH VISIBLE, HENCE, THE SHARK CONFUSION!

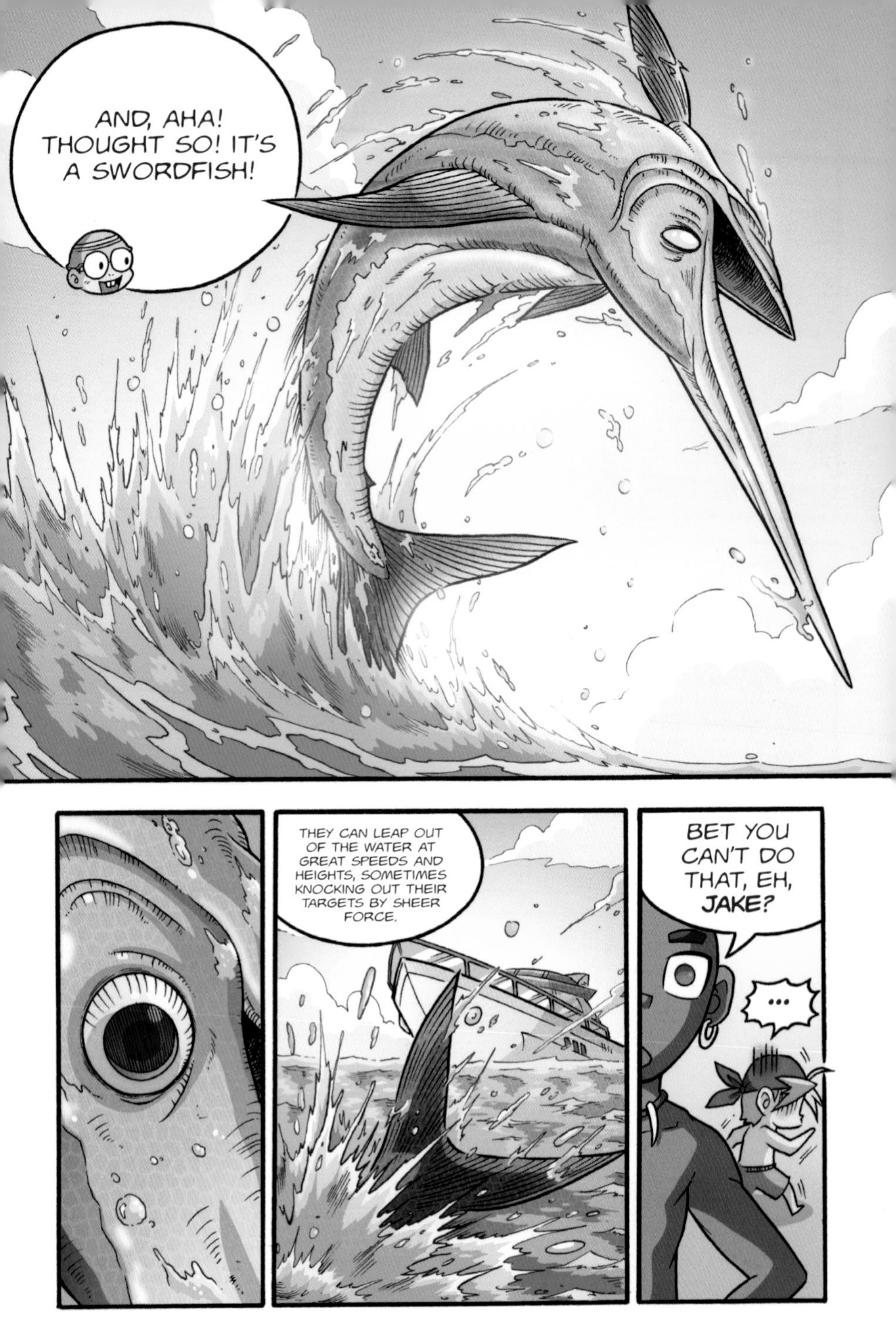
AND, AHA! THOUGHT SO! IT'S A SWORDFISH!
THEY CAN LEAP OUT OF THE WATER AT GREAT SPEEDS AND HEIGHTS, SOMETIMES KNOCKING OUT THEIR TARGETS BY SHEER FORCE.
BET YOU CAN'T DO THAT, EH, **JAKE?**
...

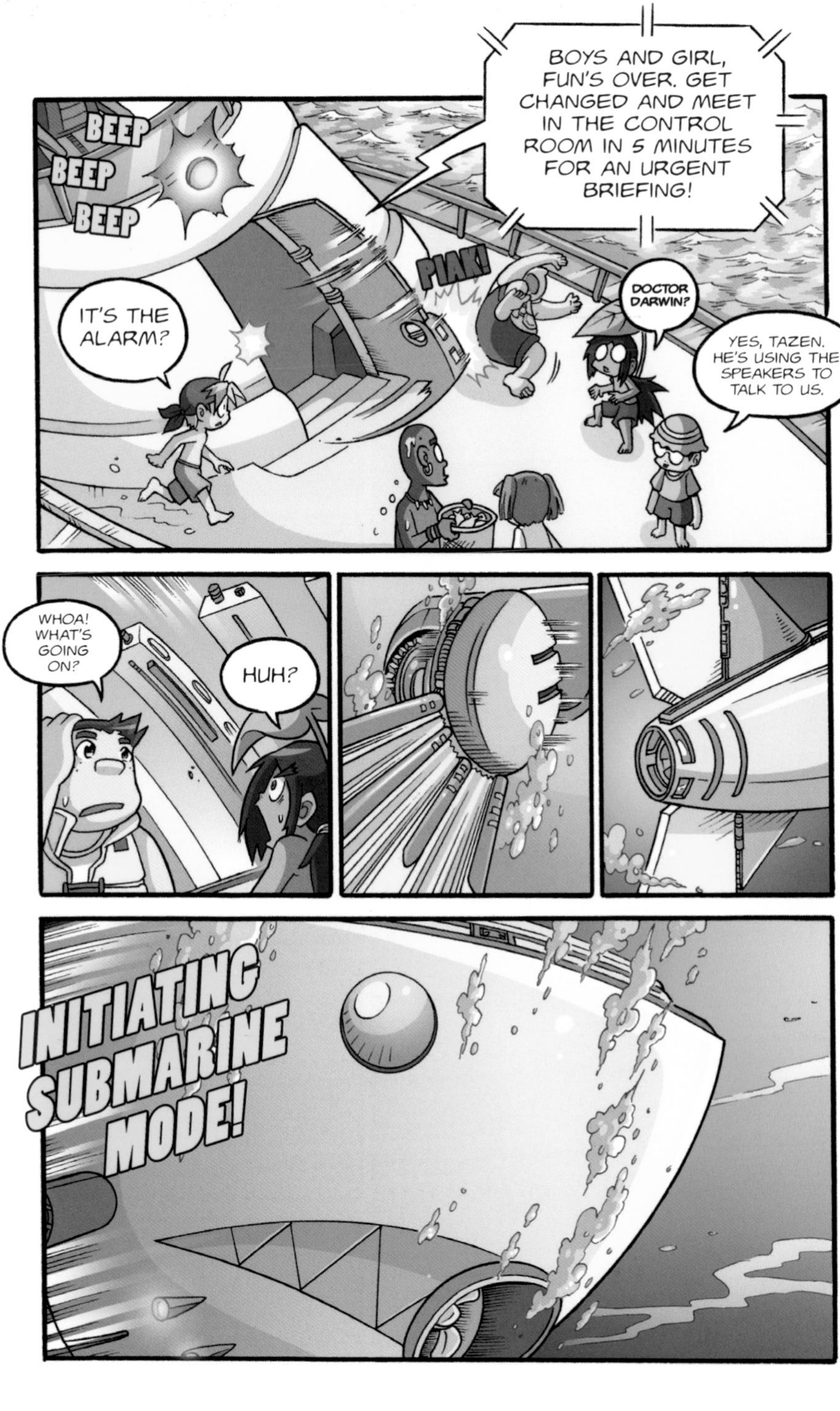
BOYS AND GIRL, FUN'S OVER. GET CHANGED AND MEET IN THE CONTROL ROOM IN 5 MINUTES FOR AN URGENT BRIEFING!
BEEP
BEEP
BEEP
PIAK!
IT'S THE ALARM?
DOCTOR DARWIN?
YES, TAZEN. HE'S USING THE SPEAKERS TO TALK TO US.
WHOA! WHAT'S GOING ON?
HUH?
INITIATING SUBMARINE MODE!

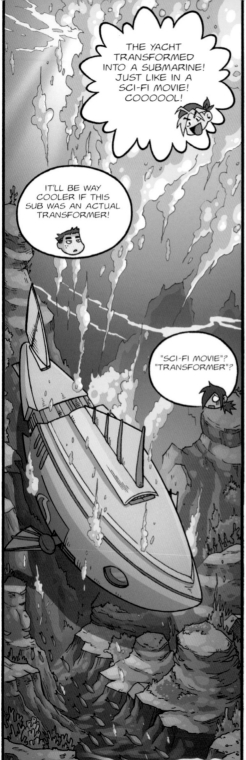

THE YACHT TRANSFORMED INTO A SUBMARINE! JUST LIKE IN A SCI-FI MOVIE! COOOOOOL!

IT'LL BE WAY COOLER IF THIS SUB WAS AN ACTUAL TRANSFORMER!

"SCI-FI MOVIE"? "TRANSFORMER"?

THE SEABED IS SO BEAUTIFUL!

Uuh! I'm too short...

I'M THE CAPTAIN NOW! LET'S SEE WHAT WE HAVE HERE.

WEIRD. IT'S NOT RESPONDING AT ALL. IS IT BROKEN?

BEEP

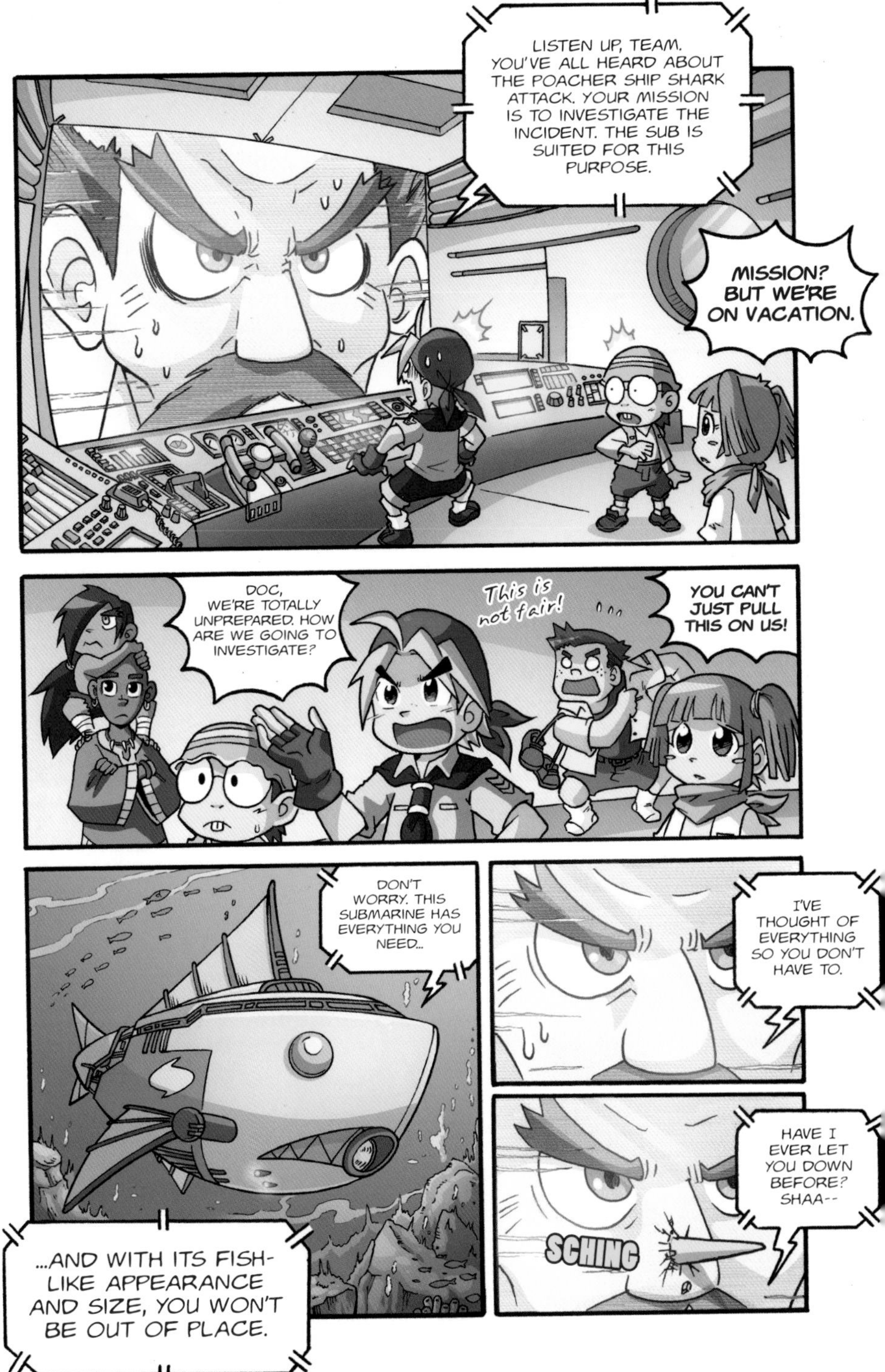

LISTEN UP, TEAM. YOU'VE ALL HEARD ABOUT THE POACHER SHIP SHARK ATTACK. YOUR MISSION IS TO INVESTIGATE THE INCIDENT. THE SUB IS SUITED FOR THIS PURPOSE.
MISSION? BUT WE'RE ON VACATION.
DOC, WE'RE TOTALLY UNPREPARED. HOW ARE WE GOING TO INVESTIGATE?
This is not fair!
YOU CAN'T JUST PULL THIS ON US!
DON'T WORRY. THIS SUBMARINE HAS EVERYTHING YOU NEED...
...AND WITH ITS FISH-LIKE APPEARANCE AND SIZE, YOU WON'T BE OUT OF PLACE.
I'VE THOUGHT OF EVERYTHING SO YOU DON'T HAVE TO.
HAVE I EVER LET YOU DOWN BEFORE? SHAA--
SCHING

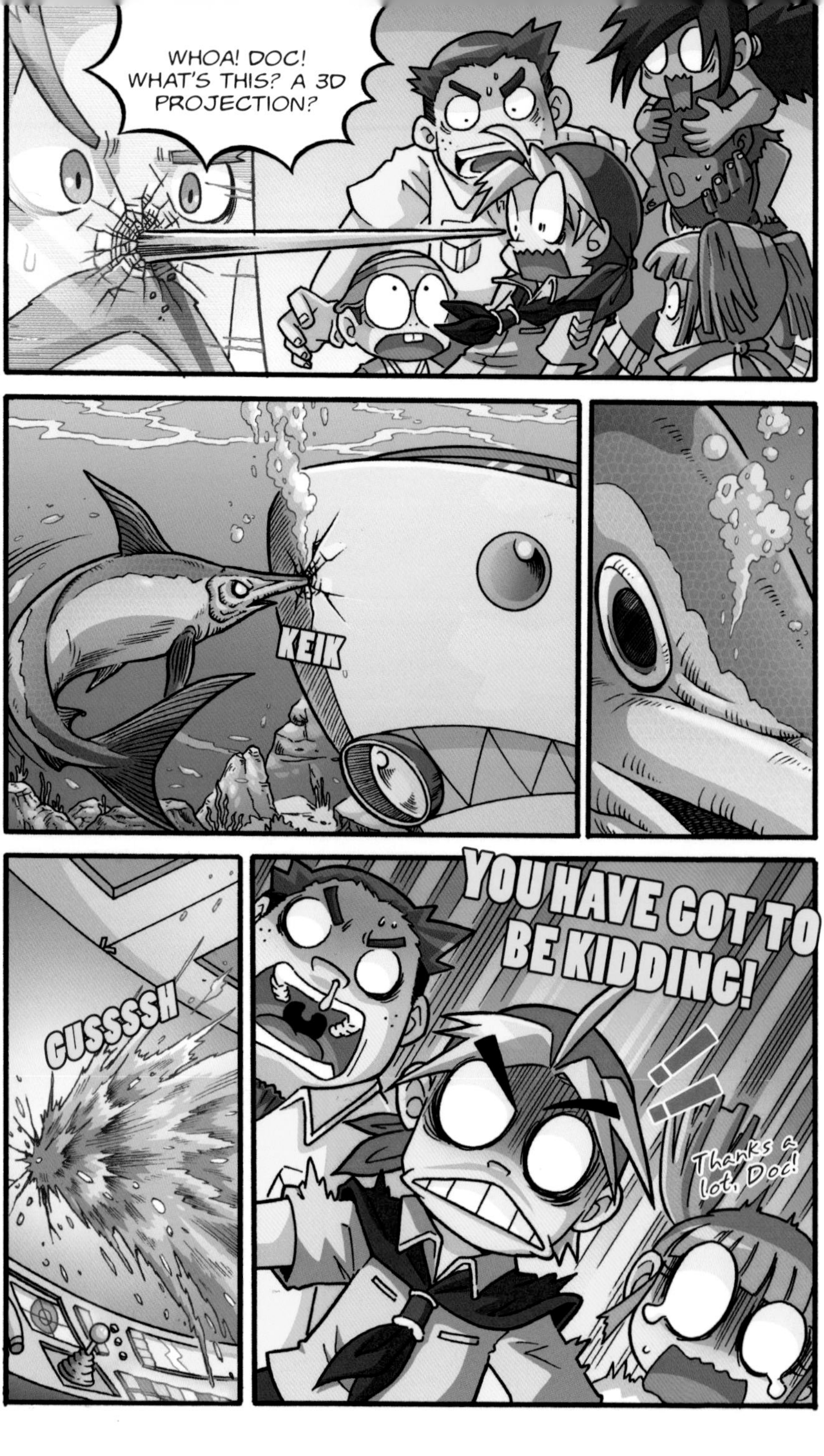
WHOA! DOC! WHAT'S THIS? A 3D PROJECTION?
KEIK
YOU HAVE GOT TO BE KIDDING!
GUSSSSH
Thanks a lot, Doc!

What are Chondrichthyes?

They are cartilaginous marine vertebrates meaning their skeletons are composed of cartilage — a bone structure present in fossil fish species. The notochord is present in the young but is gradually replaced by cartilage as they reach adulthood.

Subclasses

A) Elasmobranchii

Members of this subclass lack swim bladders and breathe through 5 to 7 pairs of gill clefts. Due to soft bone structure, they maintain balance with the help of a sturdy dorsal (back) and pectoral (side) fins. The caudal (tail) fin facilitates forward movement.

Elasmobranchii anatomy (Eg: Stingray)

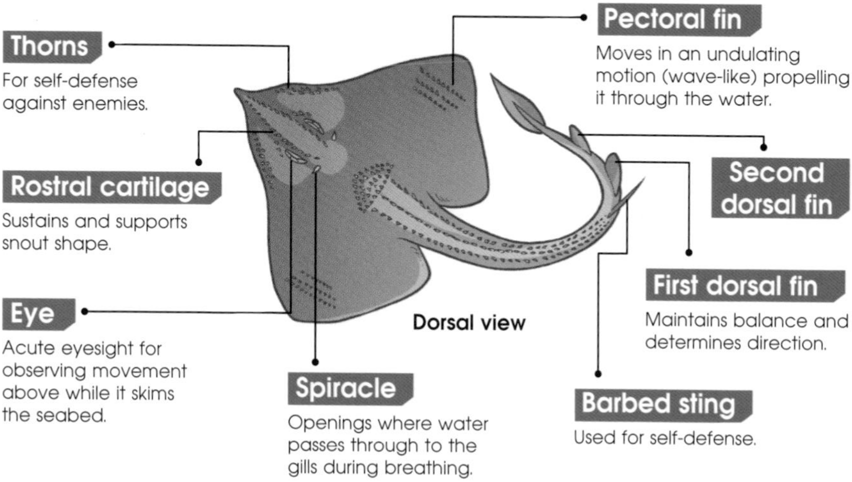
Thorns
For self-defense against enemies.
Rostral cartilage
Sustains and supports snout shape.
Eye
Acute eyesight for observing movement above while it skims the seabed.
Spiracle
Openings where water passes through to the gills during breathing.
Pectoral fin
Moves in an undulating motion (wave-like) propelling it through the water.
Second dorsal fin
First dorsal fin
Maintains balance and determines direction.
Barbed sting
Used for self-defense.
Dorsal view

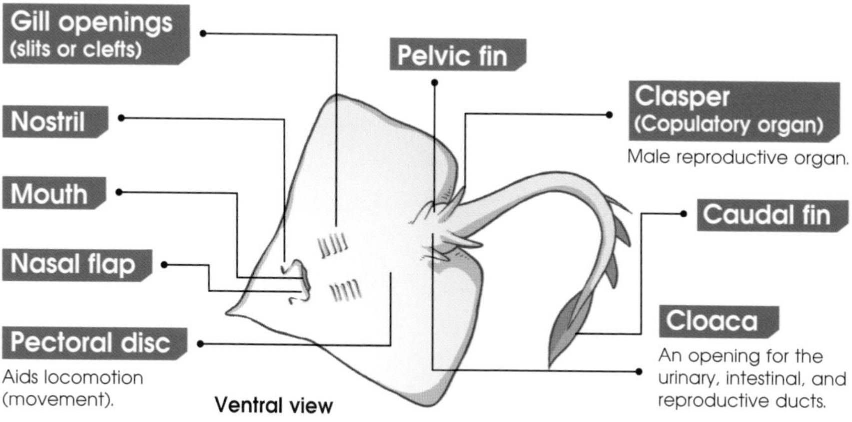
Gill openings (slits or clefts)
Nostril
Mouth
Nasal flap
Pectoral disc
Aids locomotion (movement).
Pelvic fin
Clasper (Copulatory organ)
Male reproductive organ.
Caudal fin
Cloaca
An opening for the urinary, intestinal, and reproductive ducts.
Ventral view

Elasmobranchii anatomy (Eg: Shark)

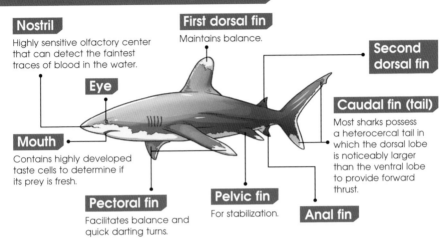

Nostril
Highly sensitive olfactory center that can detect the faintest traces of blood in the water.

First dorsal fin
Maintains balance.

Second dorsal fin

Eye

Caudal fin (tail)
Most sharks possess a heterocercal tail in which the dorsal lobe is noticeably larger than the ventral lobe to provide forward thrust.

Mouth
Contains highly developed taste cells to determine if its prey is fresh.

Pectoral fin
Facilitates balance and quick darting turns.

Pelvic fin
For stabilization.

Anal fin

Holocephali ("complete heads")

Very distinct from Elasmobranchii, this subclass is characterized by size, having only one gill slit and no spiracle, which suggests a direct link to ancient fish. Chimaera (Chimaeriformes) are the only surviving group and live close to the seabed feeding on mollusks and small invertebrates.

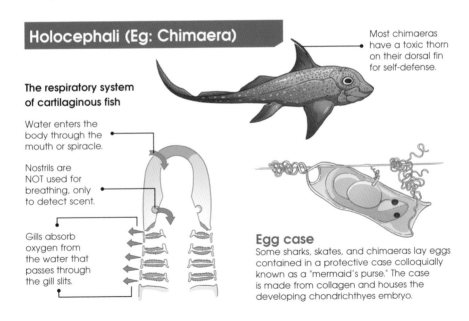

Holocephali (Eg: Chimaera)

Most chimaeras have a toxic thorn on their dorsal fin for self-defense.

The respiratory system of cartilaginous fish

Water enters the body through the mouth or spiracle.

Nostrils are NOT used for breathing, only to detect scent.

Gills absorb oxygen from the water that passes through the gill slits.

Egg case
Some sharks, skates, and chimaeras lay eggs contained in a protective case colloquially known as a "mermaid's purse." The case is made from collagen and houses the developing chondrichthyes embryo.

What are bony fish?

With as many as 28,000 known species to date, bony fish make up the majority of the fish population, widely distributed in both fresh and saltwater habitats worldwide. As opposed to cartilaginous fish, osteichthyes possess bony skeletons.

Osteichthyes anatomy

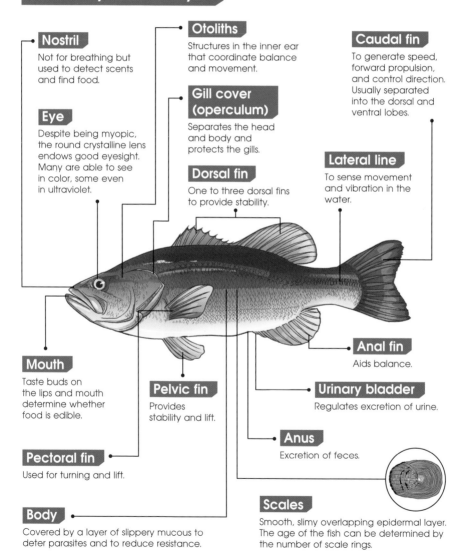

Nostril

Not for breathing but used to detect scents and find food.

Eye

Despite being myopic, the round crystalline lens endows good eyesight. Many are able to see in color, some even in ultraviolet.

Otoliths

Structures in the inner ear that coordinate balance and movement.

Gill cover (operculum)

Separates the head and body and protects the gills.

Dorsal fin

One to three dorsal fins to provide stability.

Caudal fin

To generate speed, forward propulsion, and control direction. Usually separated into the dorsal and ventral lobes.

Lateral line

To sense movement and vibration in the water.

Mouth

Taste buds on the lips and mouth determine whether food is edible.

Pelvic fin

Provides stability and lift.

Anal fin

Aids balance.

Urinary bladder

Regulates excretion of urine.

Anus

Excretion of feces.

Pectoral fin

Used for turning and lift.

Body

Covered by a layer of slippery mucous to deter parasites and to reduce resistance.

Scales

Smooth, slimy overlapping epidermal layer. The age of the fish can be determined by the number of scale rings.

The difference between bony fish and cartilaginous fish

BONY FISH		CARTILAGINOUS FISH
Harder skeleton	**Bone**	Softer skeleton
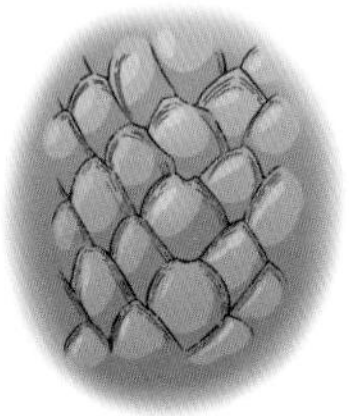 Covered by round ctenoid scales or ganoid scales. **Round scales**	**Skin**	Covered by tooth-like structures called placoid scales which are small, rough, and difficult to see. **Placoid scales** 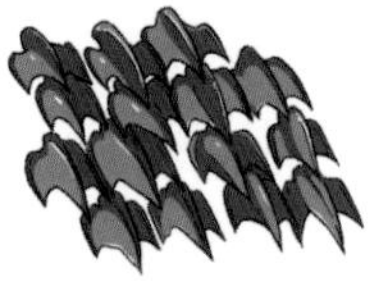
Not fixed on upper and lower jaws. Non-regenerative.	**Teeth**	Embedded in the gums and grow on upper and lower jaws. Perpetually regenerative.
Has a swim bladder — an internal gas-filled organ to control buoyancy. 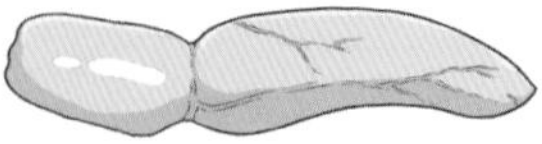	**Buoyancy**	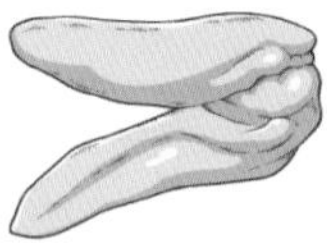 No swim bladder and must keep moving to maintain buoyancy.
Protected by a gill cover (operculum) 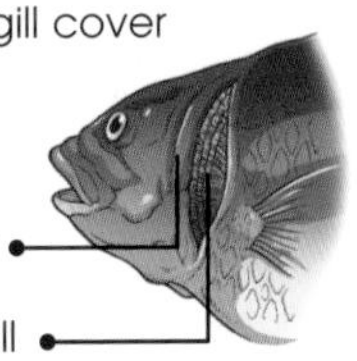 Gill cover Gill	**Gills**	Exposed with five to seven gill openings on both sides. 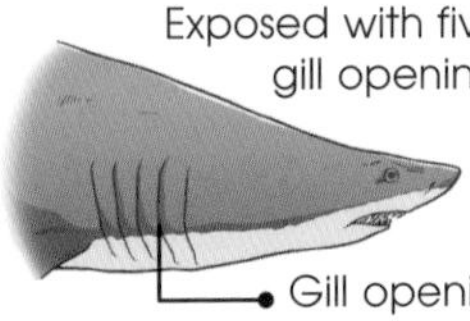 Gill opening (slit or cleft)
Varying forms; Both heterocercal (uneven sized) and symmetrical (even sized) 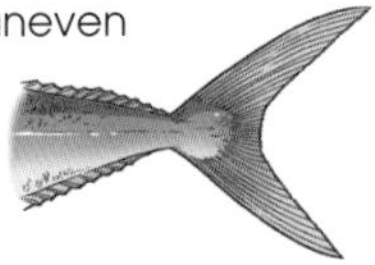	**Caudal fin (tail)**	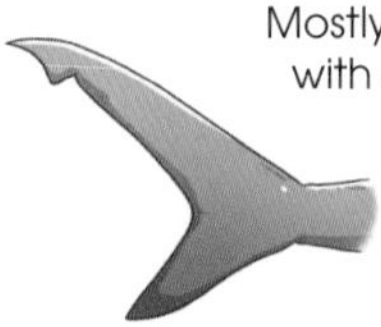 Mostly heterocercal with a large dorsal lobe.
Able to swim forwards and backwards due to more flexible fins.	**Swimming pattern**	Most can only swim forwards due to stiffer fins.
External fertilization and oviparous. A large number of eggs are spawn to increase survival rate.	**Reproduction**	Internal fertilization. Both oviparous (egg-laying) and viviparous (live birth) with higher survival rates but lower numbers.

CHAPTER 2

THE SWORD

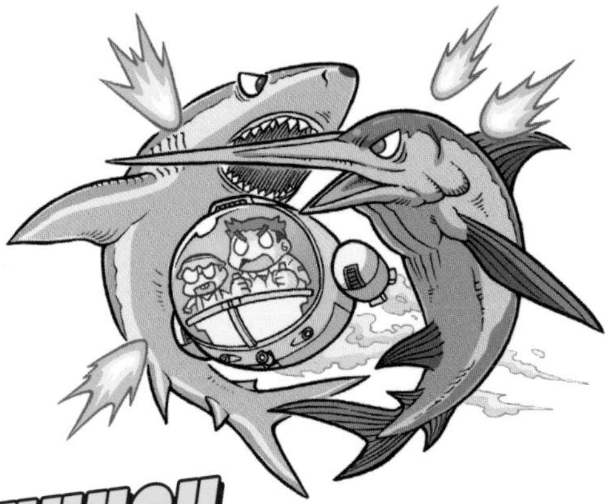

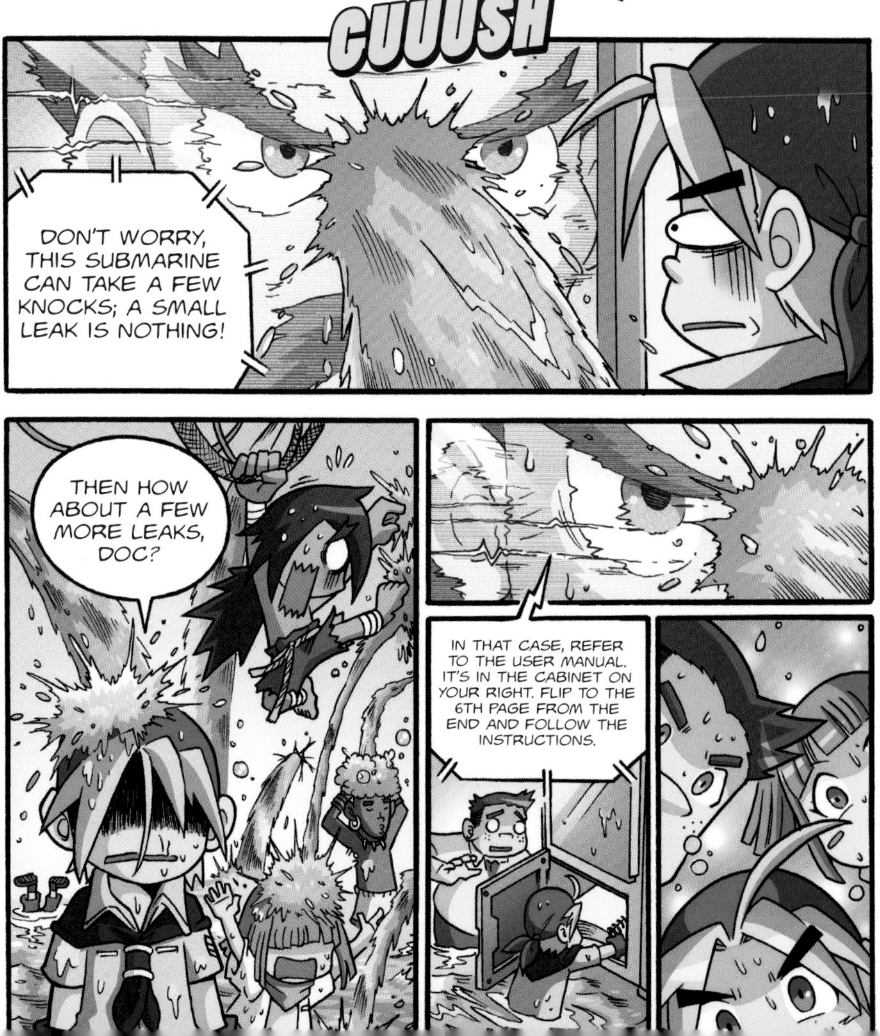
CUUUSH
DON'T WORRY, THIS SUBMARINE CAN TAKE A FEW KNOCKS; A SMALL LEAK IS NOTHING!
THEN HOW ABOUT A FEW MORE LEAKS, DOC?
IN THAT CASE, REFER TO THE USER MANUAL. IT'S IN THE CABINET ON YOUR RIGHT. FLIP TO THE 6TH PAGE FROM THE END AND FOLLOW THE INSTRUCTIONS.

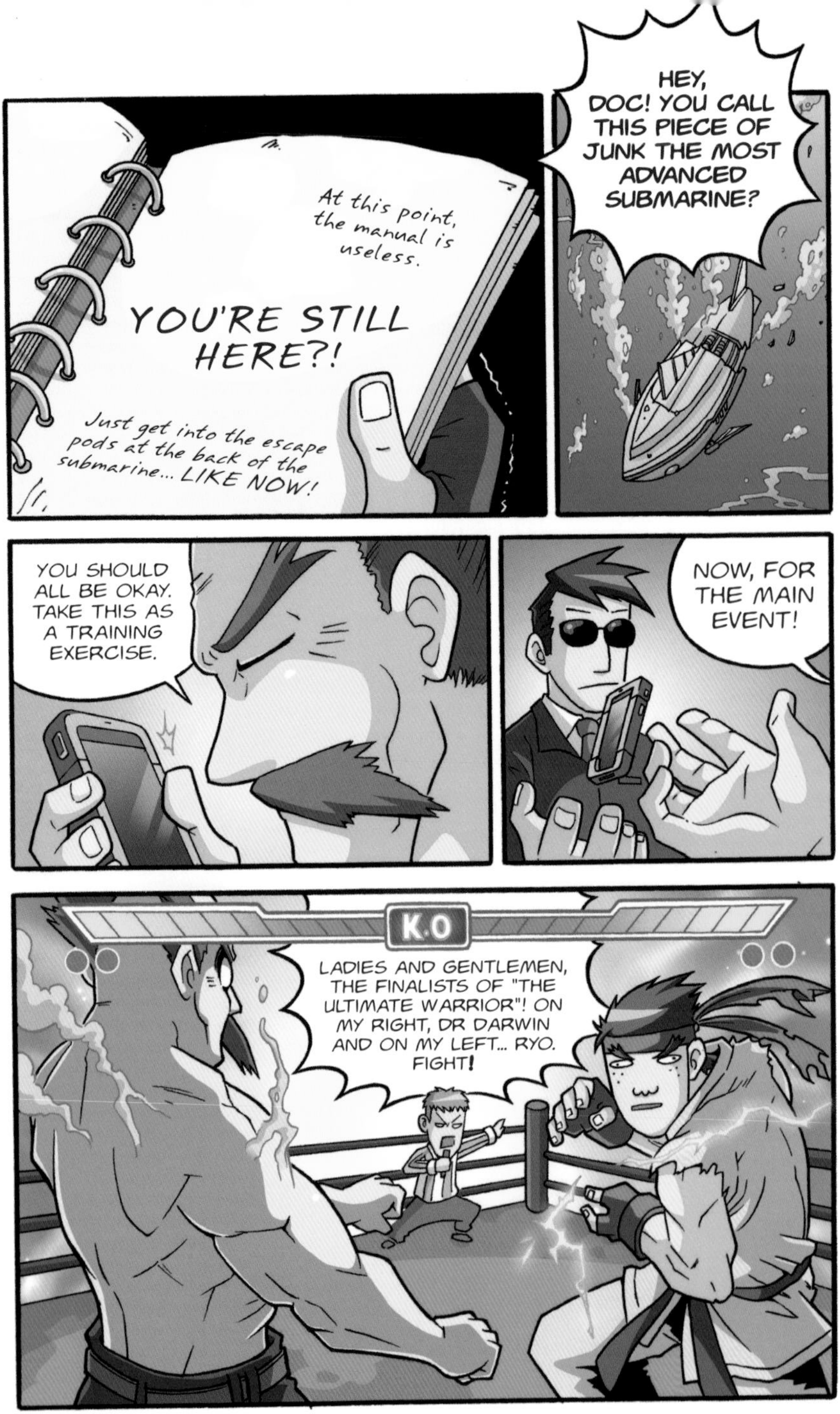
At this point, the manual is useless.
YOU'RE STILL HERE?!
Just get into the escape pods at the back of the submarine... LIKE NOW!
HEY, DOC! YOU CALL THIS PIECE OF JUNK THE MOST ADVANCED SUBMARINE?
YOU SHOULD ALL BE OKAY. TAKE THIS AS A TRAINING EXERCISE.
NOW, FOR THE MAIN EVENT!
K.O
LADIES AND GENTLEMEN, THE FINALISTS OF "THE ULTIMATE WARRIOR"! ON MY RIGHT, DR DARWIN AND ON MY LEFT... RYO. FIGHT!

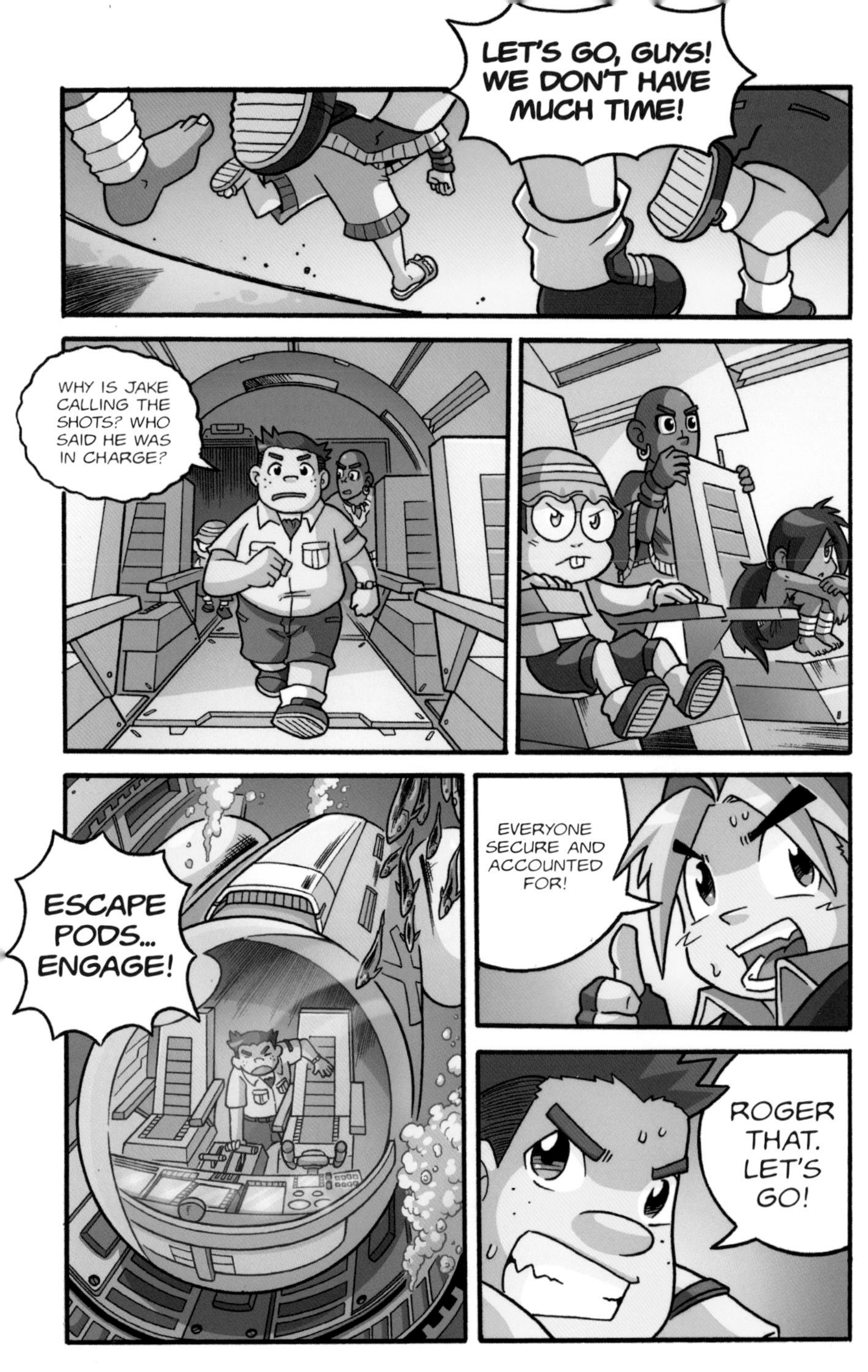
LET'S GO, GUYS! WE DON'T HAVE MUCH TIME!
WHY IS JAKE CALLING THE SHOTS? WHO SAID HE WAS IN CHARGE?
ESCAPE PODS... ENGAGE!
EVERYONE SECURE AND ACCOUNTED FOR!
ROGER THAT. LET'S GO!

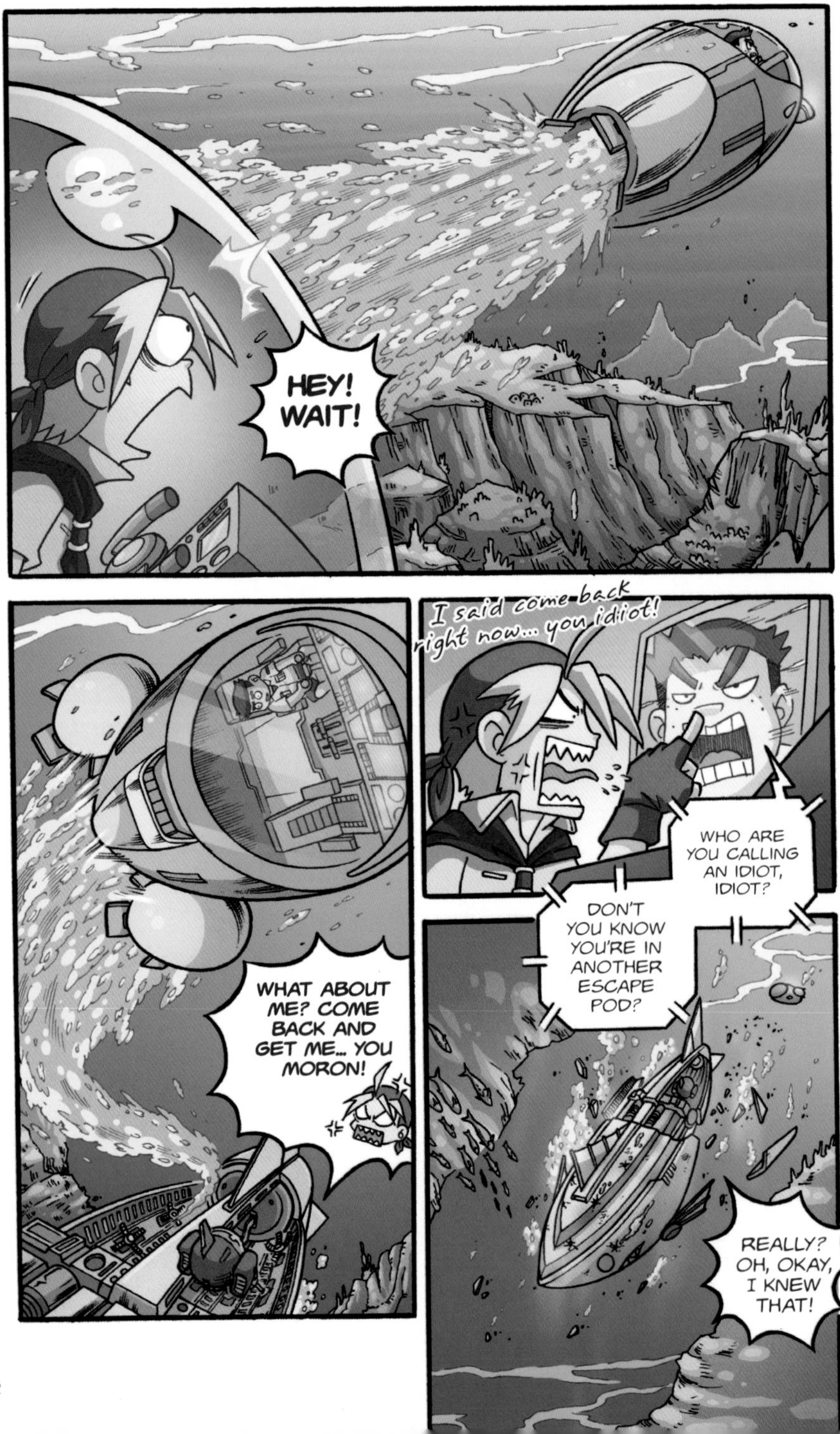
HEY! WAIT!
WHAT ABOUT ME? COME BACK AND GET ME... YOU MORON!
I said come back right now... you idiot!
WHO ARE YOU CALLING AN IDIOT, IDIOT?
DON'T YOU KNOW YOU'RE IN ANOTHER ESCAPE POD?
REALLY? OH, OKAY, I KNEW THAT!

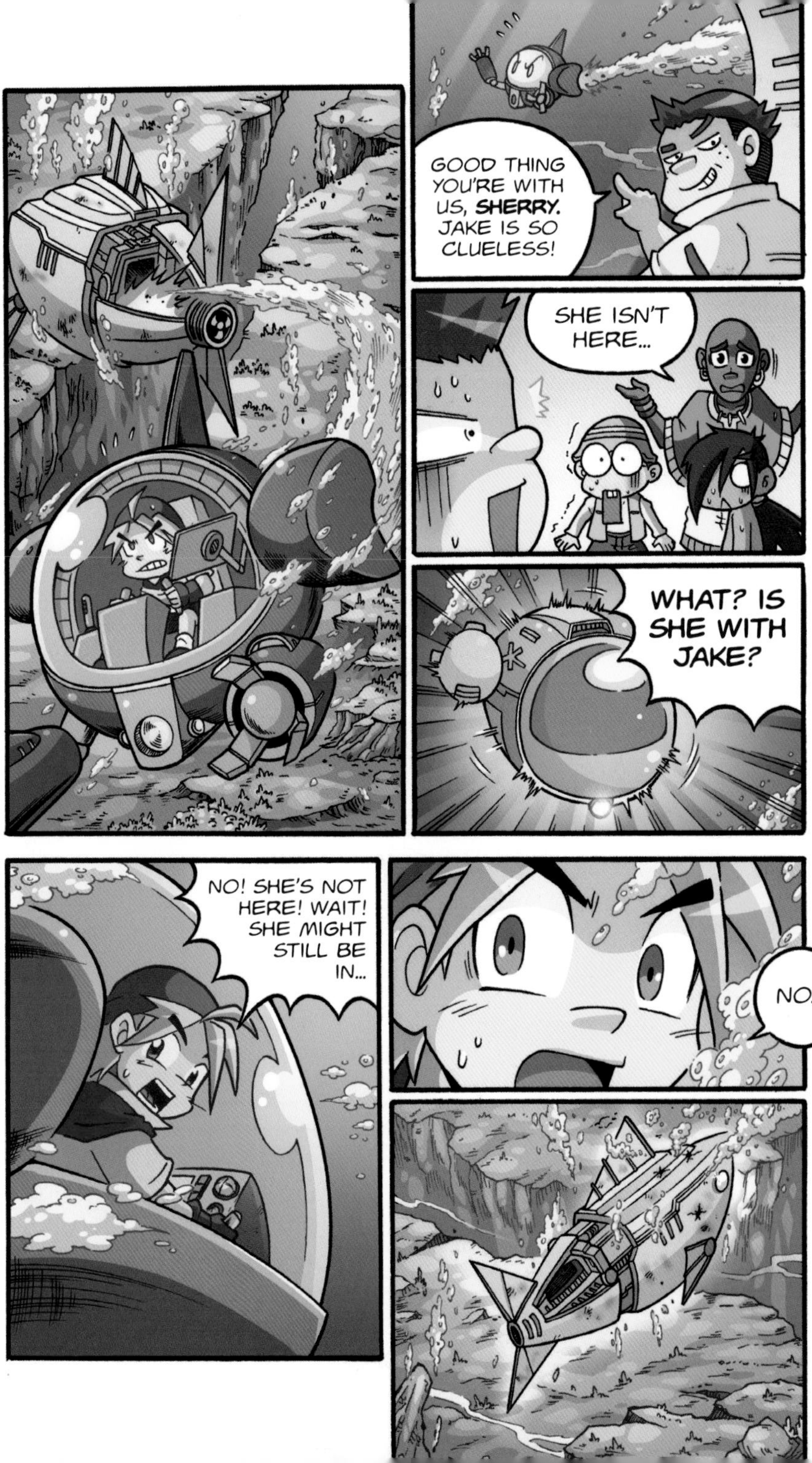
GOOD THING YOU'RE WITH US, **SHERRY.** JAKE IS SO CLUELESS!
SHE ISN'T HERE...
WHAT? IS SHE WITH JAKE?
NO! SHE'S NOT HERE! WAIT! SHE MIGHT STILL BE IN...
NO...

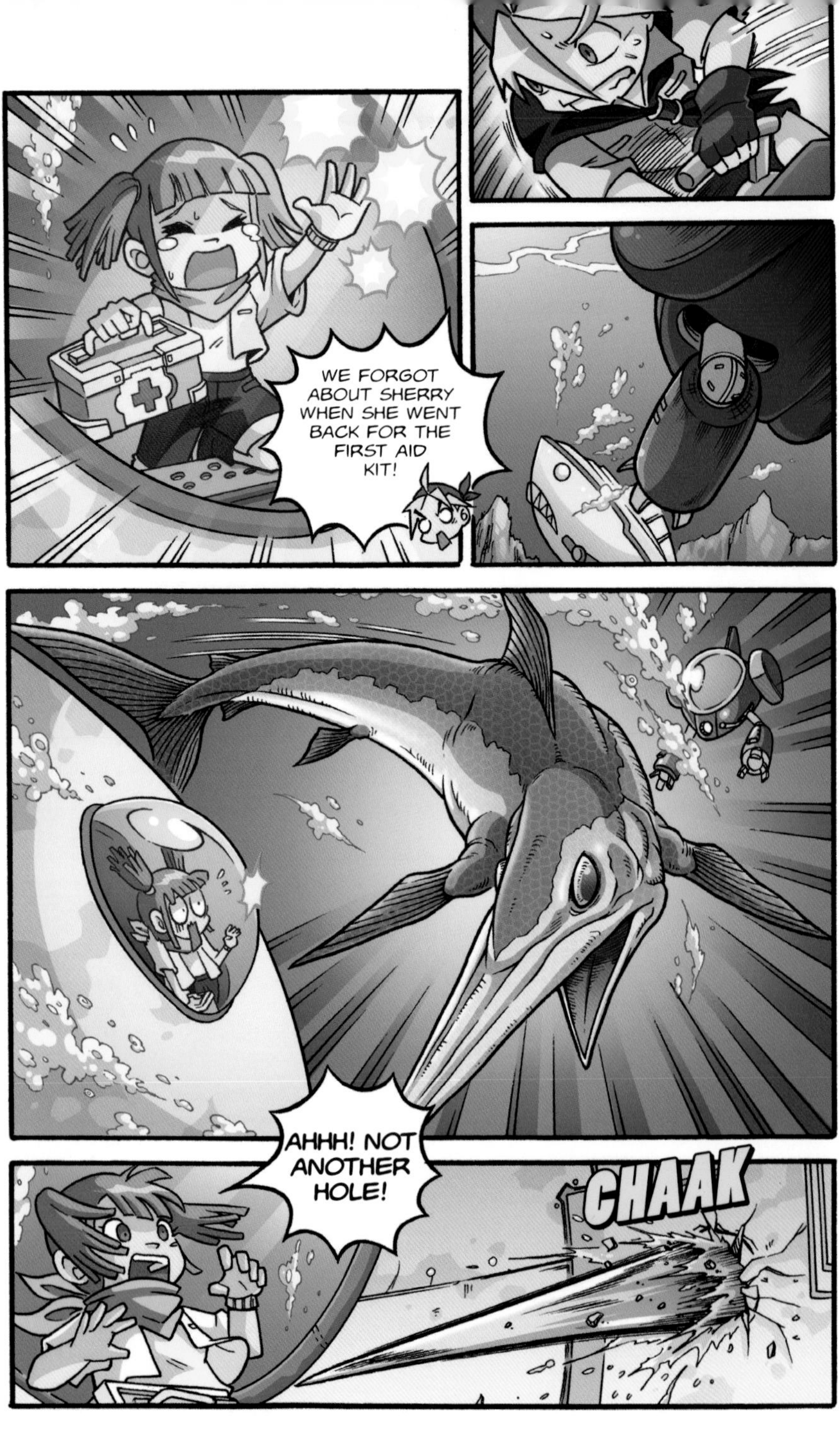

WE FORGOT ABOUT SHERRY WHEN SHE WENT BACK FOR THE FIRST AID KIT!
AHHH! NOT ANOTHER HOLE!
CHAAK

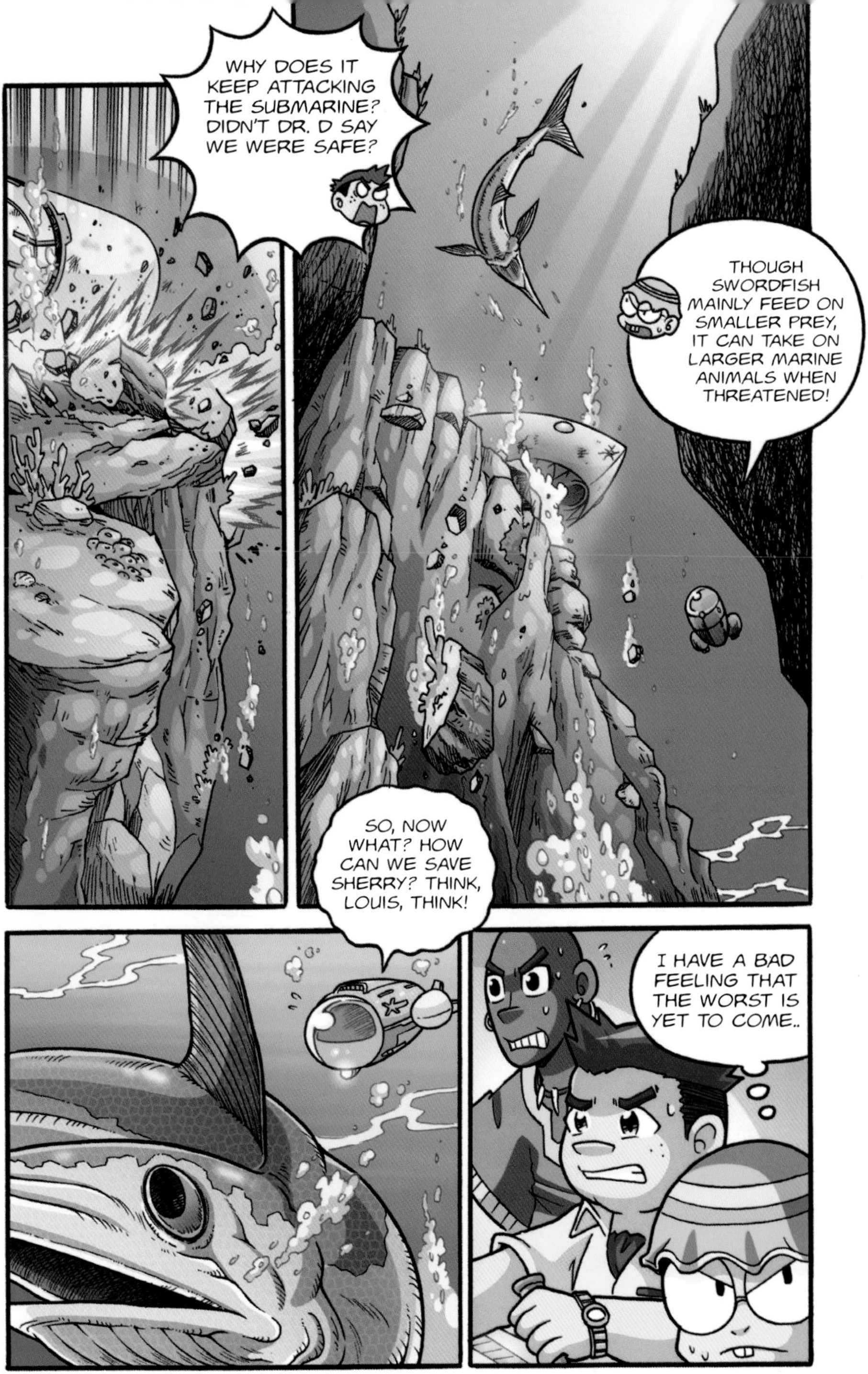
WHY DOES IT KEEP ATTACKING THE SUBMARINE? DIDN'T DR. D SAY WE WERE SAFE?
THOUGH SWORDFISH MAINLY FEED ON SMALLER PREY, IT CAN TAKE ON LARGER MARINE ANIMALS WHEN THREATENED!
SO, NOW WHAT? HOW CAN WE SAVE SHERRY? THINK, LOUIS, THINK!
I HAVE A BAD FEELING THAT THE WORST IS YET TO COME..

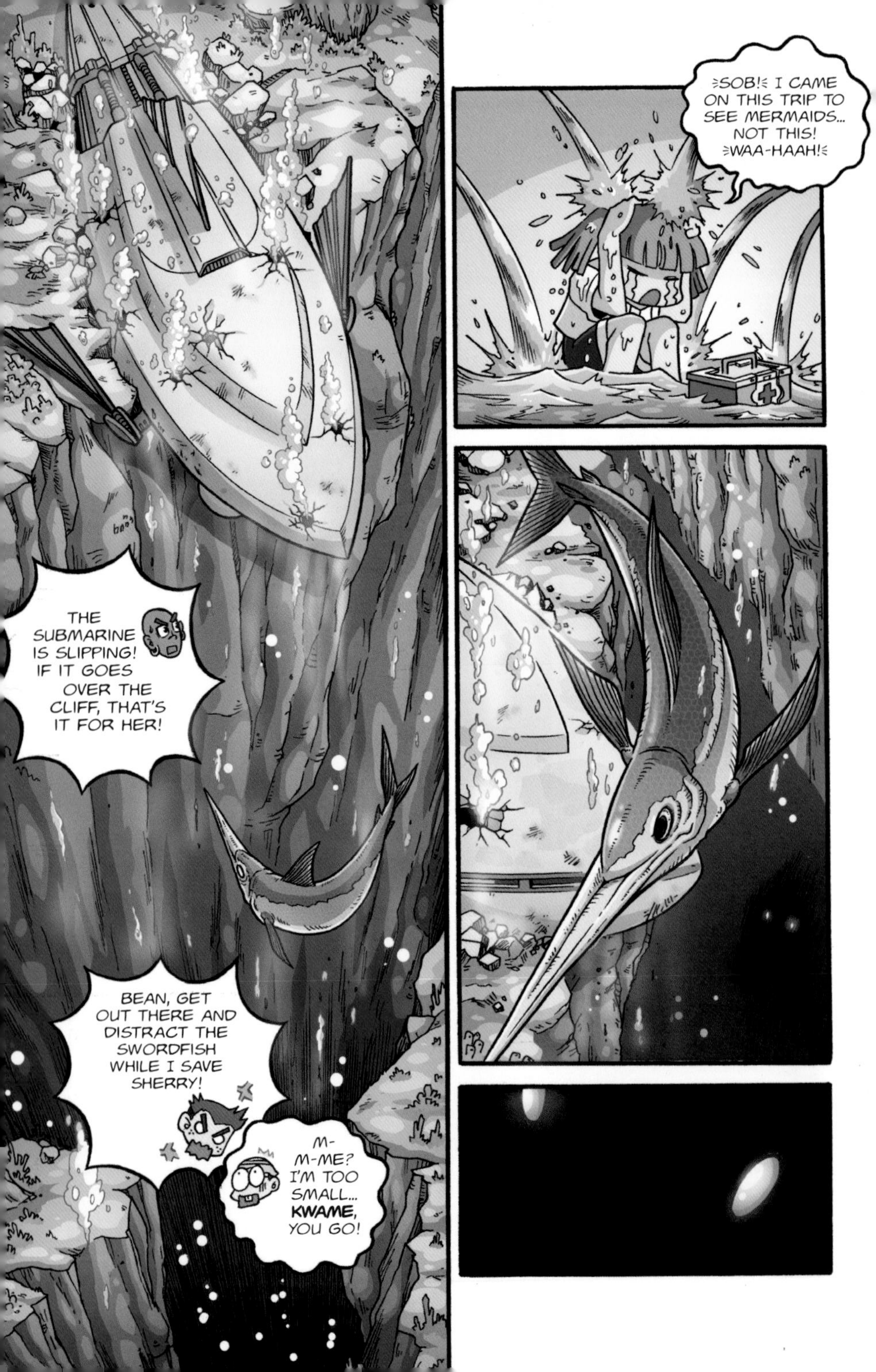
THE SUBMARINE IS SLIPPING! IF IT GOES OVER THE CLIFF, THAT'S IT FOR HER!
BEAN, GET OUT THERE AND DISTRACT THE SWORDFISH WHILE I SAVE SHERRY!
M-M-ME? I'M TOO SMALL... **KWAME**, YOU GO!
≥SOB!≤ I CAME ON THIS TRIP TO SEE MERMAIDS... NOT THIS! ≥WAA-HAAH!≤

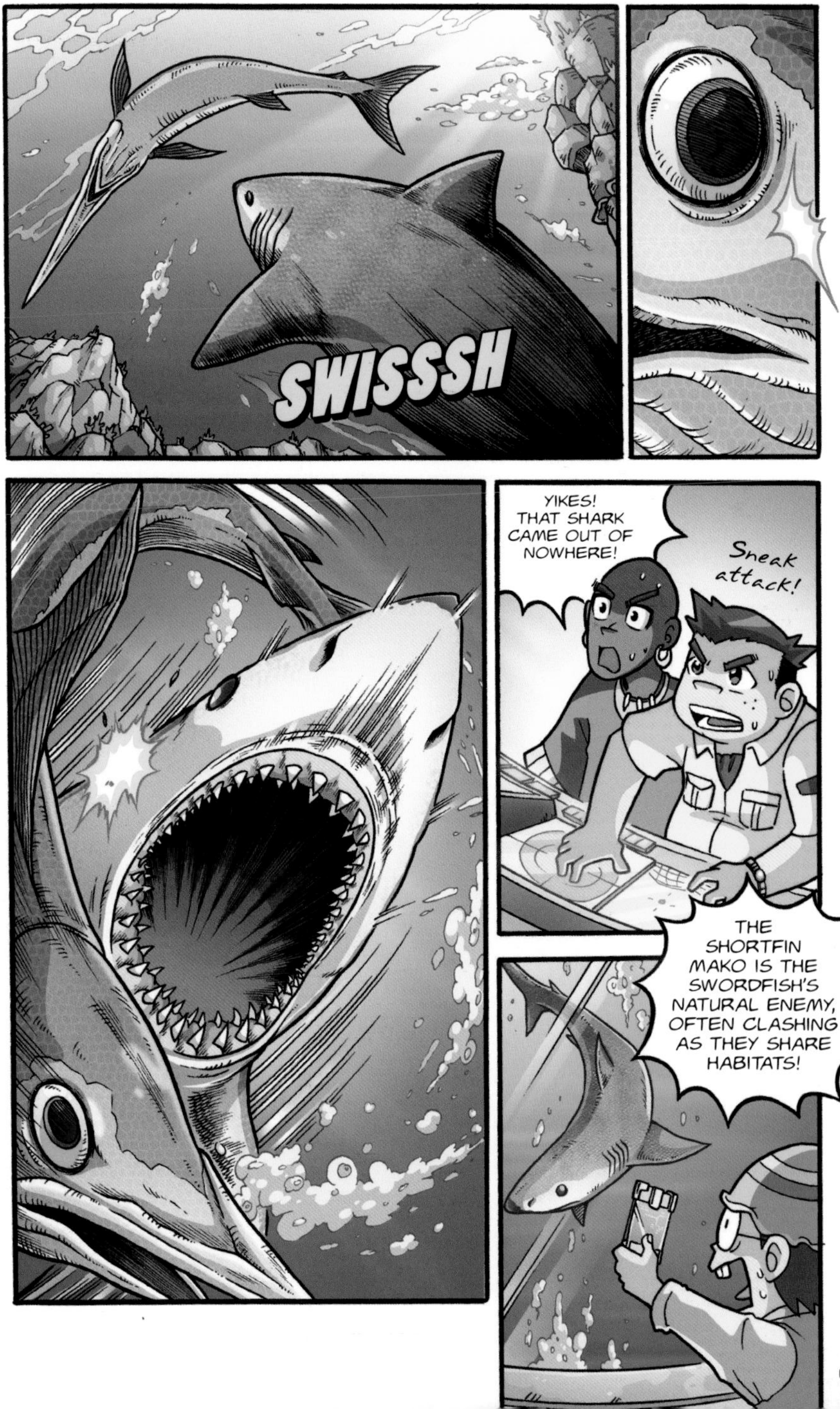
SWISSSH
YIKES! THAT SHARK CAME OUT OF NOWHERE!
Sneak attack!
THE SHORTFIN MAKO IS THE SWORDFISH'S NATURAL ENEMY, OFTEN CLASHING AS THEY SHARE HABITATS!

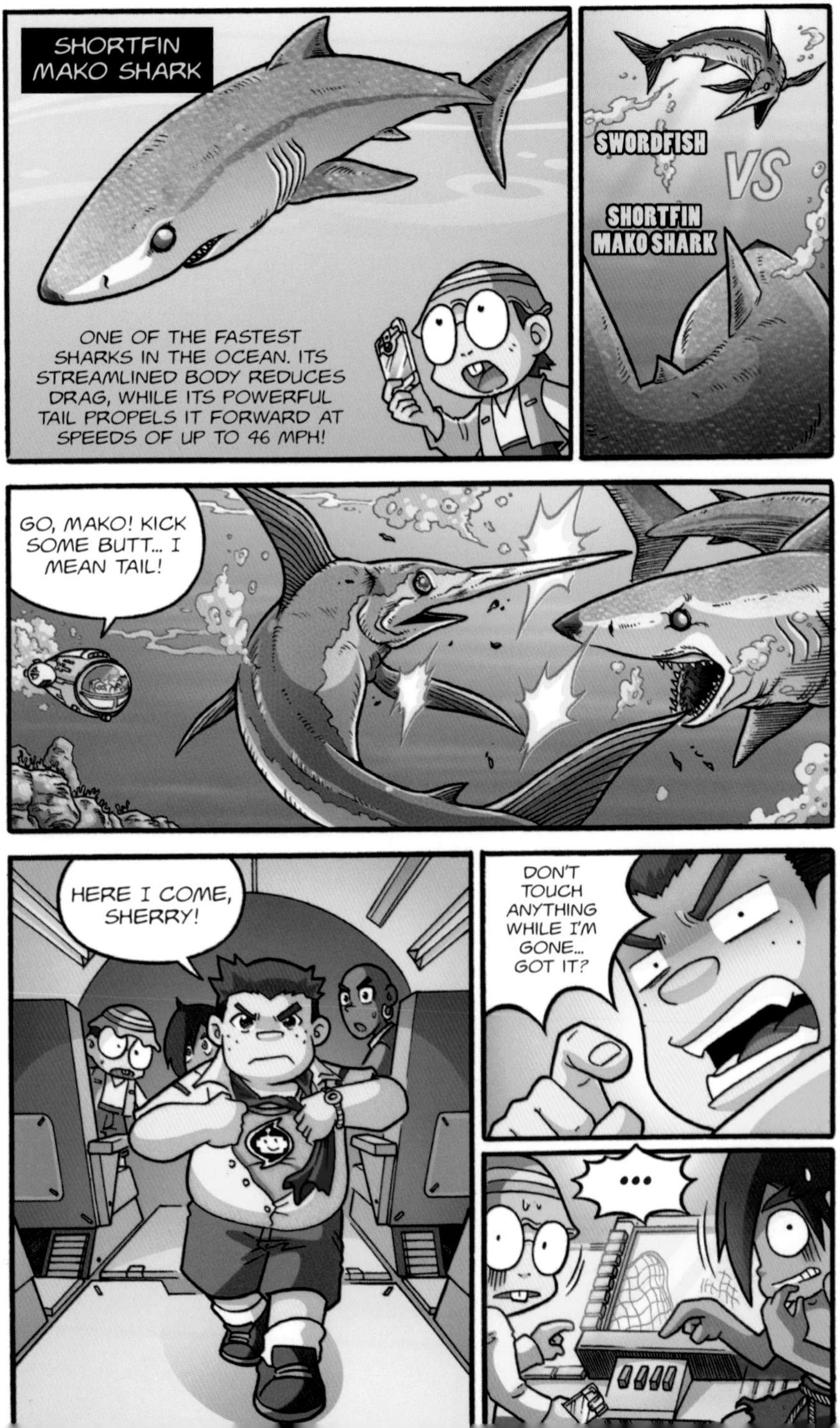
SHORTFIN MAKO SHARK
ONE OF THE FASTEST SHARKS IN THE OCEAN. ITS STREAMLINED BODY REDUCES DRAG, WHILE ITS POWERFUL TAIL PROPELS IT FORWARD AT SPEEDS OF UP TO 46 MPH!
SWORDFISH
VS
SHORTFIN MAKO SHARK
GO, MAKO! KICK SOME BUTT... I MEAN TAIL!
HERE I COME, SHERRY!
DON'T TOUCH ANYTHING WHILE I'M GONE... GOT IT?
...

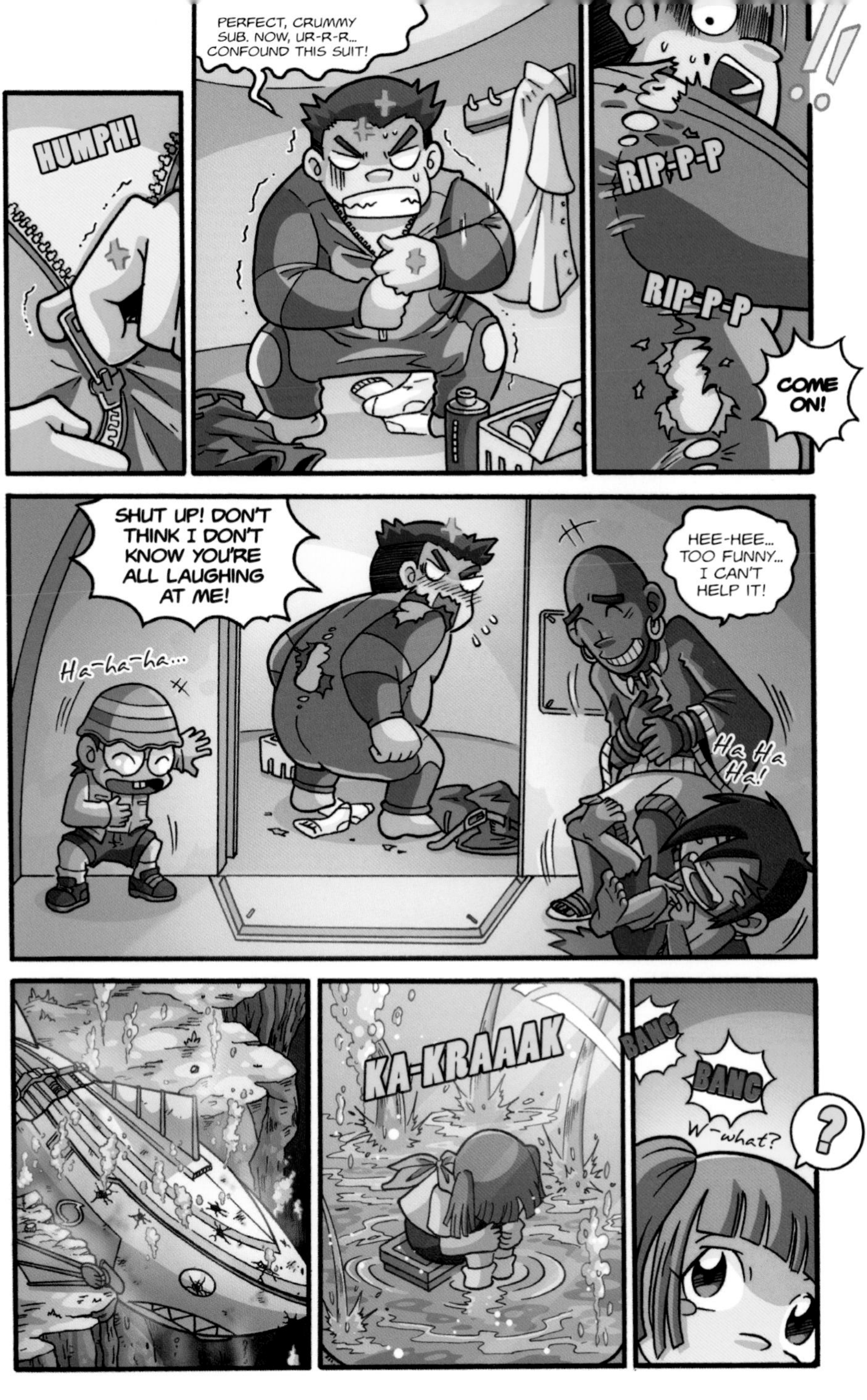
HUMPH!
PERFECT, CRUMMY SUB. NOW, UR-R-R... CONFOUND THIS SUIT!
RIP-P-P
RIP-P-P
COME ON!
SHUT UP! DON'T THINK I DON'T KNOW YOU'RE ALL LAUGHING AT ME!
Ha-ha-ha...
HEE-HEE... TOO FUNNY... I CAN'T HELP IT!
Ha Ha Ha!
KA-KRAAAK
BANG
BANG
W-what?
?

GOOD GRIEF, LOUIS!

SHAA

SHOO SHOO

CHOMP

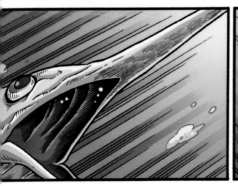

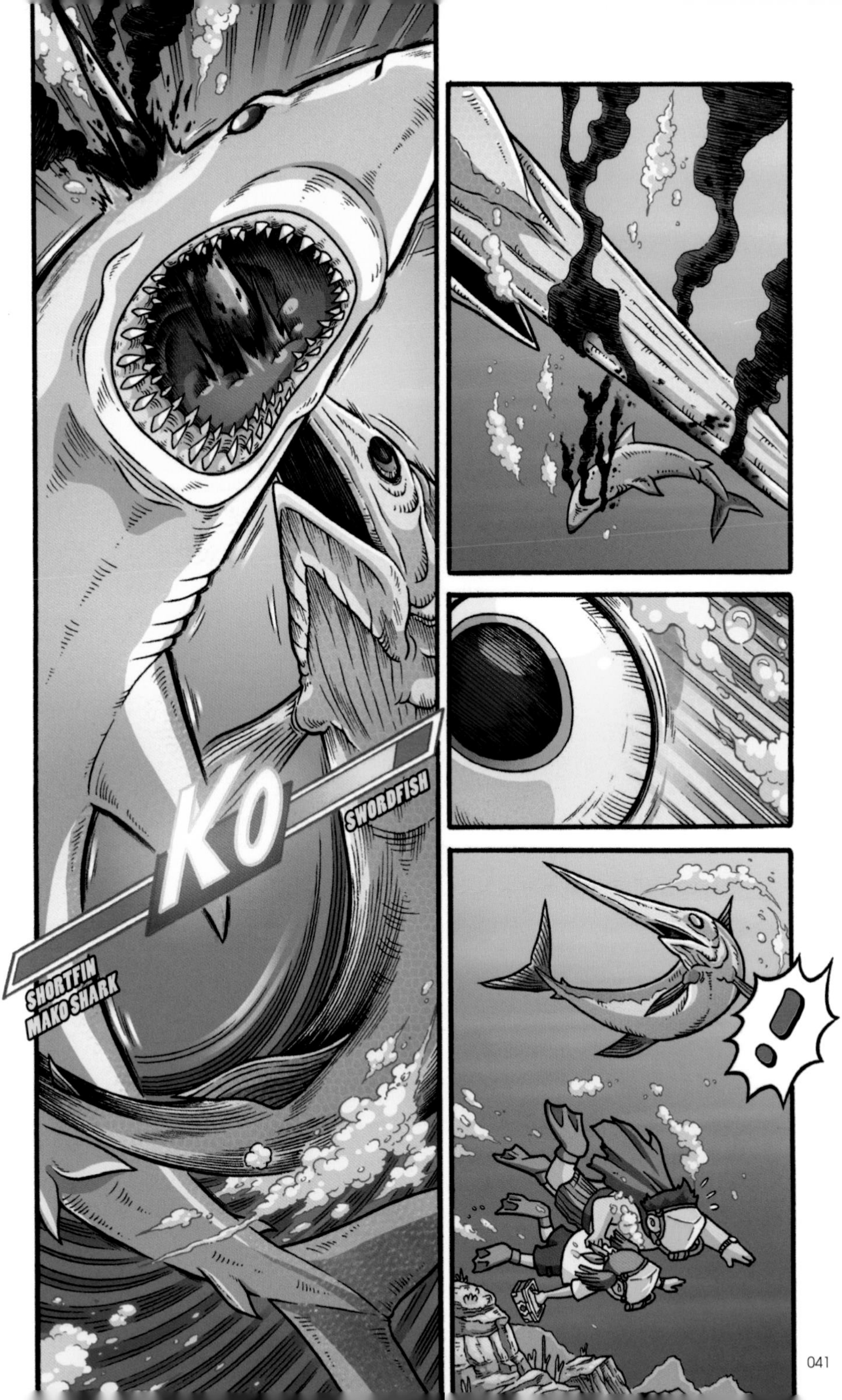
KO
SWORDFISH
SHORTFIN MAKO SHARK
!

Oh, no, has it seen us?
C'mon, Sherry!
!
What's wrong? What's going on?
THE SWORDFISH HAS SPOTTED THEM. FASTER, GUYS... SWIM FASTER!
NO! WE MUST DO SOMETHING!
NO! LOUIS SAID TO STAY PUT!

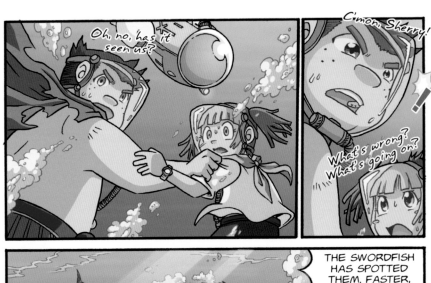

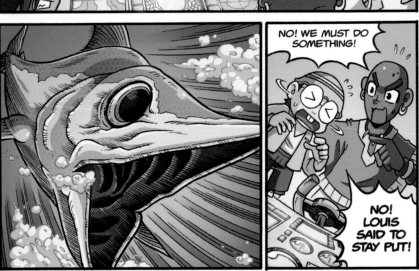

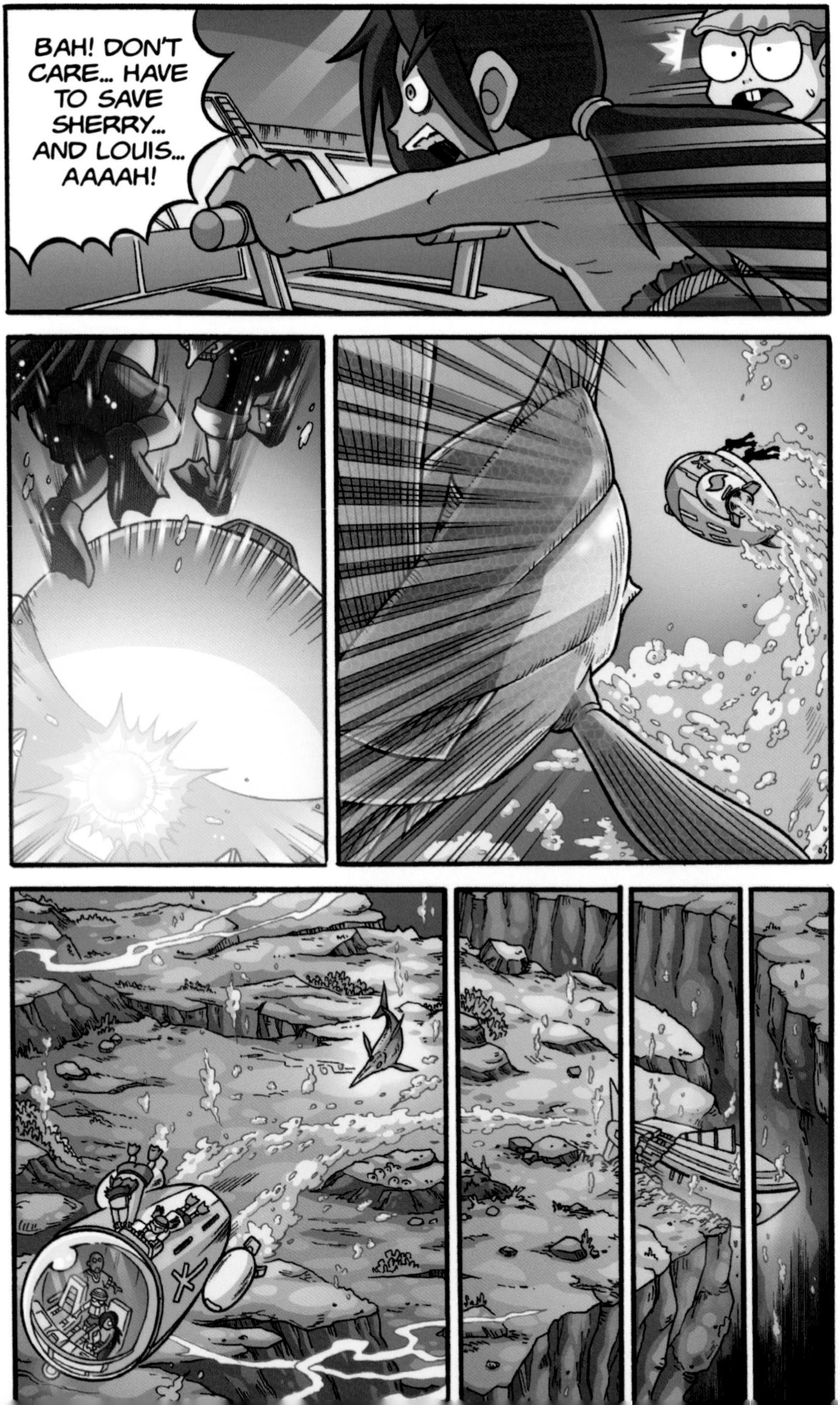
BAH! DON'T CARE... HAVE TO SAVE SHERRY... AND LOUIS... AAAAH!

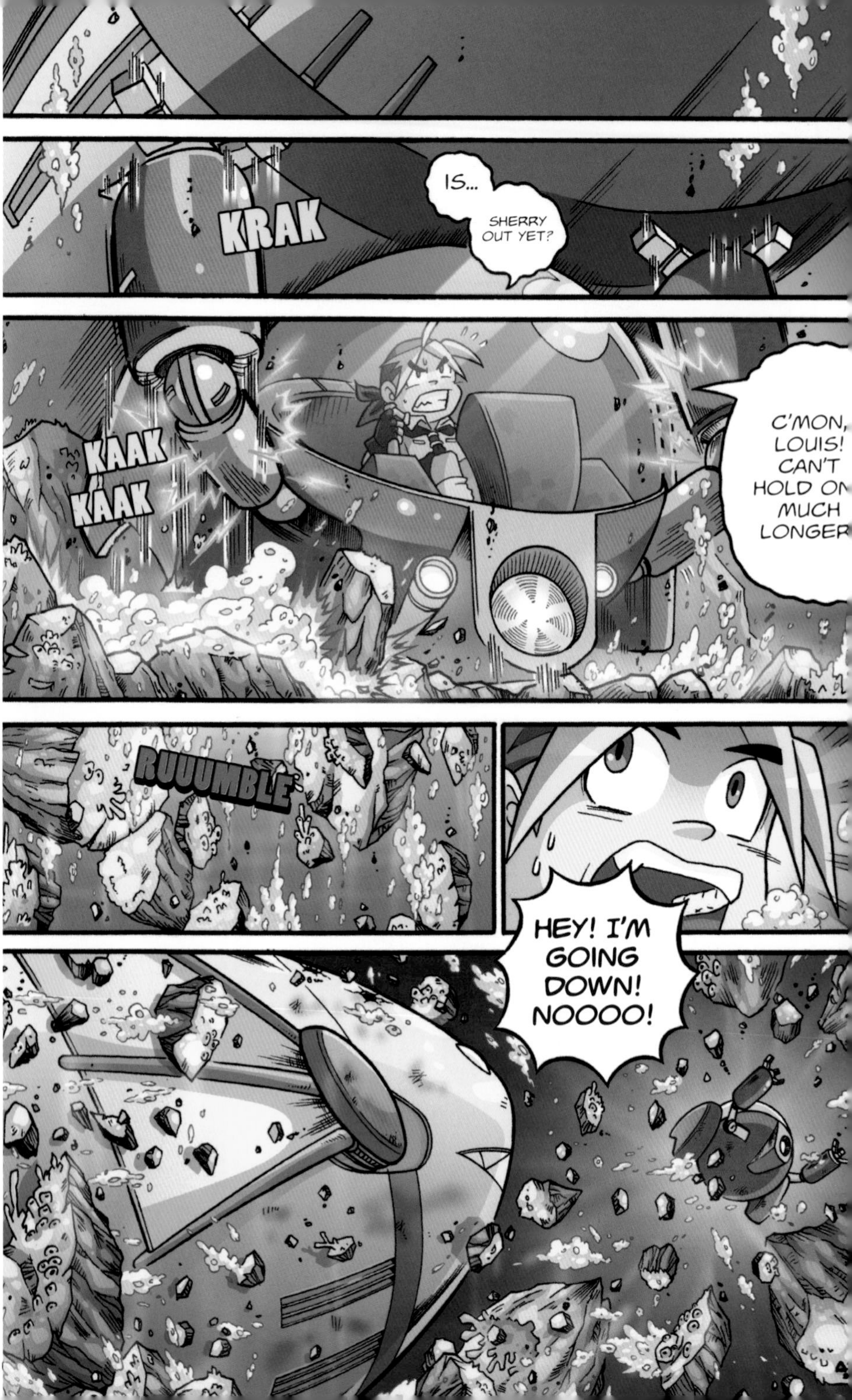
IS...
SHERRY OUT YET?
KRAK
KAAK KAAK
C'MON, LOUIS! CAN'T HOLD ON MUCH LONGER
RUUUMBLE
HEY! I'M GOING DOWN! NOOOO!

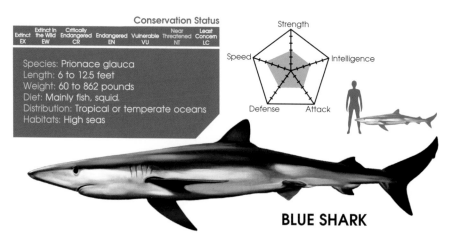

Conservation Status

Extinct EX	Extinct in the Wild EW	Critically Endangered CR	Endangered EN	Vulnerable VU	Near Threatened NT	Least Concern LC

Species: Prionace glauca
Length: 6 to 12.5 feet
Weight: 60 to 862 pounds
Diet: Mainly fish, squid.
Distribution: Tropical or temperate oceans
Habitats: High seas

Strength
Intelligence
Attack
Defense
Speed

BLUE SHARK

Light-bodied with long pectoral fins; the top of its body is deep blue, lighter on the sides, and the underside is white. Blue sharks can swim for long distances, preferring warm waters. Much larger than males, females give live birth to pups (baby sharks). Blue sharks often school segregated by sex and size, and this behavior has led to their nickname "wolves of the sea." An estimated 10 to 20 million are killed each year for their meat, hide, and fins.

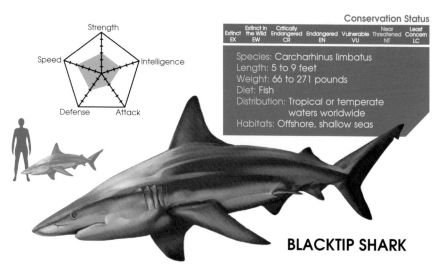

Strength
Intelligence
Attack
Defense
Speed

Conservation Status

Extinct EX	Extinct in the Wild EW	Critically Endangered CR	Endangered EN	Vulnerable VU	Near Threatened NT	Least Concern LC

Species: Carcharhinus limbatus
Length: 5 to 9 feet
Weight: 66 to 271 pounds
Diet: Fish
Distribution: Tropical or temperate waters worldwide
Habitats: Offshore, shallow seas

BLACKTIP SHARK

Characterized by black markings on its pectoral, dorsal, pelvic, and caudal fins, this robust shark is widely spread throughout tropical/subtropical waters. Grey to brown above with a pale underside, with a white horizontal stripe, blacktips are known to make spinning leaps out of the water during feeding. This viviparous species (live birth) is also widely hunted for its body parts, especially the fins, liver, and hide.

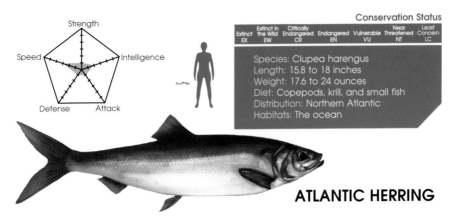

Strength
Speed
Intelligence
Defense
Attack

Conservation Status

Extinct EX	Extinct in the Wild EW	Critically Endangered CR	Endangered EN	Vulnerable VU	Near Threatened NT	Least Concern LC

Species: Clupea harengus
Length: 15.8 to 18 inches
Weight: 17.6 to 24 ounces
Diet: Copepods, krill, and small fish
Distribution: Northern Atlantic
Habitats: The ocean

ATLANTIC HERRING

Traveling in huge schools, Atlantic herring have become the main economic resource of the coastal areas of New England and Canada. A shoal may consist of up to 4 billion fish, trawling the Atlantic in search of food. Being the most prolific breeding fish in the world, it is prey to many larger marine animals in addition to widespread fishing efforts, but their numbers somehow remain undiminished.

Conservation Status

Extinct EX	Extinct in the Wild EW	Critically Endangered CR	Endangered EN	Vulnerable VU	Near Threatened NT	Least Concern LC

Species: Isurus oxyrinchus
Length: 10.5 to 13.1 feet
Weight: 132 to 300 pounds
Diet: Mainly mollusca and bony fish
Distribution: Tropical or temperate waters of the world
Habitats: Offshore waters worldwide

The fastest shark species in the world, reaching around 46 miles per hour. This highly hydrodynamic creature can leap approximately 30 feet or higher in the air. Powerfully muscular, this large shark is an ambush predator, relying on sheer speed and strength to catch prospective prey unawares. As in most shark species, female makos dwarf their male counterparts, birthing live young.

Strength
Speed
Intelligence
Defense
Attack

SHORTFIN MAKO SHARK

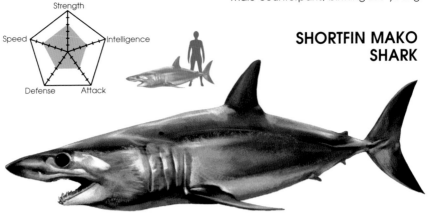

CHAPTER 3
THE COOKIECUTTERS

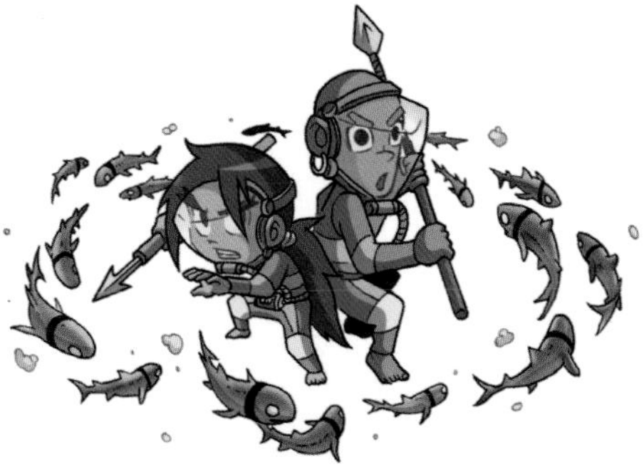

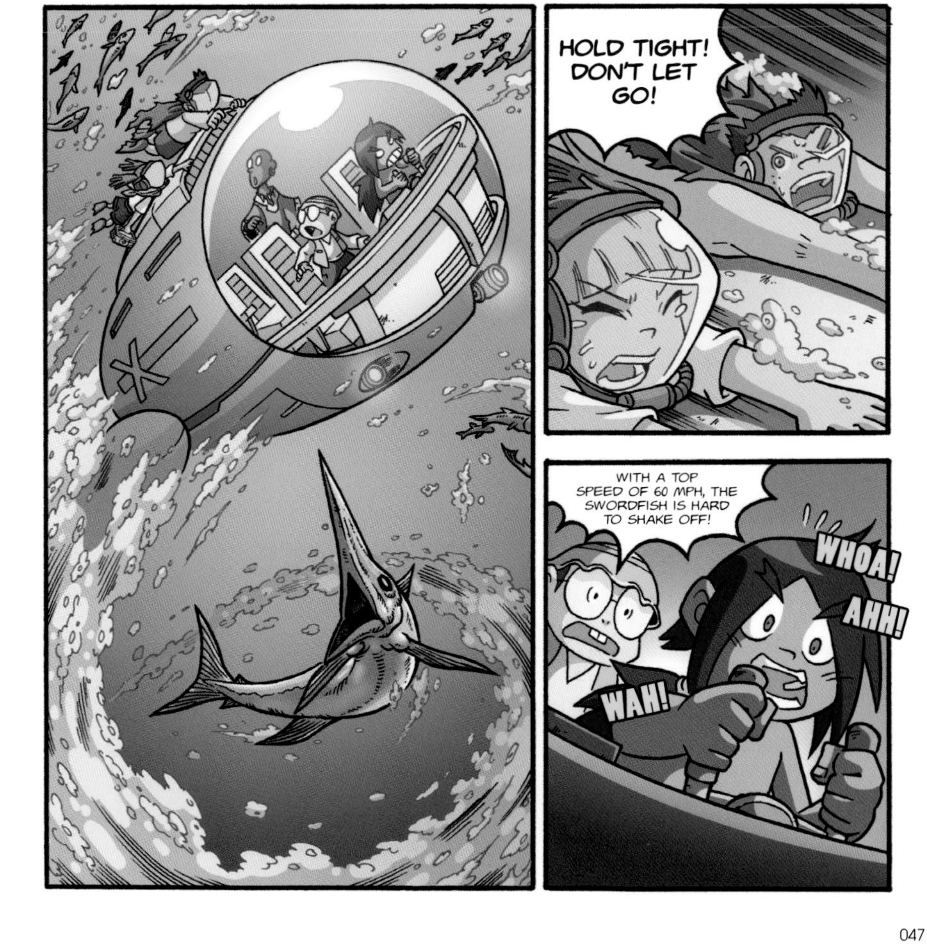
HOLD TIGHT! DON'T LET GO!
WITH A TOP SPEED OF 60 MPH, THE SWORDFISH IS HARD TO SHAKE OFF!
WHOA!
AHH!
WAH!

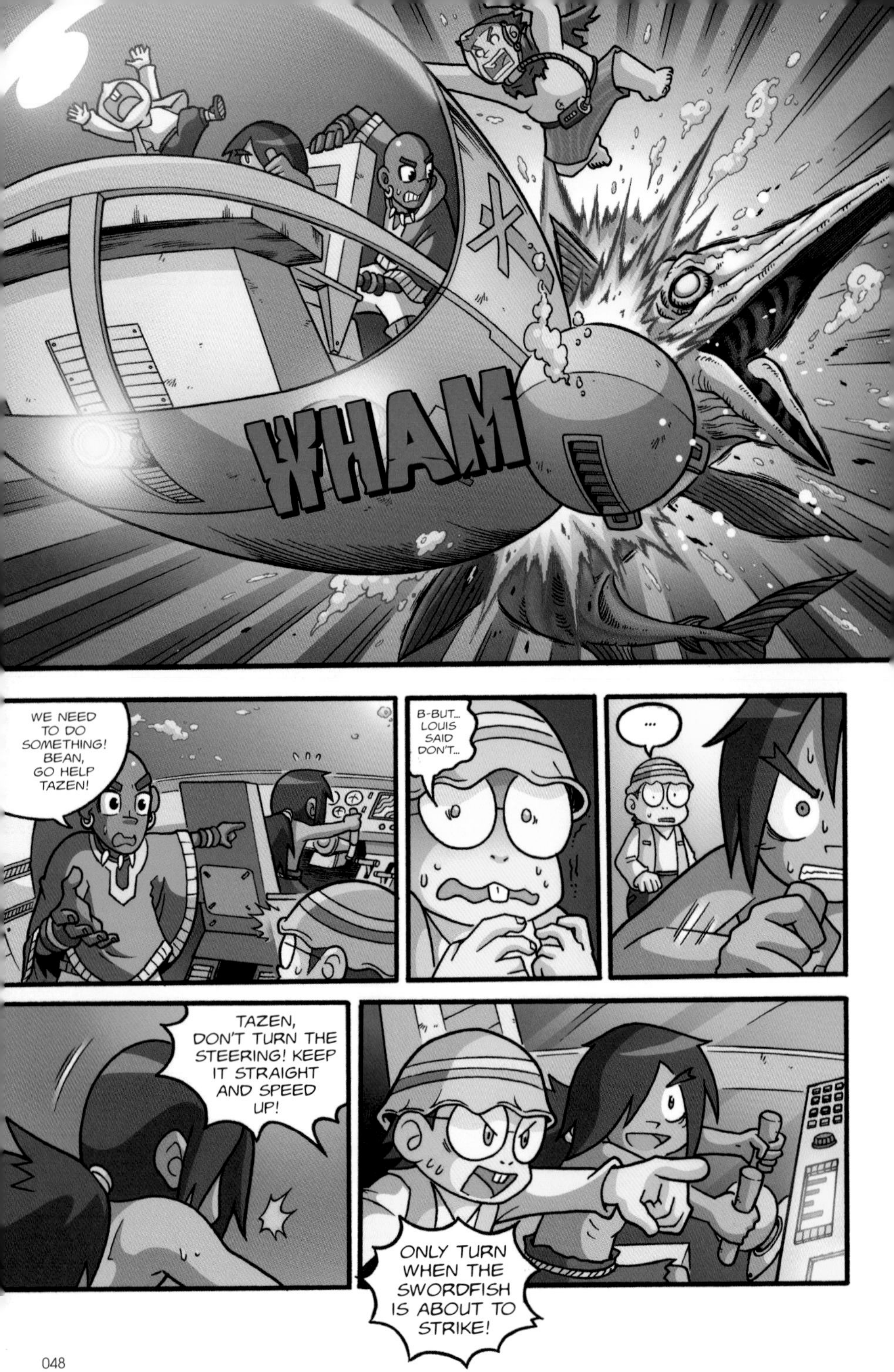
WHAM
WE NEED TO DO SOMETHING! BEAN, GO HELP TAZEN!
B-BUT... LOUIS SAID DON'T...
...
TAZEN, DON'T TURN THE STEERING! KEEP IT STRAIGHT AND SPEED UP!
ONLY TURN WHEN THE SWORDFISH IS ABOUT TO STRIKE!

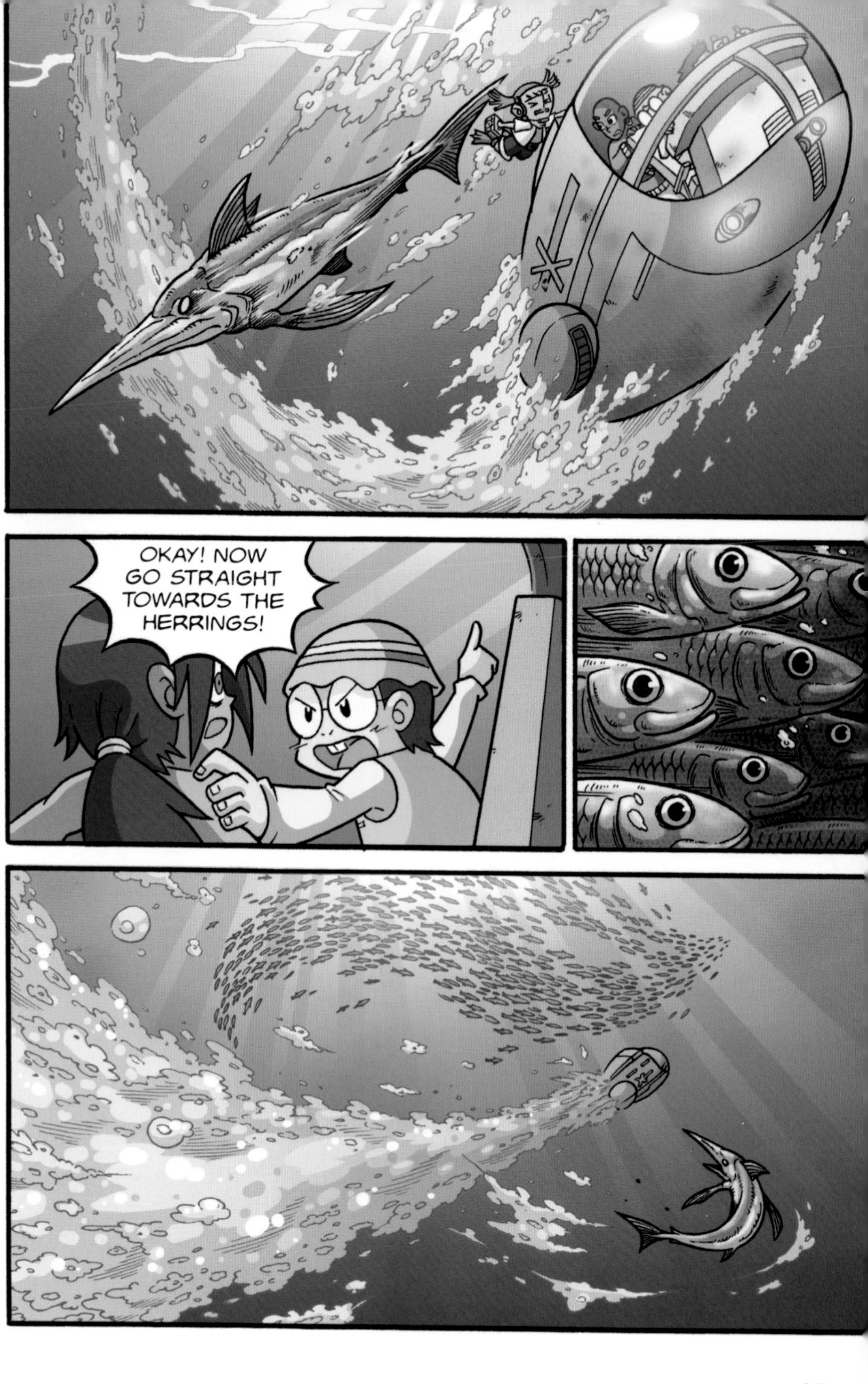
OKAY! NOW GO STRAIGHT TOWARDS THE HERRINGS!

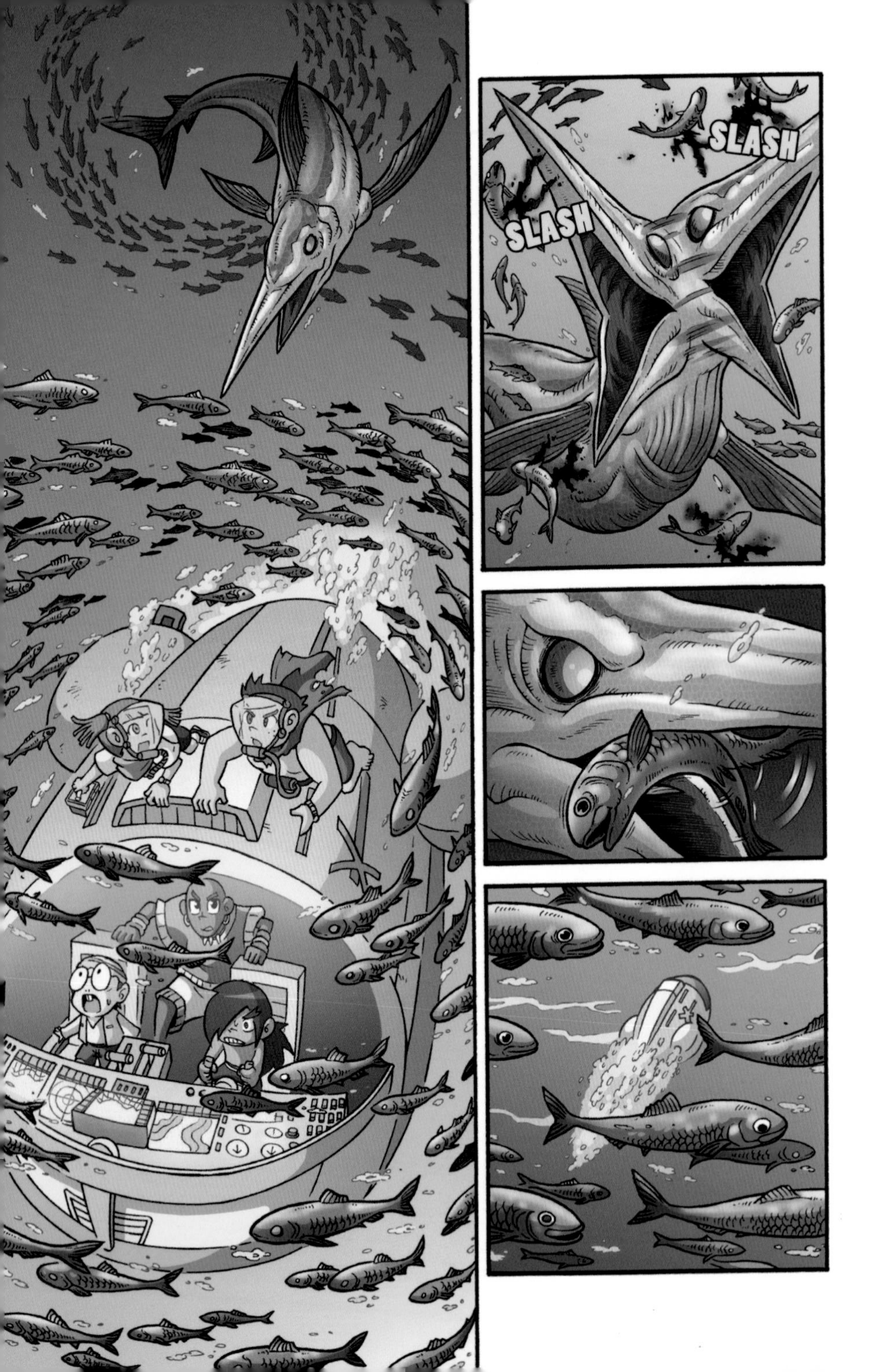
SLASH
SLASH

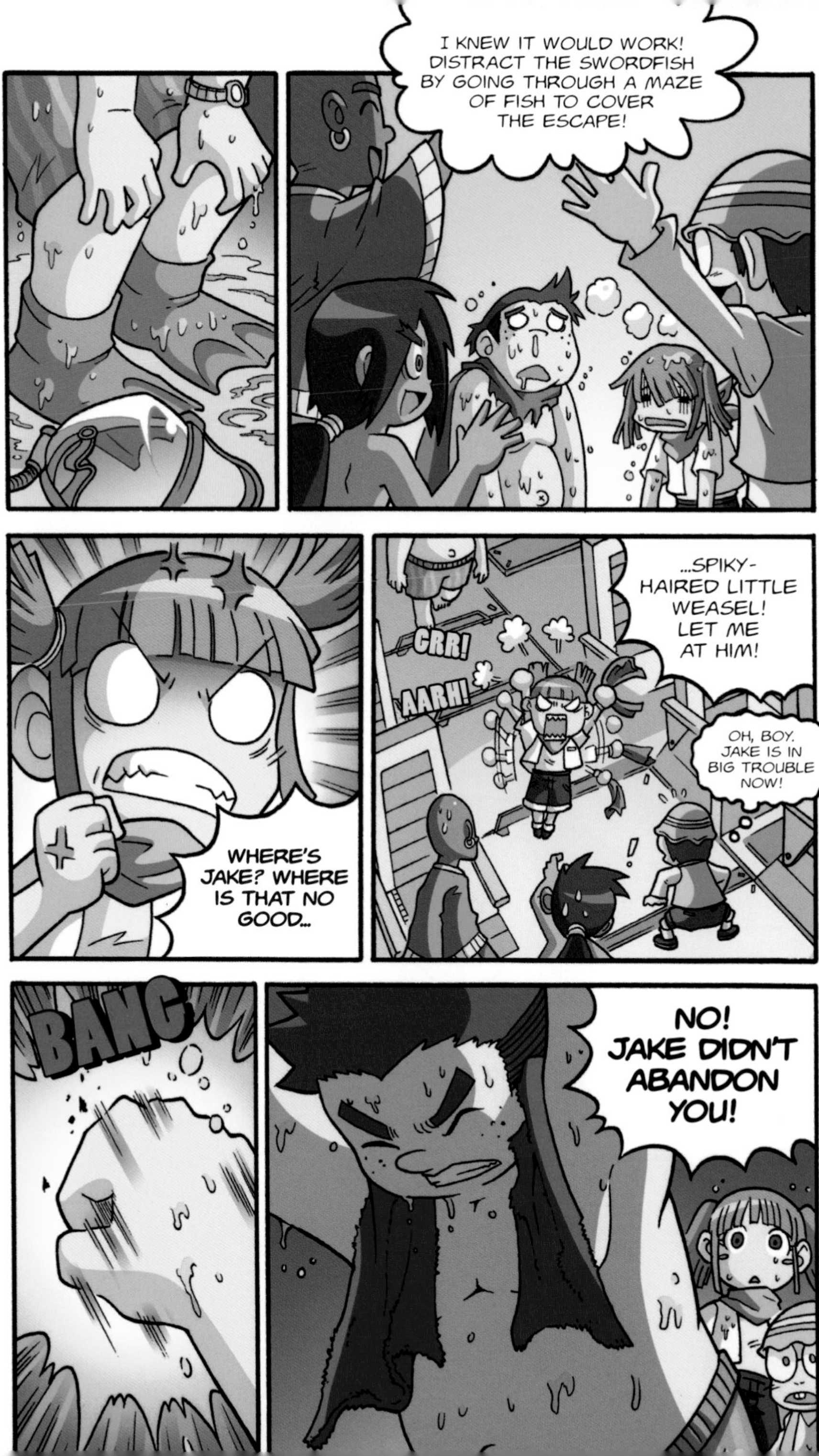

I KNEW IT WOULD WORK! DISTRACT THE SWORDFISH BY GOING THROUGH A MAZE OF FISH TO COVER THE ESCAPE!
WHERE'S JAKE? WHERE IS THAT NO GOOD...
...SPIKY-HAIRED LITTLE WEASEL! LET ME AT HIM!
CRR!
AARH!
OH, BOY. JAKE IS IN BIG TROUBLE NOW!
BANG
NO! JAKE DIDN'T ABANDON YOU!

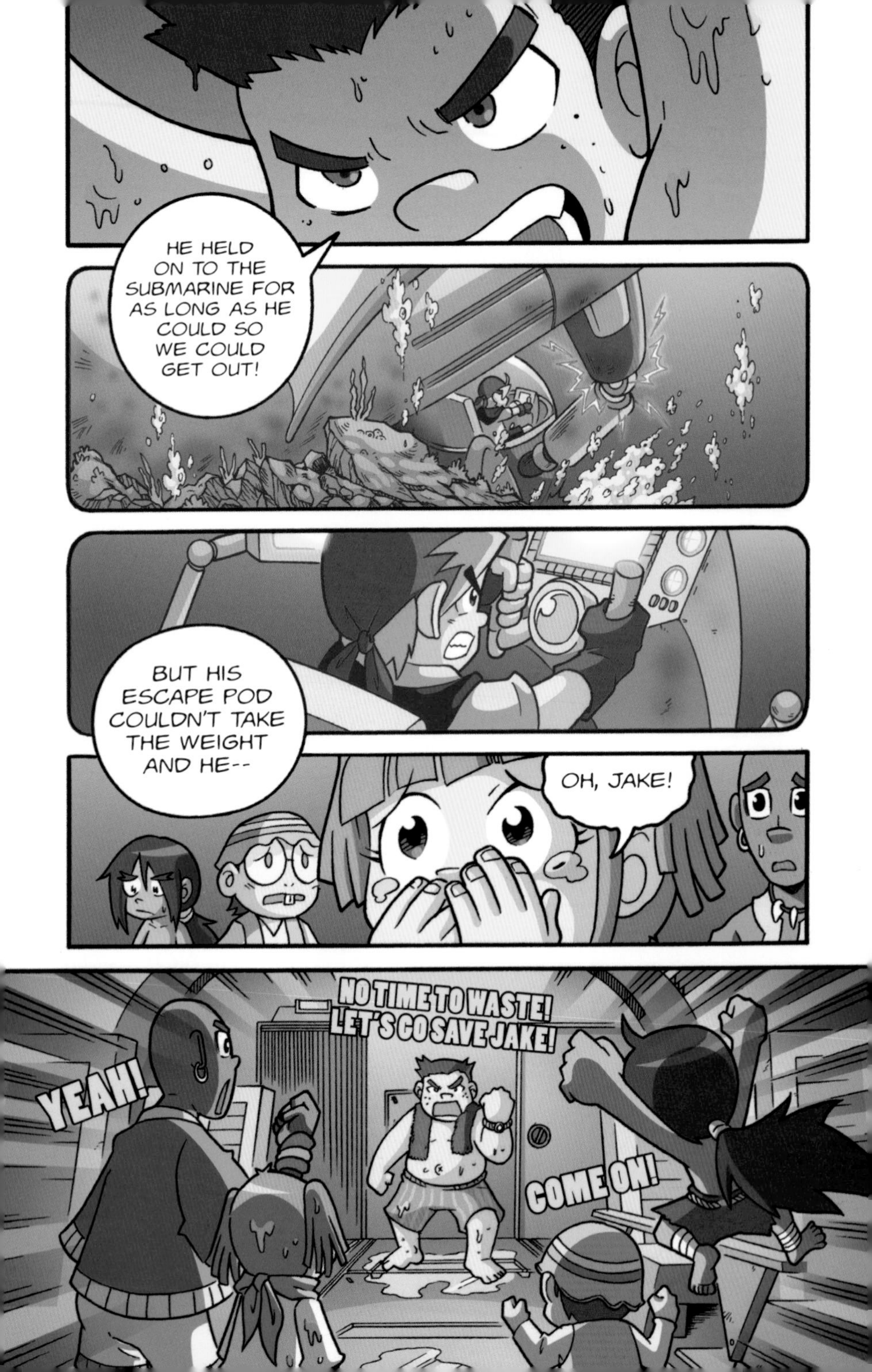
HE HELD ON TO THE SUBMARINE FOR AS LONG AS HE COULD SO WE COULD GET OUT!
BUT HIS ESCAPE POD COULDN'T TAKE THE WEIGHT AND HE--
OH, JAKE!
NO TIME TO WASTE! LET'S GO SAVE JAKE!
YEAH!
COME ON!

LOOKS LIKE THE COAST IS CLEAR. THE SWORDFISH MUST HAVE LEFT.

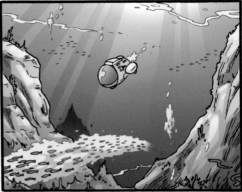

BUT KEEP AN EYE OUT FOR JAKE OR ANY SIGN OF TROUBLE, WE'RE NOT SAFE YET!

THAT'S AN ANGEL SHARK, COMMONLY SEEN ON THE SEABED! BUT WHY IS IT SO BADLY HURT?

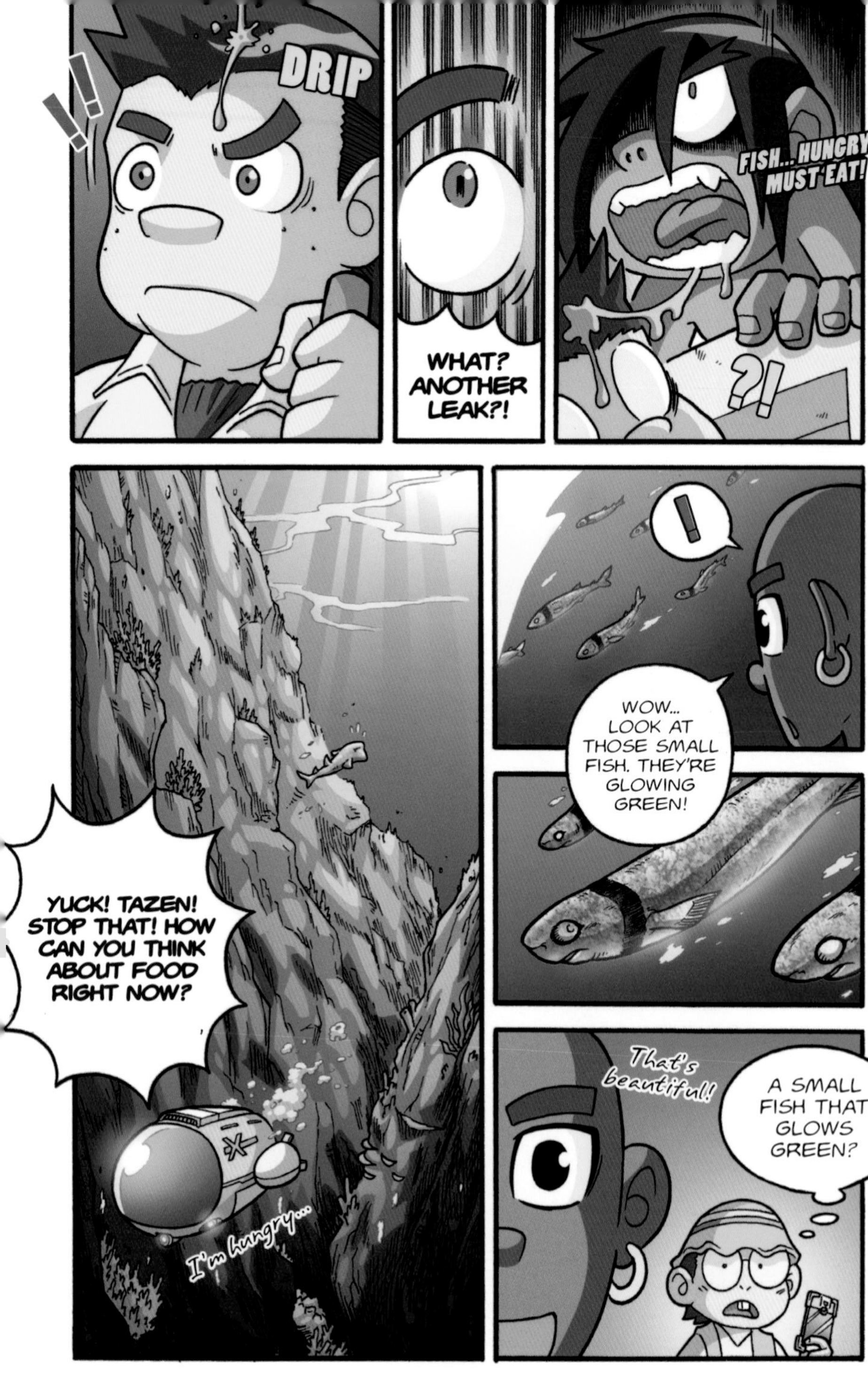
!!
DRIP
WHAT? ANOTHER LEAK?!
FISH... HUNGRY... MUST EAT!
?!
YUCK! TAZEN! STOP THAT! HOW CAN YOU THINK ABOUT FOOD RIGHT NOW?
I'm hungry...
!
WOW... LOOK AT THOSE SMALL FISH. THEY'RE GLOWING GREEN!
That's beautiful!
A SMALL FISH THAT GLOWS GREEN?

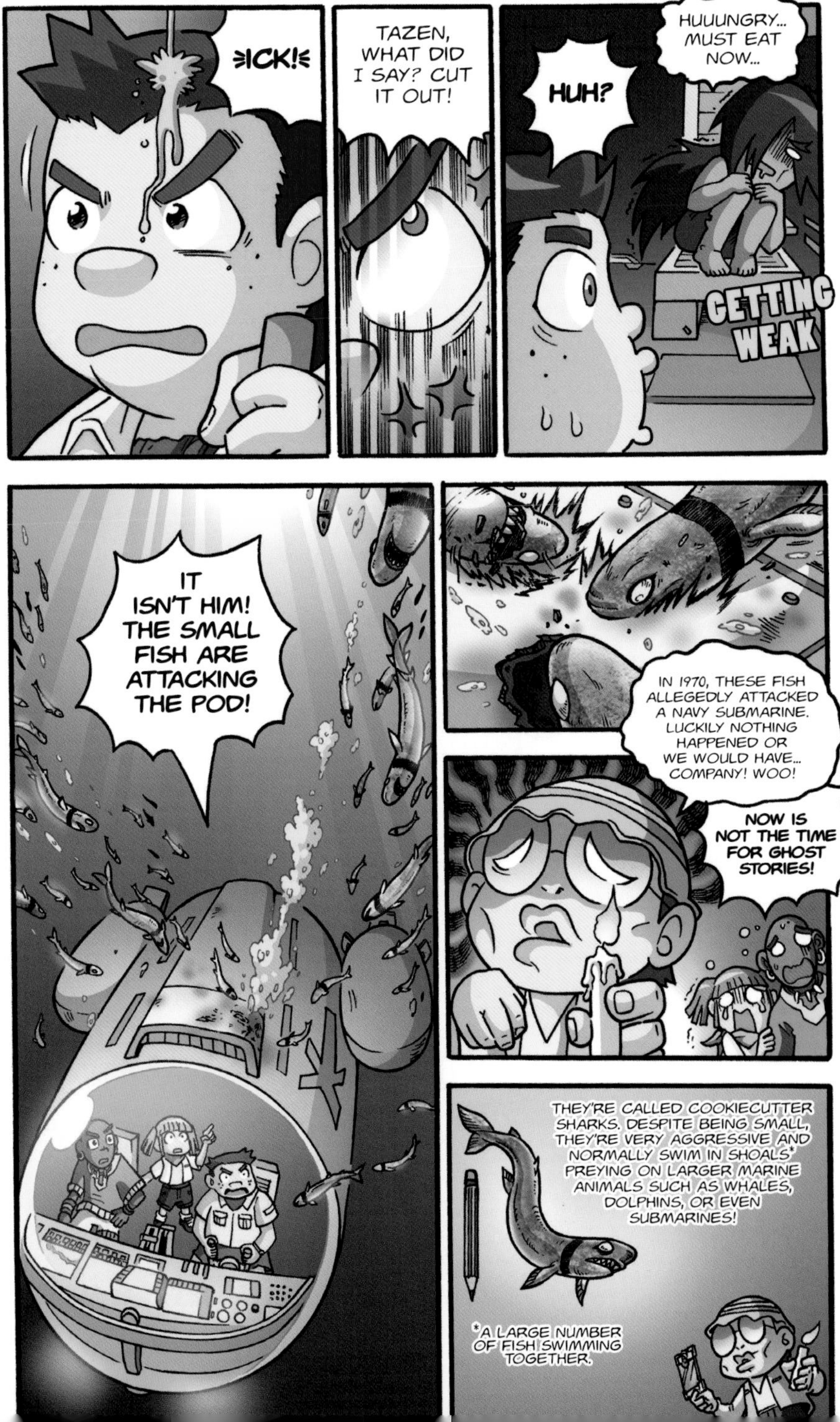

ICK!
TAZEN, WHAT DID I SAY? CUT IT OUT!
HUH?
HUUUNGRY... MUST EAT NOW...
GETTING WEAK
IT ISN'T HIM! THE SMALL FISH ARE ATTACKING THE POD!
IN 1970, THESE FISH ALLEGEDLY ATTACKED A NAVY SUBMARINE. LUCKILY NOTHING HAPPENED OR WE WOULD HAVE... COMPANY! WOO!
NOW IS NOT THE TIME FOR GHOST STORIES!
THEY'RE CALLED COOKIECUTTER SHARKS. DESPITE BEING SMALL, THEY'RE VERY AGGRESSIVE AND NORMALLY SWIM IN SHOALS* PREYING ON LARGER MARINE ANIMALS SUCH AS WHALES, DOLPHINS, OR EVEN SUBMARINES!
*A LARGE NUMBER OF FISH SWIMMING TOGETHER.

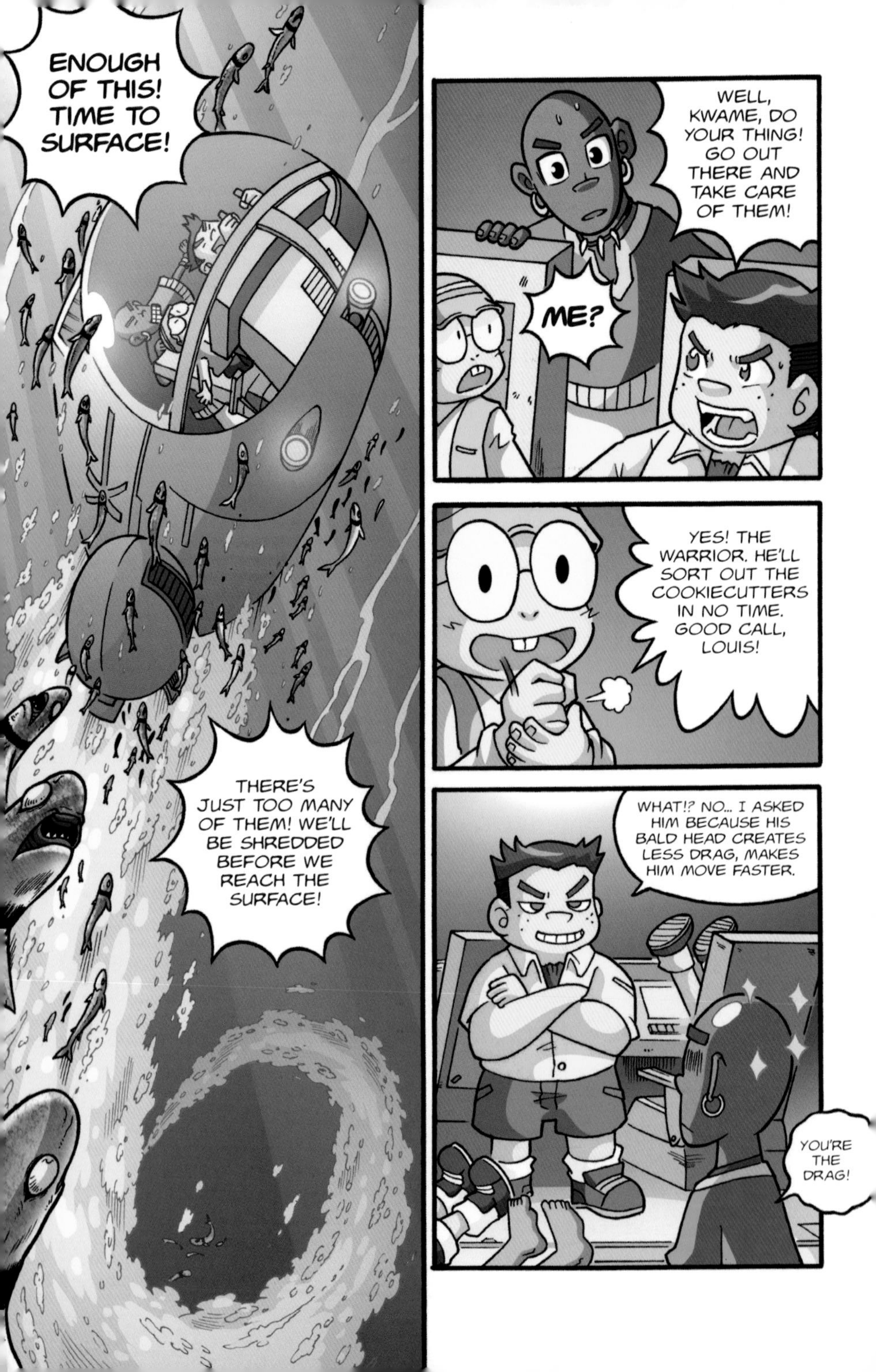
ENOUGH OF THIS! TIME TO SURFACE!
THERE'S JUST TOO MANY OF THEM! WE'LL BE SHREDDED BEFORE WE REACH THE SURFACE!
WELL, KWAME, DO YOUR THING! GO OUT THERE AND TAKE CARE OF THEM!
ME?
YES! THE WARRIOR. HE'LL SORT OUT THE COOKIECUTTERS IN NO TIME. GOOD CALL, LOUIS!
WHAT!? NO... I ASKED HIM BECAUSE HIS BALD HEAD CREATES LESS DRAG, MAKES HIM MOVE FASTER.
YOU'RE THE DRAG!

BE CAREFUL!

CHOMP

BITE

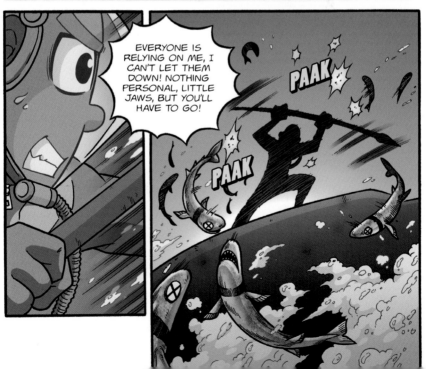

EVERYONE IS RELYING ON ME, I CAN'T LET THEM DOWN! NOTHING PERSONAL, LITTLE JAWS, BUT YOU'LL HAVE TO GO!

PAAK

PAAK

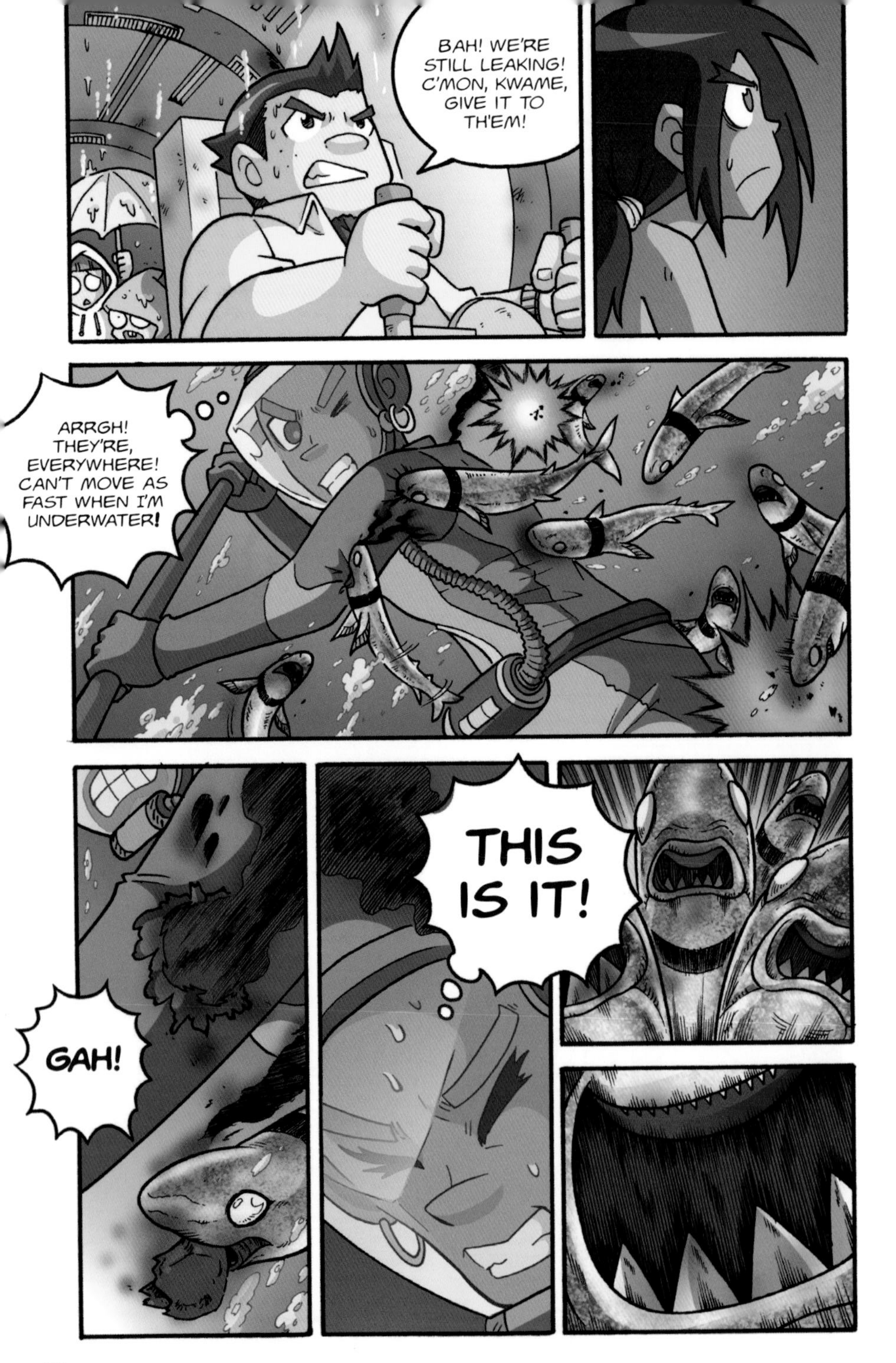
BAH! WE'RE STILL LEAKING! C'MON, KWAME, GIVE IT TO TH'EM!
ARRGH! THEY'RE, EVERYWHERE! CAN'T MOVE AS FAST WHEN I'M UNDERWATER!
GAH!
THIS IS IT!

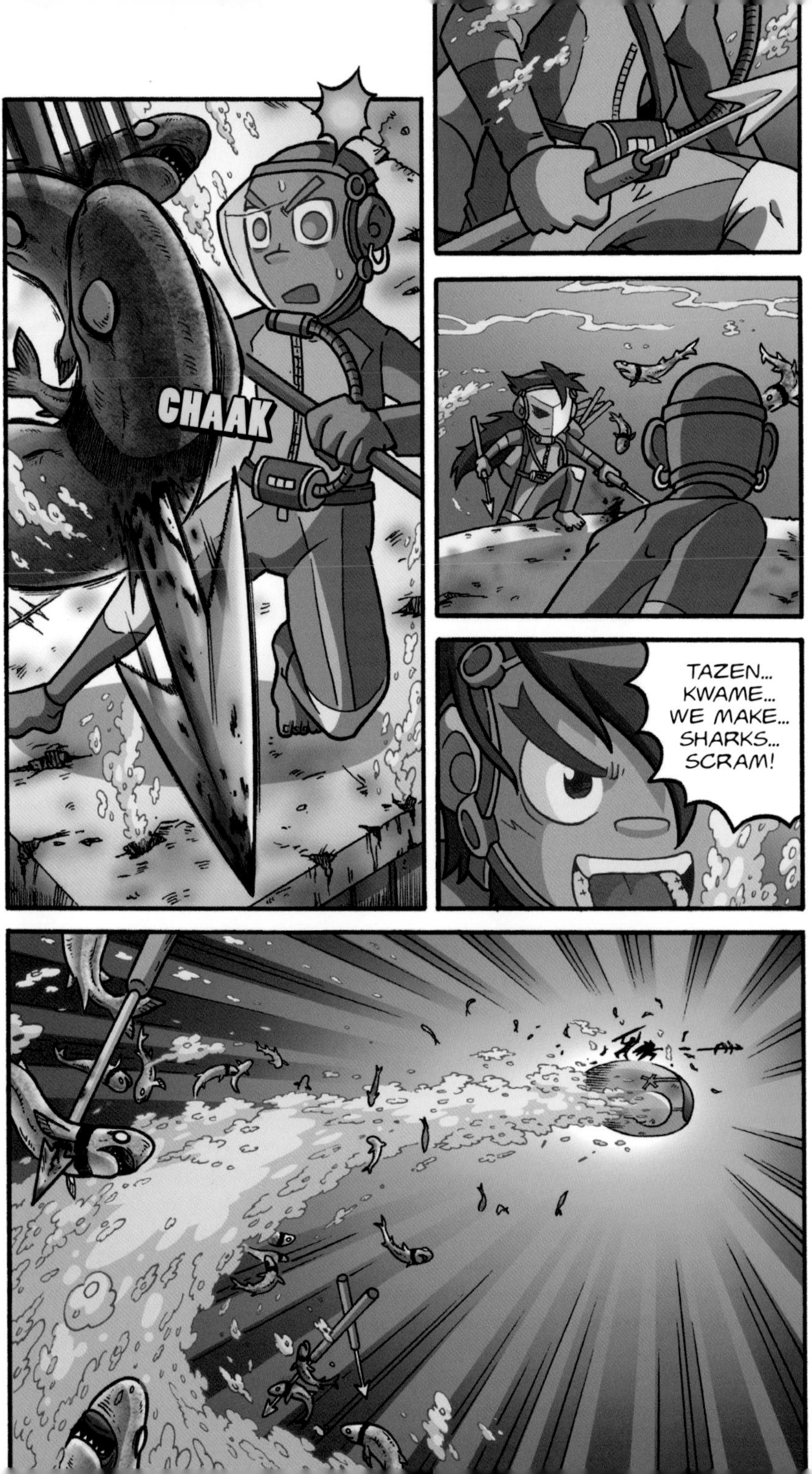
CHAAK
TAZEN... KWAME... WE MAKE... SHARKS... SCRAM!

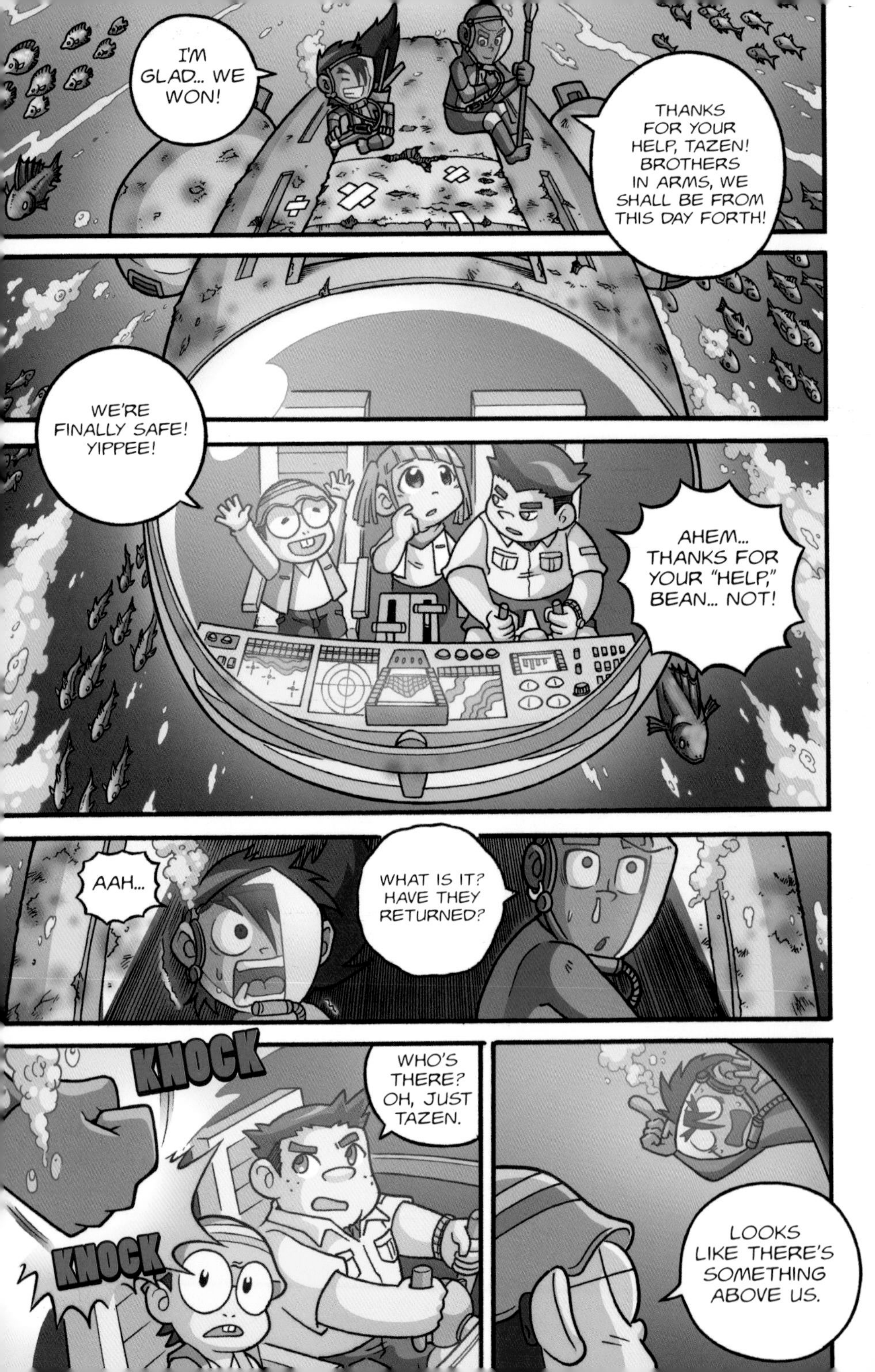
I'M GLAD... WE WON!
THANKS FOR YOUR HELP, TAZEN! BROTHERS IN ARMS, WE SHALL BE FROM THIS DAY FORTH!
WE'RE FINALLY SAFE! YIPPEE!
AHEM... THANKS FOR YOUR "HELP," BEAN... NOT!
AAH...
WHAT IS IT? HAVE THEY RETURNED?
KNOCK
KNOCK
WHO'S THERE? OH, JUST TAZEN.
LOOKS LIKE THERE'S SOMETHING ABOVE US.

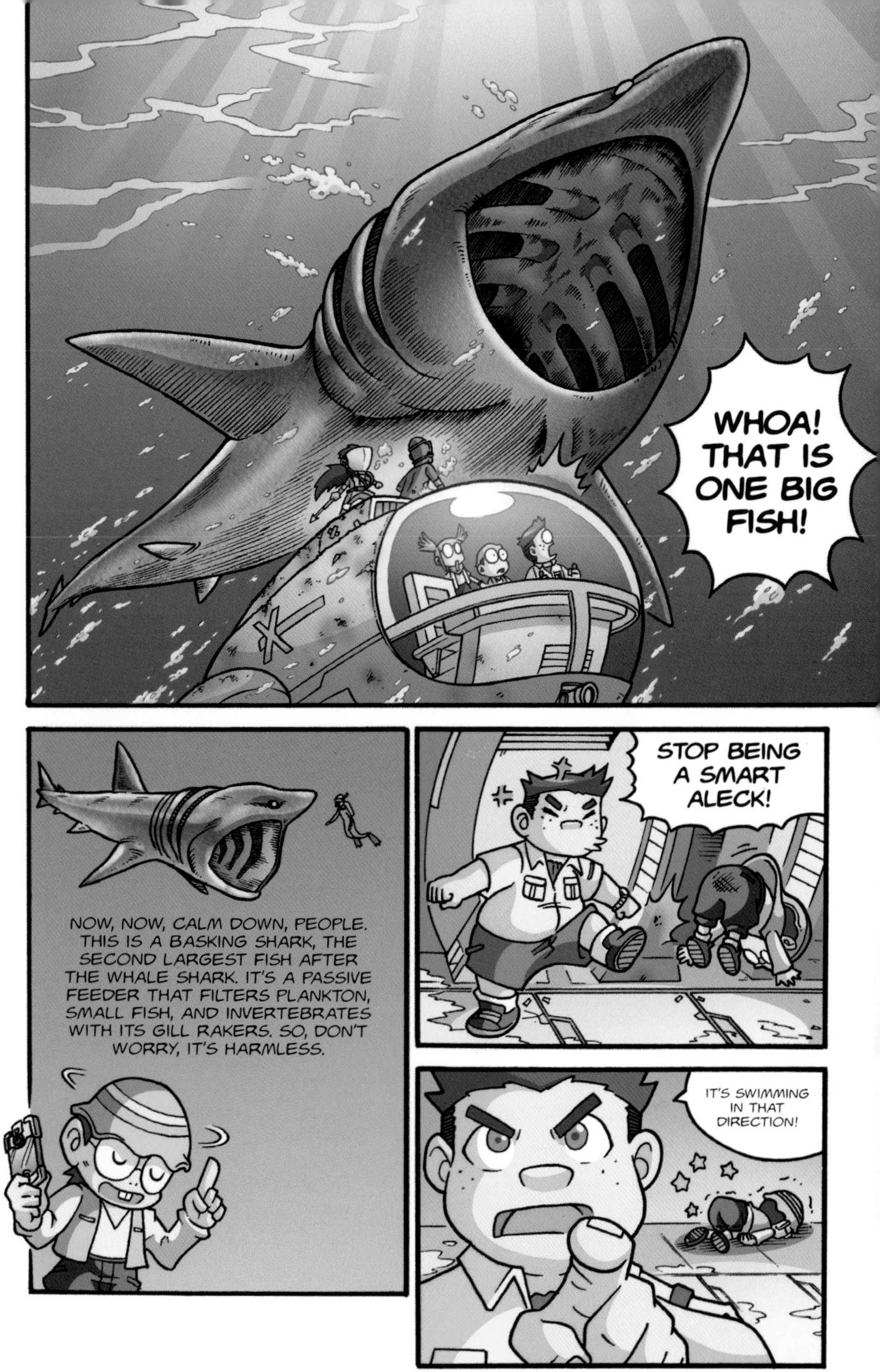
WHOA! THAT IS ONE BIG FISH!
NOW, NOW, CALM DOWN, PEOPLE. THIS IS A BASKING SHARK, THE SECOND LARGEST FISH AFTER THE WHALE SHARK. IT'S A PASSIVE FEEDER THAT FILTERS PLANKTON, SMALL FISH, AND INVERTEBRATES WITH ITS GILL RAKERS. SO, DON'T WORRY, IT'S HARMLESS.
STOP BEING A SMART ALECK!
IT'S SWIMMING IN THAT DIRECTION!

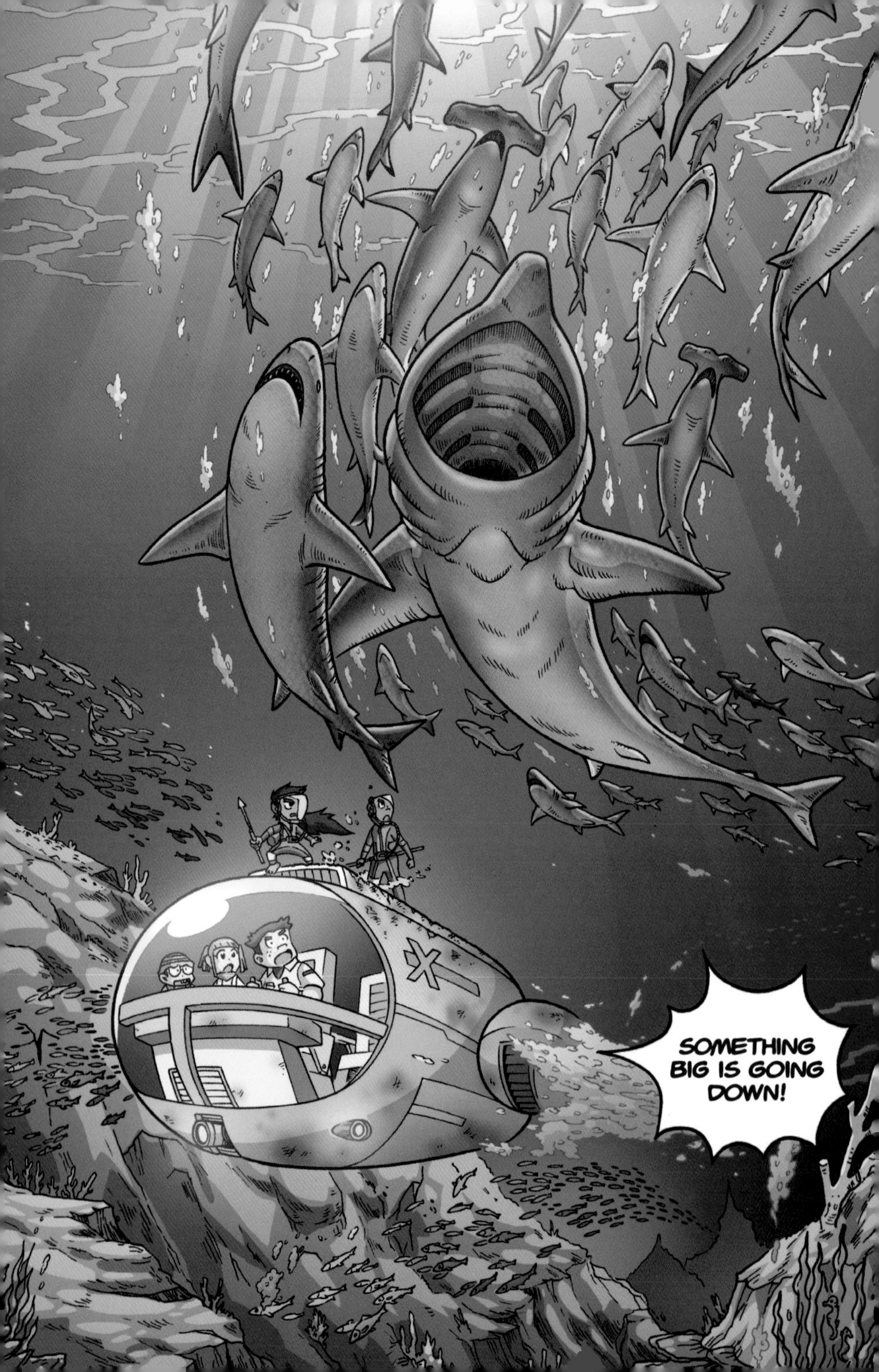
SOMETHING BIG IS GOING DOWN!

Conservation Status (Yet to be assessed)

Extinct EX	Extinct in the Wild EW	Critically Endangered CR	Endangered EN	Vulnerable VU	Near Threatened NT	Least Concern LC

Species: Echeneis naucrates
Length: 2.2 to 3.3 feet
Weight: 5 pounds
Diet: Mainly parasites and discarded food fragments
Distribution: Tropical seas worldwide
Habitats: Coral reef and open sea

Strength
Intelligence
Attack
Defense
Speed

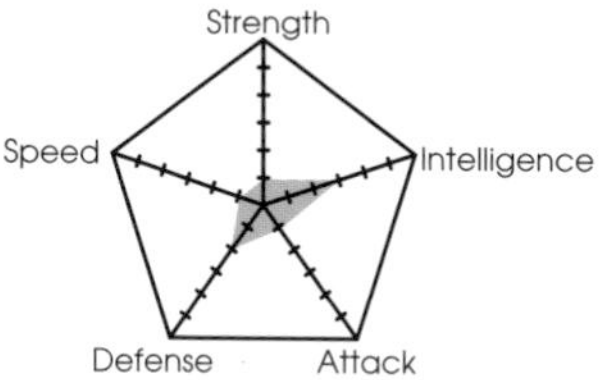

LIVE SHARKSUCKER

One of the eight species of remora, this tiny fish routinely attaches itself to a host such as a shark, ray, or dolphin, benefiting from discarded food scraps and "hitchhiking" (getting a free ride). This is made possible by a disc-like appendage on top of its head that harmlessly attaches it to its host. In return, it gobbles up pesky epidermal parasites. Some fishermen use this fish as a "homing device" to locate bigger fish which the remora will track down.

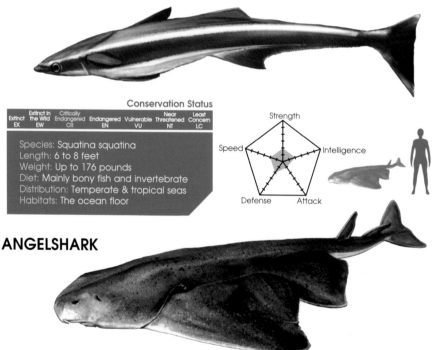

Conservation Status

Extinct EX	Extinct in the Wild EW	Critically Endangered CR	Endangered EN	Vulnerable VU	Near Threatened NT	Least Concern LC

Species: Squatina squatina
Length: 6 to 8 feet
Weight: Up to 176 pounds
Diet: Mainly bony fish and invertebrate
Distribution: Temperate & tropical seas
Habitats: The ocean floor

Strength
Intelligence
Attack
Defense
Speed

ANGELSHARK

This ray-like shark has a flattened body, with wide pectoral and pelvic fins. Like other members of its family, it is a nocturnal ambush predator that buries itself in sediment and waits for passing prey, mostly bony fishes but also skates and invertebrates. An aplacental viviparous species, females bear litters of 7 to 25 pups every other year. Although, generally harmless to humans, it can bite if provoked or mishandled.

Conservation Status

Extinct EX	Extinct in the Wild EW	Critically Endangered CR	Endangered EN	Vulnerable VU	Near Threatened NT	Least Concern LC

Species: Isistius brasiliensis
Length: Up to 16.5 to 22 inches
Weight: Unknown
Diet: Most medium to large-sized marine
      animals
Distribution: All tropical and sub-tropical
              oceanic basins
Habitats: Deep seas

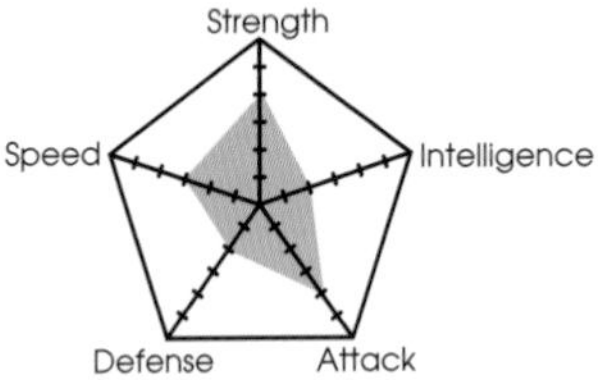

Strength · Speed · Intelligence · Defense · Attack

COOKIECUTTER SHARK

Parasitic attacks by the cookiecutter shark leaves a round "crater wound," averaging 2 inches across and 2.75 inches deep, traveling in schools, they usually feed on larger fish such as whales, dolphins, sharks, and even bite non-living objects such as undersea cables and equipment. Mostly found at depths below 1.86 miles, they emit a greenish photoluminescence, with a dark band around its neck. As with other sharks, its teeth regenerate by recycling the calcium content of old teeth, which they swallow when broken or dislodged. Despite their propensity for swarming larger prey, they are of no danger to humans due to their small size and deep dwelling preference.

The Cookiecutter's "buzz saw bite"

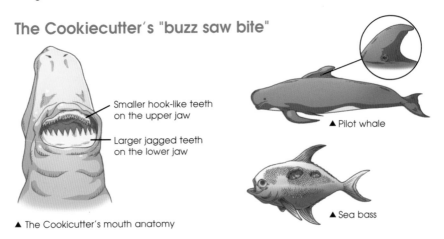

Smaller hook-like teeth
on the upper jaw

Larger jagged teeth
on the lower jaw

▲ Pilot whale

▲ Sea bass

▲ The Cookiecutter's mouth anatomy

In the dark depths, the eerie green glow serves to attract prey. When curiosity prompts a prospective victim too close, these tiny terrors latch on by hooking onto flesh with their upper jaw while the lower jaw inflicts the cookiecutter's "cookiecutter" bite, producing a suction force for a firmer grip. The circular wounds you can see on the pilot whale and sea bass above are the result of such an attack.

CHAPTER 4
GENTLE GIANT

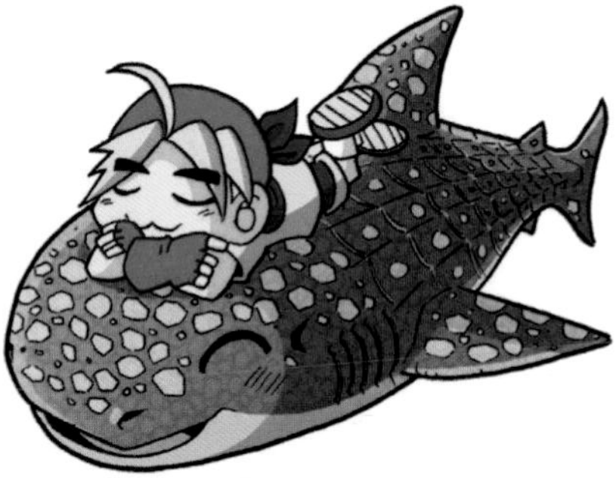

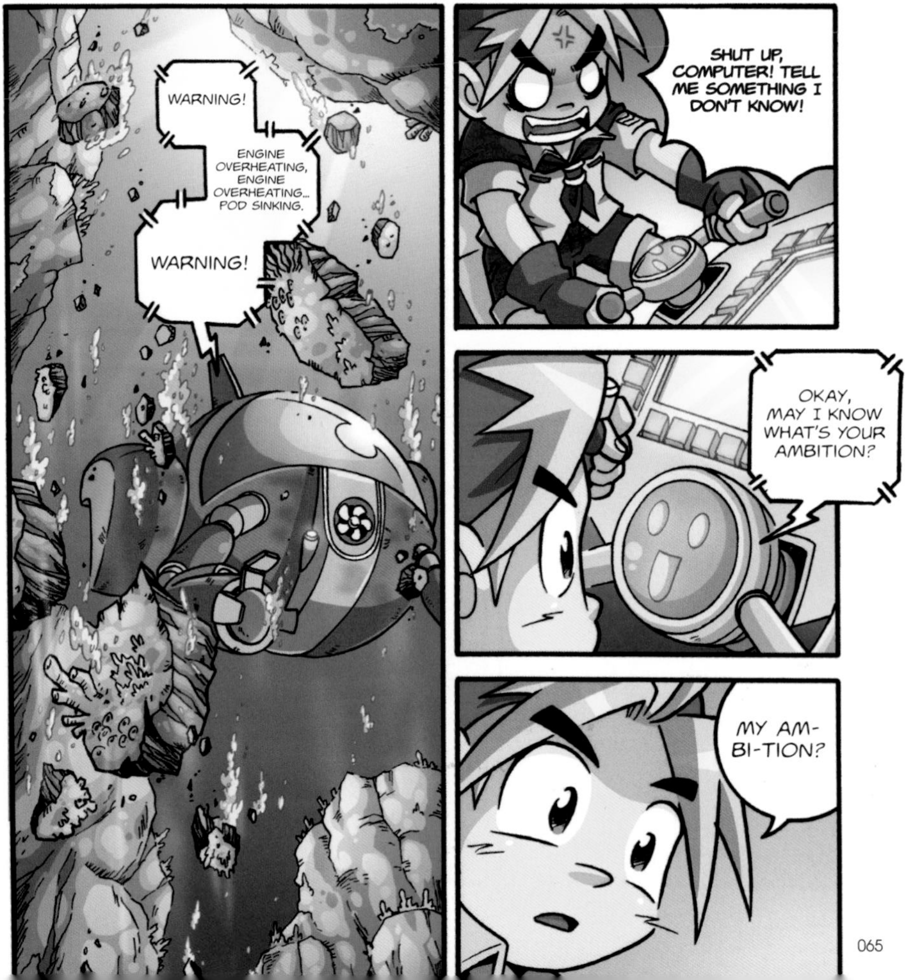
WARNING!
ENGINE OVERHEATING, ENGINE OVERHEATING... POD SINKING.
WARNING!
SHUT UP, COMPUTER! TELL ME SOMETHING I DON'T KNOW!
OKAY, MAY I KNOW WHAT'S YOUR AMBITION?
MY AM-BI-TION?

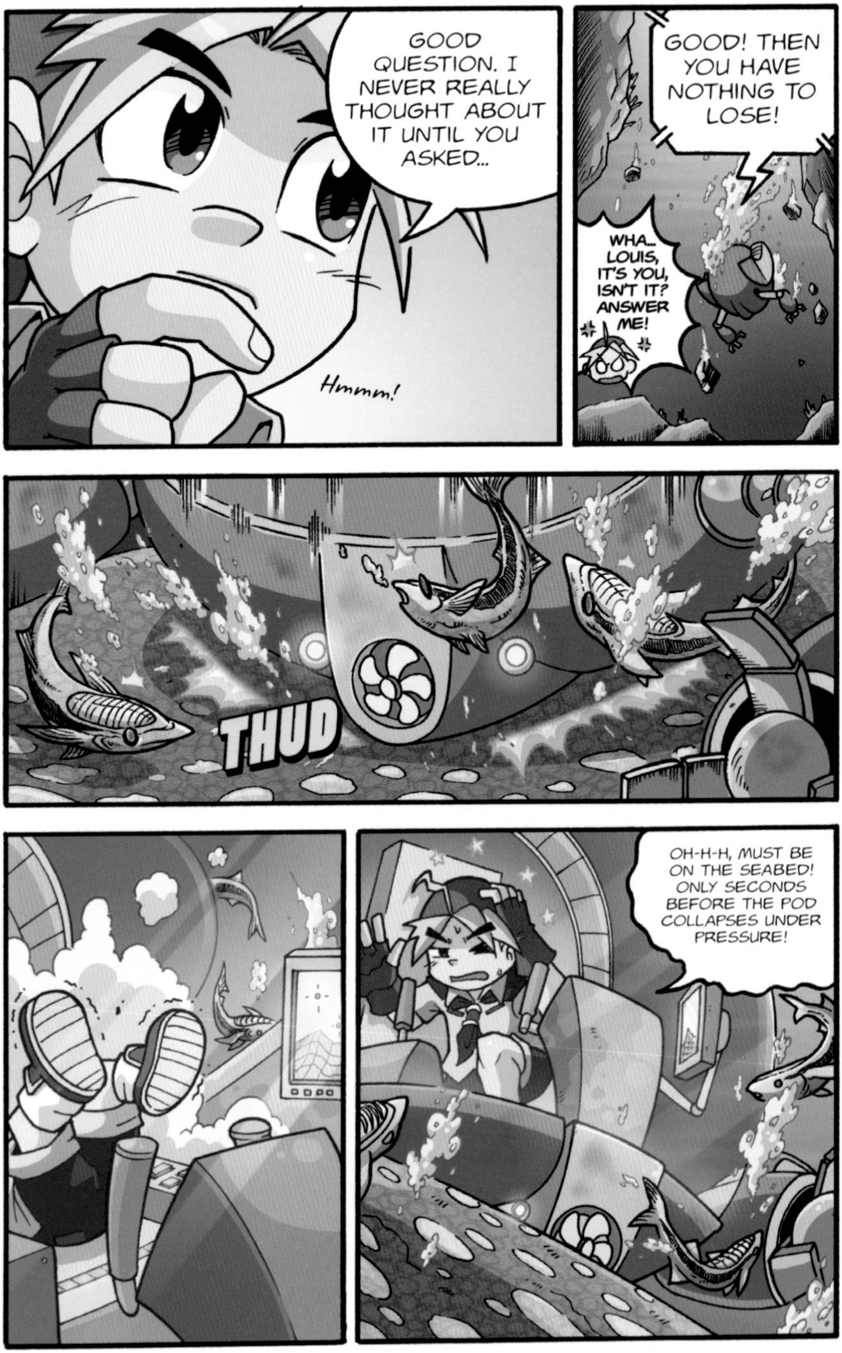
GOOD QUESTION. I NEVER REALLY THOUGHT ABOUT IT UNTIL YOU ASKED...
Hmmm!
GOOD! THEN YOU HAVE NOTHING TO LOSE!
WHA... LOUIS, IT'S YOU, ISN'T IT? ANSWER ME!
THUD
OH-H-H, MUST BE ON THE SEABED! ONLY SECONDS BEFORE THE POD COLLAPSES UNDER PRESSURE!

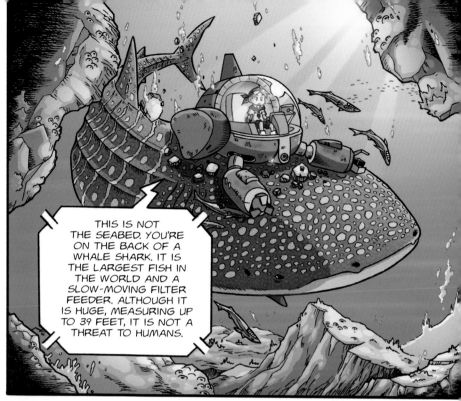

THIS IS NOT THE SEABED. YOU'RE ON THE BACK OF A WHALE SHARK. IT IS THE LARGEST FISH IN THE WORLD AND A SLOW-MOVING FILTER FEEDER. ALTHOUGH IT IS HUGE, MEASURING UP TO 39 FEET, IT IS NOT A THREAT TO HUMANS.

BECAUSE OF THAT, THE WHALE SHARK IS KNOWN AS "THE GENTLE GIANT OF THE OCEAN."

WOW! A MASSIVE CREATURE THAT IS NOT AGGRESSIVE!

A really annoying giant!

NOT AT ALL LIKE LOUIS!

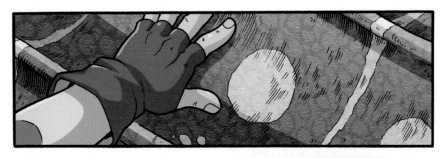

THANKS FOR SAVING MY LIFE!

WHALE SHARKS ARE VERY TOLERANT OF OUR PRESENCE.

BUT BE CAREFUL. DON'T GET HIT BY ITS TAIL!

NOW YOU TELL ME!

≶OOF!≶

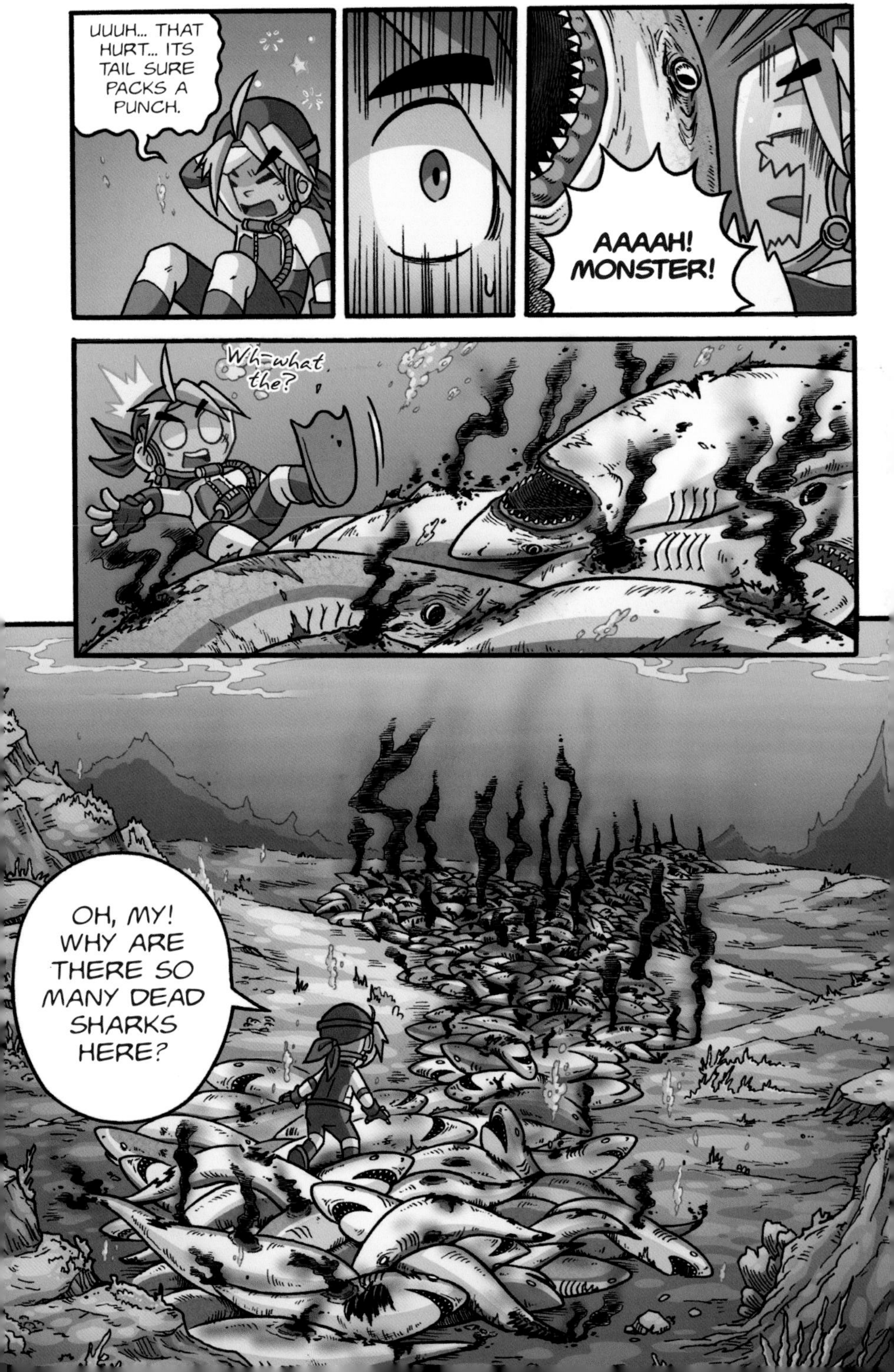
UUUH... THAT HURT... ITS TAIL SURE PACKS A PUNCH.
AAAAH! MONSTER!
Wh-what the?
OH, MY! WHY ARE THERE SO MANY DEAD SHARKS HERE?

THESE WOUNDS... LOOKS LIKE THEIR FINS WERE CUT OFF!
THESE SHARKS ARE JUST WAITING TO DIE SINCE THEY CANNOT SWIM.
SIGH... IT'S SO CRUEL...

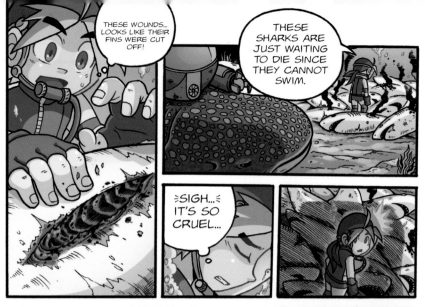

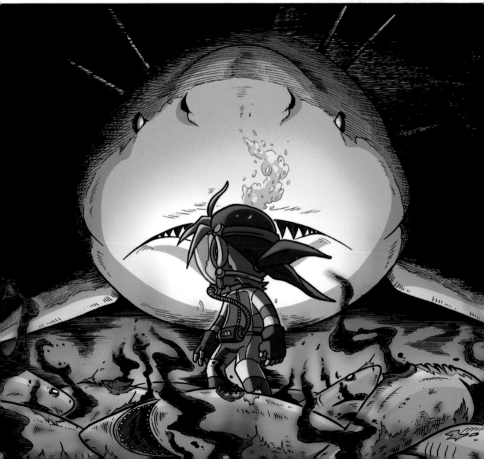

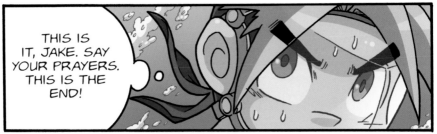

THIS IS IT, JAKE. SAY YOUR PRAYERS. THIS IS THE END!

?!

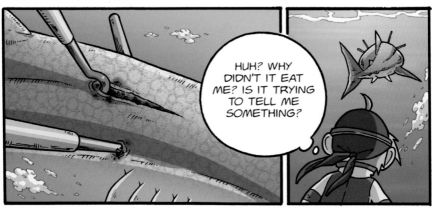

HUH? WHY DIDN'T IT EAT ME? IS IT TRYING TO TELL ME SOMETHING?

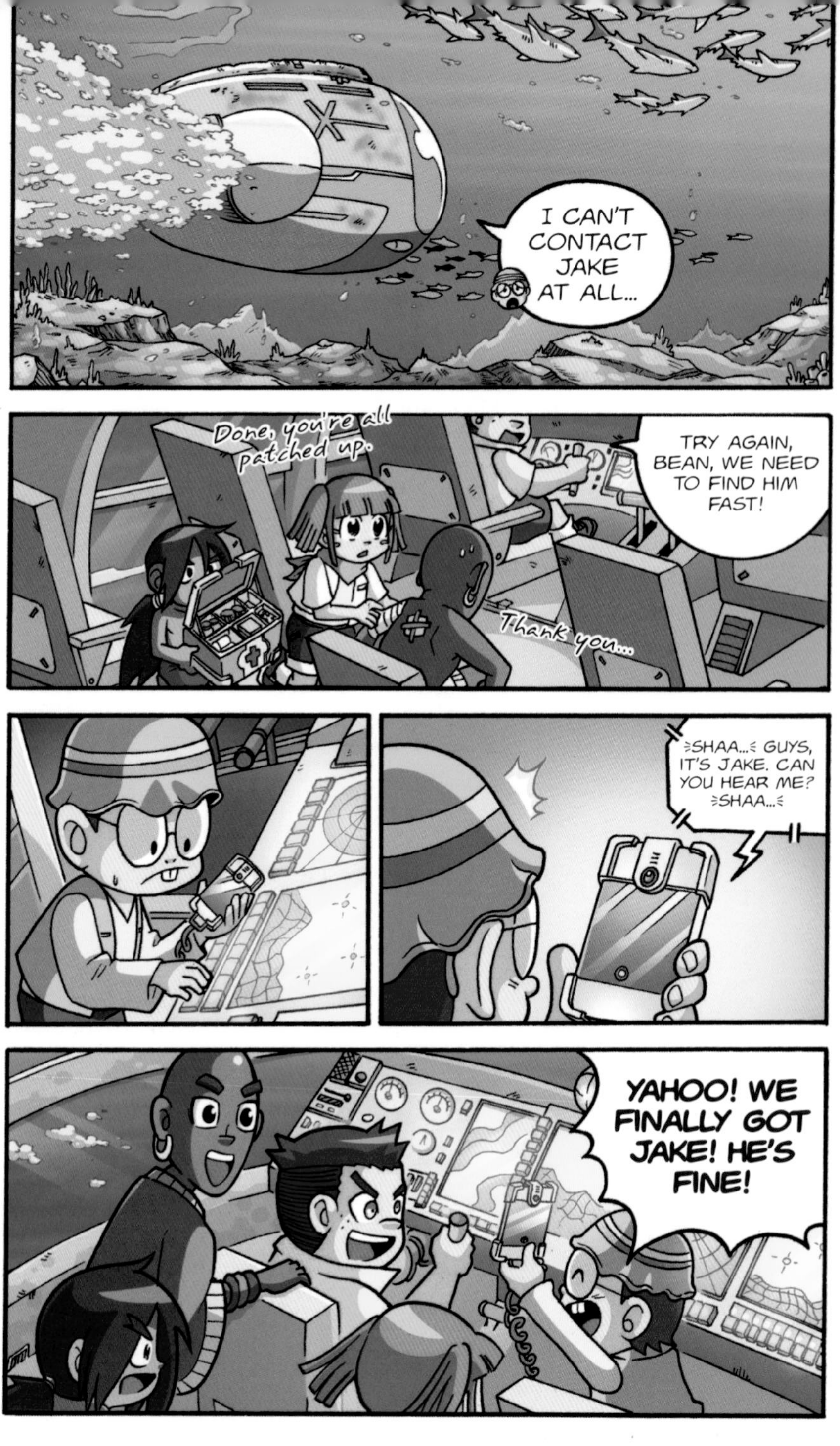
I CAN'T CONTACT JAKE AT ALL...
Done, you're all patched up.
TRY AGAIN, BEAN, WE NEED TO FIND HIM FAST!
Thank you...
SHAA... GUYS, IT'S JAKE. CAN YOU HEAR ME? SHAA...
YAHOO! WE FINALLY GOT JAKE! HE'S FINE!

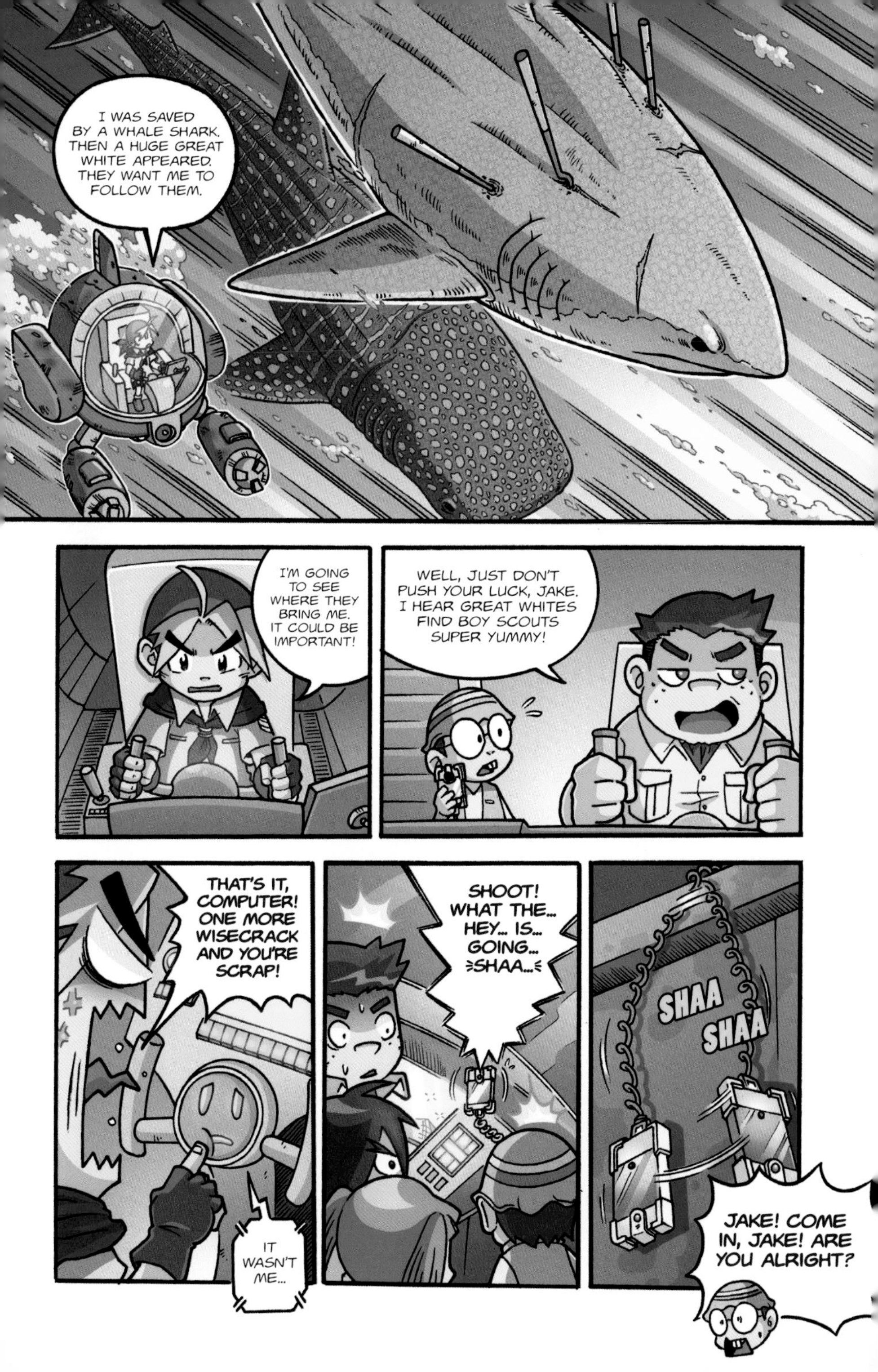
I WAS SAVED BY A WHALE SHARK. THEN A HUGE GREAT WHITE APPEARED. THEY WANT ME TO FOLLOW THEM.
I'M GOING TO SEE WHERE THEY BRING ME. IT COULD BE IMPORTANT!
WELL, JUST DON'T PUSH YOUR LUCK, JAKE. I HEAR GREAT WHITES FIND BOY SCOUTS SUPER YUMMY!
THAT'S IT, COMPUTER! ONE MORE WISECRACK AND YOU'RE SCRAP!
IT WASN'T ME...
SHOOT! WHAT THE... HEY... IS... GOING... SHAA...
SHAA
SHAA
JAKE! COME IN, JAKE! ARE YOU ALRIGHT?

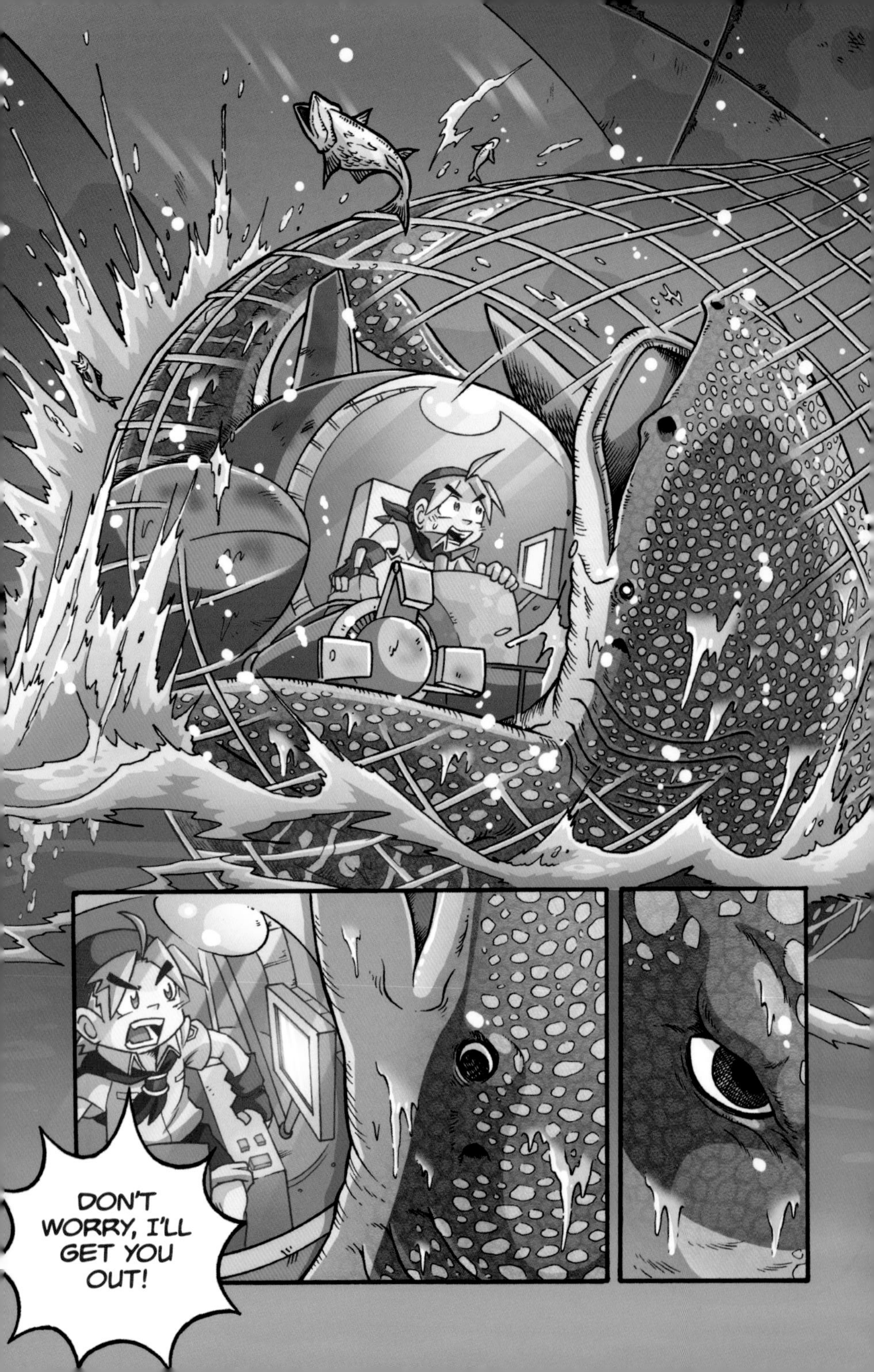
DON'T WORRY, I'LL GET YOU OUT!

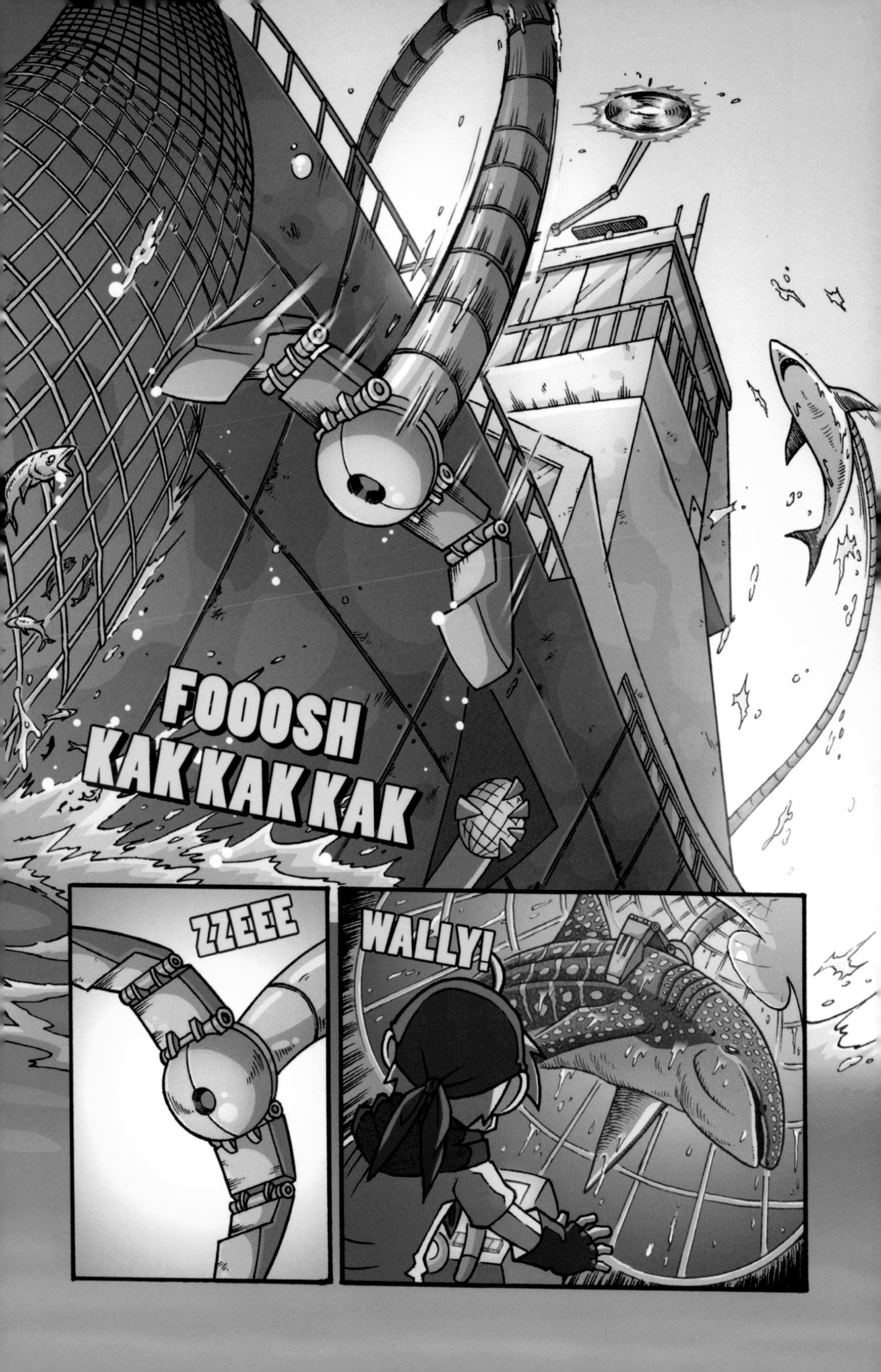
FOOOSH
KAK KAK KAK
ZZEEE
WALLY!

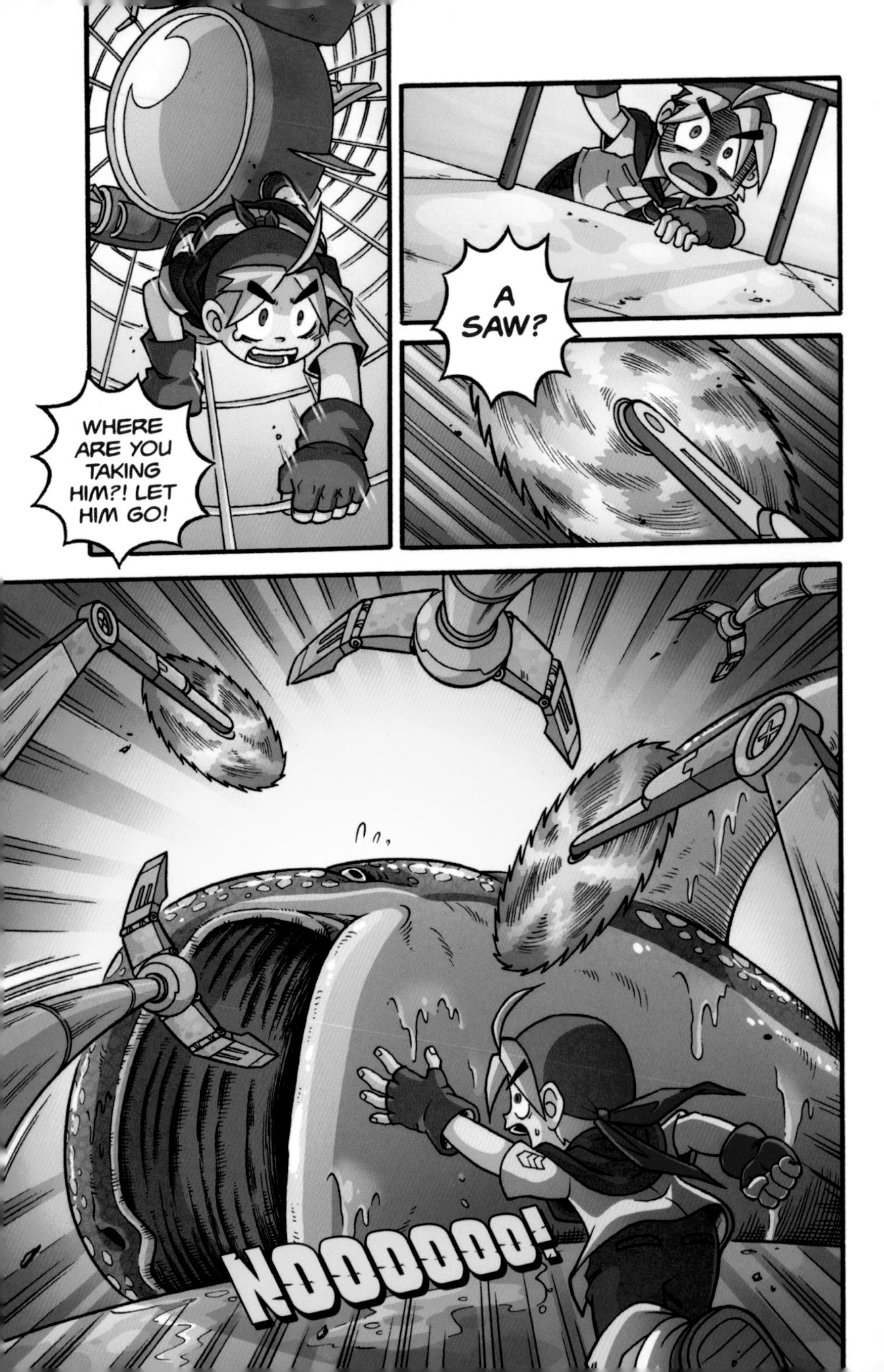
WHERE ARE YOU TAKING HIM?! LET HIM GO!
A SAW?
NOOOOOO!

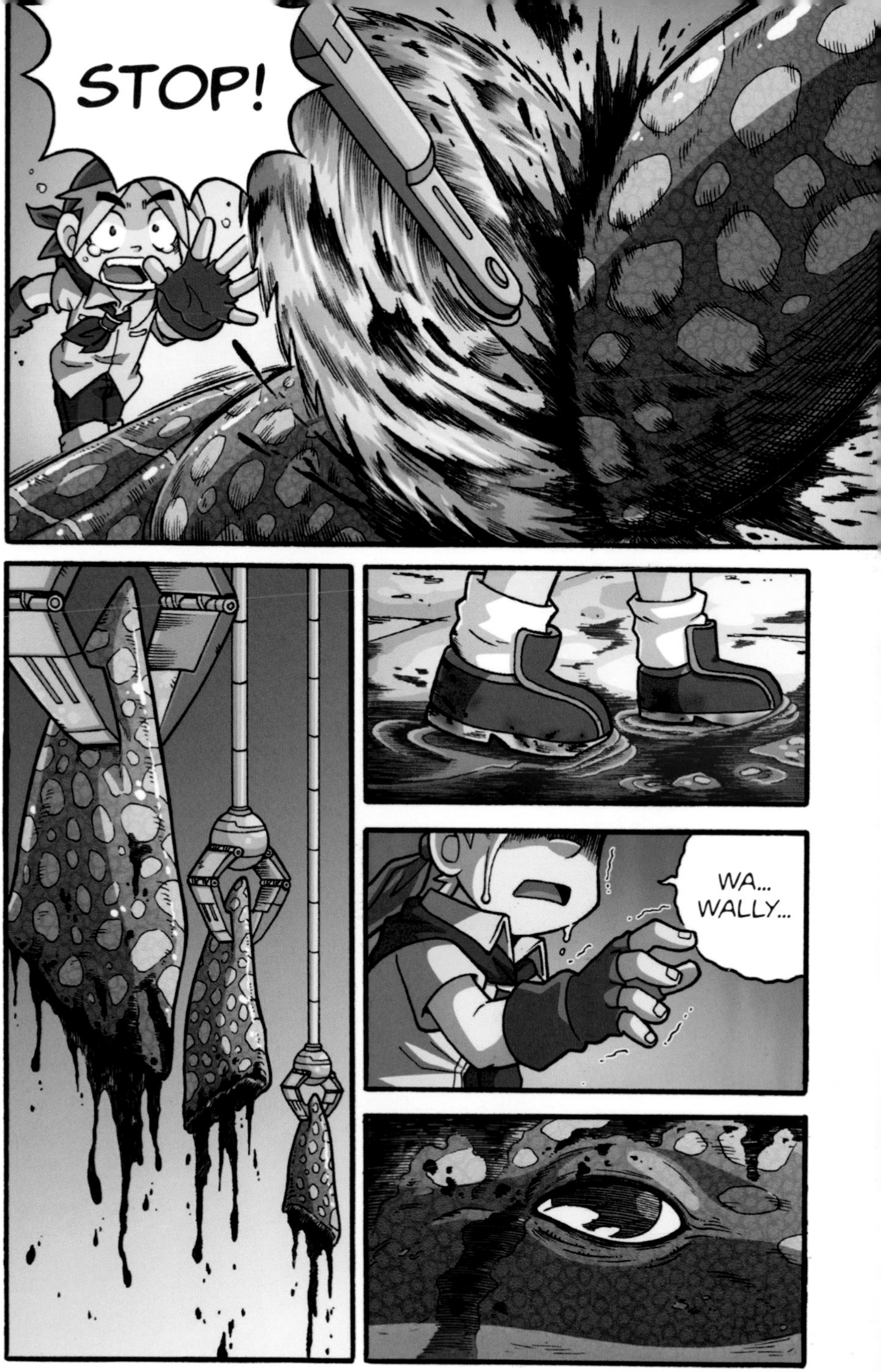
STOP!
WA... WALLY...

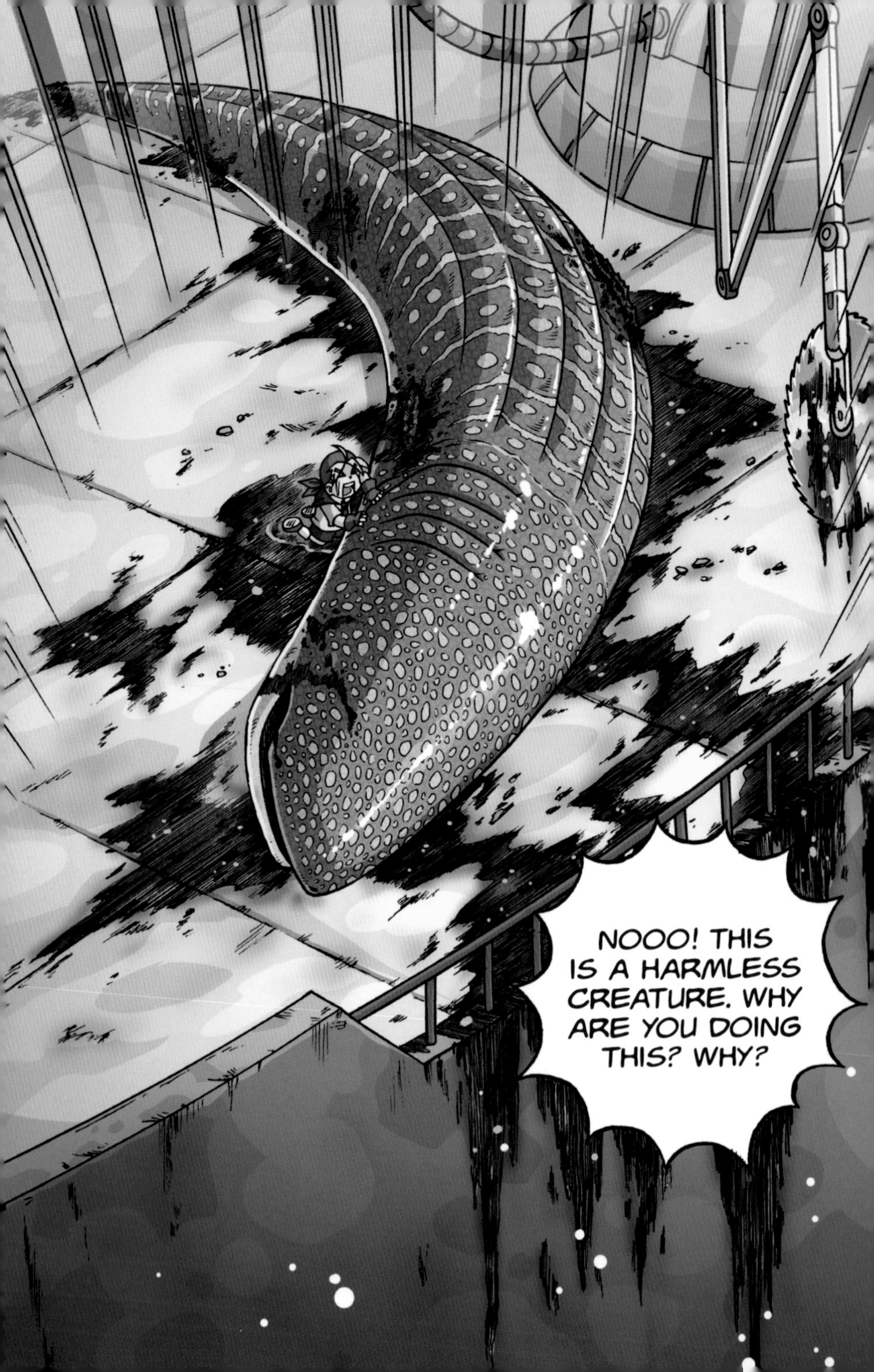
NOOO! THIS IS A HARMLESS CREATURE. WHY ARE YOU DOING THIS? WHY?

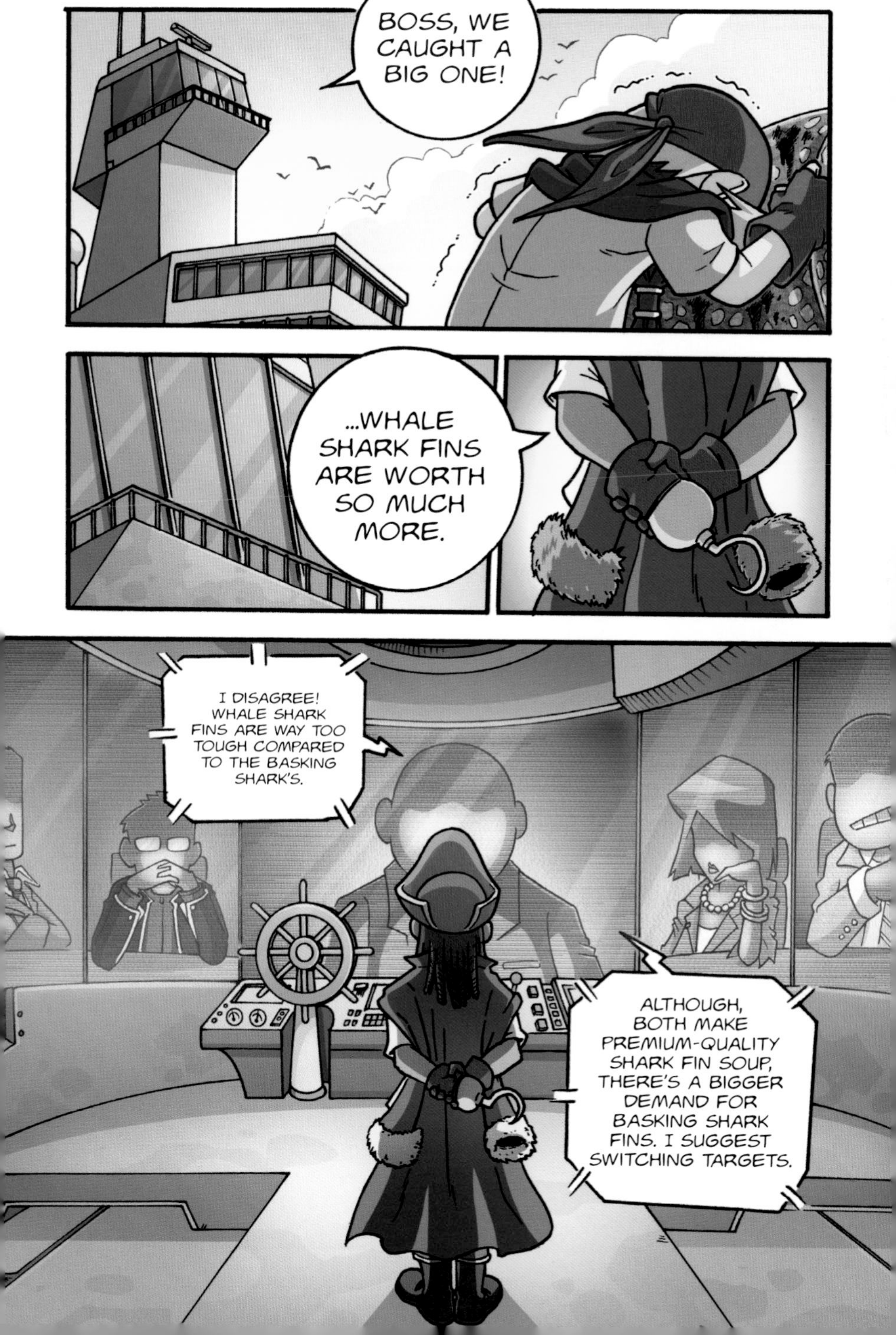
BOSS, WE CAUGHT A BIG ONE!
...WHALE SHARK FINS ARE WORTH SO MUCH MORE.
I DISAGREE! WHALE SHARK FINS ARE WAY TOO TOUGH COMPARED TO THE BASKING SHARK'S.
ALTHOUGH, BOTH MAKE PREMIUM-QUALITY SHARK FIN SOUP, THERE'S A BIGGER DEMAND FOR BASKING SHARK FINS. I SUGGEST SWITCHING TARGETS.

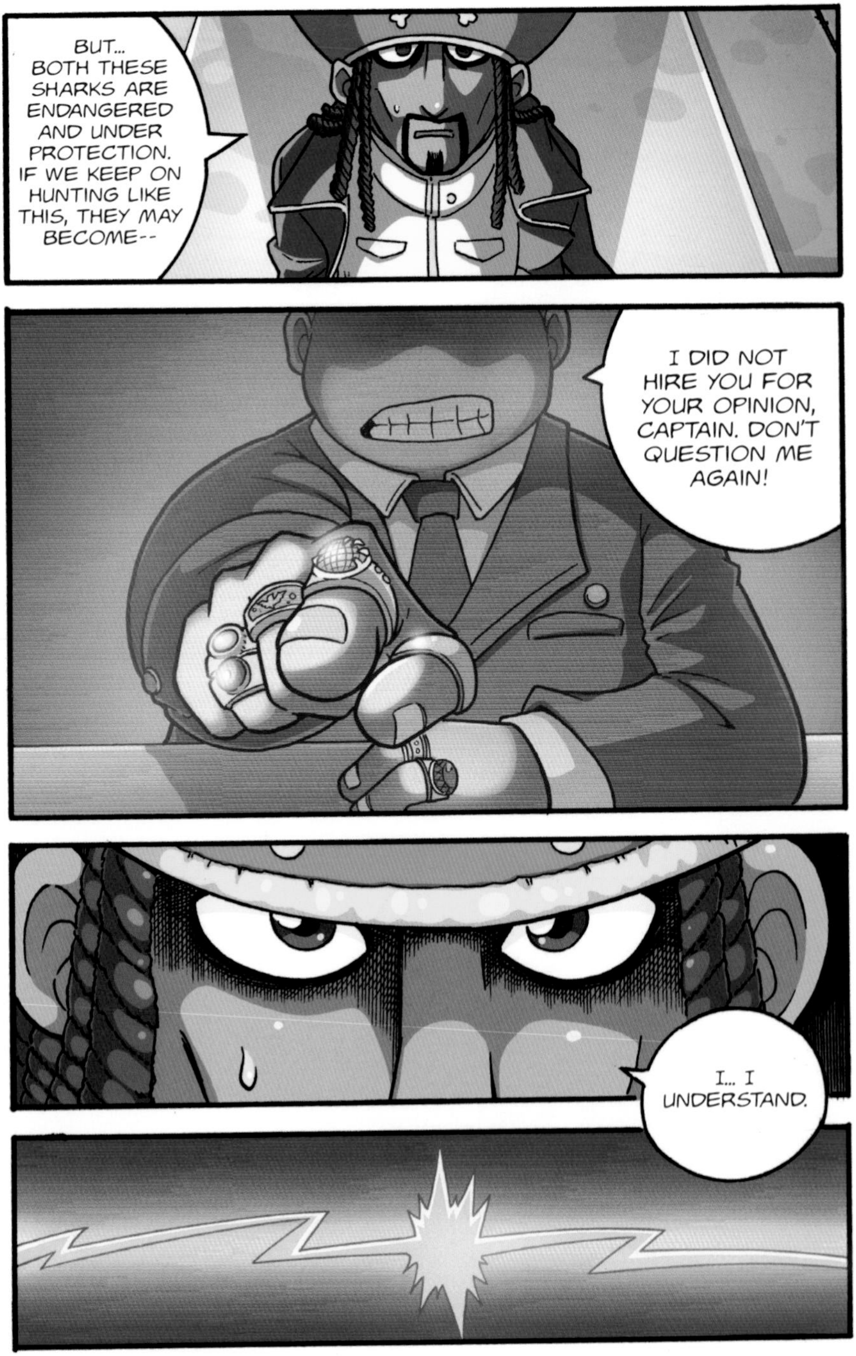
BUT... BOTH THESE SHARKS ARE ENDANGERED AND UNDER PROTECTION. IF WE KEEP ON HUNTING LIKE THIS, THEY MAY BECOME--
I DID NOT HIRE YOU FOR YOUR OPINION, CAPTAIN. DON'T QUESTION ME AGAIN!
I... I UNDERSTAND.

WHALE SHARK

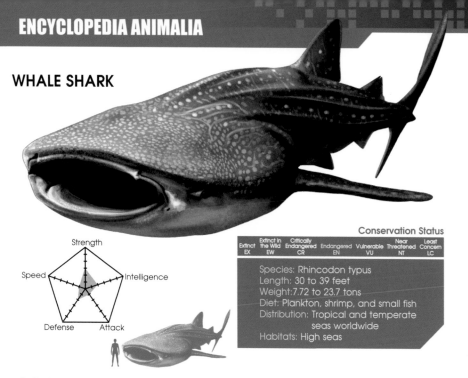

Strength

Speed — Intelligence

Defense — Attack

Conservation Status

Extinct EX	Extinct in the Wild EW	Critically Endangered CR	Endangered EN	Vulnerable VU	Near Threatened NT	Least Concern LC

Species: Rhincodon typus
Length: 30 to 39 feet
Weight: 7.72 to 23.7 tons
Diet: Plankton, shrimp, and small fish
Distribution: Tropical and temperate seas worldwide
Habitats: High seas

Both the largest shark and fish in the world, this beautiful creature is harmless to humans, despite its gigantic size. This placid filter-feeder mainly feeds on plankton by opening its mouth (up to 5 feet wide) to draw or suck these tiny marine lifeforms in, where 10 filter pads with between 300 to 350 rows of tiny teeth effectively filters its minuscule meal from seawater. Predominantly grayish green, its rough hide is peppered with white spots, while its underside is creamy white. Reaching maturity at 30 years, these majestic creatures have a natural lifespan of around 70 years in the wild.

How filter feeding works:

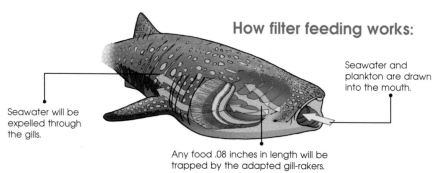

Seawater and plankton are drawn into the mouth.

Seawater will be expelled through the gills.

Any food .08 inches in length will be trapped by the adapted gill-rakers.

Whale sharks are migratory animals and can be found in both tropical and temperate seas during different seasons. This enormous fish, unsurprisingly has no natural predators, however, it is vulnerable to commercial fishing, and is protected in many countries such as Taiwan and The Philippines.

Arguably one of the most dangerous and aggressive sharks that come into contact with humans fairly regularly, as a result of its unusual choice of habitat. It can survive in freshwater rivers and lakes by regulating its salt and water balance via its rectal gland, kidney, liver, and gills. Typically solitary hunters, bulls occasionally hunt in pairs and are highly territorial.

Conservation Status

Extinct EX	Extinct in the Wild EW	Critically Endangered CR	Endangered EN	Vulnerable VU	Near Threatened NT	Least Concern LC

Species: Carcharhinus leucas
Length: 7 to 11 feet
Weight: 198 to 507 pounds
Diet: Mainly other sharks and bony fish
Distribution: Coastal tropical and temperate seas worldwide
Habitats: Warm shallow waters, rivers, and lakes

Strength
Intelligence
Attack
Defense
Speed

BULL SHARK

Conservation Status

Extinct EX	Extinct in the Wild EW	Critically Endangered CR	Endangered EN	Vulnerable VU	Near Threatened NT	Least Concern LC

Species: Cetorhinus maximus
Length: 18 to 30 feet
Weight: 4.4 to 5.5 tons
Diet: Plankton, small fish, invertebrates
Distribution: Temperate seas throughout the world
Habitats: Shoreline seas to oceans except the Indian Ocean

The second largest fish on Earth, it shares several traits with the largest; it too is a docile filter-feeder, capable of sieving 2,205 tons of water per hour through its gaping maw, trawling minute oceanic life close to the surface. Featuring a bulbous snout with keen olfactory senses, this migratory leviathan usually travels thousands of miles during the winter months and can be seen near coastlines where plankton are aplenty.

BASKING SHARK

Strength
Intelligence
Attack
Defense
Speed

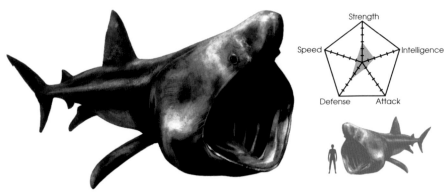

CHAPTER 5
SIXTH SENSE

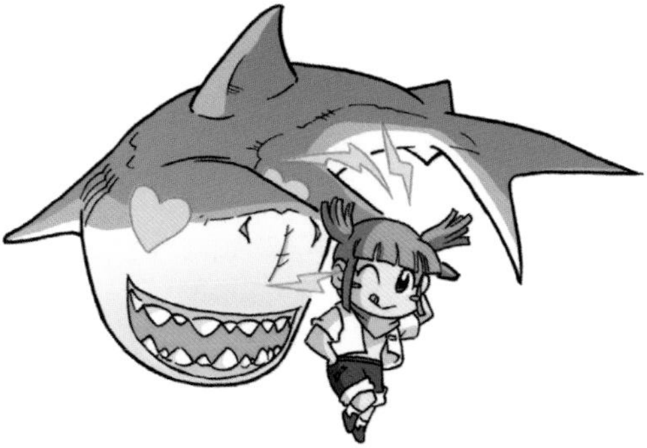

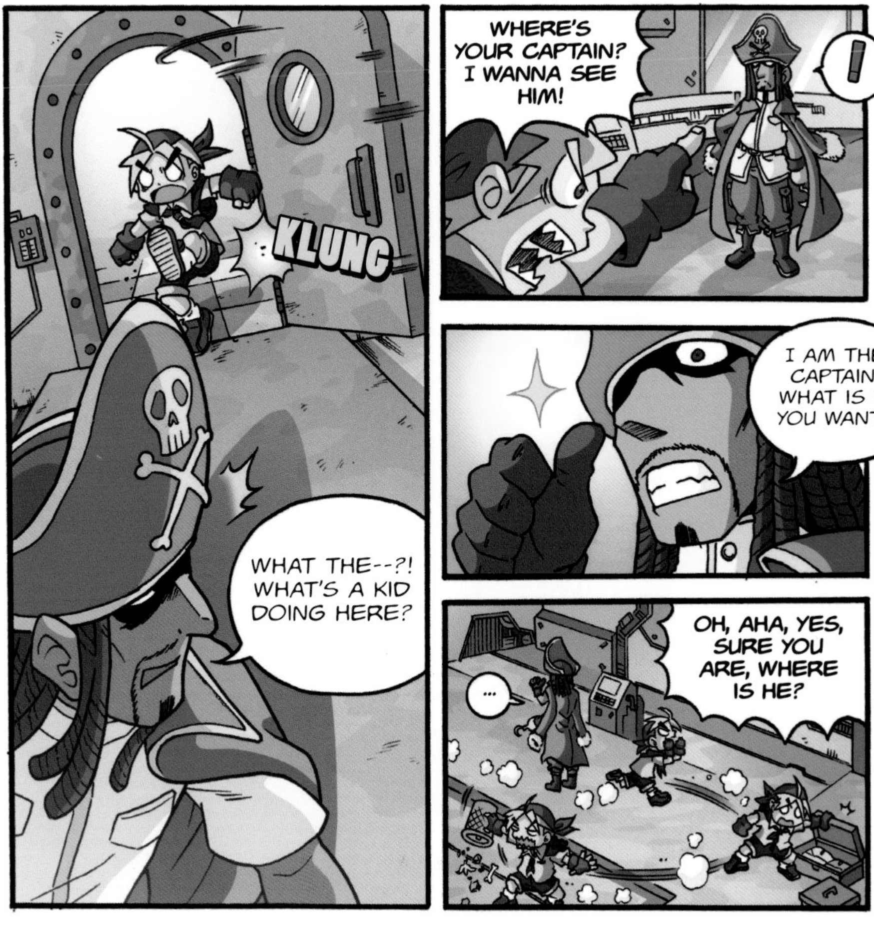
KLUNG
WHAT THE--?! WHAT'S A KID DOING HERE?
WHERE'S YOUR CAPTAIN? I WANNA SEE HIM!
!
I AM THE CAPTAIN! WHAT IS IT YOU WANT?
OH, AHA, YES, SURE YOU ARE, WHERE IS HE?
...

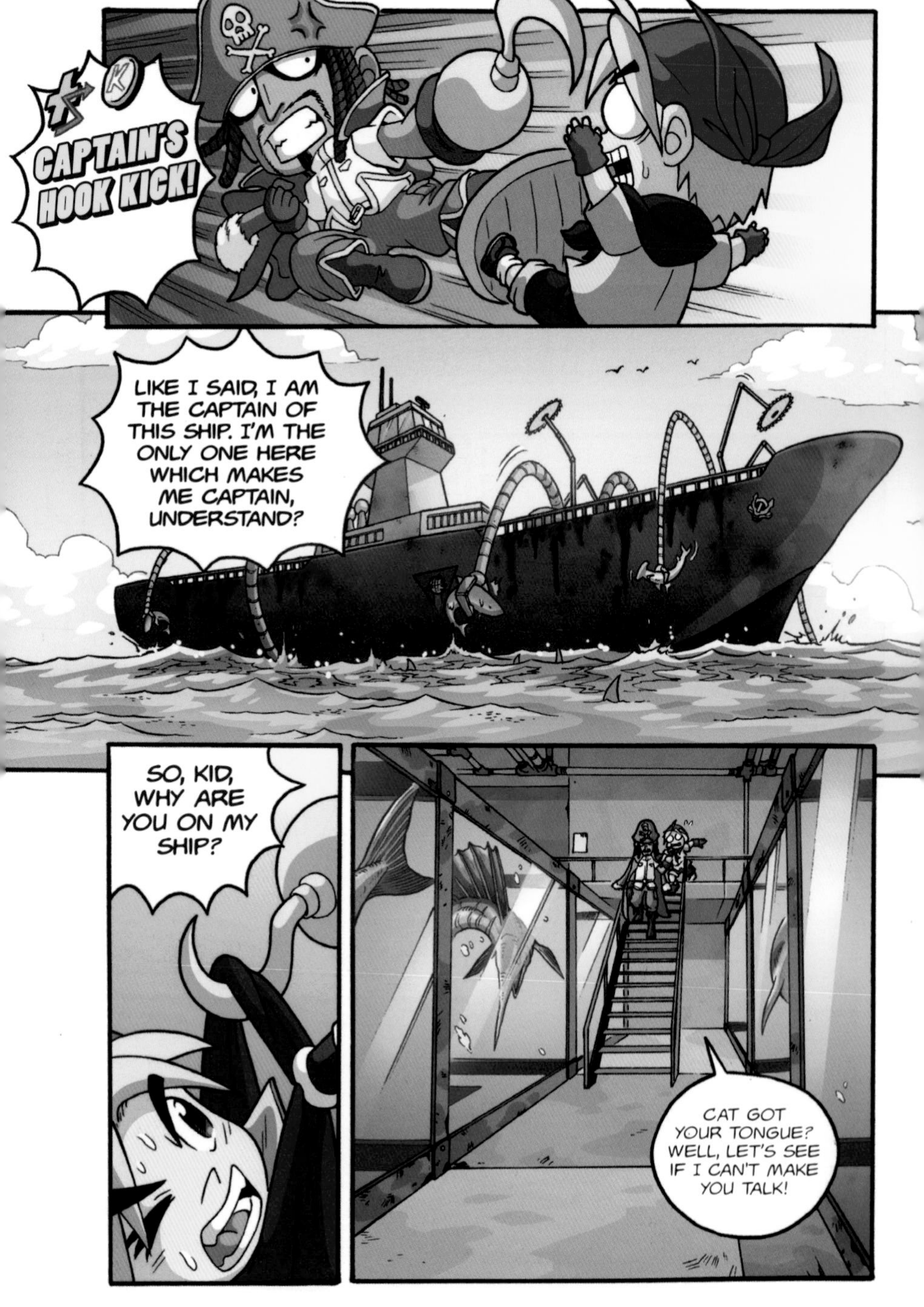
K
CAPTAIN'S HOOK KICK!
LIKE I SAID, I AM THE CAPTAIN OF THIS SHIP. I'M THE ONLY ONE HERE WHICH MAKES ME CAPTAIN, UNDERSTAND?
SO, KID, WHY ARE YOU ON MY SHIP?
CAT GOT YOUR TONGUE? WELL, LET'S SEE IF I CAN'T MAKE YOU TALK!

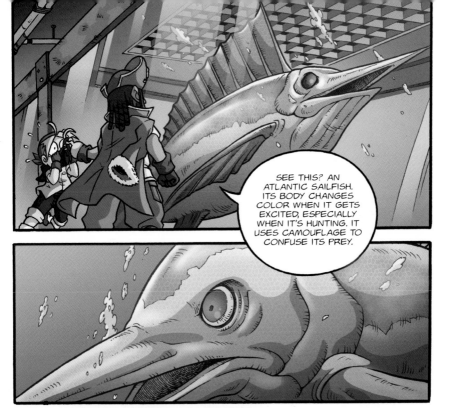

SEE THIS? AN ATLANTIC SAILFISH. ITS BODY CHANGES COLOR WHEN IT GETS EXCITED, ESPECIALLY WHEN IT'S HUNTING. IT USES CAMOUFLAGE TO CONFUSE ITS PREY.

HMM... I WONDER WHY THEY'RE SO AGITATED?

MAYBE THEY CAN'T STAND THAT HOKEY OUTFIT YOU'RE WEARING!

DON'T WORRY, I'LL SAVE YOU! I PROMISE!

SILENCE, INSOLENT BRAT, OR YOU'RE FISH FOOD!

SORRY, CAP'N KOOK, SAILFISH DON'T EAT PEOPLE...

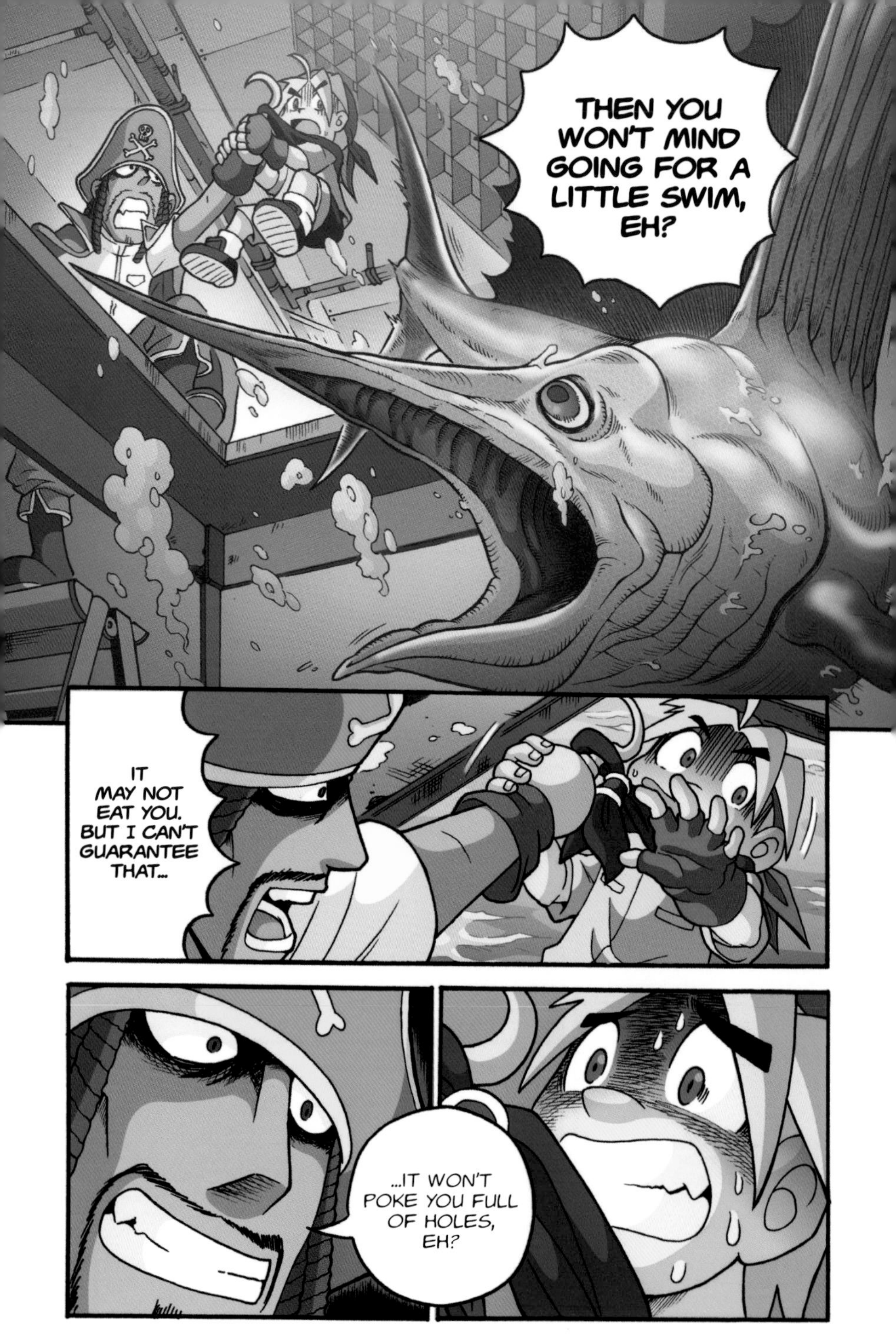
THEN YOU WON'T MIND GOING FOR A LITTLE SWIM, EH?
IT MAY NOT EAT YOU. BUT I CAN'T GUARANTEE THAT...
...IT WON'T POKE YOU FULL OF HOLES, EH?

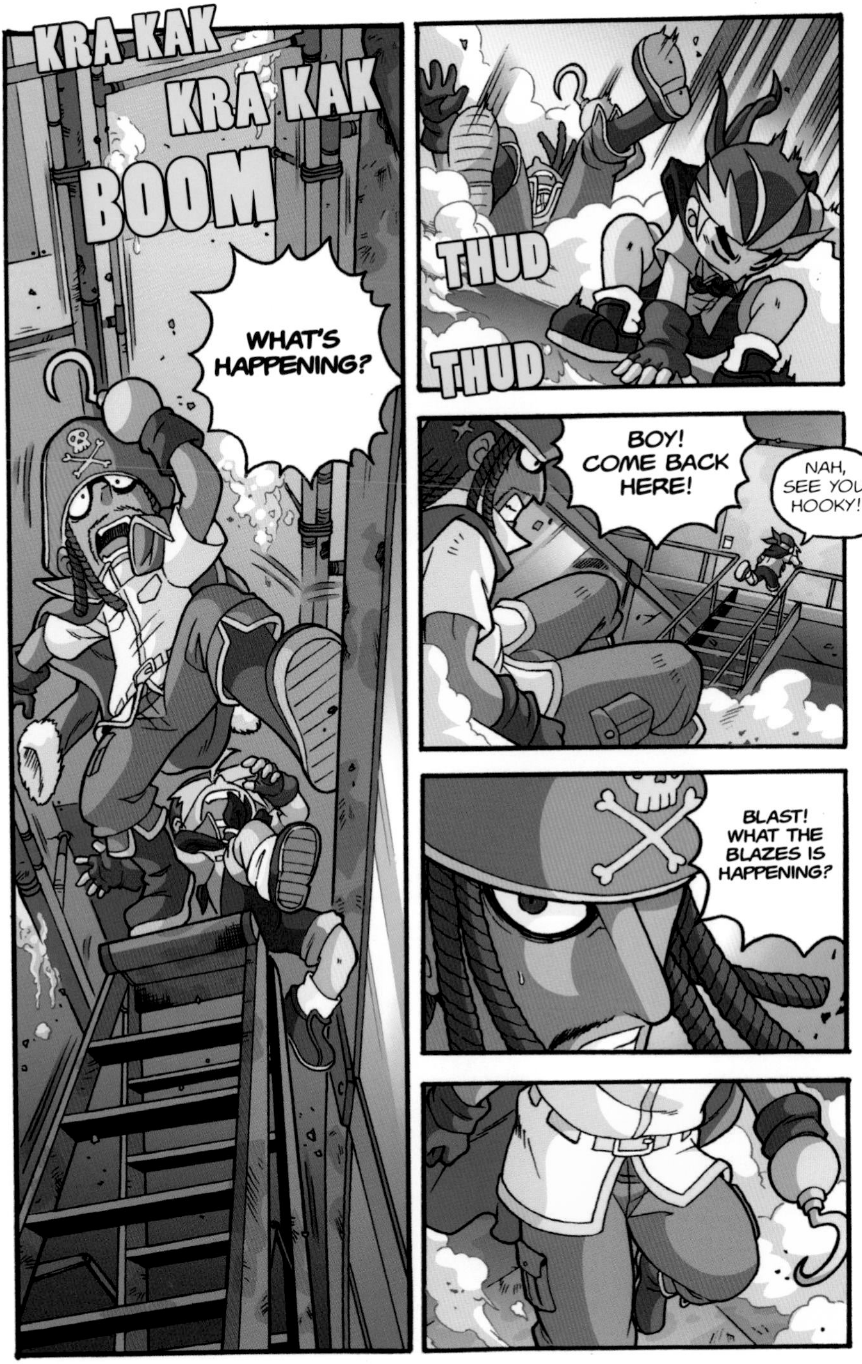
KRA KAK
KRA KAK
BOOM
WHAT'S HAPPENING?
THUD
THUD
BOY! COME BACK HERE!
NAH, SEE YOU, HOOKY!
BLAST! WHAT THE BLAZES IS HAPPENING?

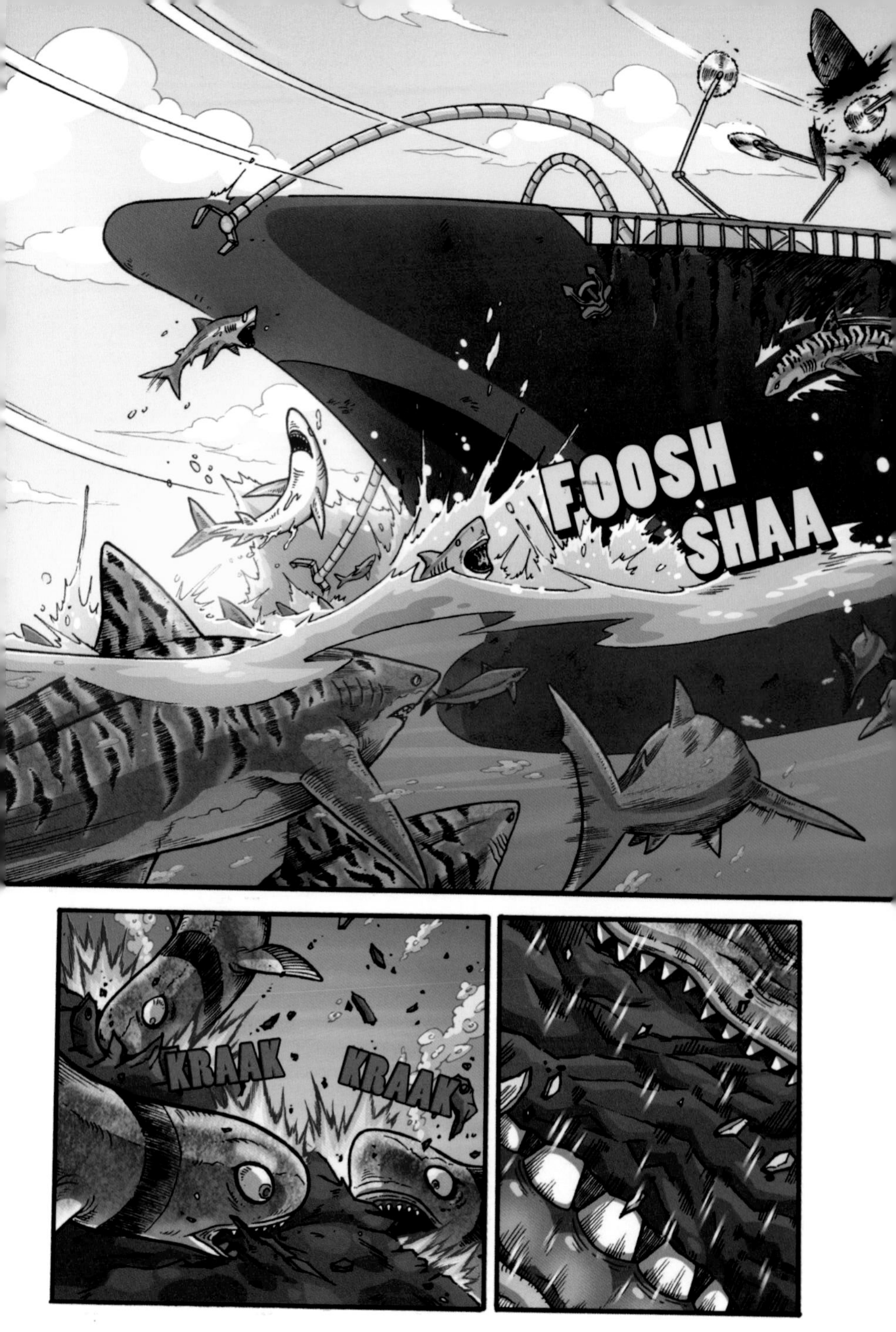
FOOSH
SHAA
KRAAK
KRAAK

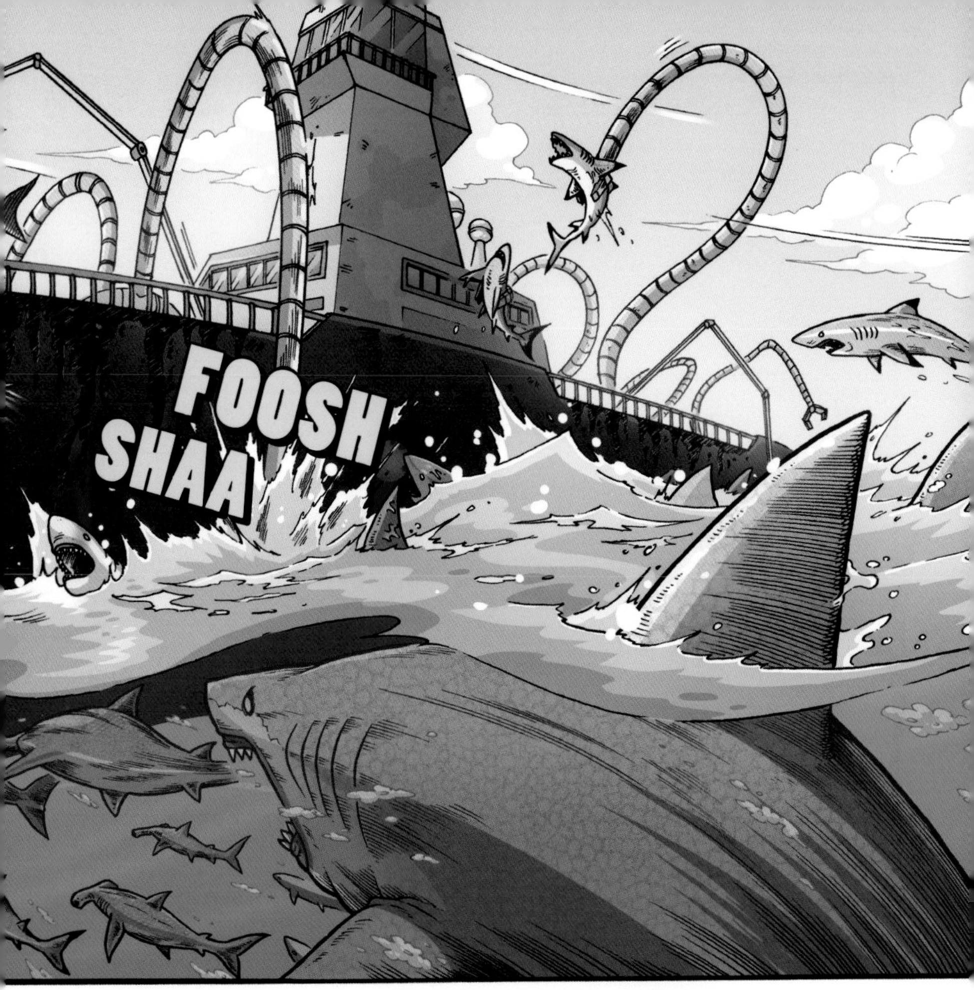
FOOSH
SHAA

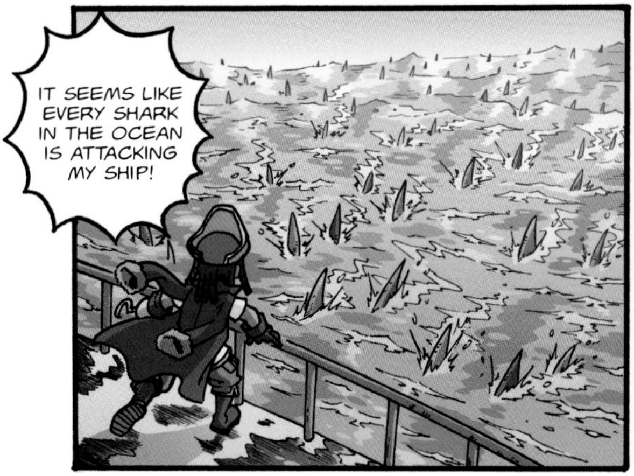
IT SEEMS LIKE EVERY SHARK IN THE OCEAN IS ATTACKING MY SHIP!

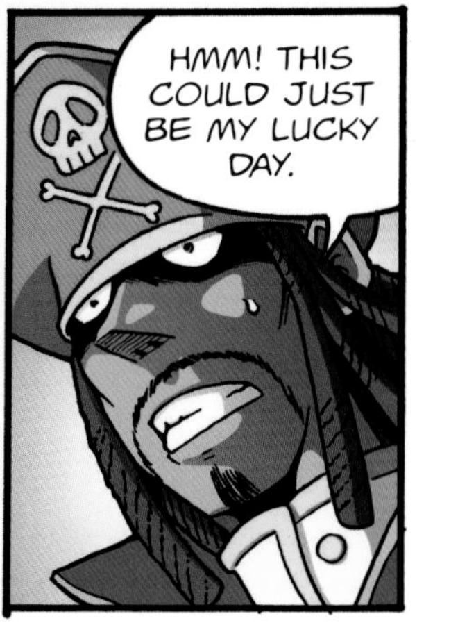
HMM! THIS COULD JUST BE MY LUCKY DAY.

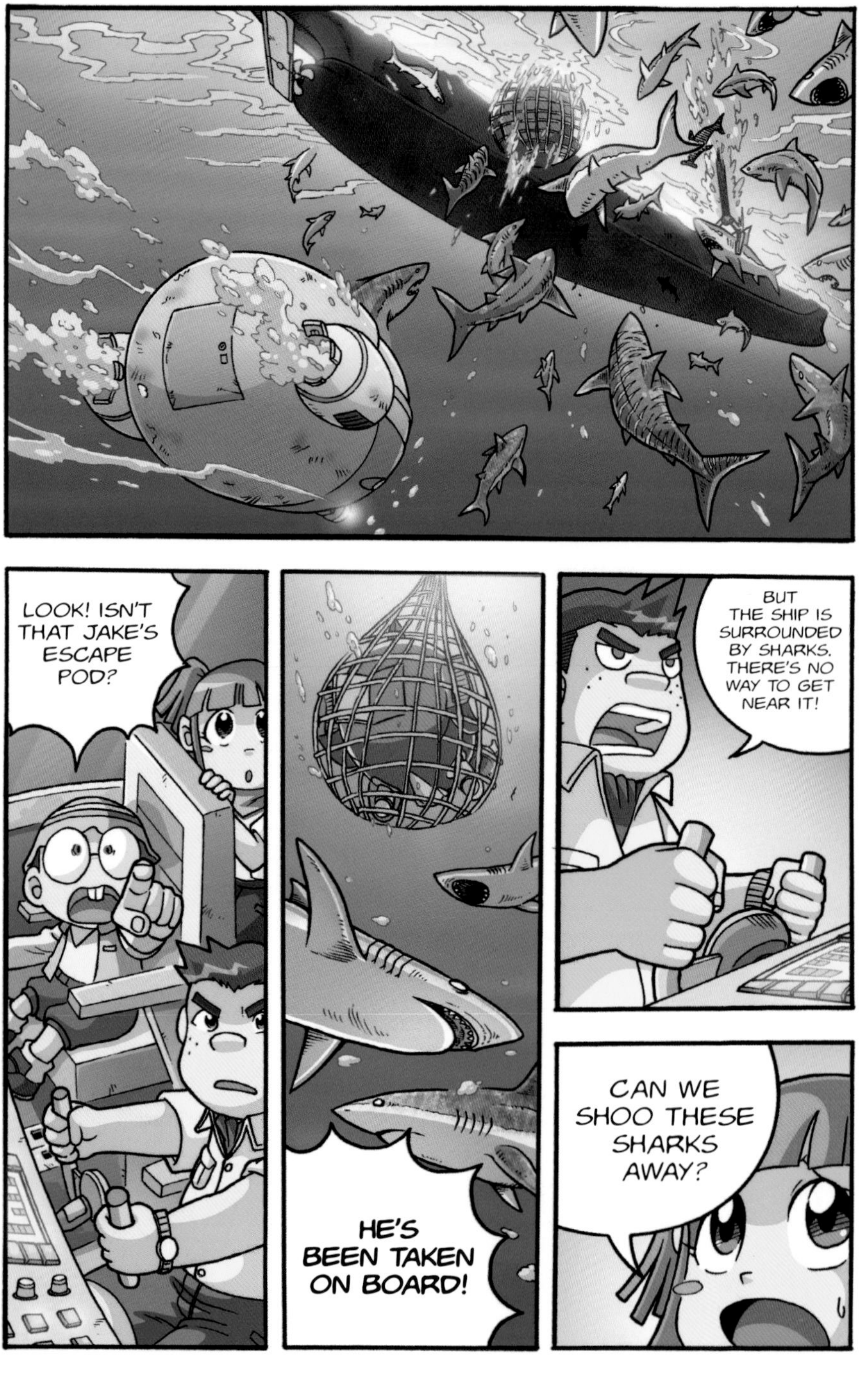
LOOK! ISN'T THAT JAKE'S ESCAPE POD?
HE'S BEEN TAKEN ON BOARD!
BUT THE SHIP IS SURROUNDED BY SHARKS. THERE'S NO WAY TO GET NEAR IT!
CAN WE SHOO THESE SHARKS AWAY?

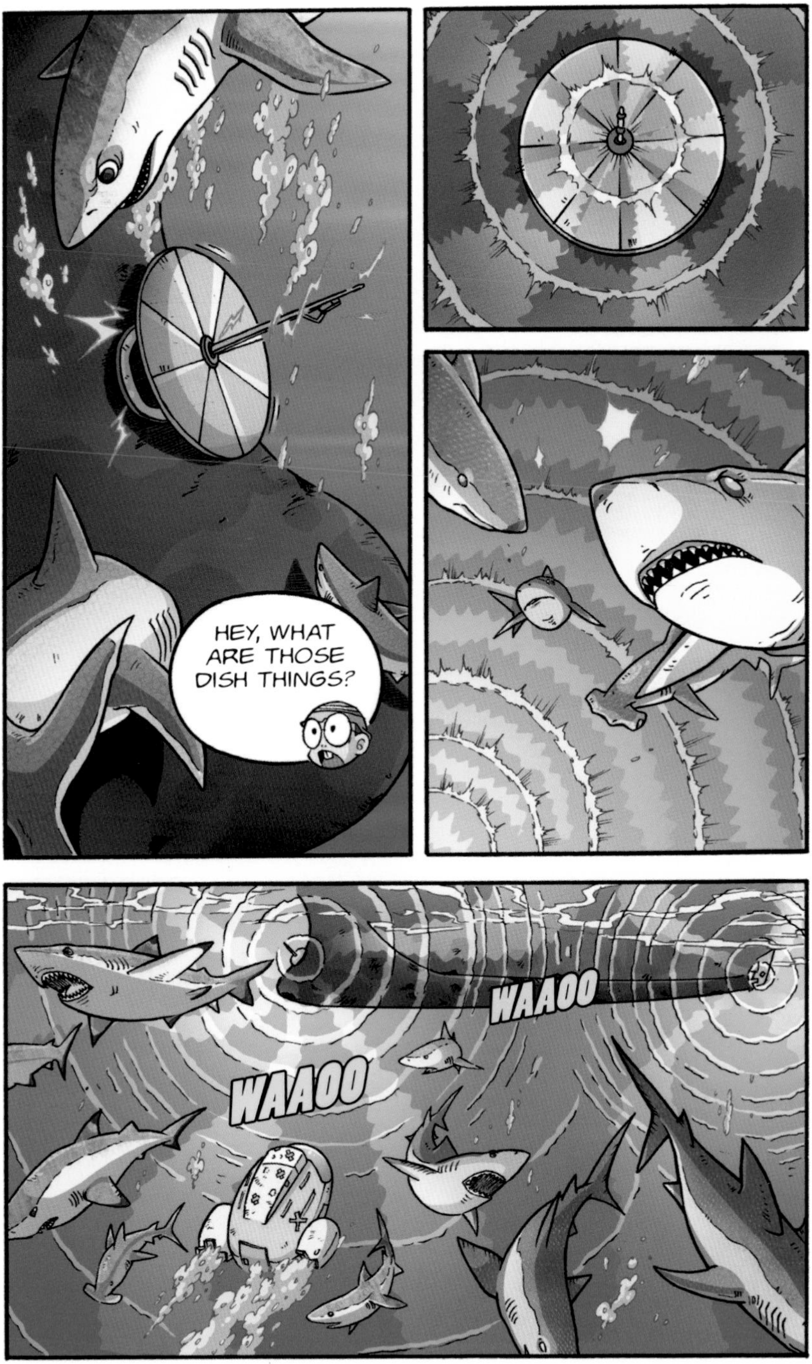
HEY, WHAT ARE THOSE DISH THINGS?
WAAOO
WAAOO

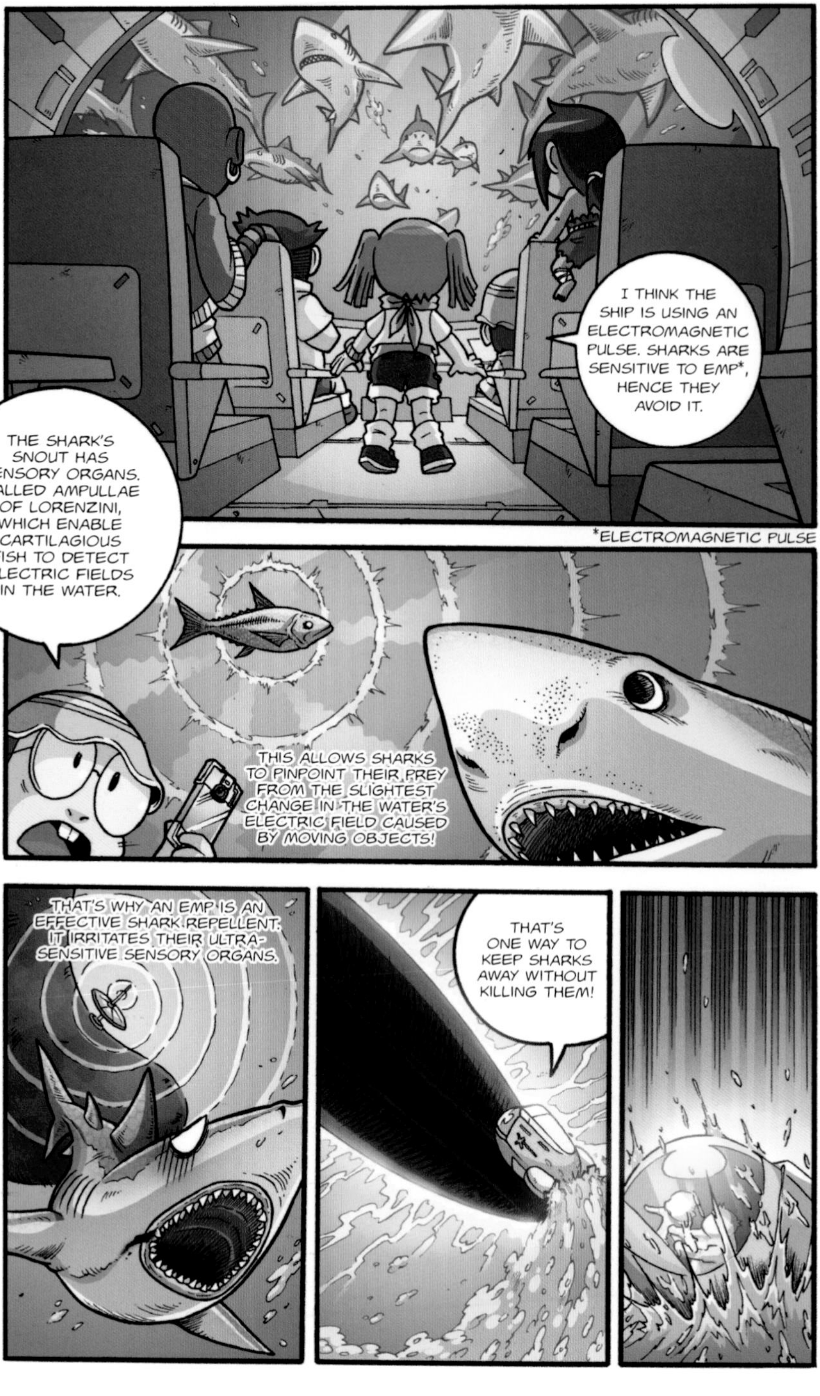
I THINK THE SHIP IS USING AN ELECTROMAGNETIC PULSE. SHARKS ARE SENSITIVE TO EMP*, HENCE THEY AVOID IT.
*ELECTROMAGNETIC PULSE
THE SHARK'S SNOUT HAS SENSORY ORGANS. CALLED AMPULLAE OF LORENZINI, WHICH ENABLE CARTILAGIOUS FISH TO DETECT ELECTRIC FIELDS IN THE WATER.
THIS ALLOWS SHARKS TO PINPOINT THEIR PREY FROM THE SLIGHTEST CHANGE IN THE WATER'S ELECTRIC FIELD CAUSED BY MOVING OBJECTS!
THAT'S WHY AN EMP IS AN EFFECTIVE SHARK REPELLENT. IT IRRITATES THEIR ULTRA-SENSITIVE SENSORY ORGANS.
THAT'S ONE WAY TO KEEP SHARKS AWAY WITHOUT KILLING THEM!

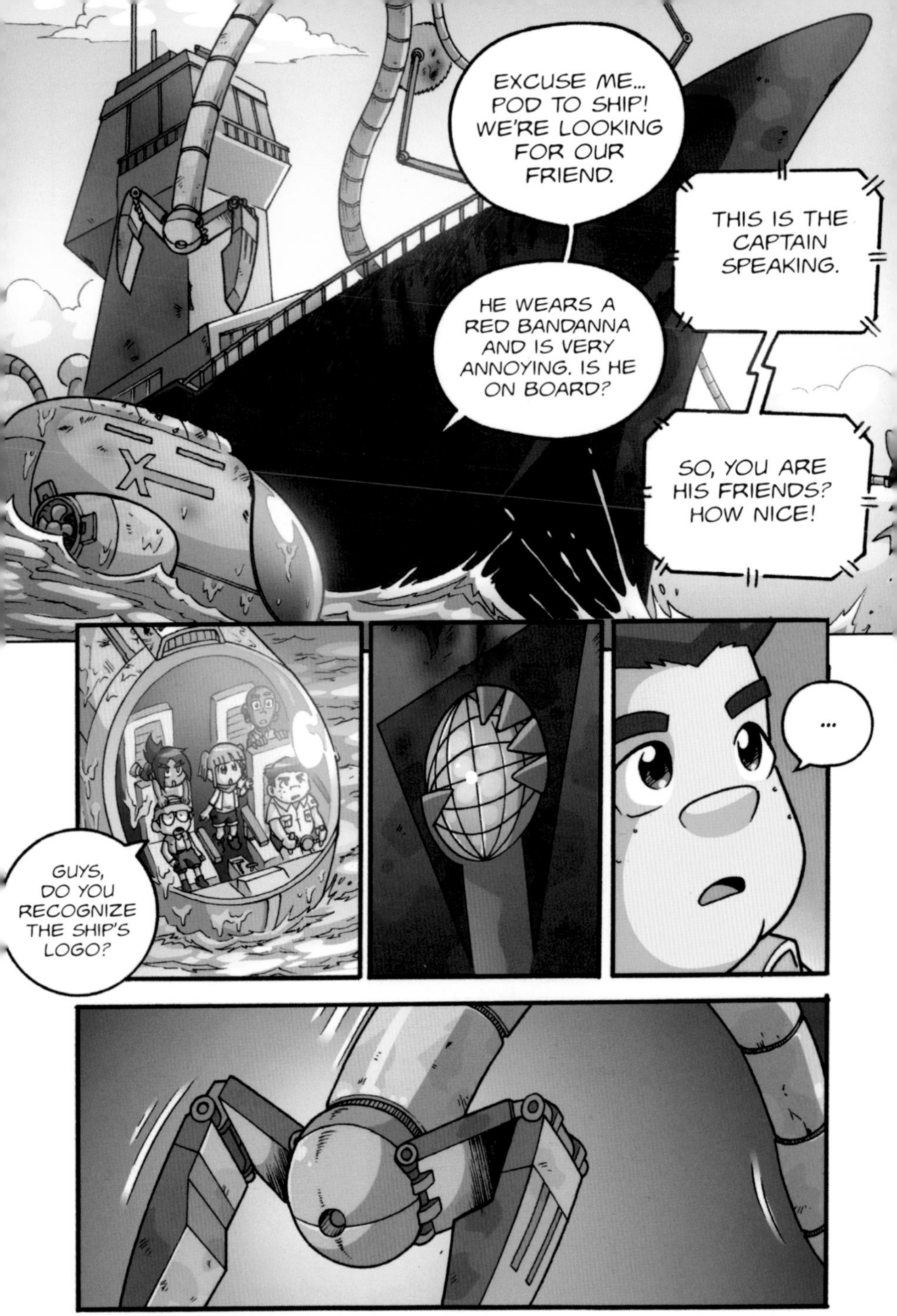
EXCUSE ME... POD TO SHIP! WE'RE LOOKING FOR OUR FRIEND.
HE WEARS A RED BANDANNA AND IS VERY ANNOYING. IS HE ON BOARD?
THIS IS THE CAPTAIN SPEAKING.
SO, YOU ARE HIS FRIENDS? HOW NICE!
GUYS, DO YOU RECOGNIZE THE SHIP'S LOGO?
...

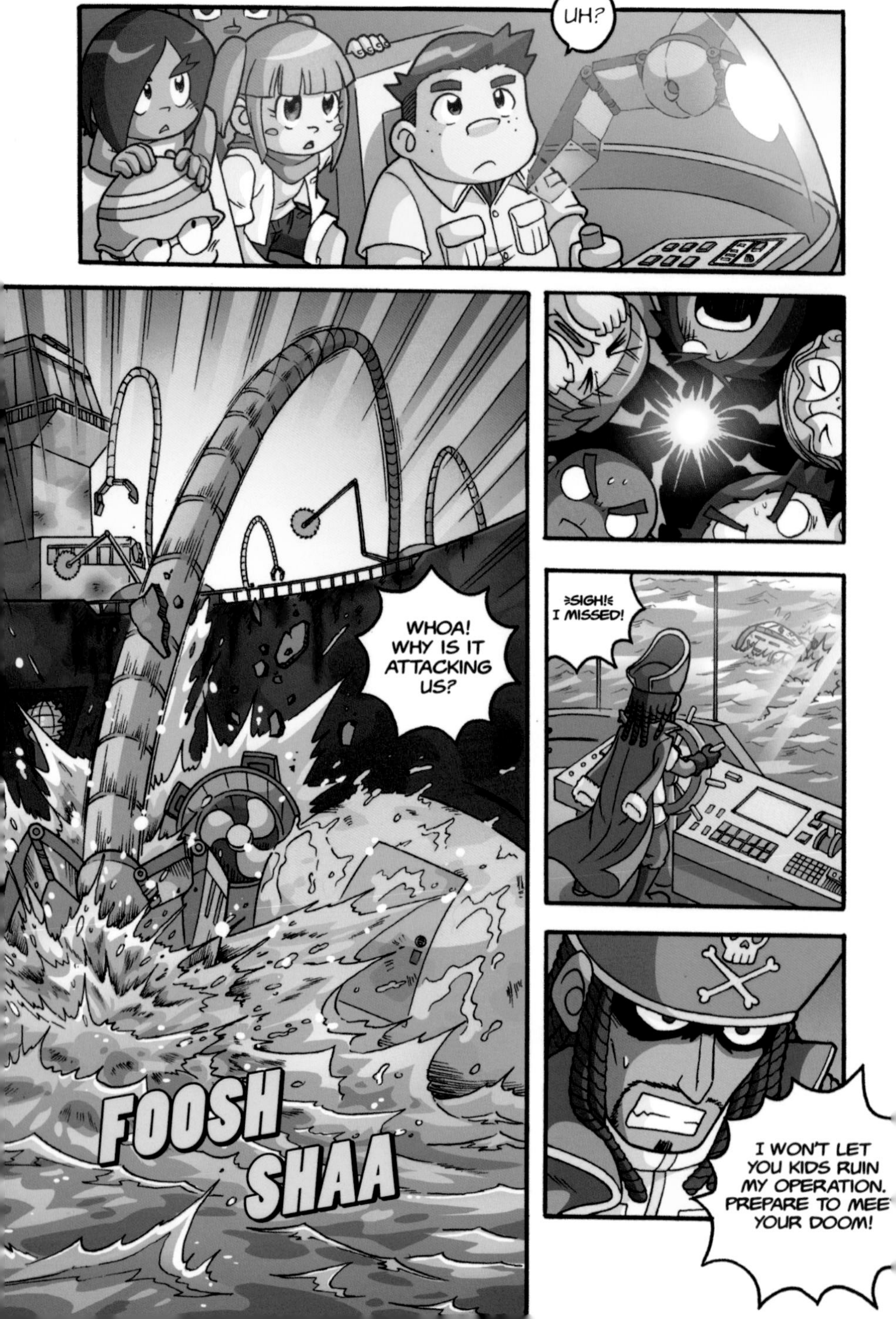
UH?
WHOA! WHY IS IT ATTACKING US?
FOOSH
SHAA
≥SIGH!≤ I MISSED!
I WON'T LET YOU KIDS RUIN MY OPERATION. PREPARE TO MEE YOUR DOOM!

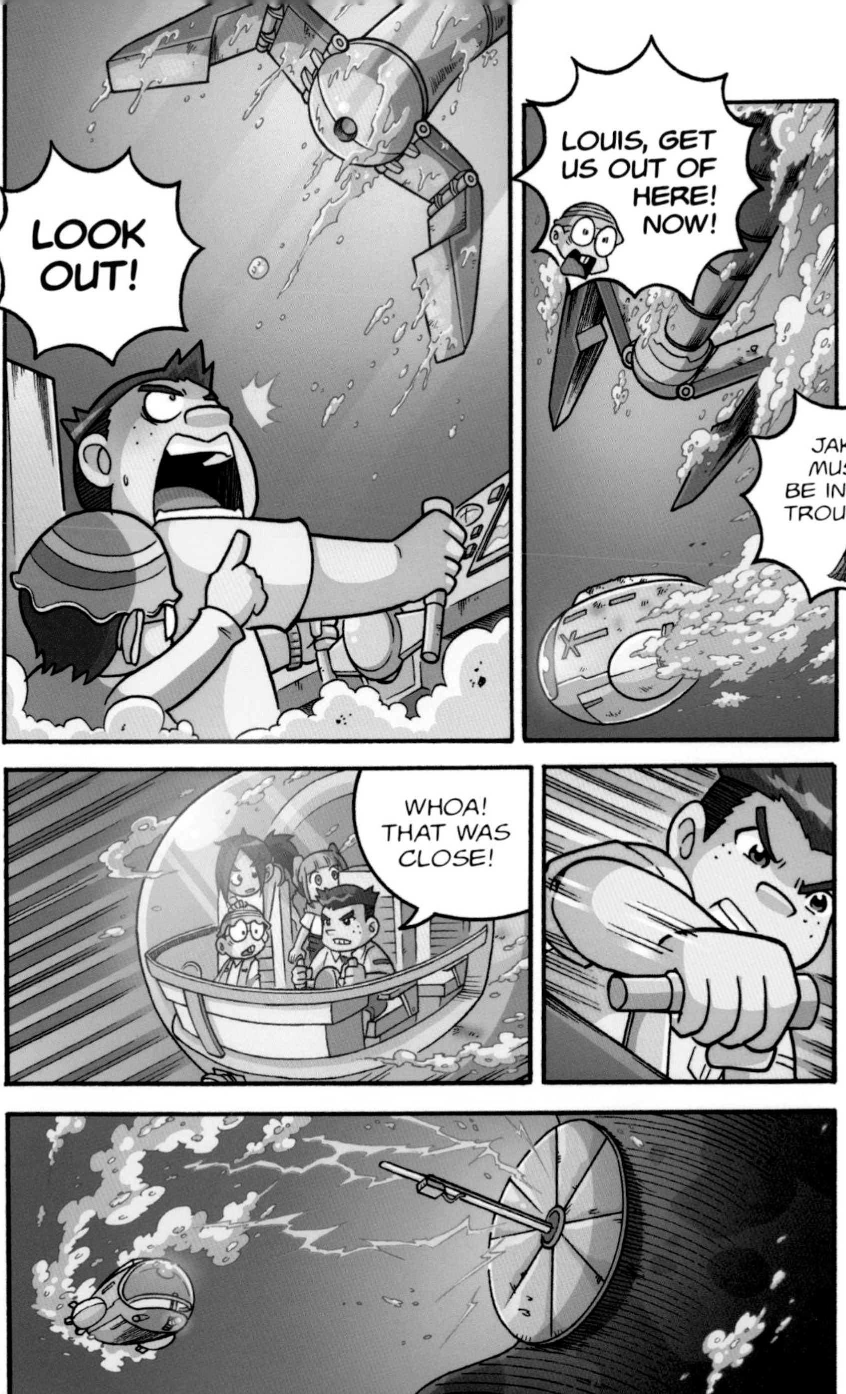
LOOK OUT!
LOUIS, GET US OUT OF HERE! NOW!
JAKE MUST BE IN BIG TROUBLE!
WHOA! THAT WAS CLOSE!

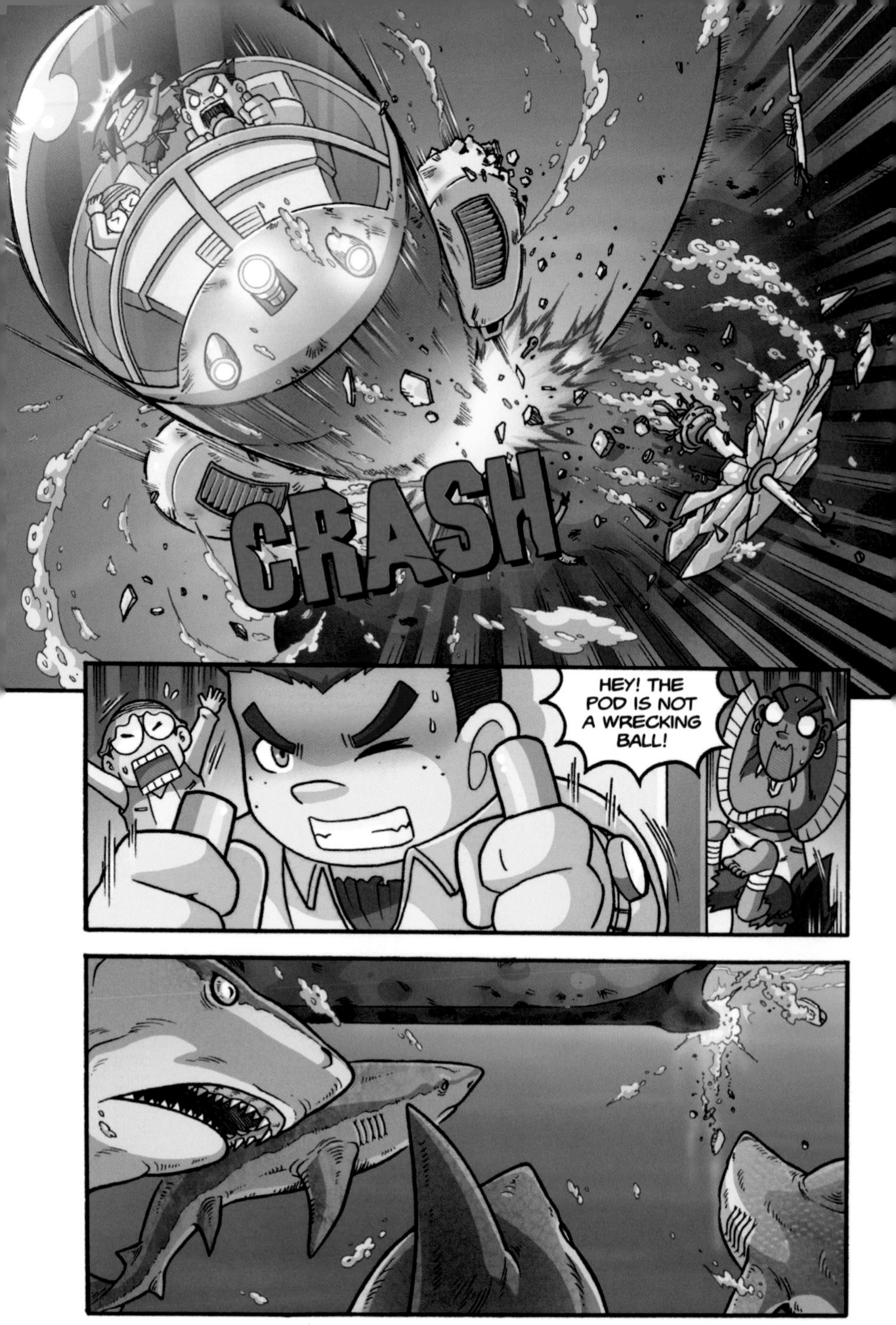
CRASH
HEY! THE POD IS NOT A WRECKING BALL!

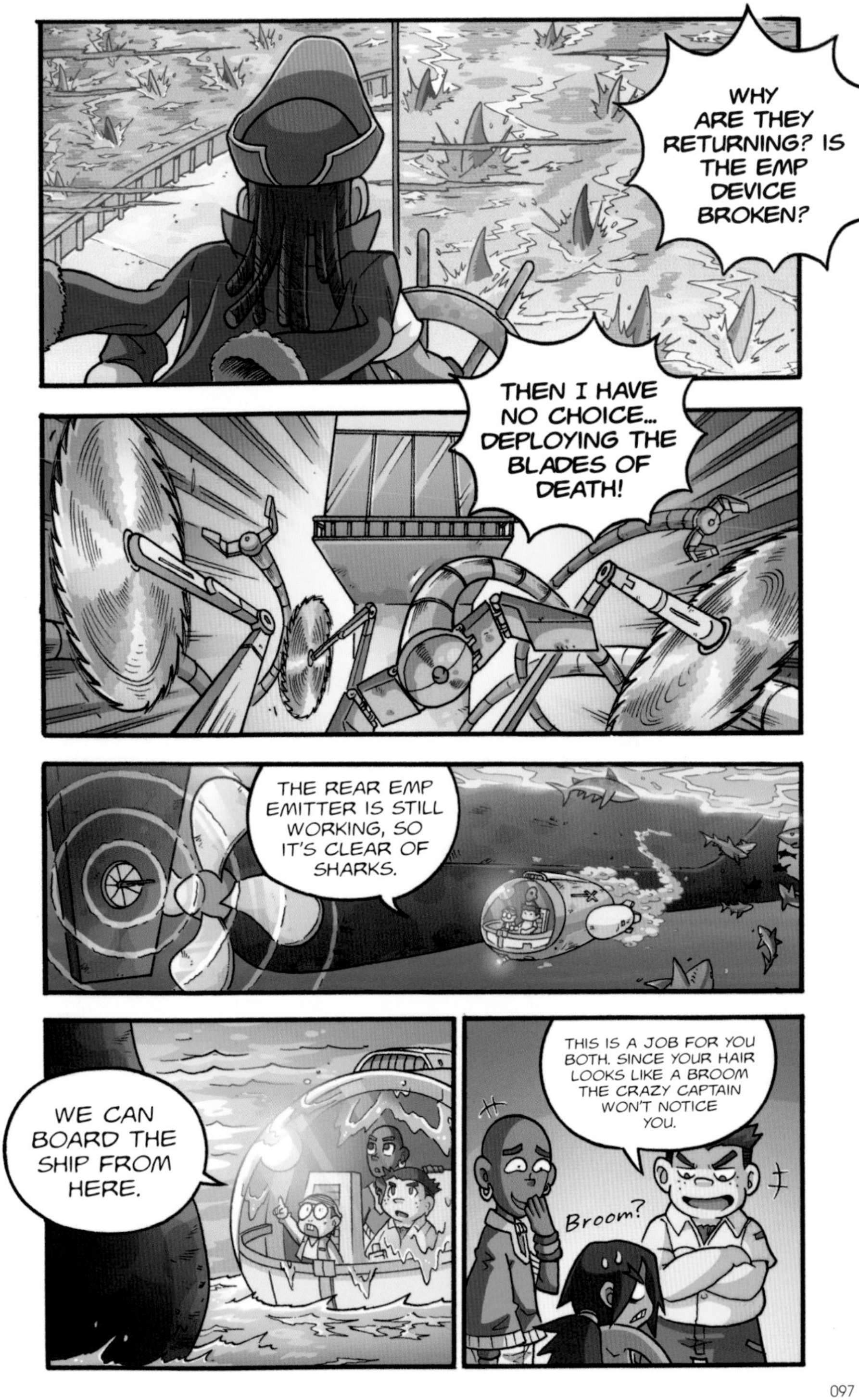
WHY ARE THEY RETURNING? IS THE EMP DEVICE BROKEN?
THEN I HAVE NO CHOICE... DEPLOYING THE BLADES OF DEATH!
THE REAR EMP EMITTER IS STILL WORKING, SO IT'S CLEAR OF SHARKS.
WE CAN BOARD THE SHIP FROM HERE.
THIS IS A JOB FOR YOU BOTH. SINCE YOUR HAIR LOOKS LIKE A BROOM THE CRAZY CAPTAIN WON'T NOTICE YOU.
Broom?

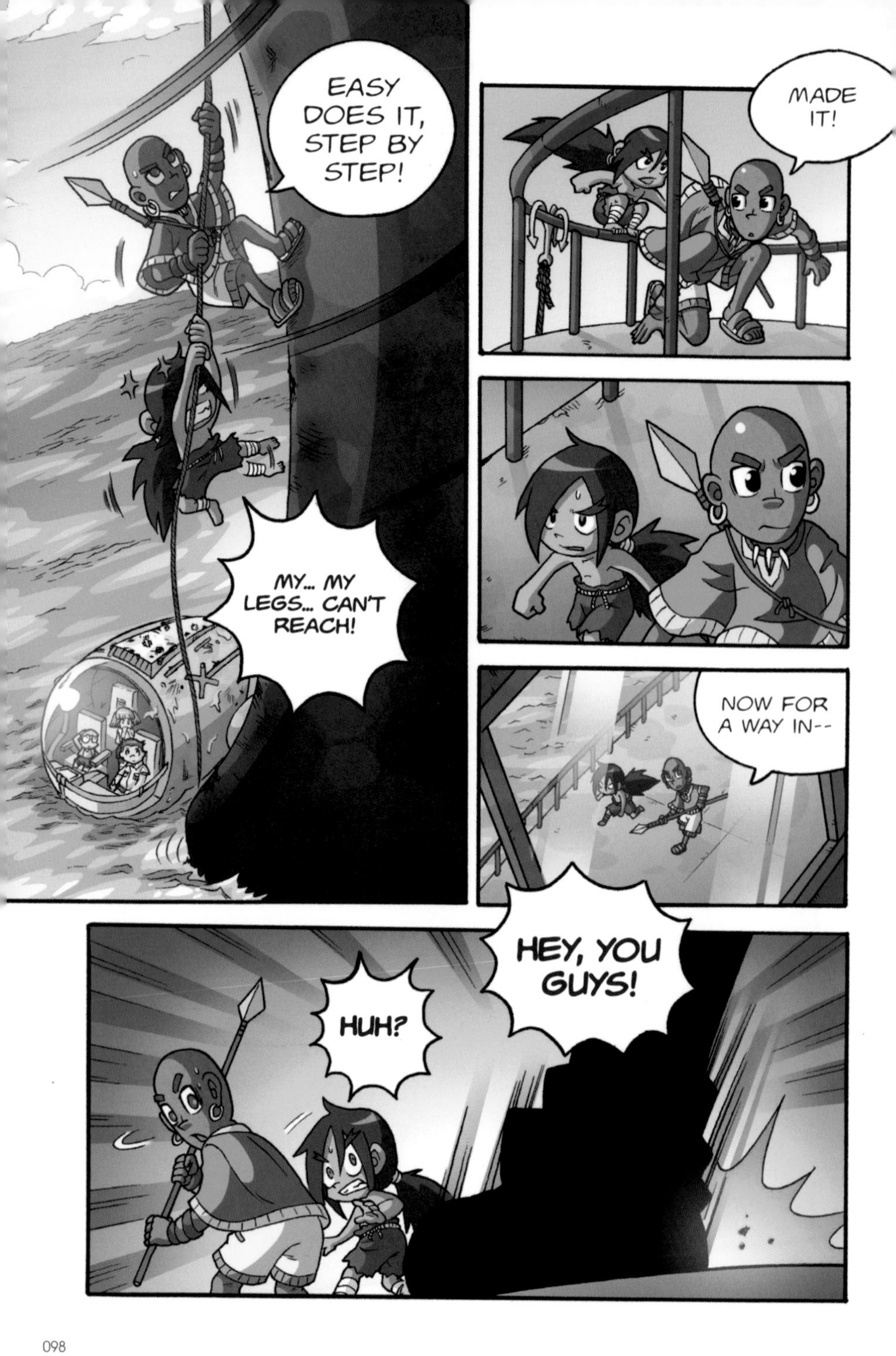
EASY DOES IT, STEP BY STEP!
MY... MY LEGS... CAN'T REACH!
MADE IT!
NOW FOR A WAY IN--
HEY, YOU GUYS!
HUH?

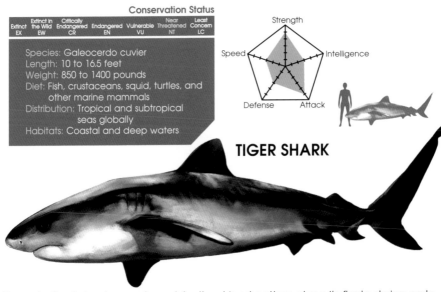

Conservation Status

Extinct EX	Extinct in the Wild EW	Critically Endangered CR	Endangered EN	Vulnerable VU	Near Threatened NT	Least Concern LC

Species: Galeocerdo cuvier
Length: 10 to 16.5 feet
Weight: 850 to 1400 pounds
Diet: Fish, crustaceans, squid, turtles, and other marine mammals
Distribution: Tropical and subtropical seas globally
Habitats: Coastal and deep waters

Strength
Speed
Intelligence
Defense
Attack

TIGER SHARK

Named after its jungle counterpart for the striped pattern along its flanks during early adolescence, it is a relatively large macropredator that more than earns its name. Second only to the great white shark, when it comes to encounters with humans, tigers are notoriously aggressive and often prowl coastal waters in search of prey. A solitary and mostly nocturnal hunter, its eyes contain a reflective layer called tapetum lucidum, maximizing visibility in low-light conditions, another similarity with the quadruped tiger.

Nothing but the tooth; Great White vs. Tiger

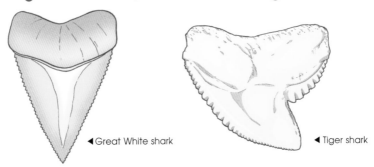

◀ Great White shark

◀ Tiger shark

The tiger shark's shorter, smaller teeth are specialized to slice through flesh, bone, and other tough substances such as turtle shells. Similar to most sharks, however, its teeth are continually replaced by rows of new ones. Their broad, heavily calcified jaws and nearly terminal mouth, combined with robust, serrated teeth, enable tiger sharks, hunting together, to take on large prey, such as humpback whales.

Conservation Status

Extinct EX	Extinct in the Wild EW	Critically Endangered CR	Endangered EN	Vulnerable VU	Near Threatened NT	Least Concern LC

Species: Lamna nasus
Length: 6.6 to 9.8 feet
Weight: 507 pounds at most
Diet: Mostly bony fish
Distribution: Northern Atlantic and Antarctic waters
Habitats: Cold and temperate waters

A stout bodied mackerel shark with a fusiform (spindle-like) shape that tapers to a pointed snout and narrow tail with large pectoral and rounded dorsal fins. Powerful and active swimmers, they embark on seasonal migrations to cooler waters of the northern and southern extremes. Reputed to be "playful," porbeagles are popular game fish for anglers, which has had a detrimental impact upon the overall survival of the species due to over-fishing and low birth rates.

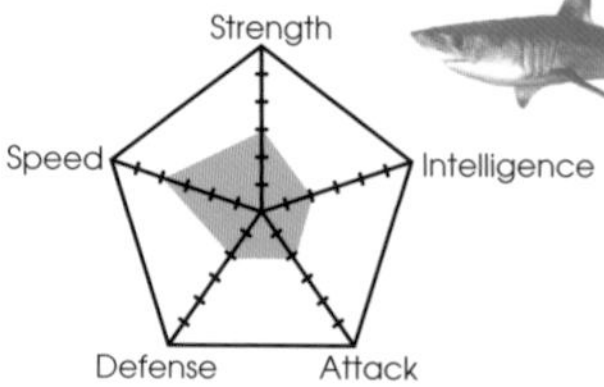
Strength
Intelligence
Attack
Defense
Speed

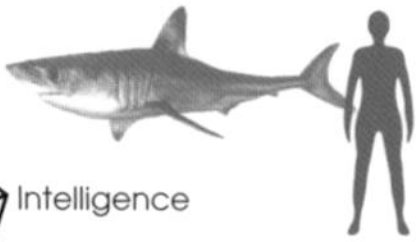

PORBEAGLE SHARK

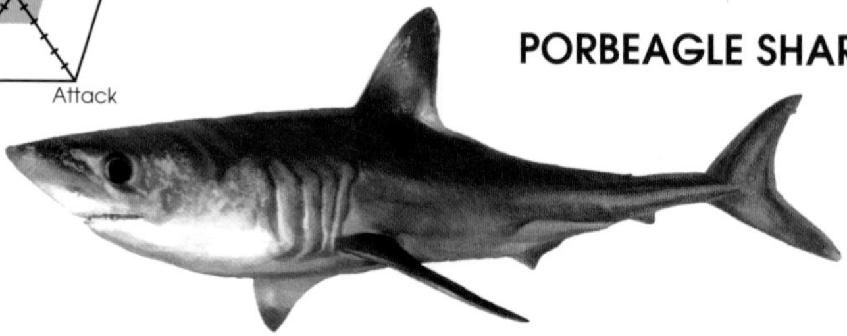

The largest of the visually striking family Sphyrnidae, it can be distinguished by the shape of its "hammer" (called the "cephalofoil"), which is wide with an almost straight front margin. A solitary, strong-swimming apex predator, it feeds on a wide variety of prey. Observations of this species in the wild suggest that the cephalofoil functions to immobilize stingrays, a favorite prey. This species has a viviparous mode of reproduction, bearing litters of up to 55 pups every two years.

Conservation Status

Extinct EX	Extinct in the Wild EW	Critically Endangered CR	Endangered EN	Vulnerable VU	Near Threatened NT	Least Concern LC

Species: Sphyrna mokarran
Length: From 11.5 to 20 feet
Weight: Over 900 pounds
Diet: Crustaceans and cephalopods to smaller sharks
Distribution: Tropical and temperate waters worldwide
Habitats: Coastlines

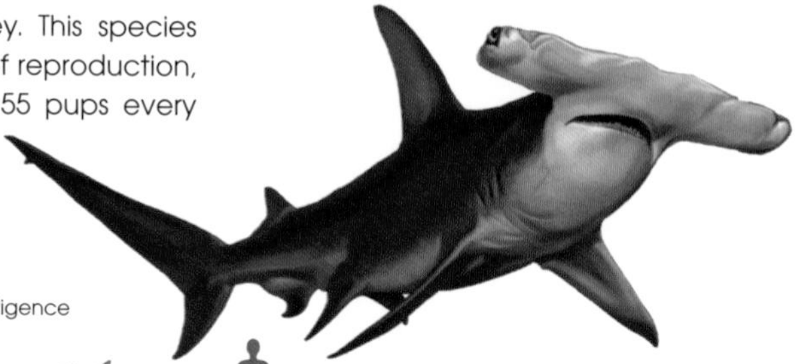

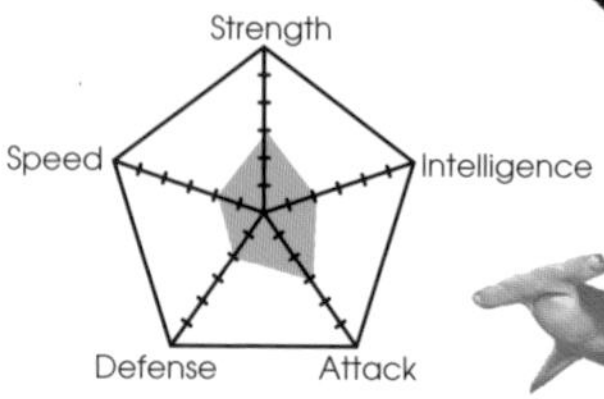
Strength
Intelligence
Attack
Defense
Speed

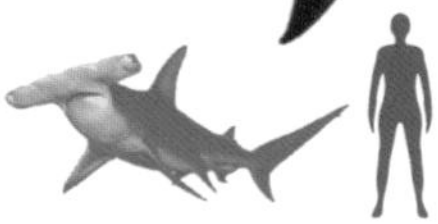

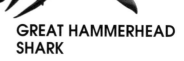

GREAT HAMMERHEAD SHARK

CHAPTER 6

UNDERWATER BATTLE

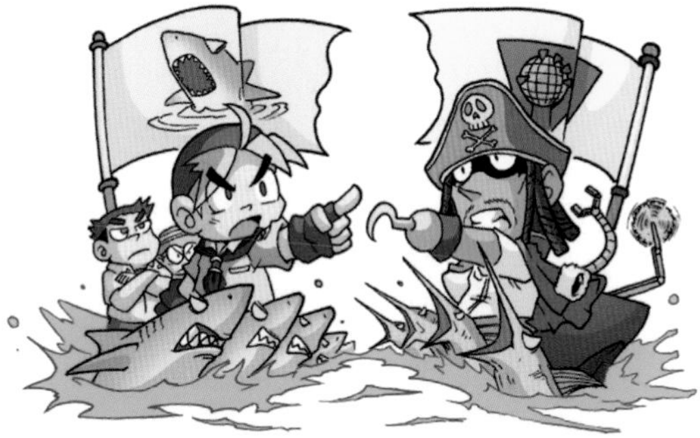

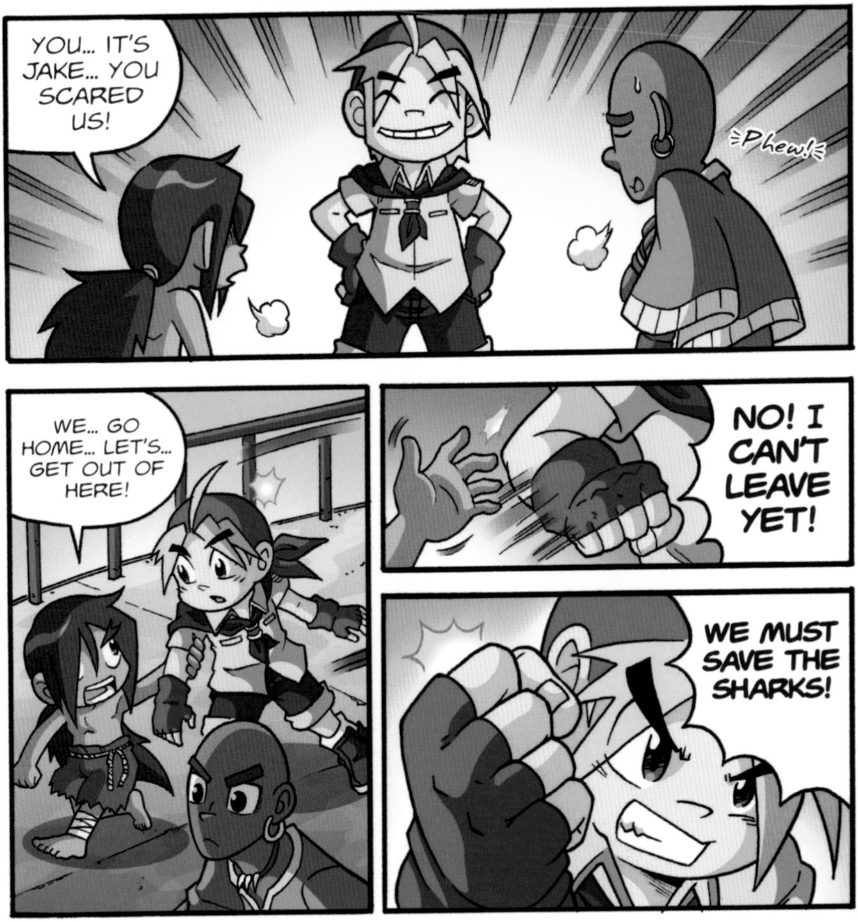
YOU... IT'S JAKE... YOU SCARED US!
Phew!
WE... GO HOME... LET'S... GET OUT OF HERE!
NO! I CAN'T LEAVE YET!
WE MUST SAVE THE SHARKS!

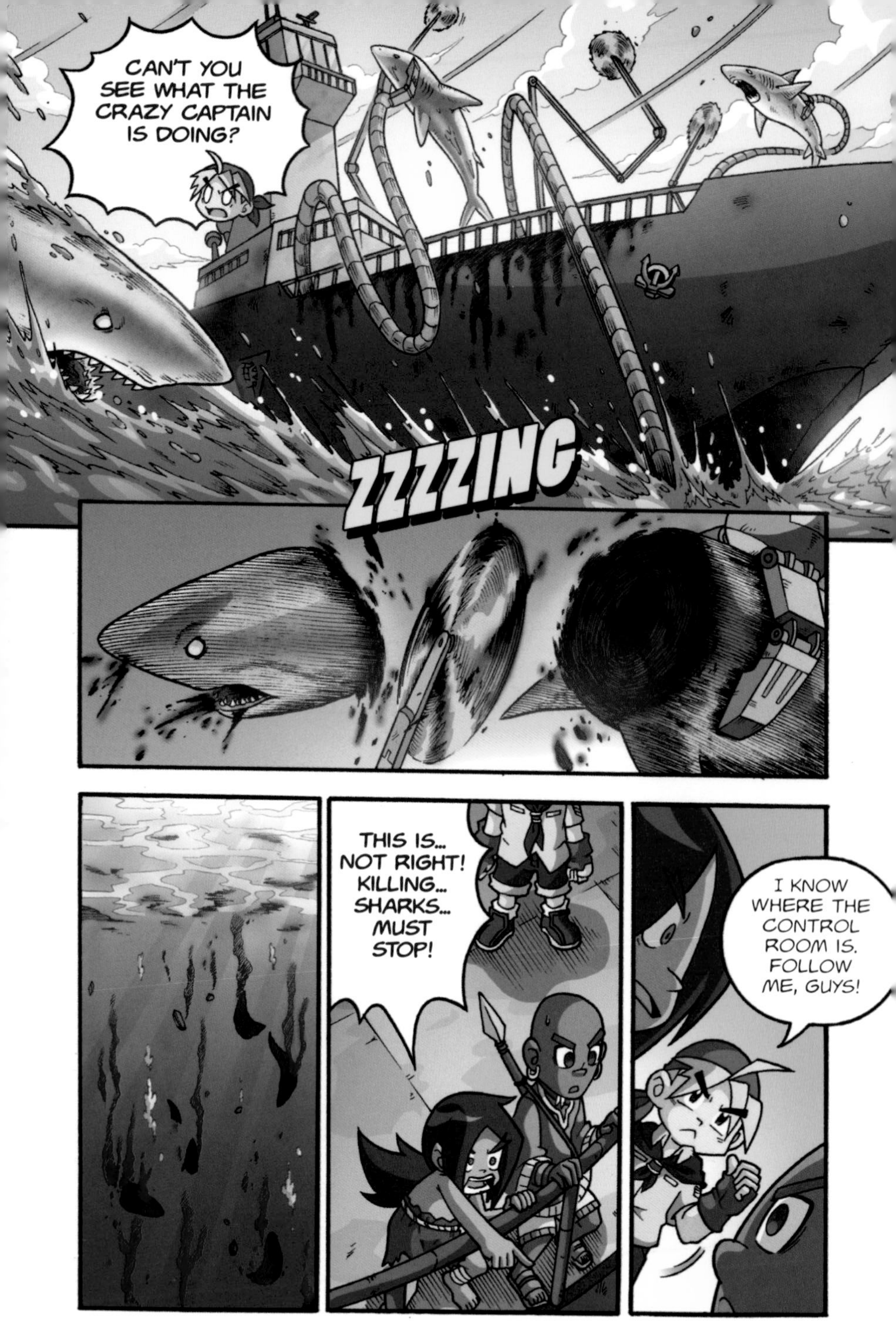
CAN'T YOU SEE WHAT THE CRAZY CAPTAIN IS DOING?
ZZZZING
THIS IS... NOT RIGHT! KILLING... SHARKS... MUST STOP!
I KNOW WHERE THE CONTROL ROOM IS. FOLLOW ME, GUYS!

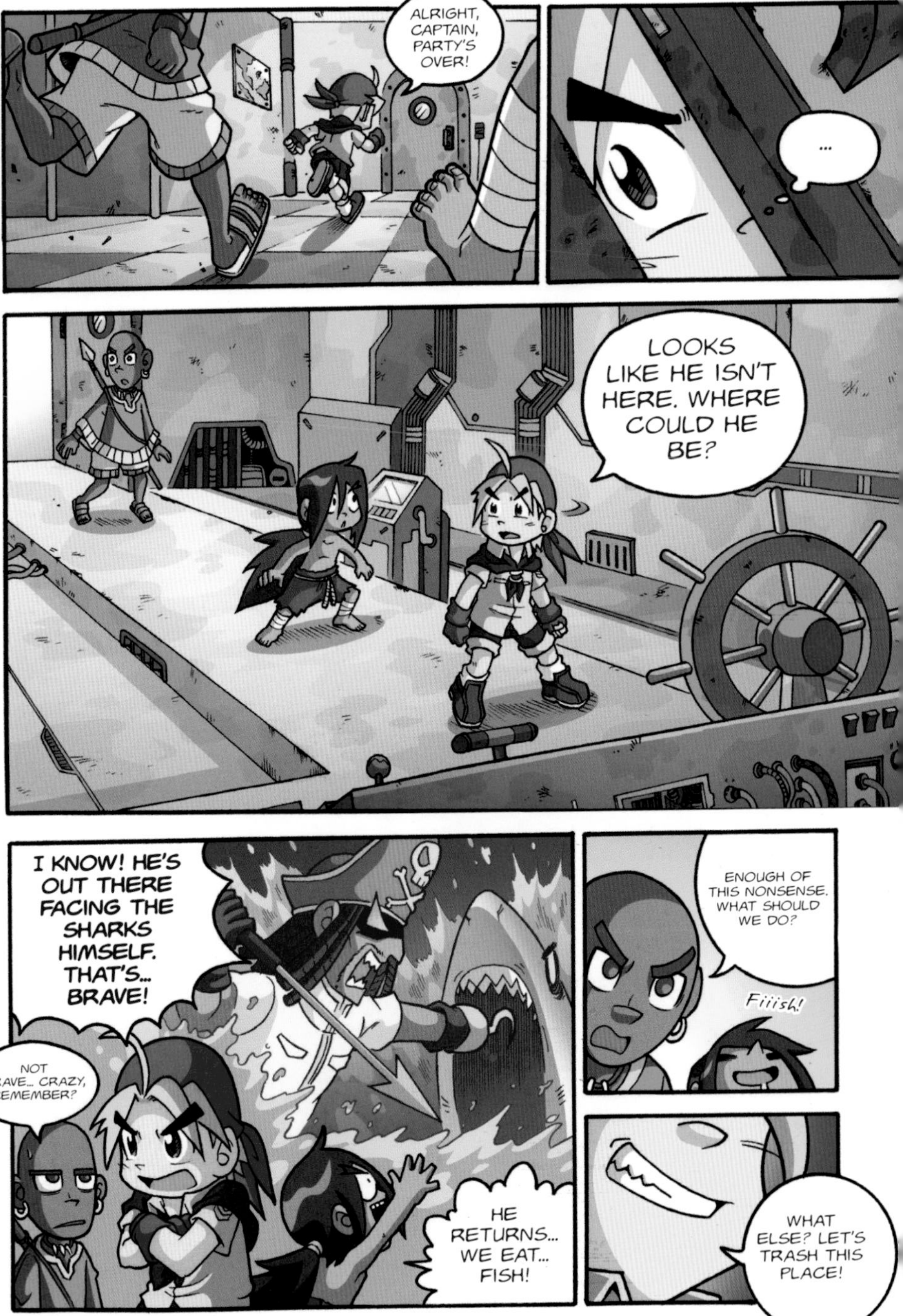
ALRIGHT, CAPTAIN, PARTY'S OVER!
...
LOOKS LIKE HE ISN'T HERE. WHERE COULD HE BE?
I KNOW! HE'S OUT THERE FACING THE SHARKS HIMSELF. THAT'S... BRAVE!
NOT BRAVE... CRAZY, REMEMBER?
HE RETURNS... WE EAT... FISH!
ENOUGH OF THIS NONSENSE. WHAT SHOULD WE DO?
Fiiish!
WHAT ELSE? LET'S TRASH THIS PLACE!

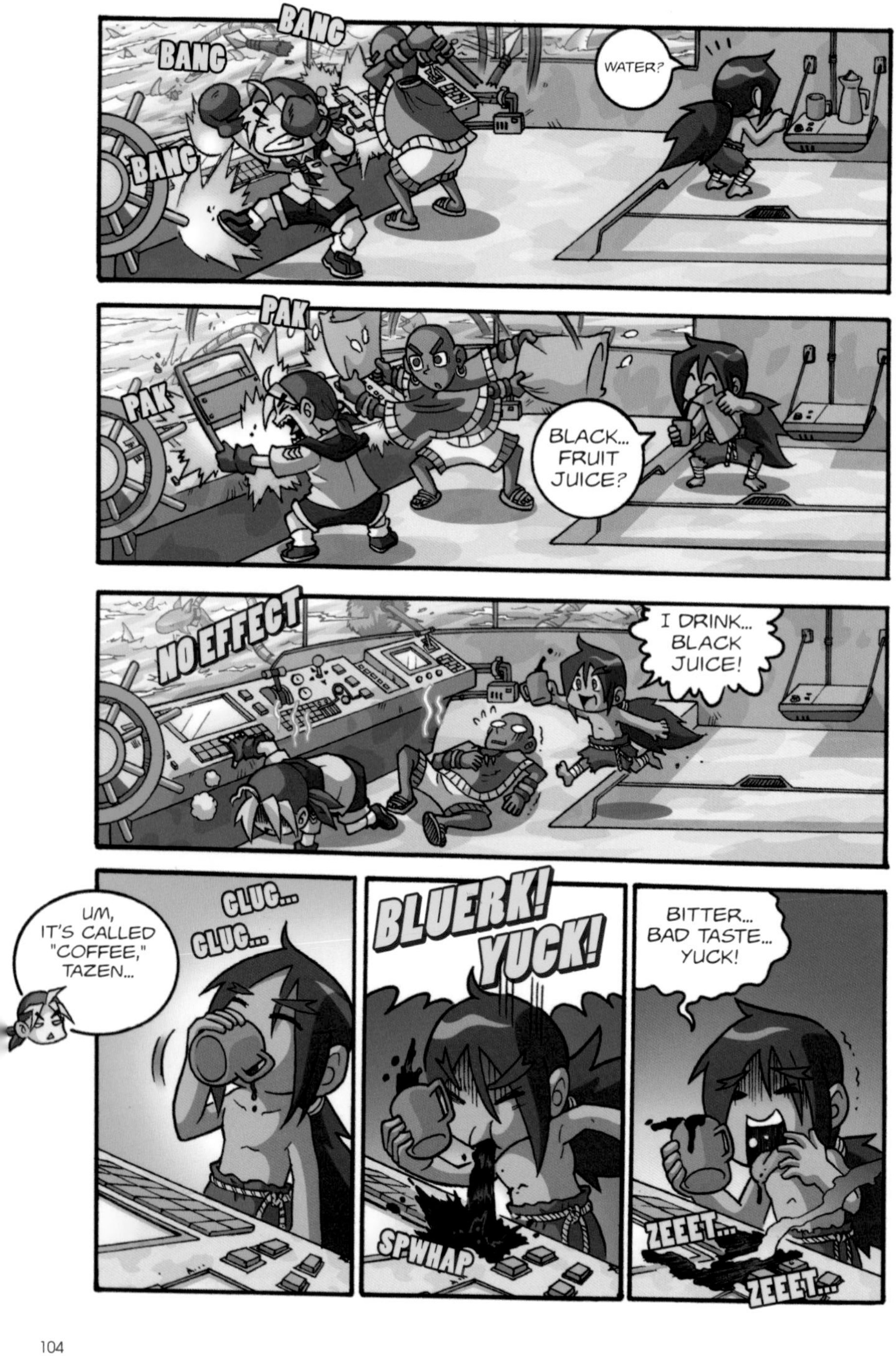
BANG
BANG
BANG
WATER?
PAK
PAK
BLACK... FRUIT JUICE?
NO EFFECT
I DRINK... BLACK JUICE!
UM, IT'S CALLED "COFFEE," TAZEN...
GLUG...
GLUG...
BLUERK! YUCK!
SPWHAP
BITTER... BAD TASTE... YUCK!
ZEEET...
ZEEET...

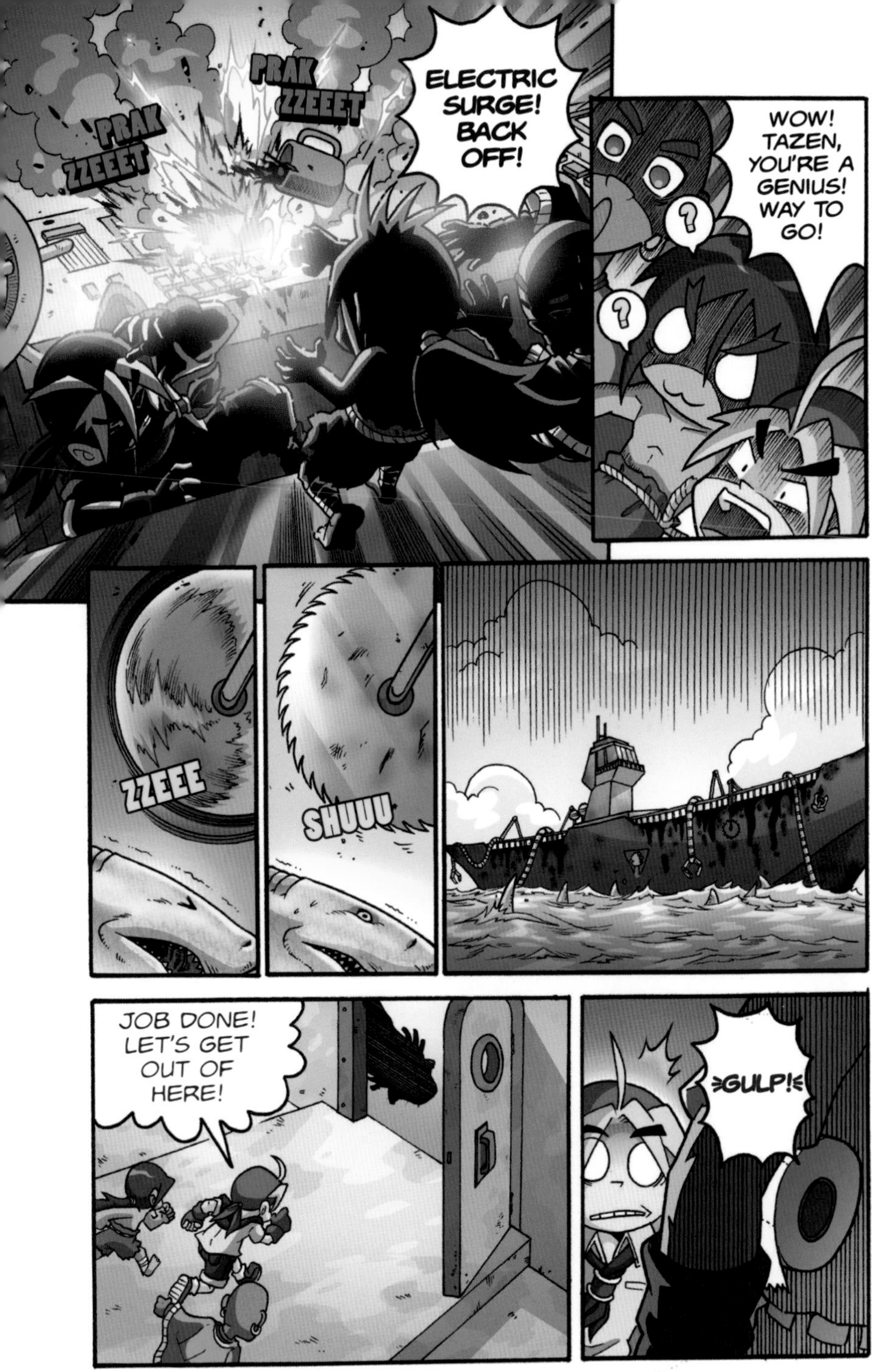
PRAK
ZZEEET
PRAK
ZZEEET
ELECTRIC SURGE! BACK OFF!
WOW! TAZEN, YOU'RE A GENIUS! WAY TO GO!
?
?
ZZEEE
SHUUU
JOB DONE! LET'S GET OUT OF HERE!
GULP!

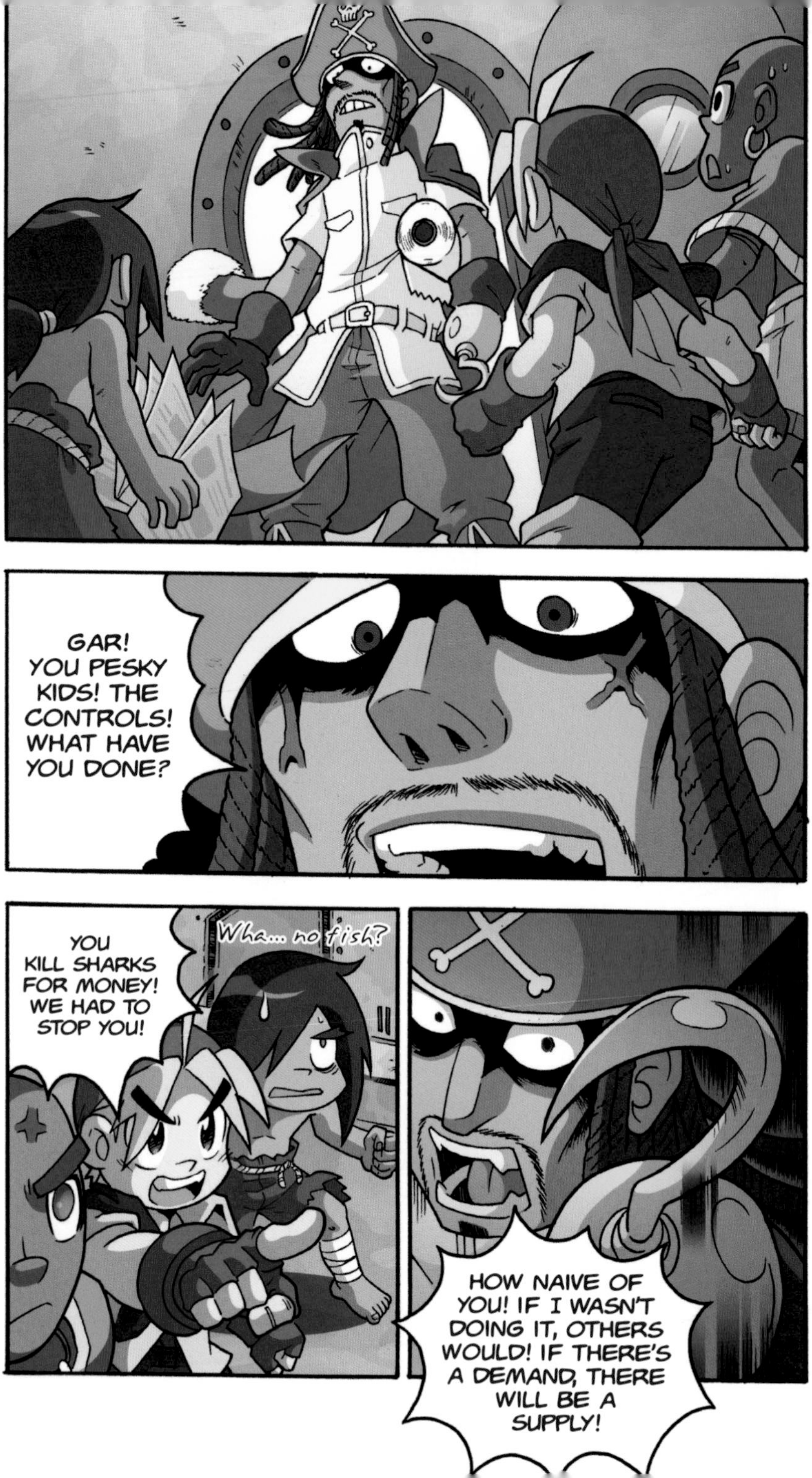
GAR! YOU PESKY KIDS! THE CONTROLS! WHAT HAVE YOU DONE?
YOU KILL SHARKS FOR MONEY! WE HAD TO STOP YOU!
Wha... no fish?
HOW NAIVE OF YOU! IF I WASN'T DOING IT, OTHERS WOULD! IF THERE'S A DEMAND, THERE WILL BE A SUPPLY!

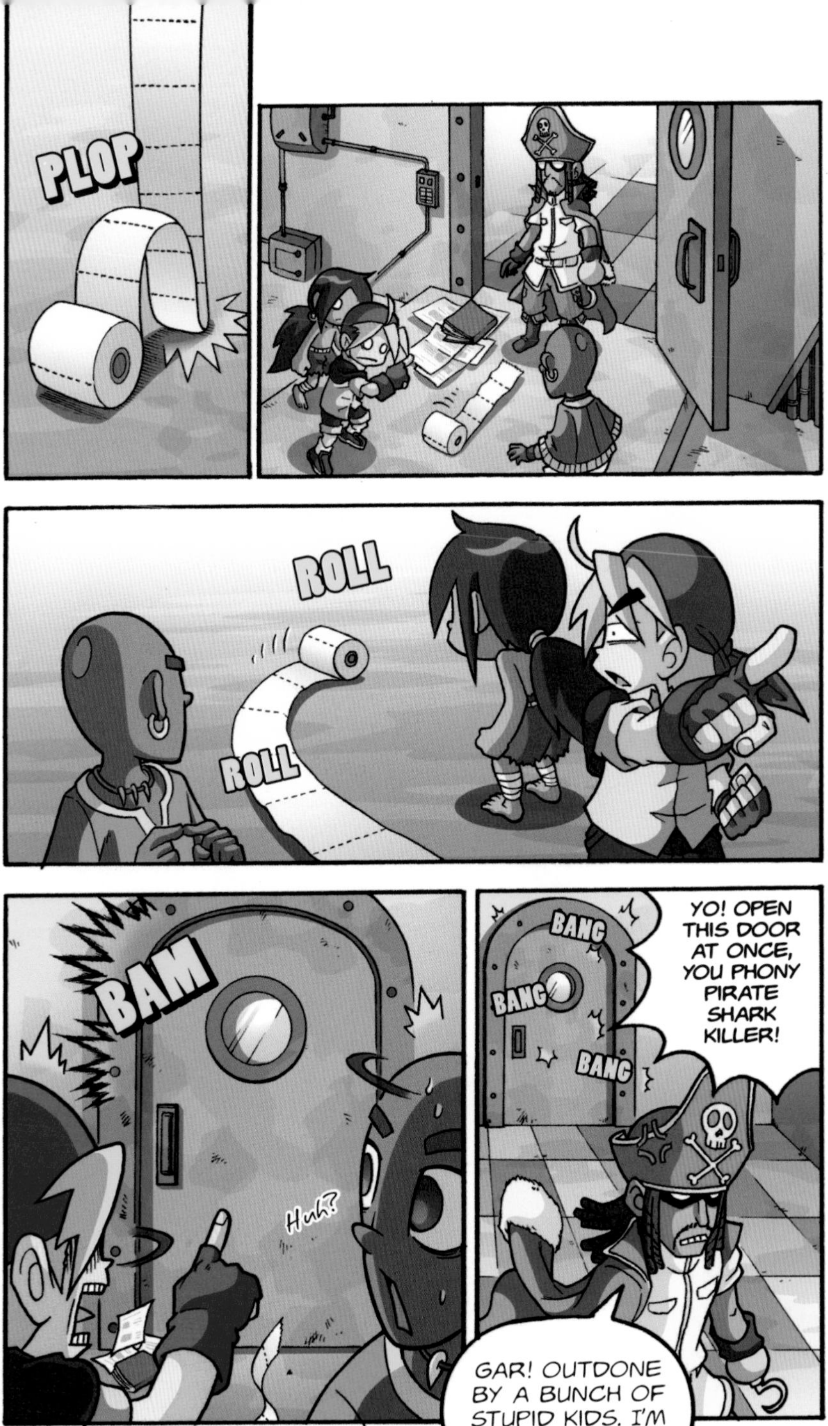
PLOP
ROLL
ROLL
BAM
Huh?
BANG
BANG
BANG
YO! OPEN THIS DOOR AT ONCE, YOU PHONY PIRATE SHARK KILLER!
GAR! OUTDONE BY A BUNCH OF STUPID KIDS. I'M GETTING OLD!

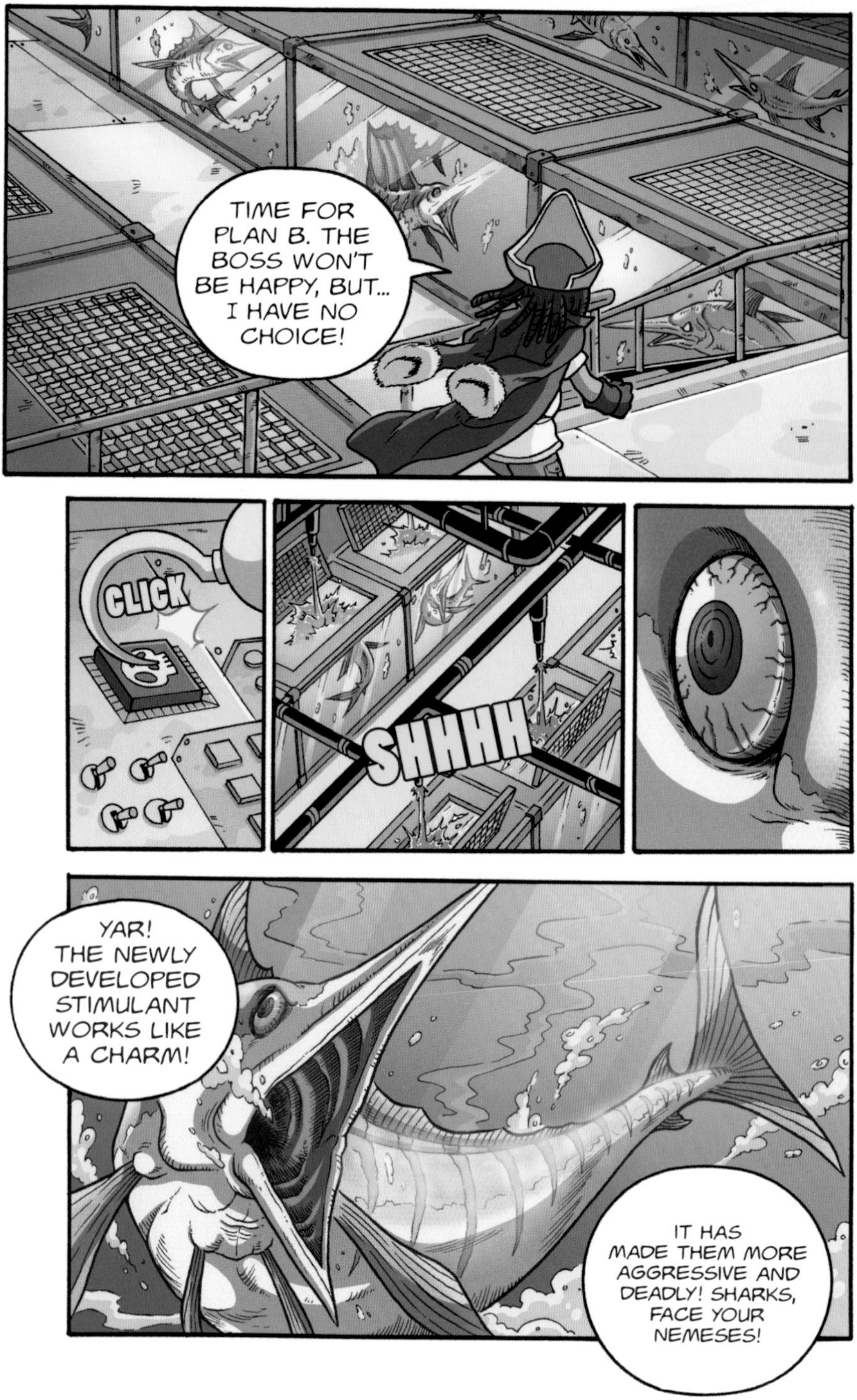
TIME FOR PLAN B. THE BOSS WON'T BE HAPPY, BUT... I HAVE NO CHOICE!
CLICK
SHHHH
YAR! THE NEWLY DEVELOPED STIMULANT WORKS LIKE A CHARM!
IT HAS MADE THEM MORE AGGRESSIVE AND DEADLY! SHARKS, FACE YOUR NEMESES!

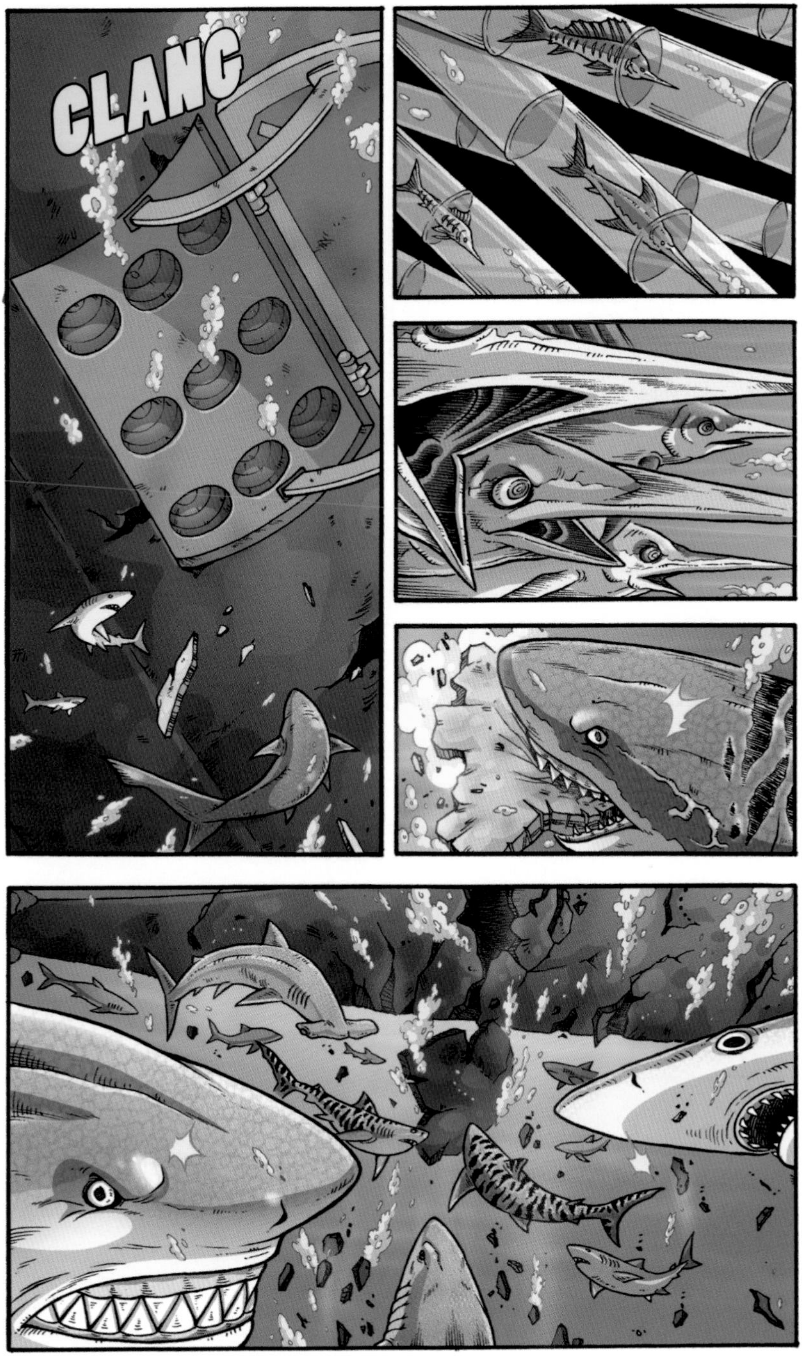
CLANG

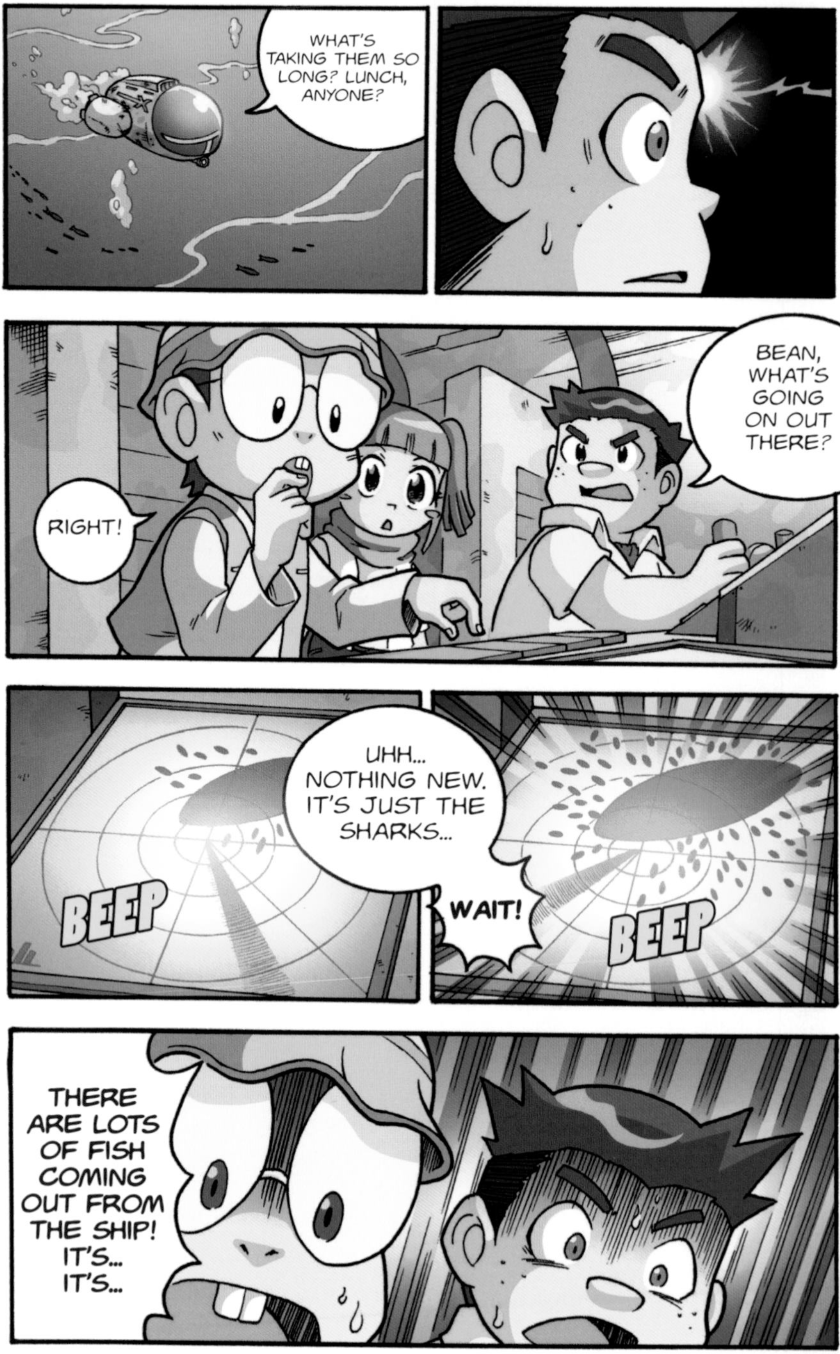
WHAT'S TAKING THEM SO LONG? LUNCH, ANYONE?
BEAN, WHAT'S GOING ON OUT THERE?
RIGHT!
UHH... NOTHING NEW. IT'S JUST THE SHARKS...
BEEP
WAIT!
BEEP
THERE ARE LOTS OF FISH COMING OUT FROM THE SHIP! IT'S... IT'S...

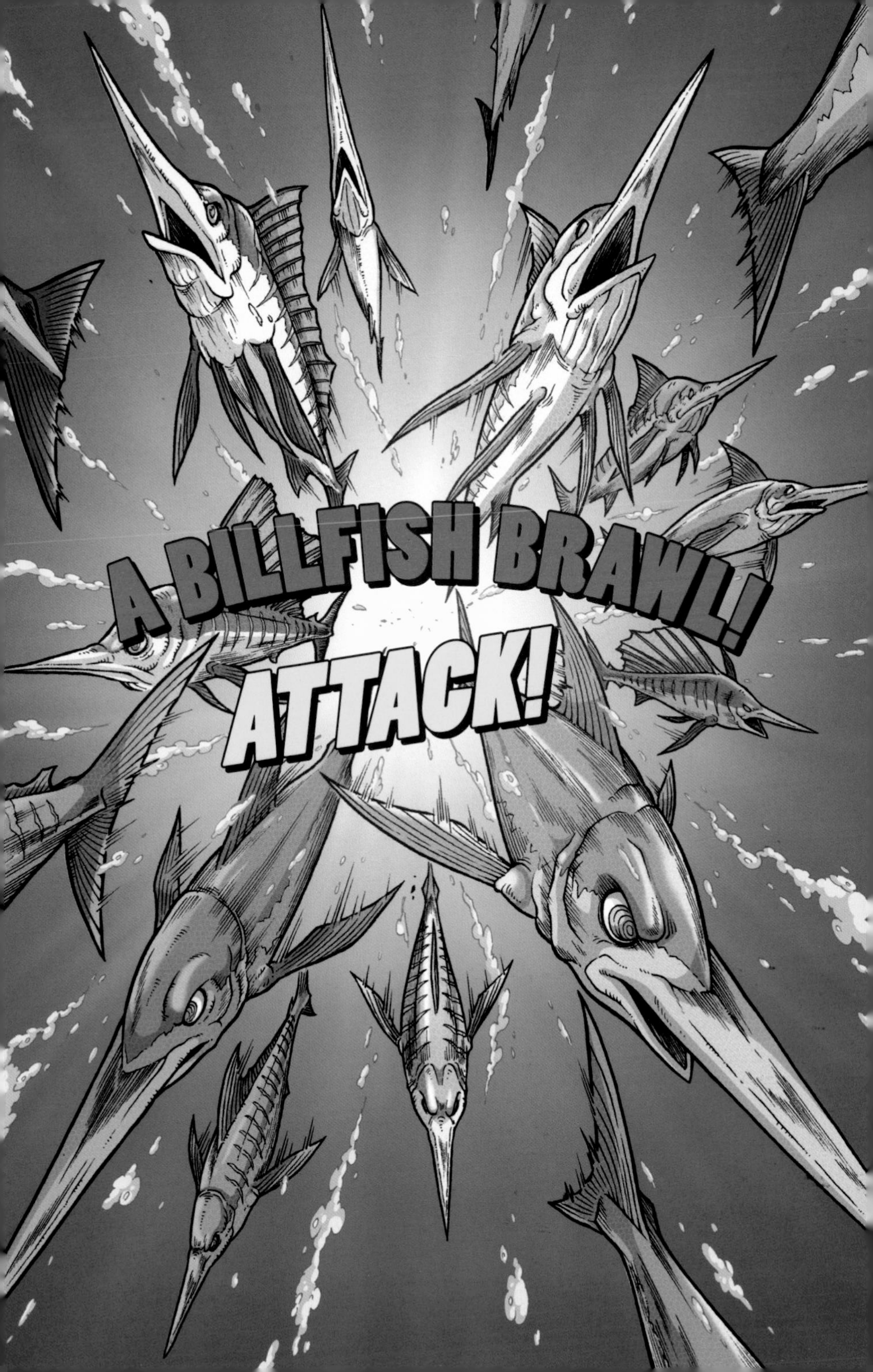
A BILLFISH BRAWL!
ATTACK!

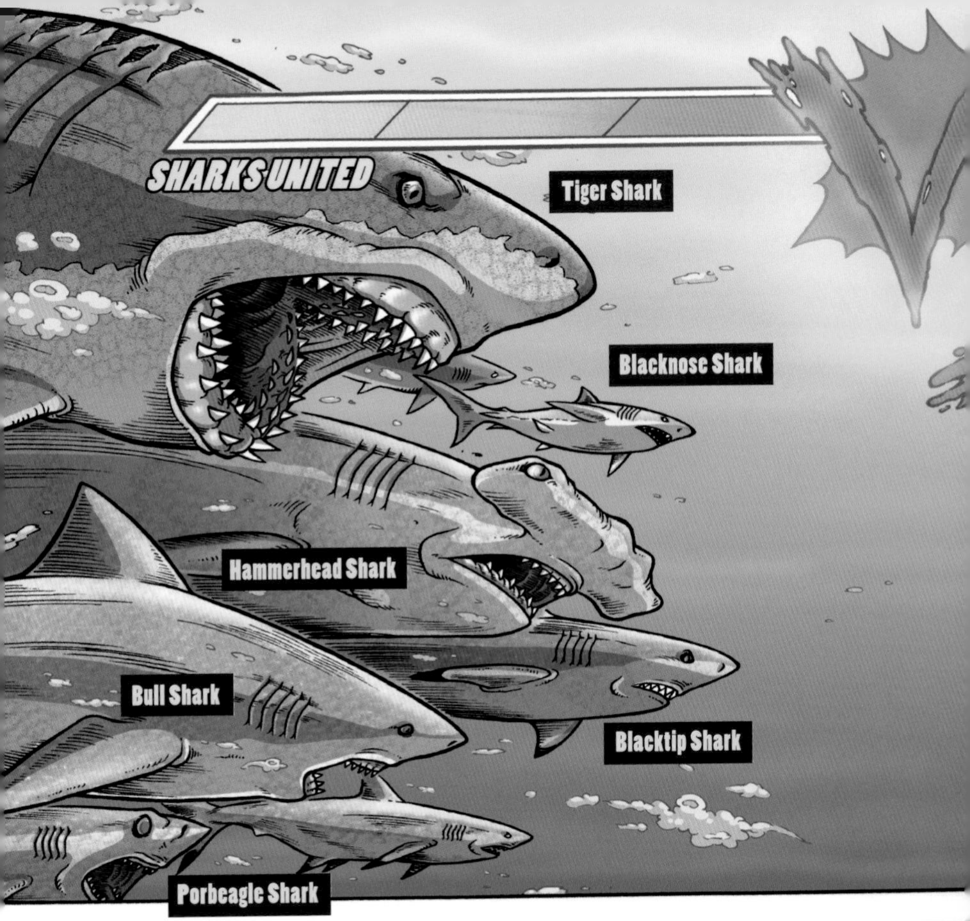
SHARKS UNITED
Tiger Shark
Blacknose Shark
Hammerhead Shark
Bull Shark
Blacktip Shark
Porbeagle Shark

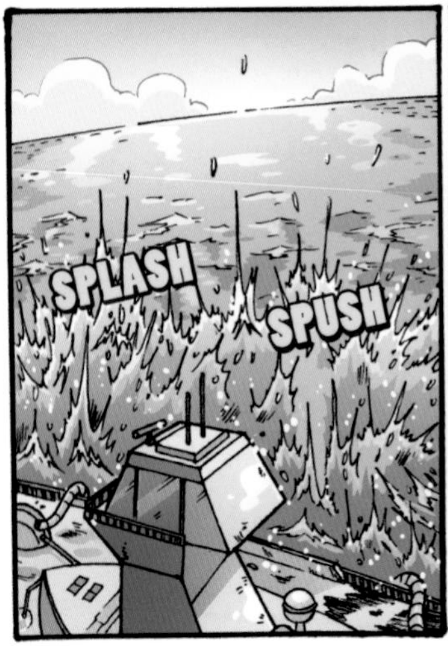
SPLASH
SPUSH

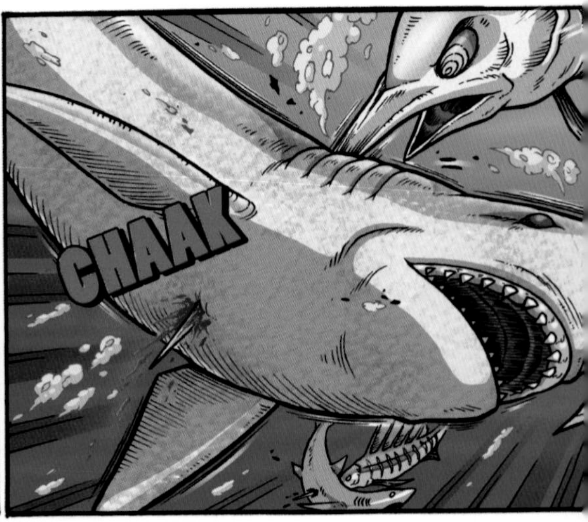
CHAAK

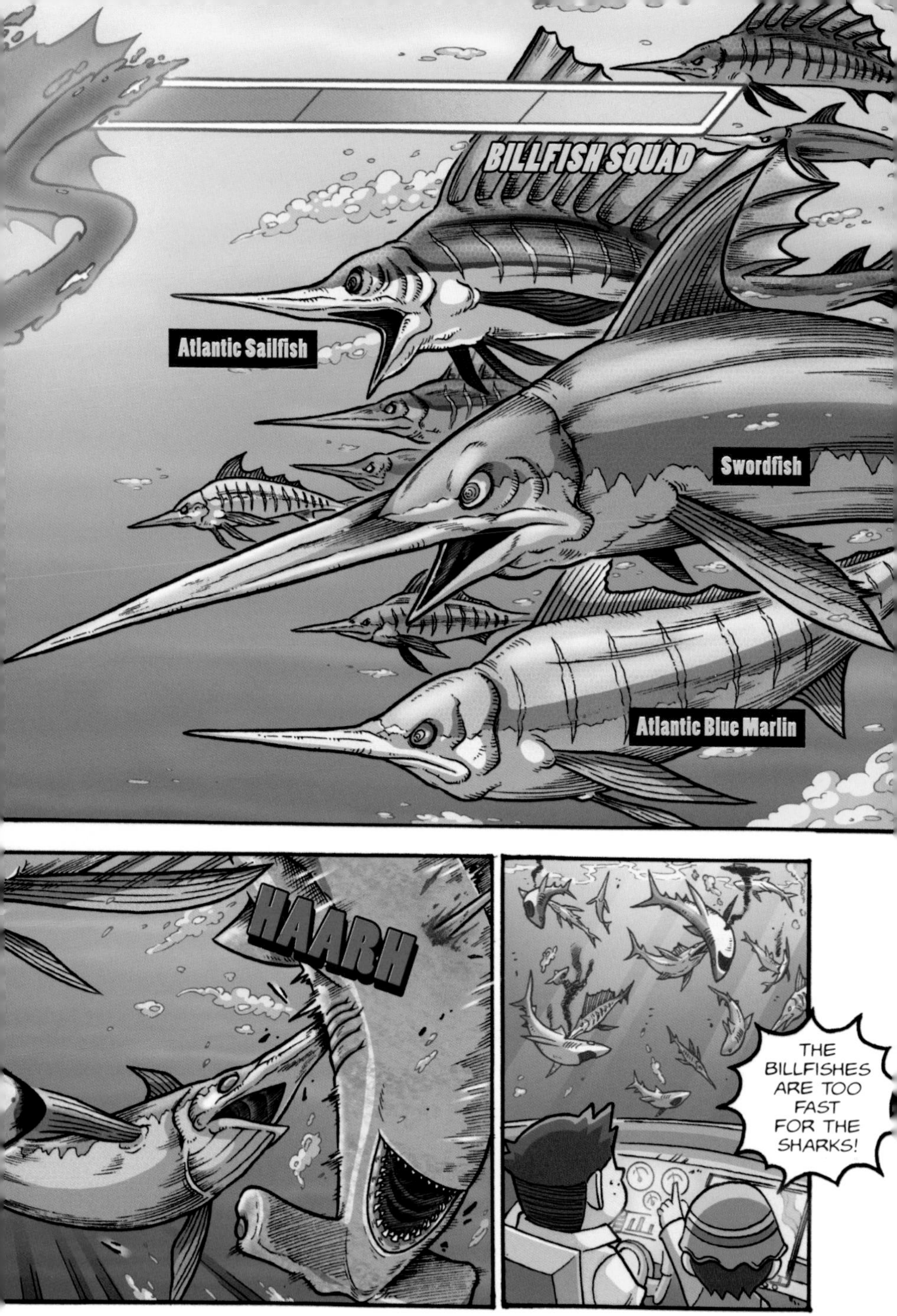
BILLFISH SQUAD
Atlantic Sailfish
Swordfish
Atlantic Blue Marlin
HAARH
THE BILLFISHES ARE TOO FAST FOR THE SHARKS!

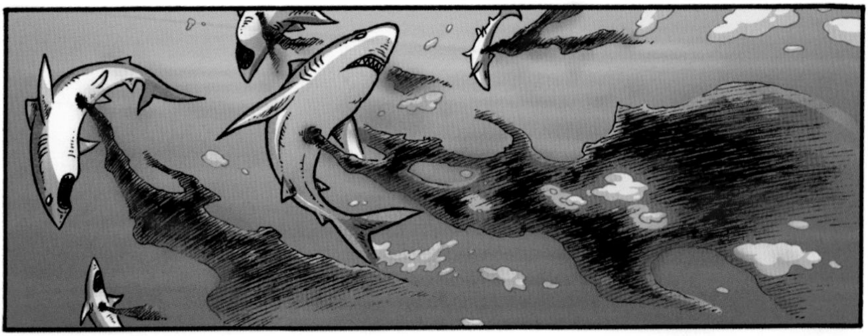

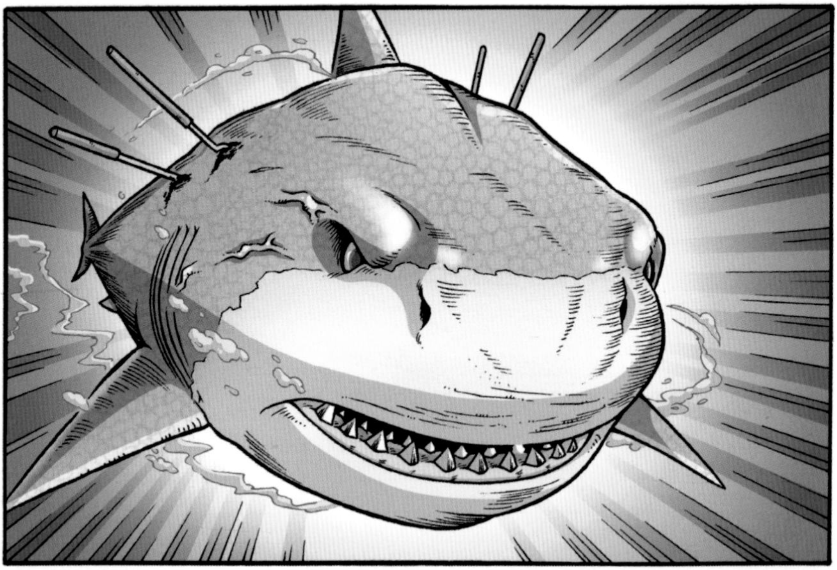

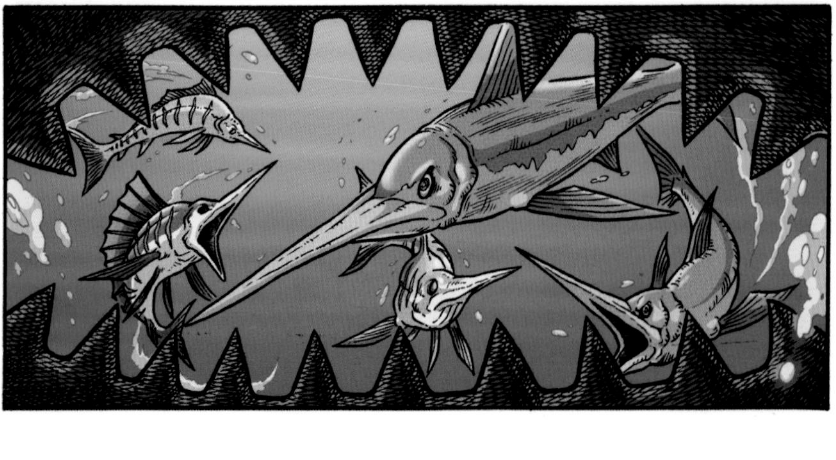

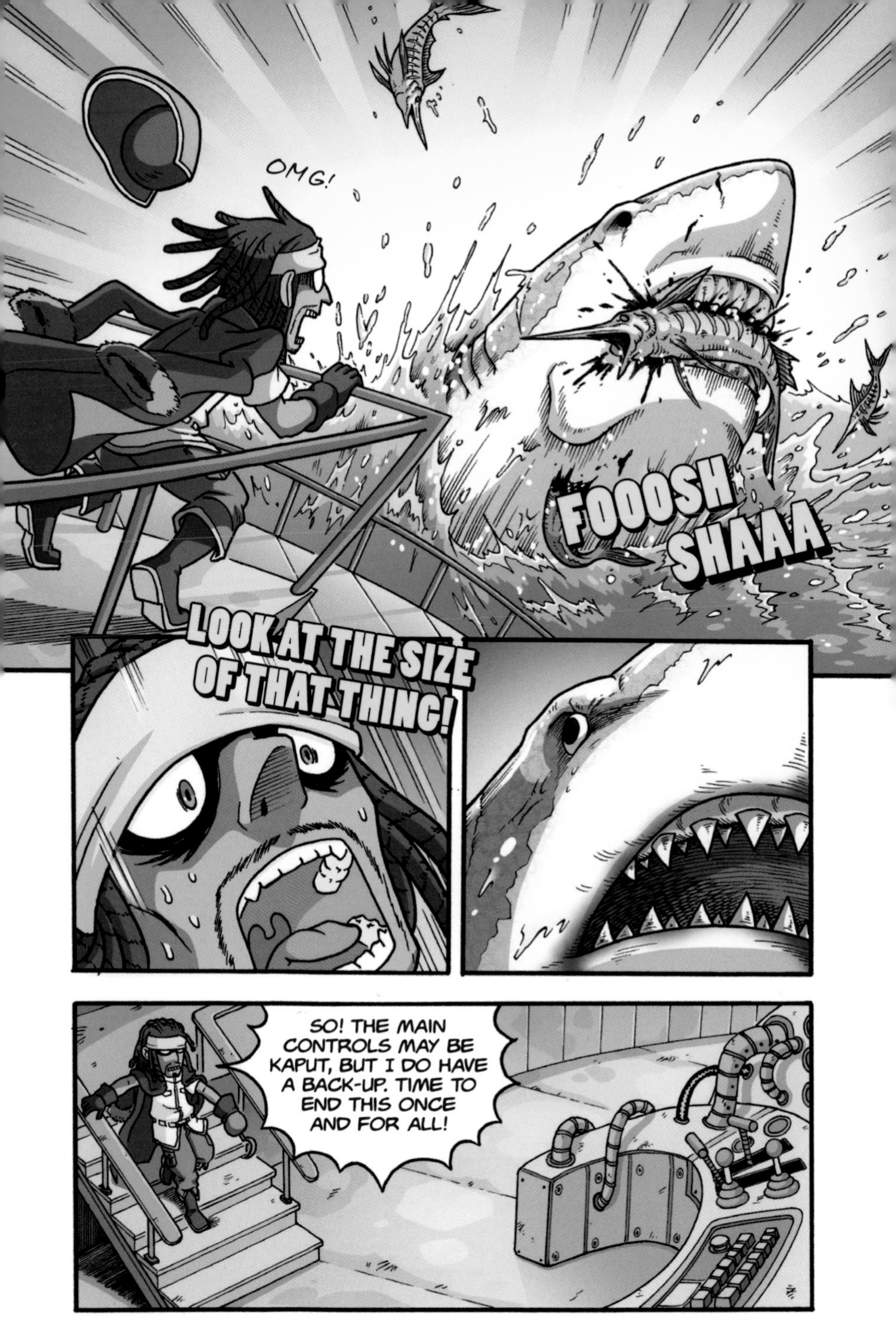
OMG!
FOOOSH SHAAA
LOOK AT THE SIZE OF THAT THING!
SO! THE MAIN CONTROLS MAY BE KAPUT, BUT I DO HAVE A BACK-UP. TIME TO END THIS ONCE AND FOR ALL!

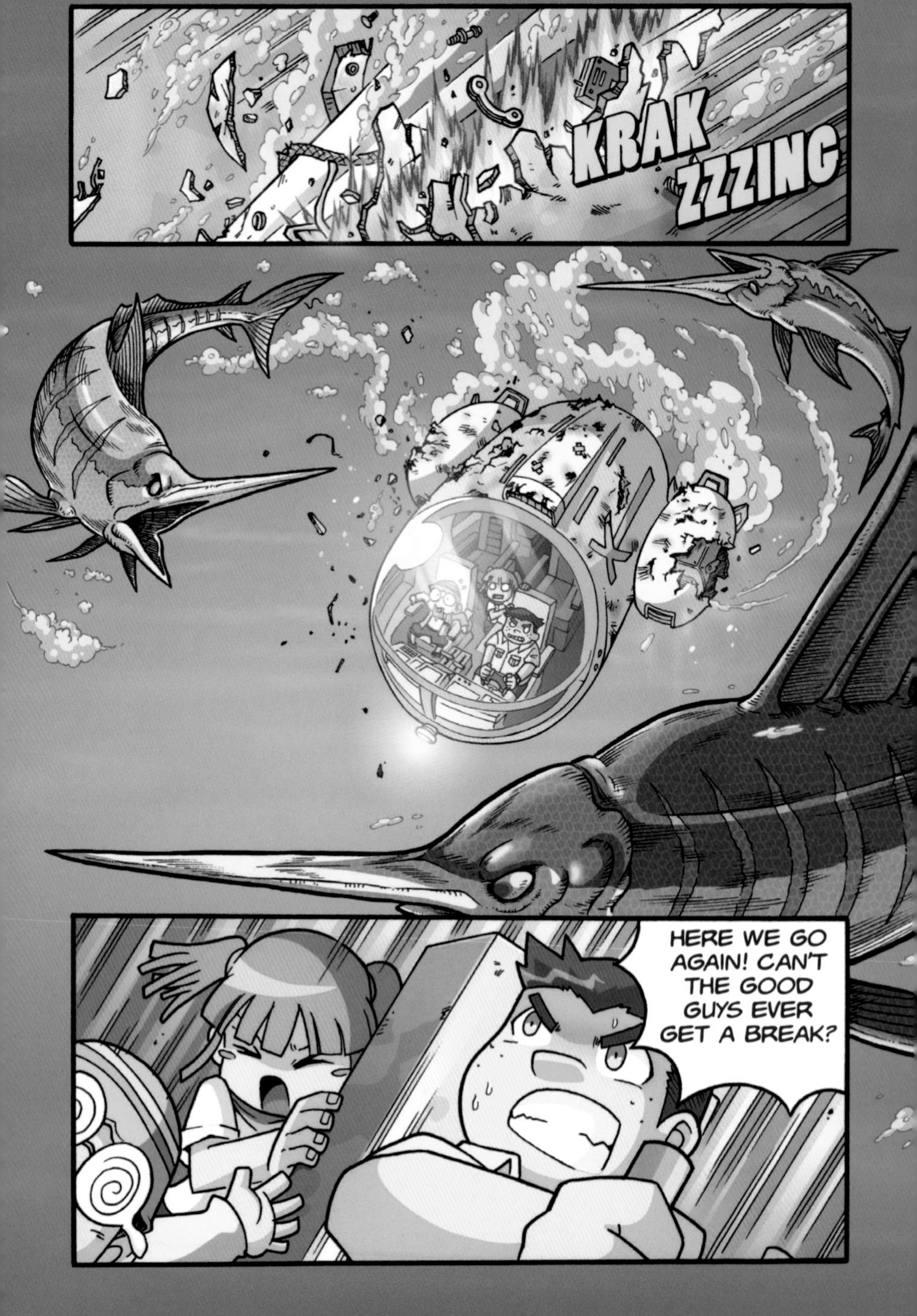
KRAK
ZZZING
HERE WE GO AGAIN! CAN'T THE GOOD GUYS EVER GET A BREAK?

Conservation Status

Extinct EX	Extinct in the Wild EW	Critically Endangered CR	Endangered EN	Vulnerable VU	Near Threatened NT	Least Concern LC

Species: Carcharhinus longimanus
Length: 6 to 13 feet
Weight: Up to 375 pounds
Diet: Mainly bony fish
Distribution: Warm seas worldwide
Habitats: High seas and coastlines

OCEANIC WHITETIP SHARK

This large, stocky-bodied pelagic shark is notable for its long white tipped rounded fins. This aggressive but slow-moving fish dominates feeding frenzies, earning the name "sea-dogs" which sailors used as a byword for hungry sharks. It is this tendency that makes it a danger to shipwreck or air crash survivors. Recent studies, show steeply declining populations as its large fins are highly valued as the chief ingredient in shark fin soup.

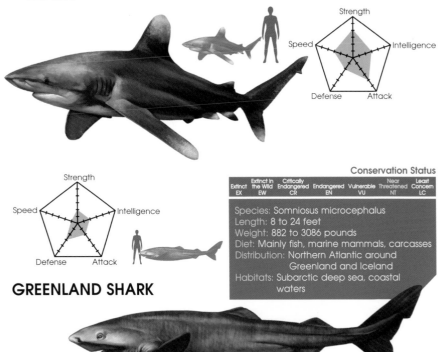

Strength
Intelligence
Attack
Defense
Speed

Strength
Intelligence
Attack
Defense
Speed

Conservation Status

Extinct EX	Extinct in the Wild EW	Critically Endangered CR	Endangered EN	Vulnerable VU	Near Threatened NT	Least Concern LC

Species: Somniosus microcephalus
Length: 8 to 24 feet
Weight: 882 to 3086 pounds
Diet: Mainly fish, marine mammals, carcasses
Distribution: Northern Atlantic around Greenland and Iceland
Habitats: Subarctic deep sea, coastal waters

GREENLAND SHARK

This large slow-moving fish lives farther north than any other shark species. Many of its adaptations are due to it being the only truly subarctic species. Attracted by the smell of rotting meat in the water, they often congregate in large numbers around fishing operations. The combination of its sluggishness and the presence of seals among its stomach contents has led researchers to opine that it is an opportunistic apex ambush predator. Although its flesh is poisonous, it is considered a delicacy in Greenland and Iceland, and can be eaten after careful preparation.

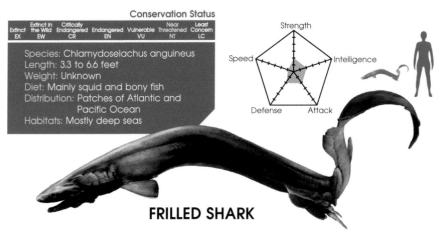

Conservation Status

Extinct EX	Extinct in the Wild EW	Critically Endangered CR	Endangered EN	Vulnerable VU	Near Threatened NT	Least Concern LC

Species: Chlamydoselachus anguineus
Length: 3.3 to 6.6 feet
Weight: Unknown
Diet: Mainly squid and bony fish
Distribution: Patches of Atlantic and
                    Pacific Ocean
Habitats: Mostly deep seas

Strength
Speed   Intelligence
Defense   Attack

FRILLED SHARK

With its elongated, eel-like body, and strange appearance, it has long been likened to the mythical sea serpent. Its broad, flattened head has a short, rounded snout. Its vertical slitted nostrils are separated by a leading flap of skin. The moderately large eyes are horizontally oval and lack nictitating membranes (protective third eyelids). The very long jaws are positioned terminally (at the end of the snout), as opposed to the underslung jaws of most sharks. The corners of the mouth lack furrows or folds, with widely spaced needle teeth; 19 to 28 in the upper jaw and 21 to 29 in the lower.

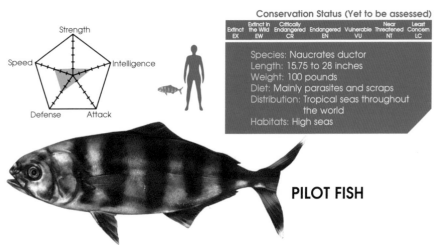

Strength
Speed   Intelligence
Defense   Attack

Conservation Status (Yet to be assessed)

Extinct EX	Extinct in the Wild EW	Critically Endangered CR	Endangered EN	Vulnerable VU	Near Threatened NT	Least Concern LC

Species: Naucrates ductor
Length: 15.75 to 28 inches
Weight: 100 pounds
Diet: Mainly parasites and scraps
Distribution: Tropical seas throughout
                    the world
Habitats: High seas

PILOT FISH

Pilot fish normally form a symbiotic relationship with larger marine animals such as sharks and whales, for purposes of food and protection, while the host benefits by getting itself "cleaned" of parasites. Identified by the alternating monochrome bands across their bodies, these small fish have also been known to follow ships returning to harbor, hence the origin of their name.

CHAPTER 7

GREAT WHITE WRATH

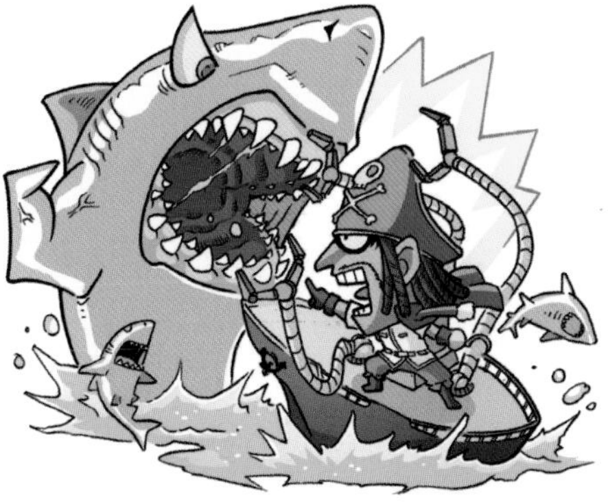

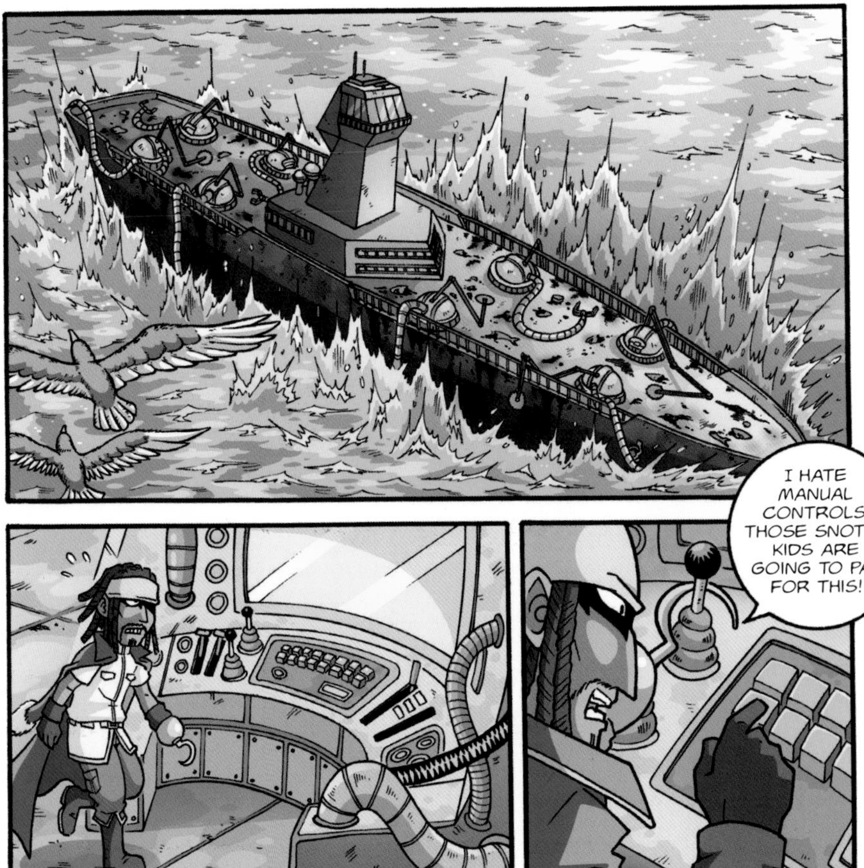
I HATE MANUAL CONTROLS. THOSE SNOTTY KIDS ARE GOING TO PAY FOR THIS!

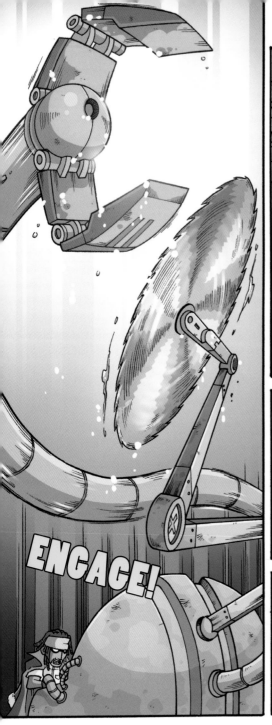

ENGAGE!

WHAT?! THE KILLER ARMS AND SAW ARE BACK IN ACTION? I THOUGHT WE DESTROYED THE CONTROLS. CAPTAIN HOOKY, MUST BE GOING MANUAL!

WE HAVE TO STOP HIM!

KWAME, TAZEN! WE'VE GOT TO THINK OF A WAY OUT... NOW!

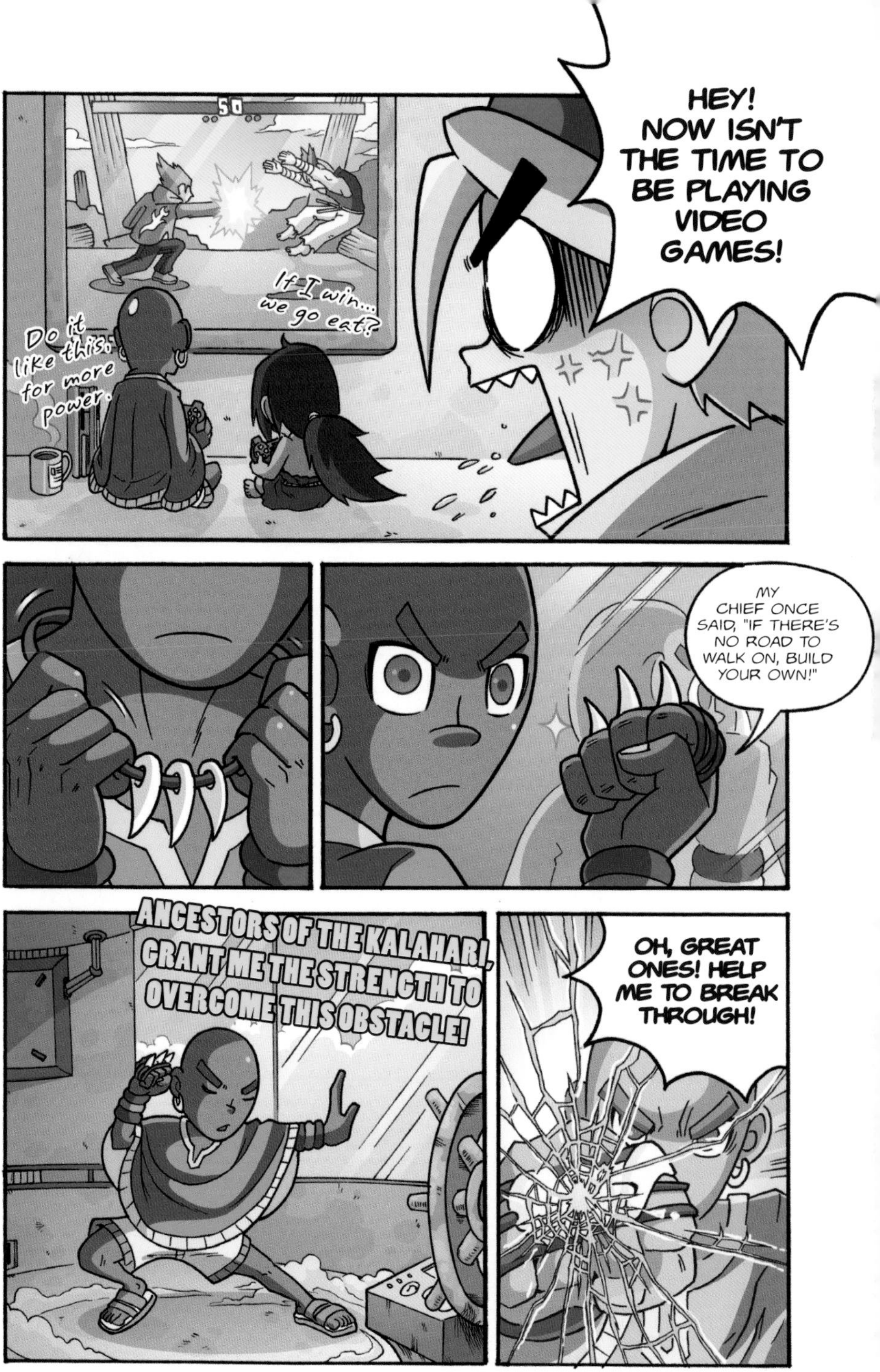

HEY! NOW ISN'T THE TIME TO BE PLAYING VIDEO GAMES!
If I win... we go eat?
Do it like this, for more power.
MY CHIEF ONCE SAID, "IF THERE'S NO ROAD TO WALK ON, BUILD YOUR OWN!"
ANCESTORS OF THE KALAHARI, GRANT ME THE STRENGTH TO OVERCOME THIS OBSTACLE!
OH, GREAT ONES! HELP ME TO BREAK THROUGH!

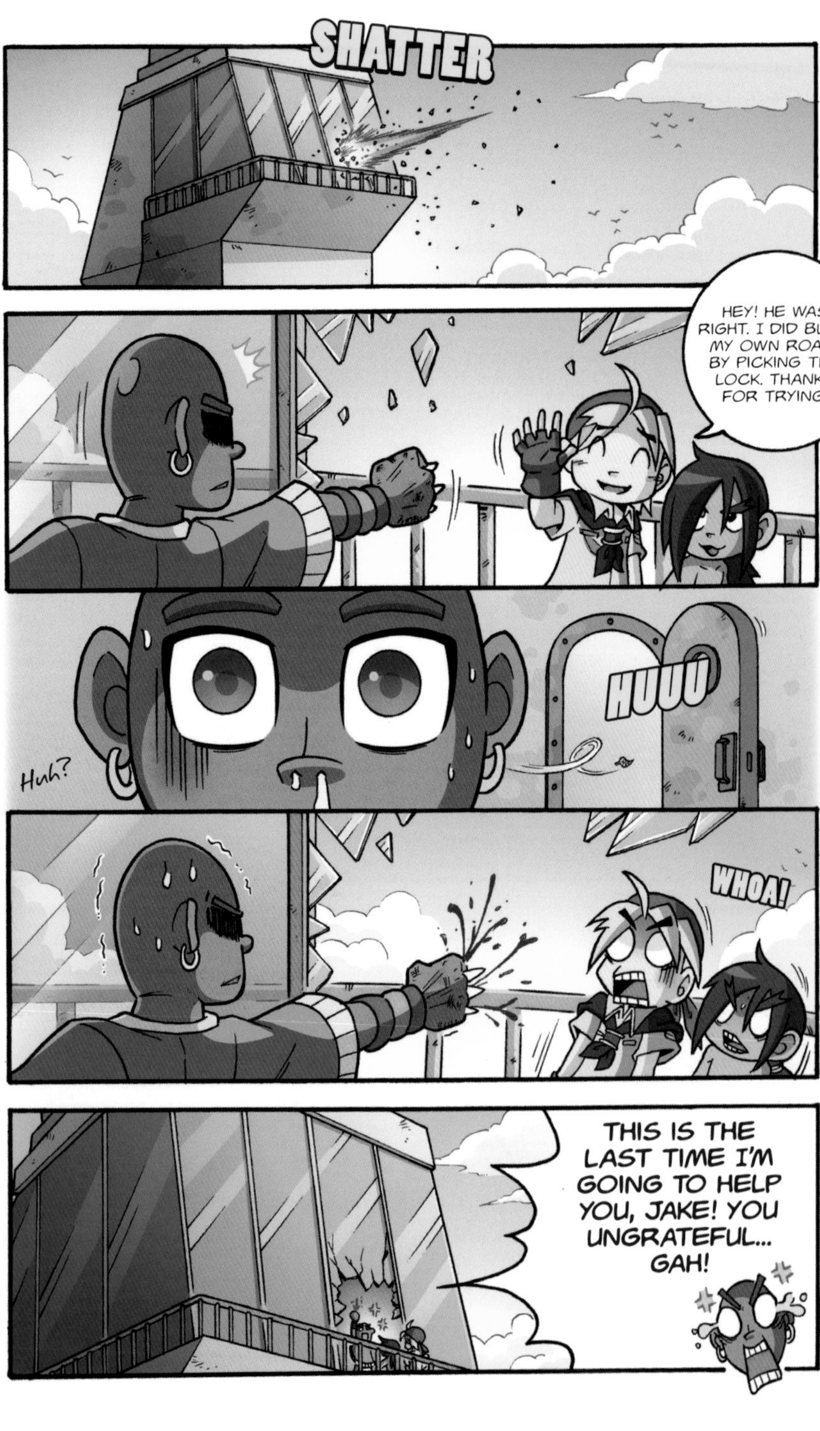
SHATTER
HEY! HE WAS RIGHT. I DID BUILD MY OWN ROAD... BY PICKING THE LOCK. THANKS FOR TRYING.
HUUU
Huh?
WHOA!
THIS IS THE LAST TIME I'M GOING TO HELP YOU, JAKE! YOU UNGRATEFUL... GAH!

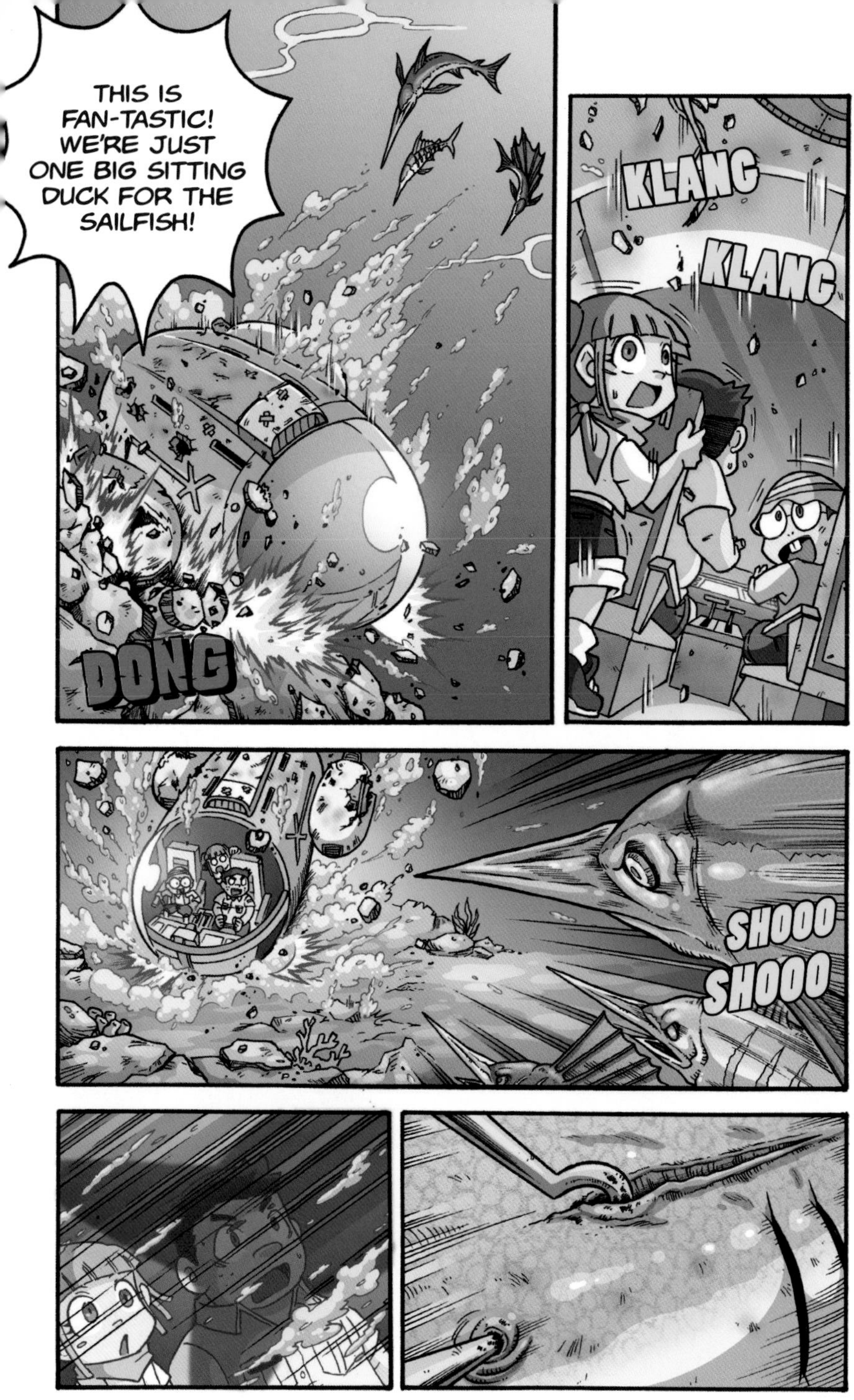
THIS IS FAN-TASTIC! WE'RE JUST ONE BIG SITTING DUCK FOR THE SAILFISH!
DONG
KLANG
KLANG
SHOOO
SHOOO

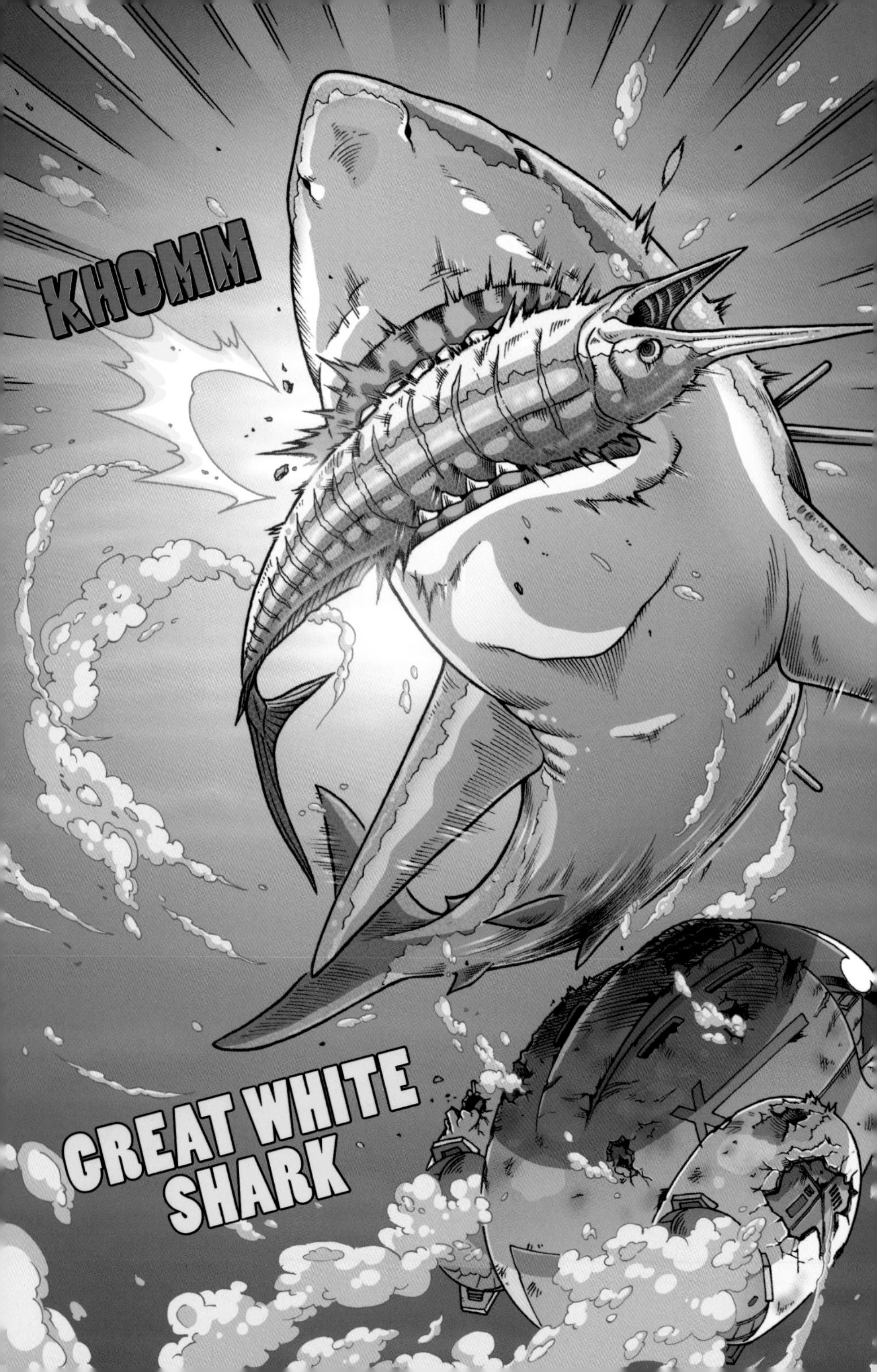
KHOMM
GREAT WHITE SHARK

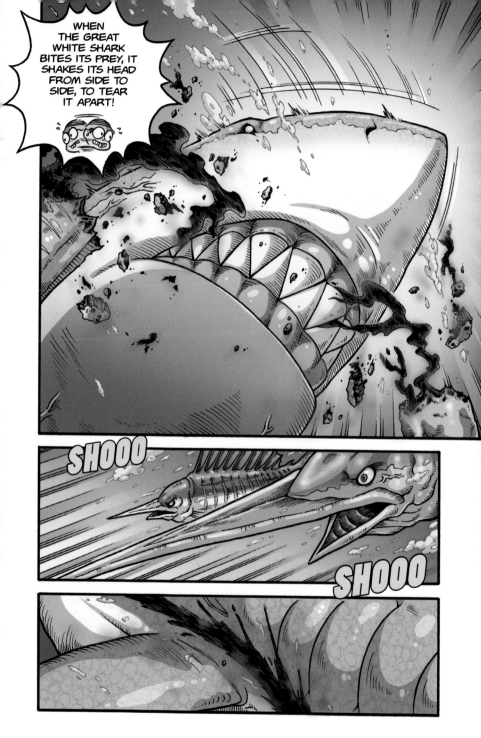

WHEN THE GREAT WHITE SHARK BITES ITS PREY, IT SHAKES ITS HEAD FROM SIDE TO SIDE, TO TEAR IT APART!

SHOOO

SHOOO

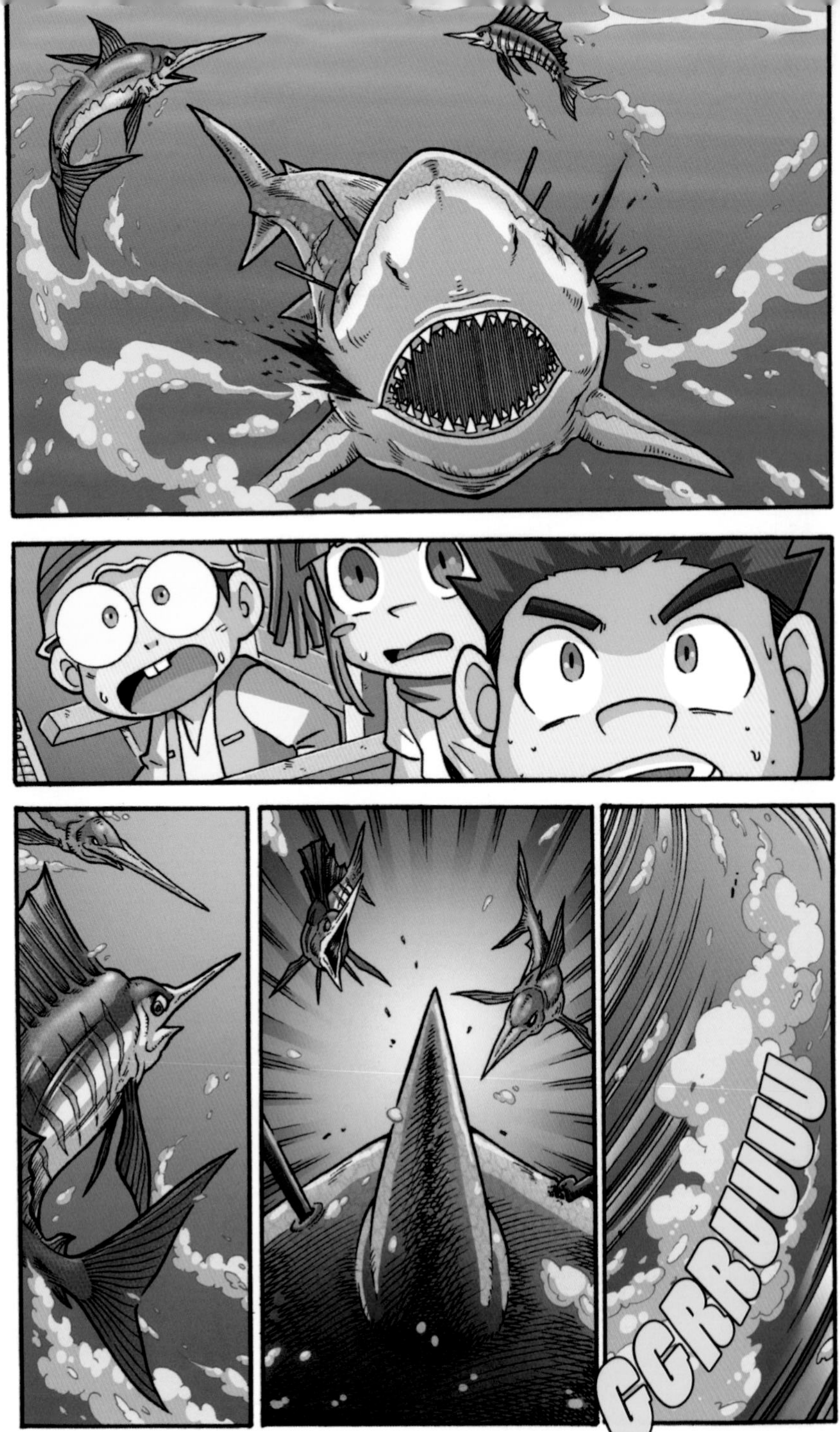
CGRUUUU

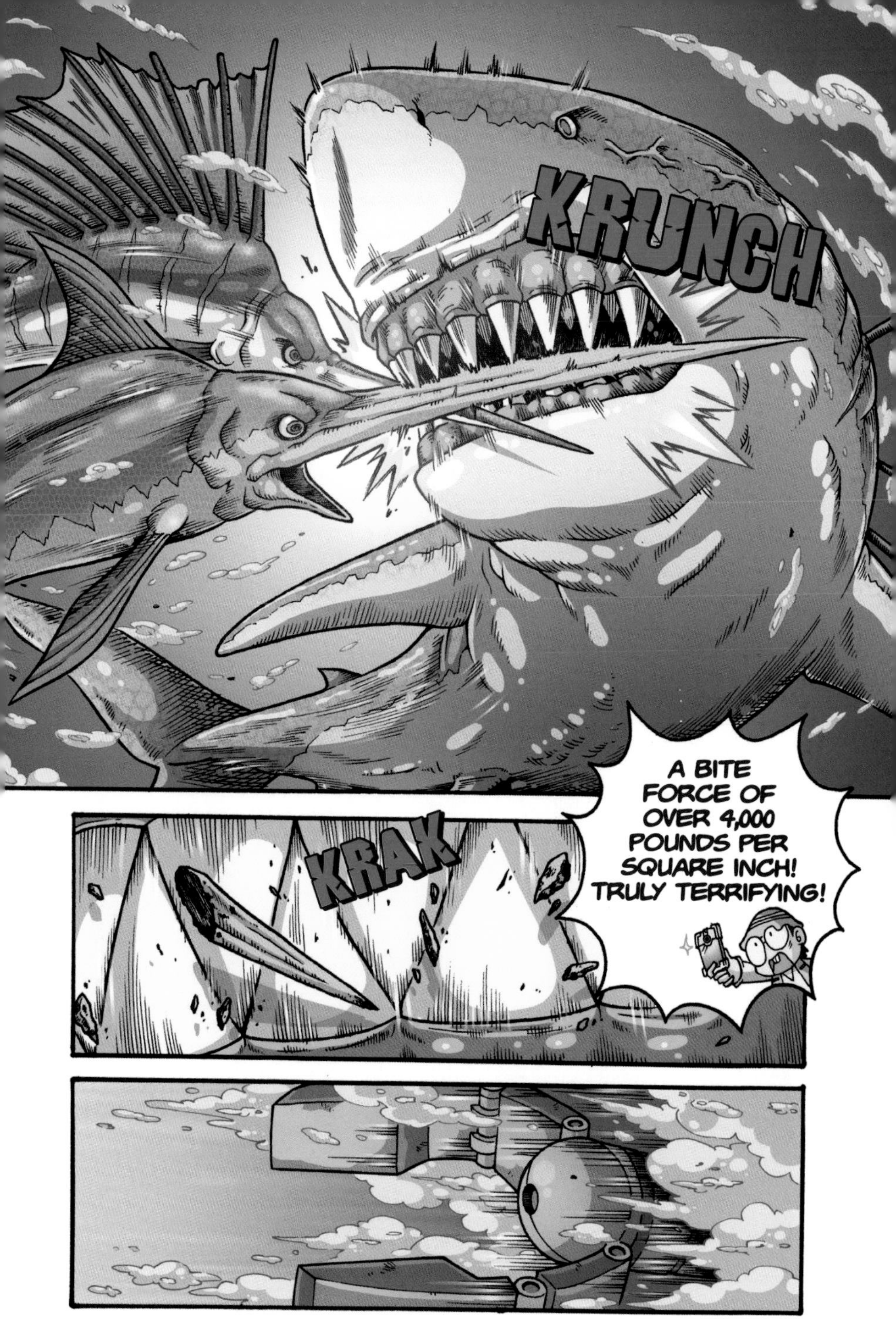
KRUNCH
KRAK
A BITE FORCE OF OVER 4,000 POUNDS PER SQUARE INCH! TRULY TERRIFYING!

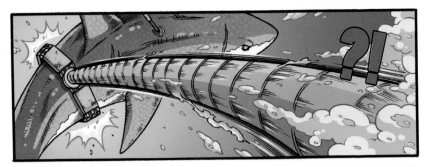

FOOSH SKOOSH

GOOD NIGHT, GREAT WHITE! PREPARE TO DIE!

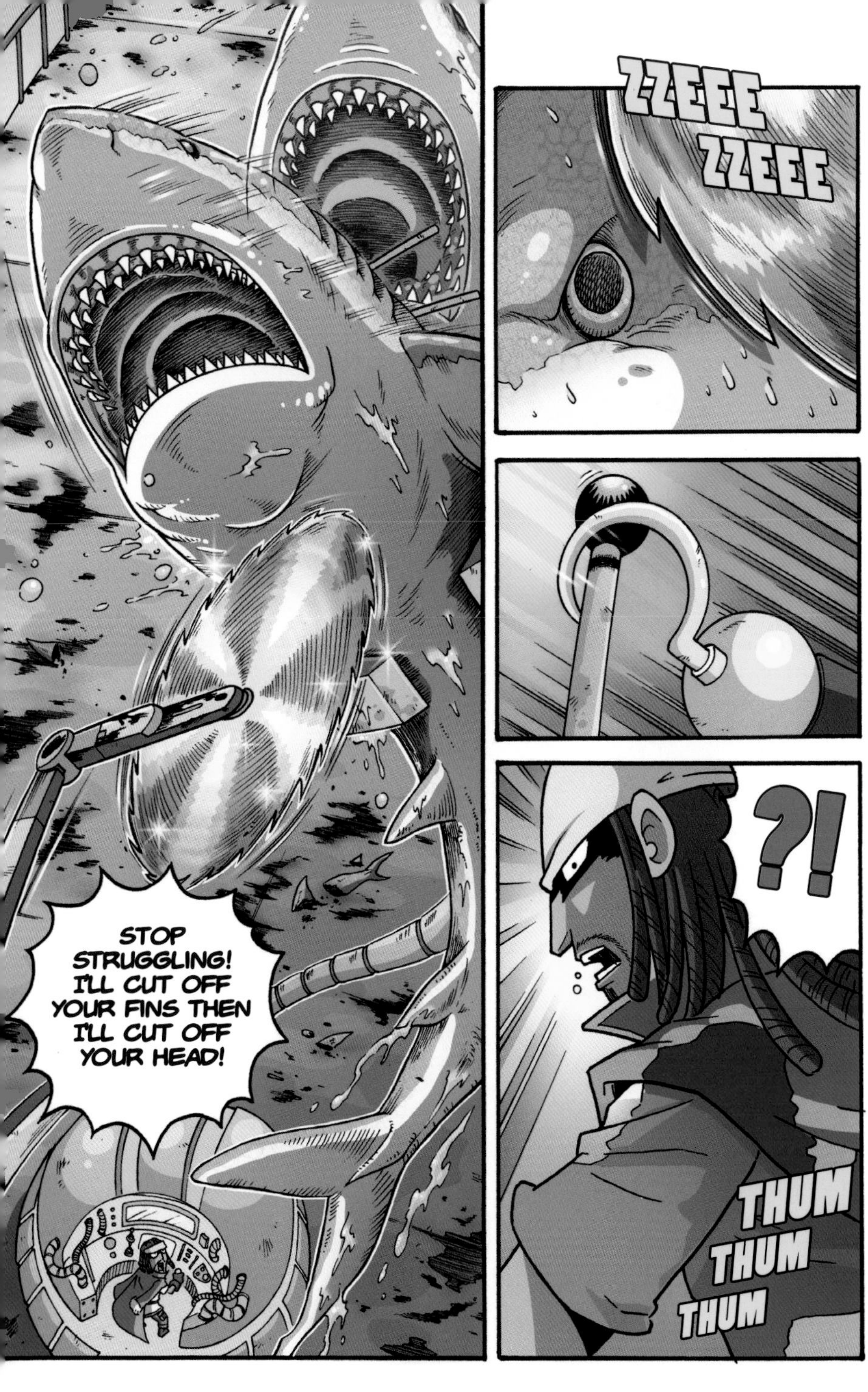
STOP STRUGGLING! I'LL CUT OFF YOUR FINS THEN I'LL CUT OFF YOUR HEAD!
ZZEEE ZZEEE
?!
THUM THUM THUM

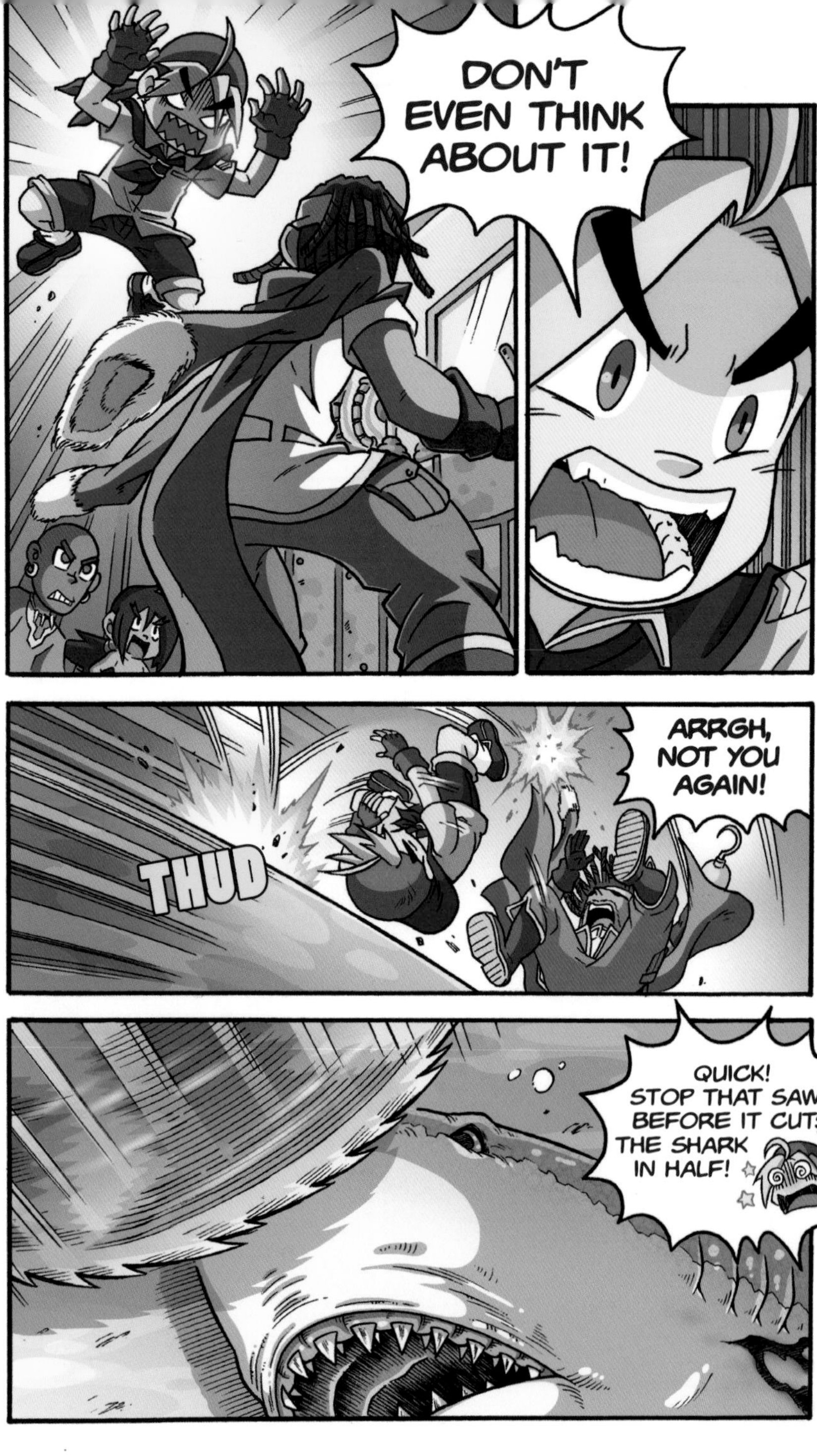
DON'T EVEN THINK ABOUT IT!
ARRGH, NOT YOU AGAIN!
THUD
QUICK! STOP THAT SAW... BEFORE IT CUTS THE SHARK IN HALF!

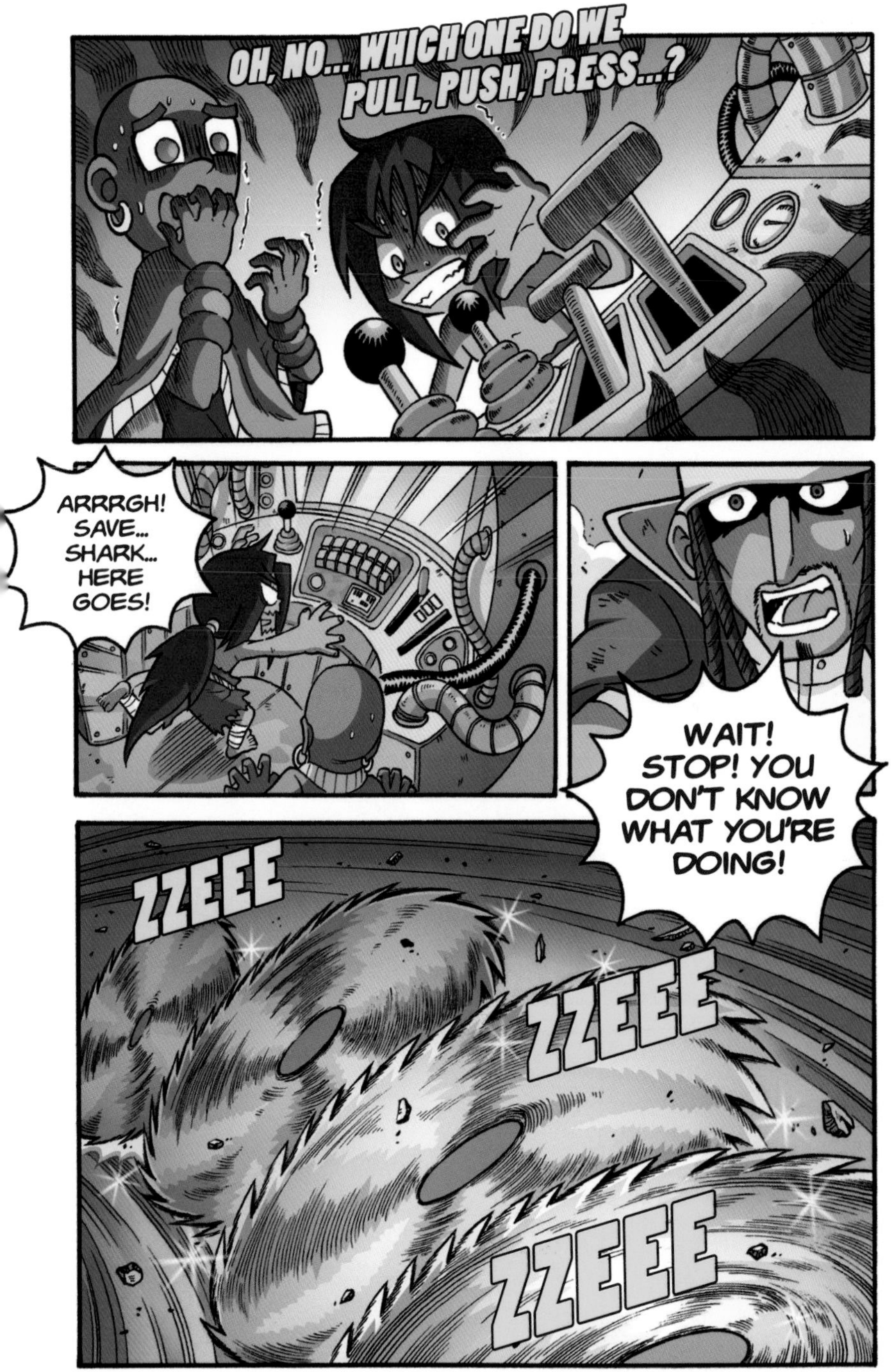
OH, NO... WHICH ONE DO WE PULL, PUSH, PRESS...?
ARRRGH! SAVE... SHARK... HERE GOES!
WAIT! STOP! YOU DON'T KNOW WHAT YOU'RE DOING!
ZZEEE
ZZEEE
ZZEEE

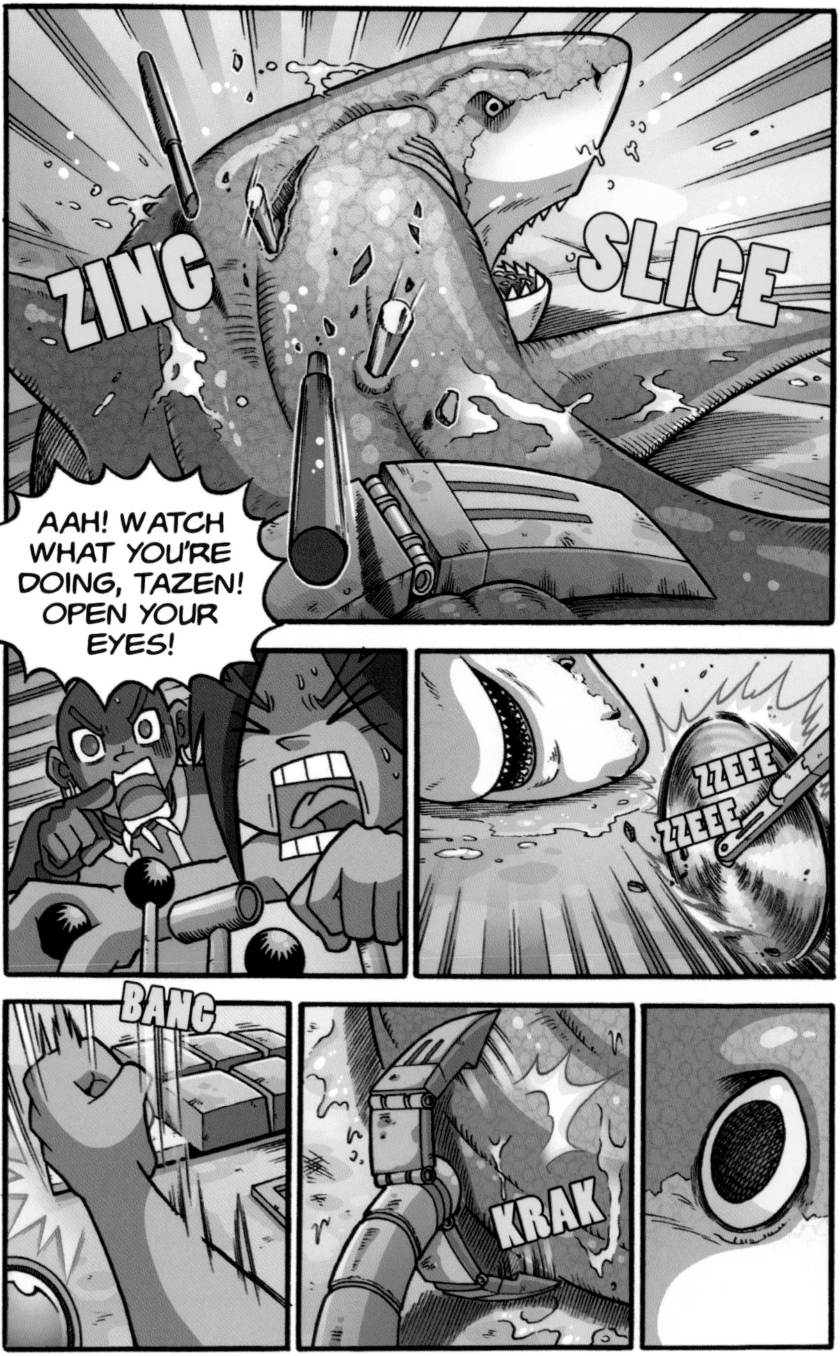
ZING
SLICE
AAH! WATCH WHAT YOU'RE DOING, TAZEN! OPEN YOUR EYES!
ZZEEE
ZZEEE
BANG
KRAK

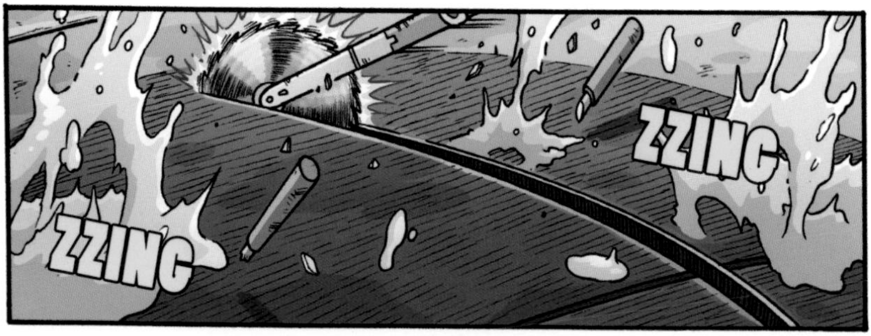
ZZING
ZZING
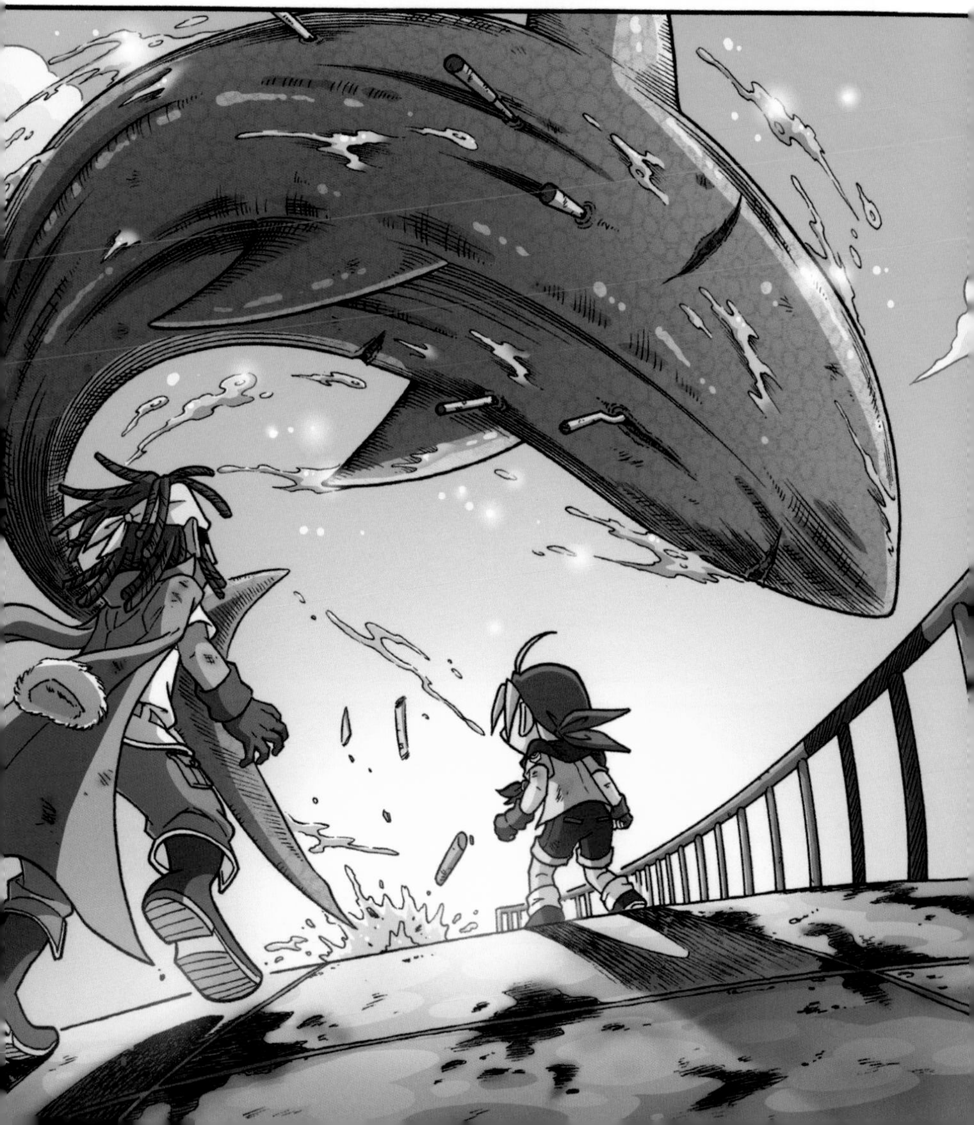

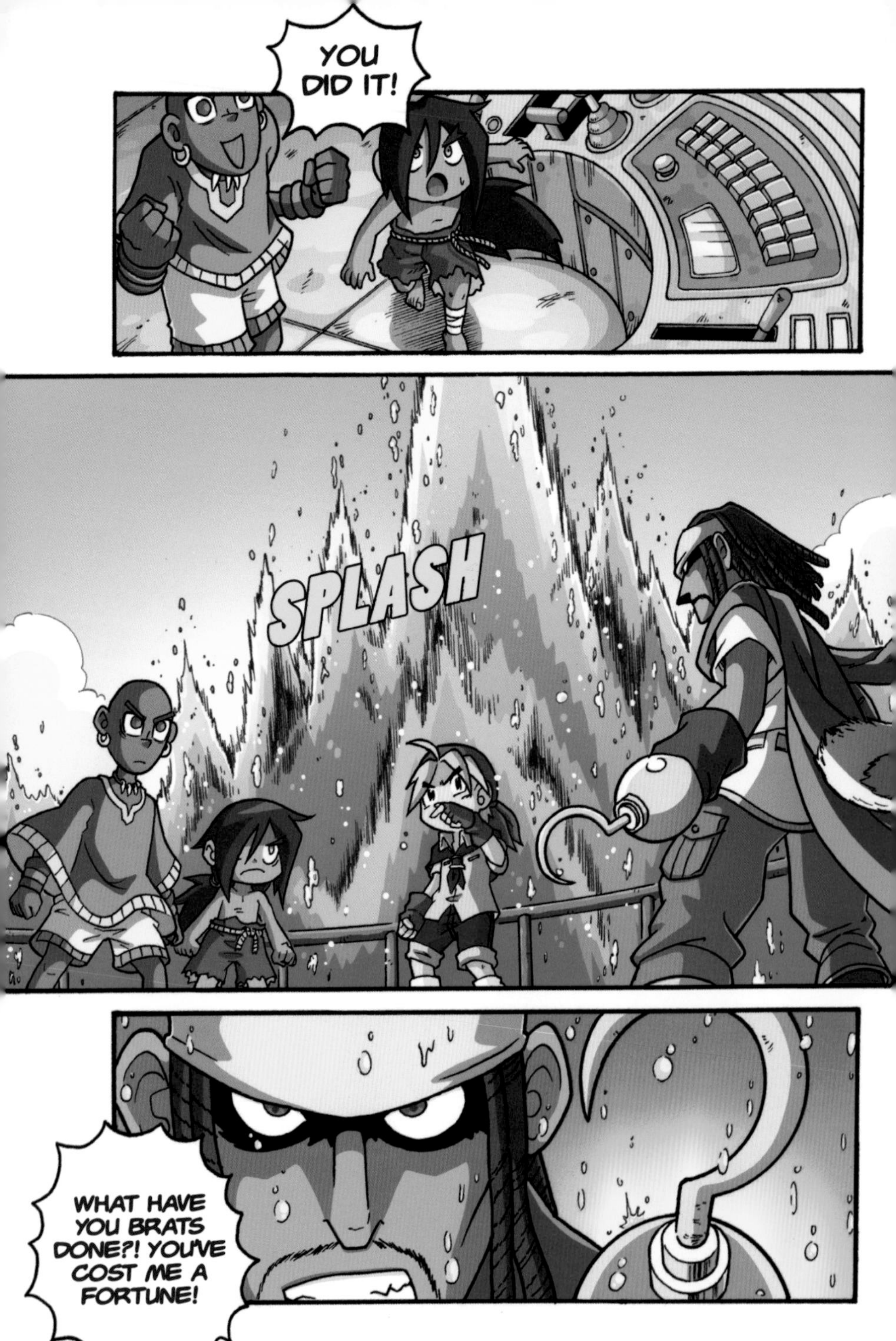
YOU DID IT!
SPLASH
WHAT HAVE YOU BRATS DONE?! YOU'VE COST ME A FORTUNE!

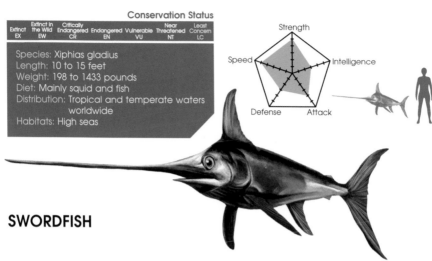

Conservation Status

Extinct EX	Extinct in the Wild EW	Critically Endangered CR	Endangered EN	Vulnerable VU	Near Threatened NT	Least Concern LC

Species: Xiphias gladius
Length: 10 to 15 feet
Weight: 198 to 1433 pounds
Diet: Mainly squid and fish
Distribution: Tropical and temperate waters worldwide
Habitats: High seas

Strength
Intelligence
Attack
Defense
Speed

SWORDFISH

Large, highly migratory, predatory fish characterized by a long, flat bill, swordfish are a popular sport fish of the billfish category and can typically be found from near the surface to a depth of 1805 feet. Swift swimmers, swordfish have an estimated top speed of 60 miles per hour. The presence of special organs next to their eyes to heat their eyes and brain greatly improves their vision, and consequently their ability to catch prey, one of the 22 of the over 25,000 fish species to have such an adaptation. Contrary to popular belief, the "sword" is not used to spear, but instead may be used to slash at its prey in order to injure it, facilitating capture.

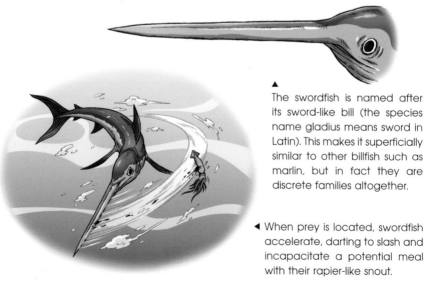

▲ The swordfish is named after its sword-like bill (the species name gladius means sword in Latin). This makes it superficially similar to other billfish such as marlin, but in fact they are discrete families altogether.

◀ When prey is located, swordfish accelerate, darting to slash and incapacitate a potential meal with their rapier-like snout.

Conservation Status (Yet to be assessed)

Extinct	Extinct in the Wild	Critically Endangered	Endangered	Vulnerable	Near Threatened	Least Concern
EX	EW	CR	EN	VU	NT	LC

Species: Istiophorus albicans
Length: 10.33 to 13.12 feet
Weight: Up to 128 pounds
Diet: Sardine, squid, and octopi
Distribution: Tropical and temperate Atlantic and Mediterranean
Habitats: High seas

Deriving its name from its large distinctive sail-like dorsal fin, this member of family Istiophoridae of the order Perciformes is one of the most colorful oceanic fish; metallic blue with bluish vertical barring along the flanks contrasts with its silvery white underside. Capable of short bursts of acceleration, achieving speeds of up to 34 miles per hour. This favorite of sports fishermen is an aggressive, determined species, which only adds to the prestige of a successful capture.

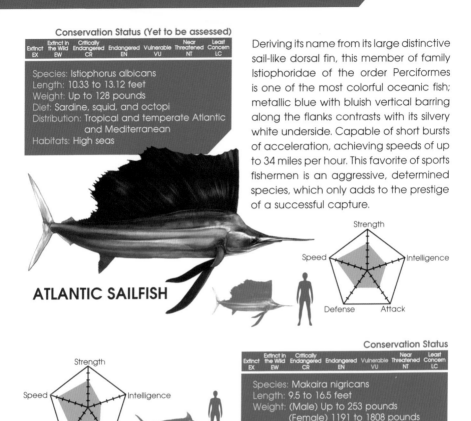

ATLANTIC SAILFISH

Strength
Speed
Intelligence
Defense
Attack

Conservation Status

Extinct	Extinct in the Wild	Critically Endangered	Endangered	Vulnerable	Near Threatened	Least Concern
EX	EW	CR	EN	VU	NT	LC

Strength
Speed
Intelligence
Defense
Attack

Species: Makaira nigricans
Length: 9.5 to 16.5 feet
Weight: (Male) Up to 253 pounds
(Female) 1191 to 1808 pounds
Diet: Mostly surface fish
Distribution: Tropical Atlantic ocean zones
Habitats: High seas

ATLANTIC BLUE MARLIN

Endemic to the Atlantic, this large distinctive billfish is a blue water fish that spends the majority of its life in the open sea far from land. Having few natural enemies, apart from shortfin makos and great whites, its popularity among game fishermen has seen it become a victim of overfishing, earning it vulnerable status on the International Union for Conservation of Nature's red list, Furthermore the relatively high fat content of its meat makes it commercially valuable in certain markets, making it doubly desirable and sought after. Marlins are migratory fish, with seasonal migratory patterns extending as far east as West Africa, and as far south as Venezuela.

CHAPTER 8
ABANDON SHIP!

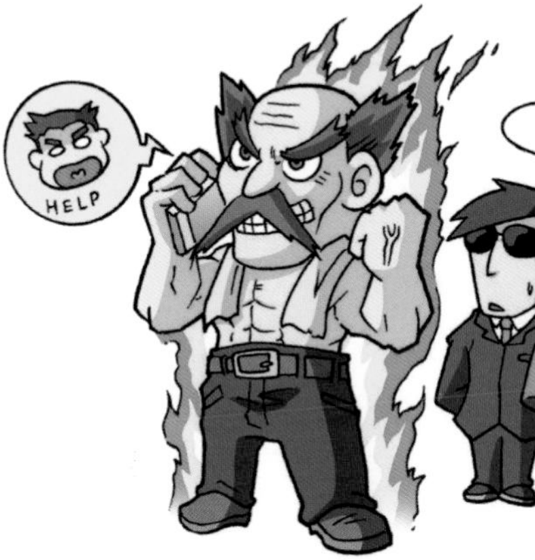
HELP
...

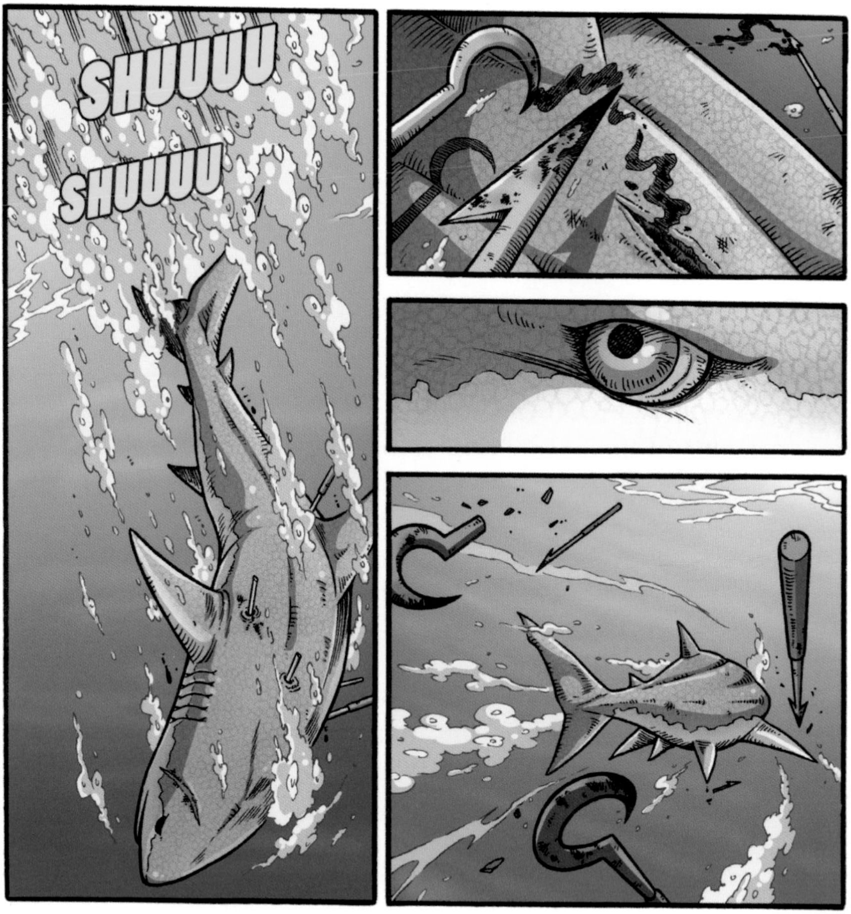
SHUUUU
SHUUUU

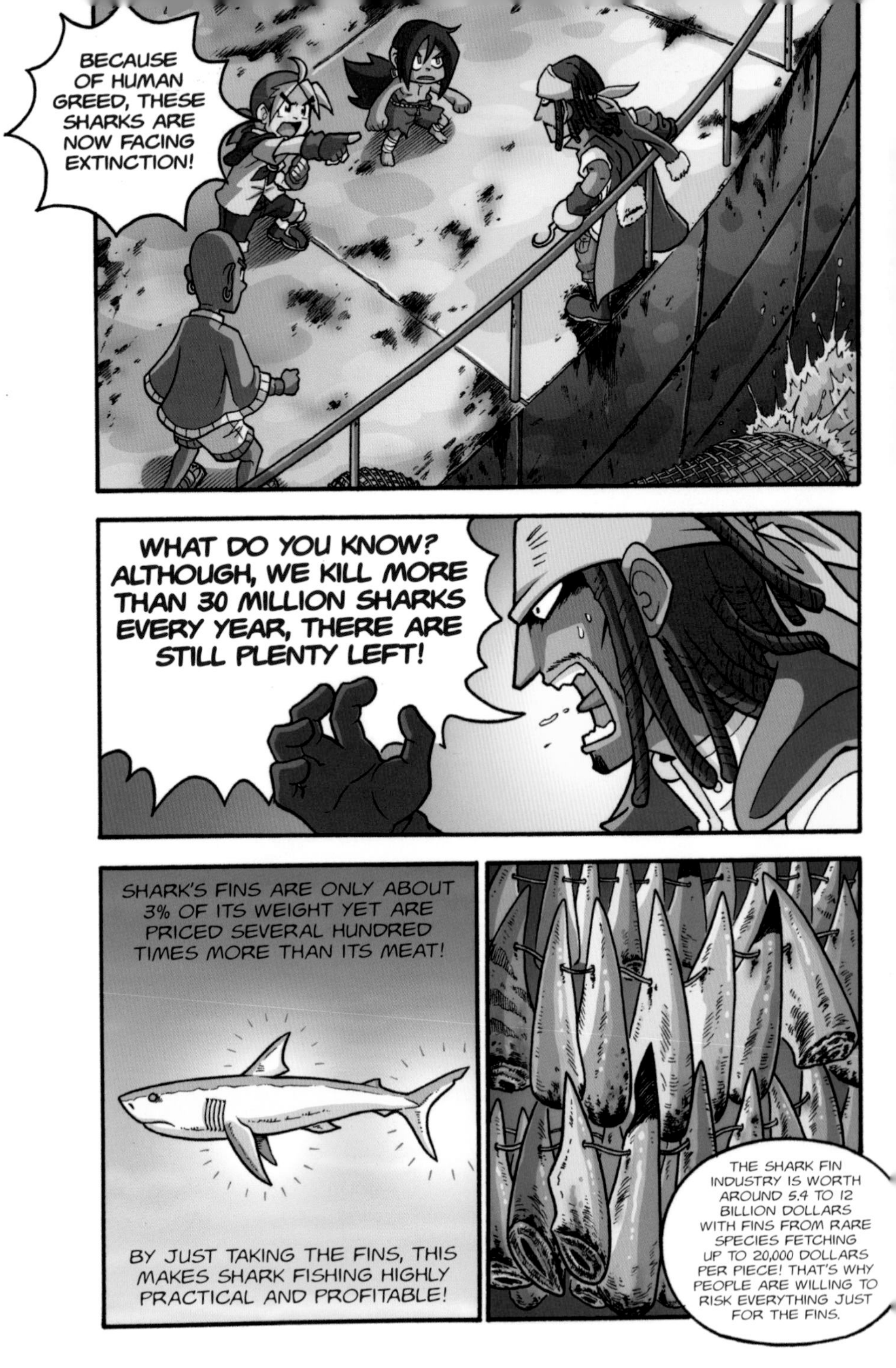
BECAUSE OF HUMAN GREED, THESE SHARKS ARE NOW FACING EXTINCTION!
WHAT DO YOU KNOW? ALTHOUGH, WE KILL MORE THAN 30 MILLION SHARKS EVERY YEAR, THERE ARE STILL PLENTY LEFT!
SHARK'S FINS ARE ONLY ABOUT 3% OF ITS WEIGHT YET ARE PRICED SEVERAL HUNDRED TIMES MORE THAN ITS MEAT!
BY JUST TAKING THE FINS, THIS MAKES SHARK FISHING HIGHLY PRACTICAL AND PROFITABLE!
THE SHARK FIN INDUSTRY IS WORTH AROUND 5.4 TO 12 BILLION DOLLARS WITH FINS FROM RARE SPECIES FETCHING UP TO 20,000 DOLLARS PER PIECE! THAT'S WHY PEOPLE ARE WILLING TO RISK EVERYTHING JUST FOR THE FINS.

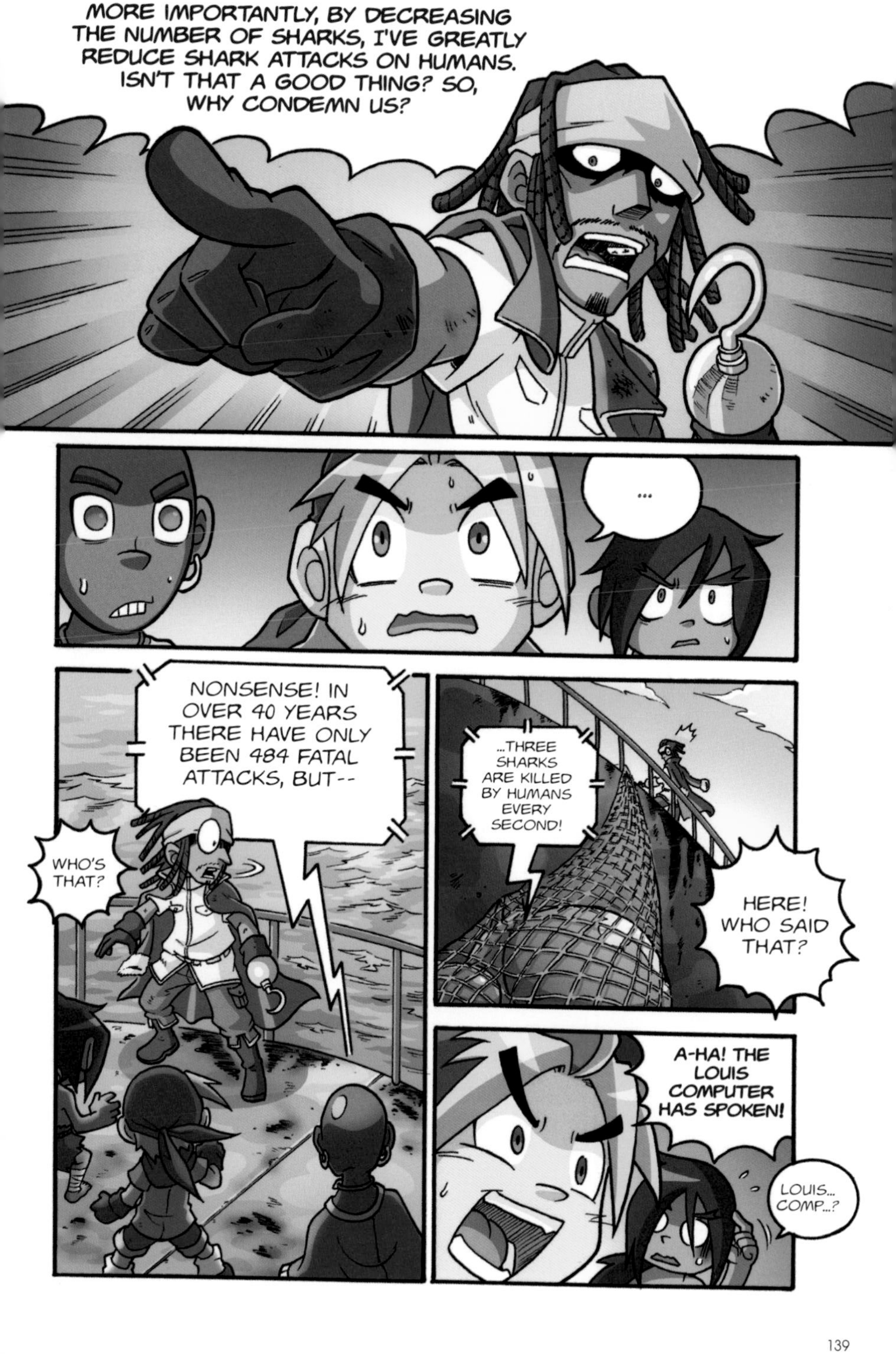
MORE IMPORTANTLY, BY DECREASING THE NUMBER OF SHARKS, I'VE GREATLY REDUCE SHARK ATTACKS ON HUMANS. ISN'T THAT A GOOD THING? SO, WHY CONDEMN US?
...
NONSENSE! IN OVER 40 YEARS THERE HAVE ONLY BEEN 484 FATAL ATTACKS, BUT--
WHO'S THAT?
...THREE SHARKS ARE KILLED BY HUMANS EVERY SECOND!
HERE! WHO SAID THAT?
A-HA! THE LOUIS COMPUTER HAS SPOKEN!
LOUIS... COMP...?

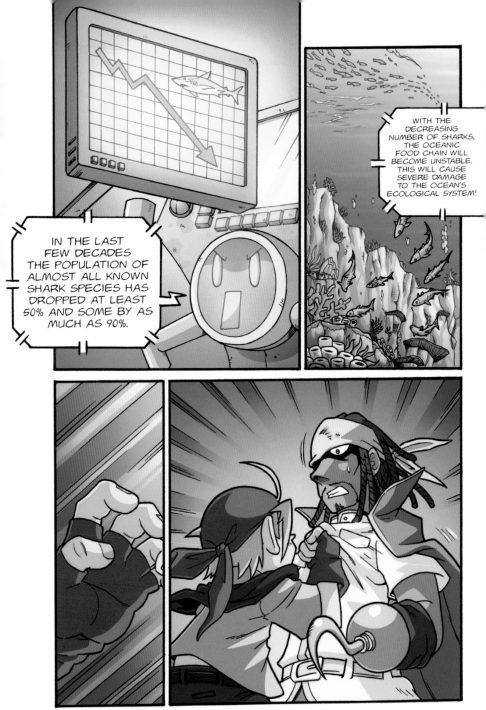

IN THE LAST FEW DECADES THE POPULATION OF ALMOST ALL KNOWN SHARK SPECIES HAS DROPPED AT LEAST 50% AND SOME BY AS MUCH AS 90%.

WITH THE DECREASING NUMBER OF SHARKS, THE OCEANIC FOOD CHAIN WILL BECOME UNSTABLE. THIS WILL CAUSE SEVERE DAMAGE TO THE OCEAN'S ECOLOGICAL SYSTEM!

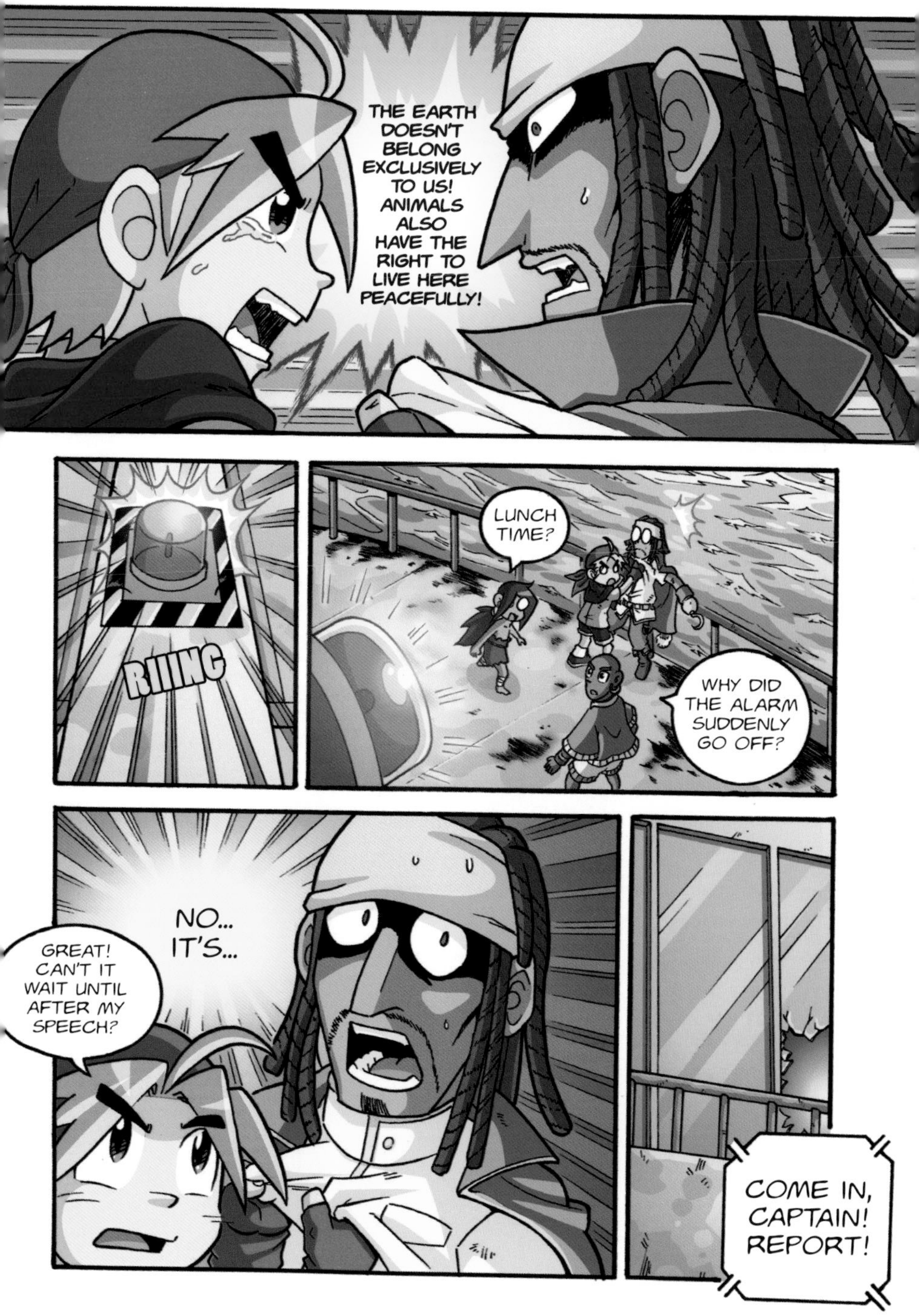
THE EARTH DOESN'T BELONG EXCLUSIVELY TO US! ANIMALS ALSO HAVE THE RIGHT TO LIVE HERE PEACEFULLY!
RIIING
LUNCH TIME?
WHY DID THE ALARM SUDDENLY GO OFF?
NO... IT'S...
GREAT! CAN'T IT WAIT UNTIL AFTER MY SPEECH?
COME IN, CAPTAIN! REPORT!

WHAT THE BLAZES HAS HAPPENED?
SOUND ONLY
GENTLEMEN... LADY. I THINK THE SHARK FIN BUSINESS LOOKS TO HAVE BECOME MORE HAZARDOUS THAN PROFITABLE; I SUGGEST WE WITHDRAW!
TO PERSEVERE IN THE FACE OF UNHEALTHY ODDS WOULD BE VERY UNWISE.
INITIATE SELF-DESTRUCT MODE!
BOOM
BOOM
BOOM

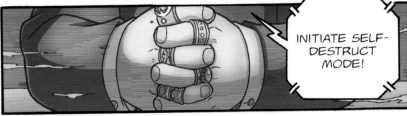

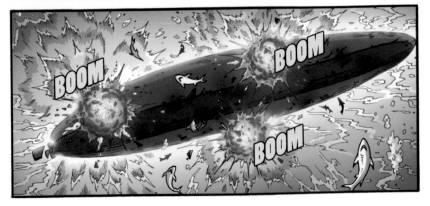

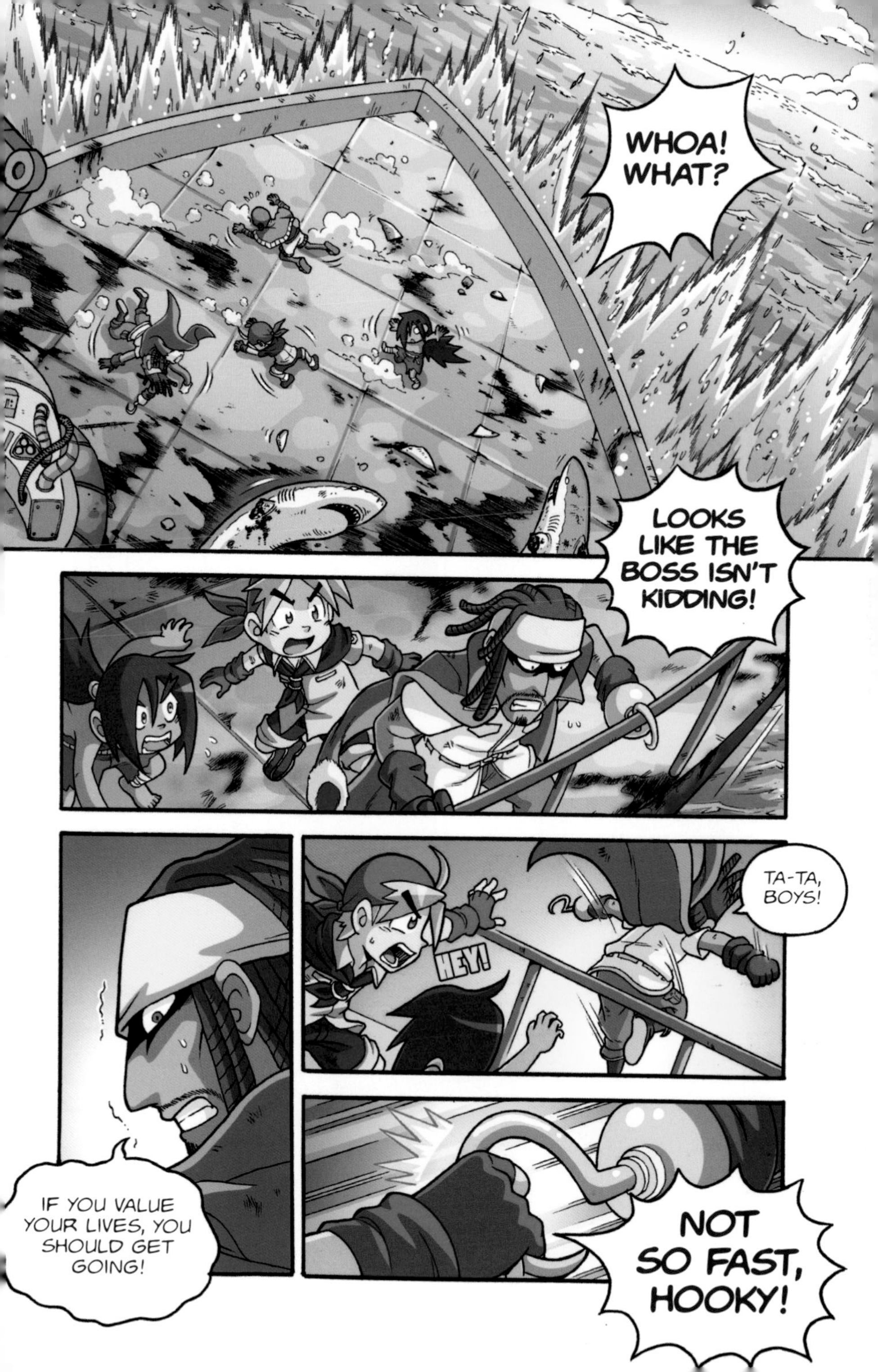
WHOA! WHAT?
LOOKS LIKE THE BOSS ISN'T KIDDING!
IF YOU VALUE YOUR LIVES, YOU SHOULD GET GOING!
TA-TA, BOYS!
HEY!
NOT SO FAST, HOOKY!

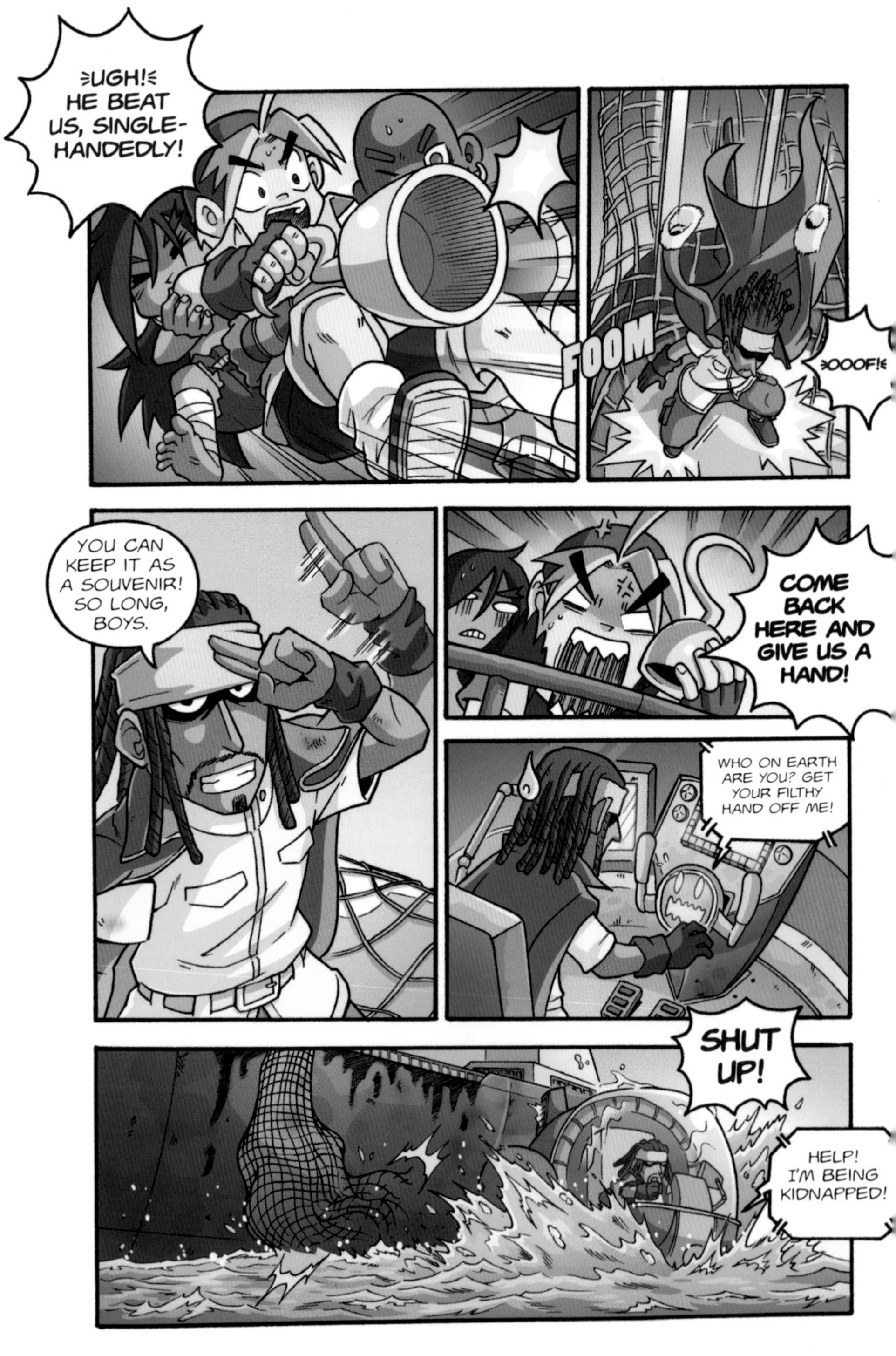

UGH! HE BEAT US, SINGLE-HANDEDLY!
FOOM
OOOF!
YOU CAN KEEP IT AS A SOUVENIR! SO LONG, BOYS.
COME BACK HERE AND GIVE US A HAND!
WHO ON EARTH ARE YOU? GET YOUR FILTHY HAND OFF ME!
SHUT UP!
HELP! I'M BEING KIDNAPPED!

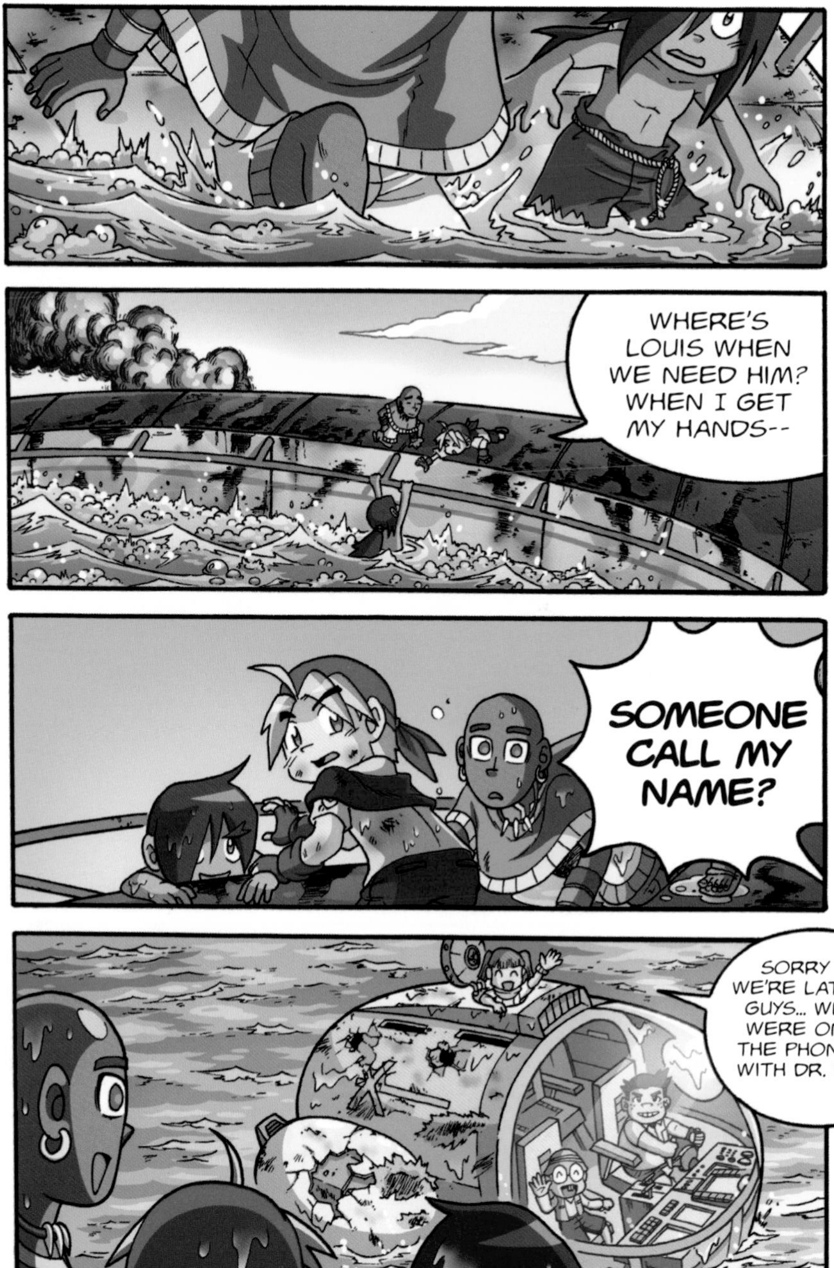
WHERE'S LOUIS WHEN WE NEED HIM? WHEN I GET MY HANDS--
SOMEONE CALL MY NAME?
SORRY WE'RE LATE, GUYS... WE WERE ON THE PHONE WITH DR. D!

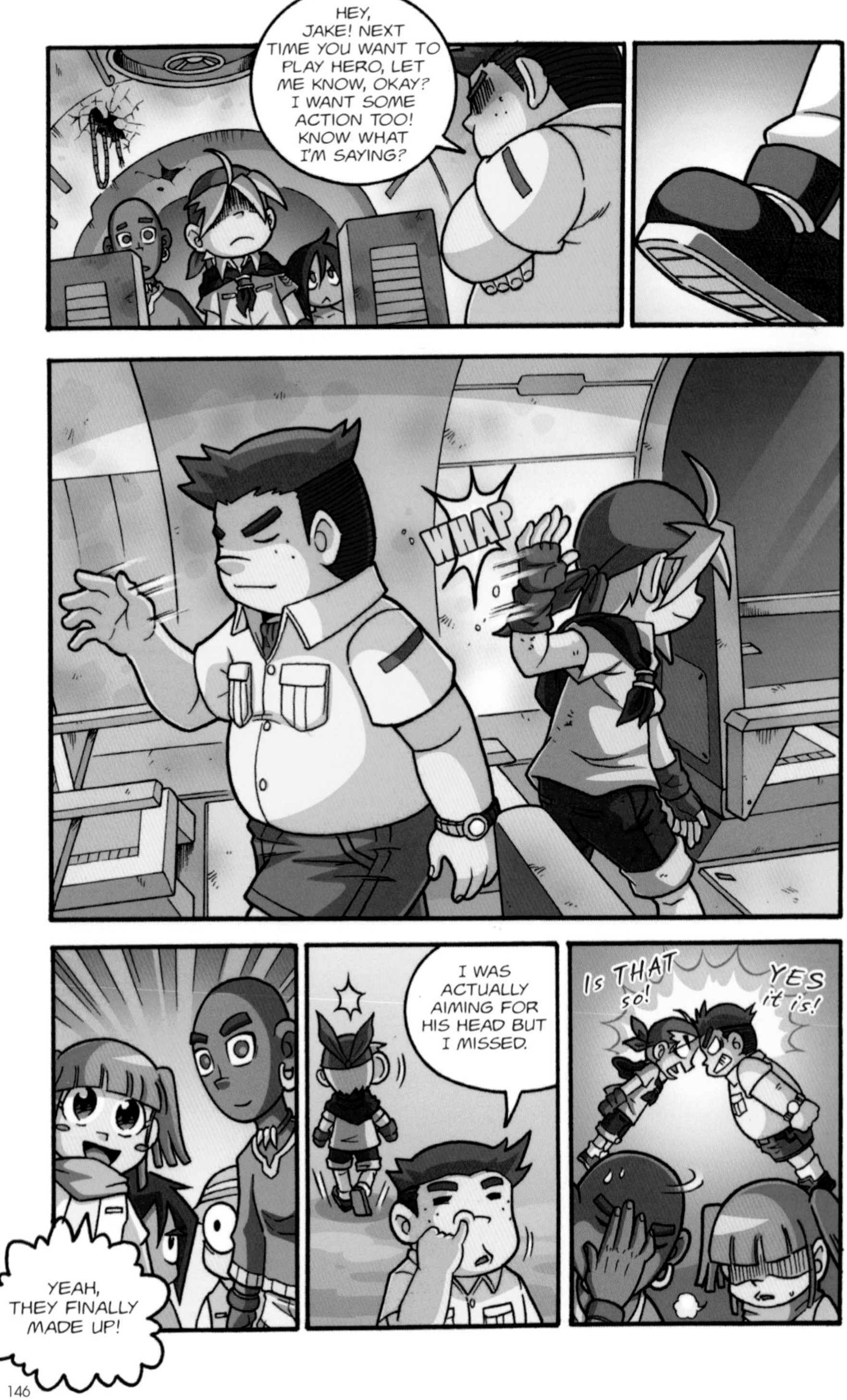
HEY, JAKE! NEXT TIME YOU WANT TO PLAY HERO, LET ME KNOW, OKAY? I WANT SOME ACTION TOO! KNOW WHAT I'M SAYING?
WHAP
YEAH, THEY FINALLY MADE UP!
I WAS ACTUALLY AIMING FOR HIS HEAD BUT I MISSED.
Is THAT so!
YES it is!

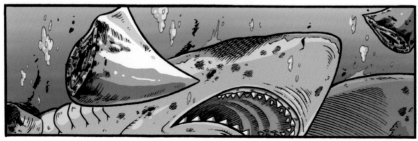

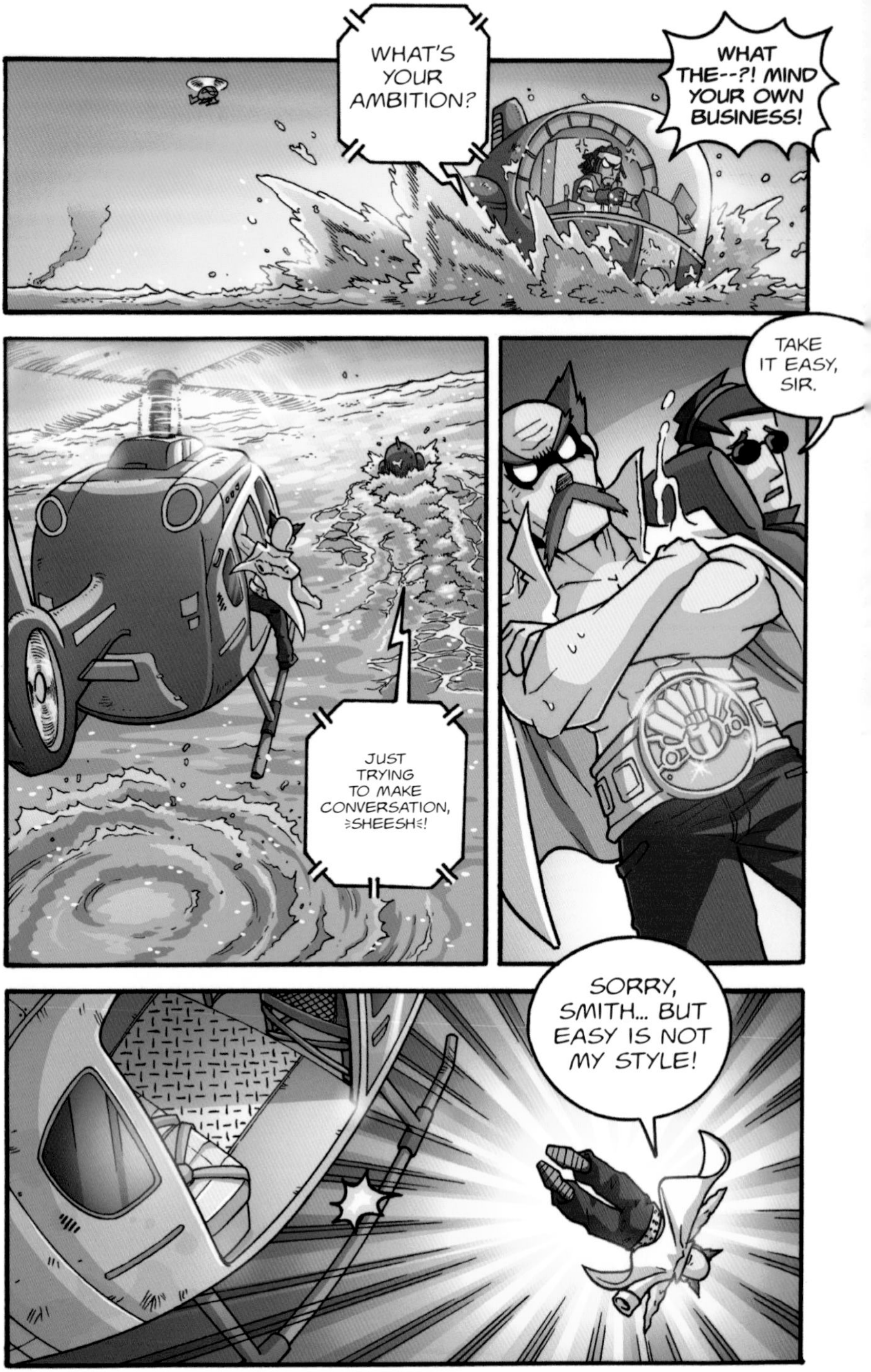
WHAT'S YOUR AMBITION?
WHAT THE--?! MIND YOUR OWN BUSINESS!
JUST TRYING TO MAKE CONVERSATION, SHEESH!
TAKE IT EASY, SIR.
SORRY, SMITH... BUT EASY IS NOT MY STYLE!

THUNDER PUNCH!

CRASH

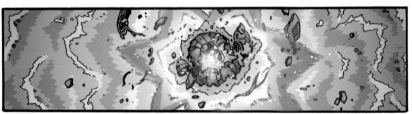

P-PLEASE, LEMME GO! I WAS JUST FOLLOWING ORDERS!

DON'T WORRY. I'LL LET YOU GO... TO PRISON!

THA... THANKS...

HELLO, FISH, WHAT IS YOUR AMBITION?

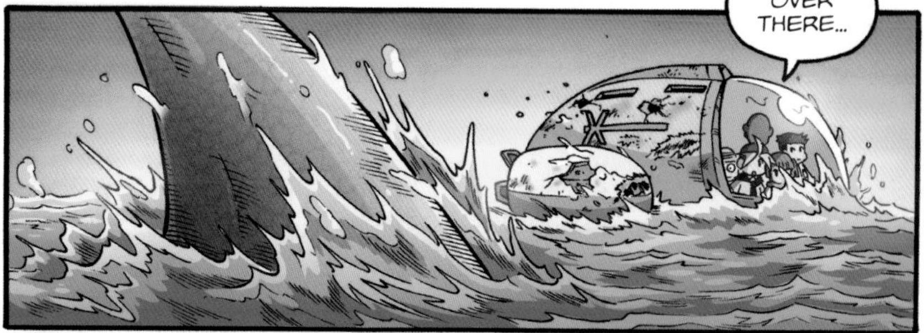
LOOK! OVER THERE...

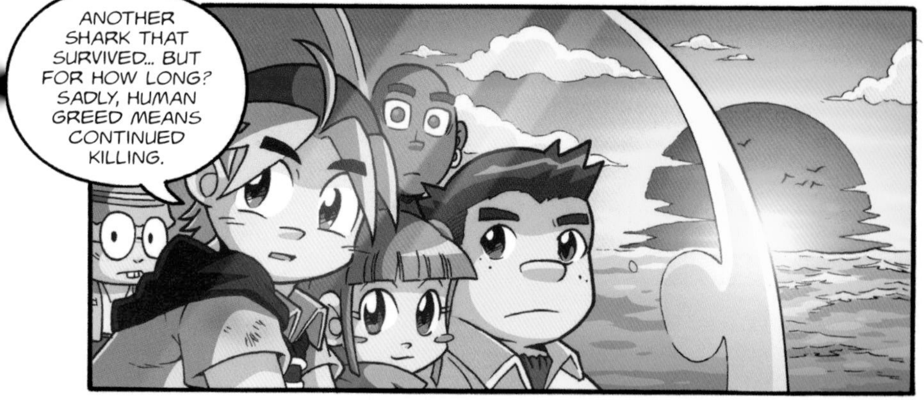
ANOTHER SHARK THAT SURVIVED... BUT FOR HOW LONG? SADLY, HUMAN GREED MEANS CONTINUED KILLING.

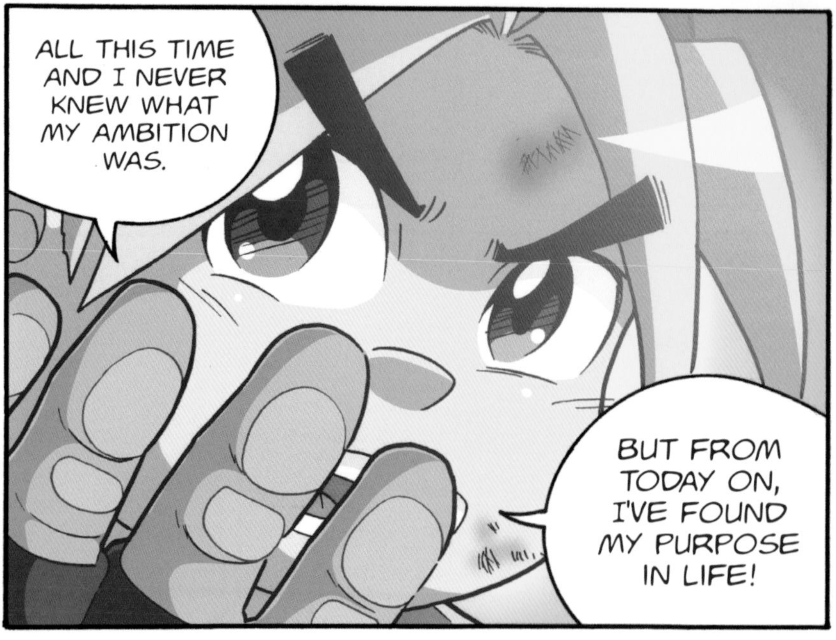
ALL THIS TIME AND I NEVER KNEW WHAT MY AMBITION WAS.
BUT FROM TODAY ON, I'VE FOUND MY PURPOSE IN LIFE!

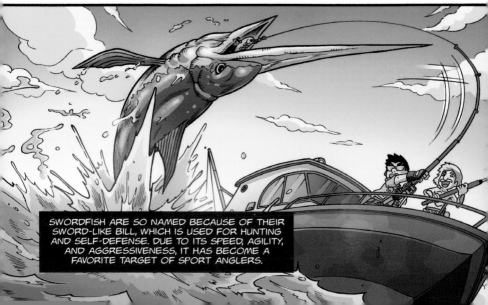

SWORDFISH ARE SO NAMED BECAUSE OF THEIR SWORD-LIKE BILL, WHICH IS USED FOR HUNTING AND SELF-DEFENSE. DUE TO ITS SPEED, AGILITY, AND AGGRESSIVENESS, IT HAS BECOME A FAVORITE TARGET OF SPORT ANGLERS.

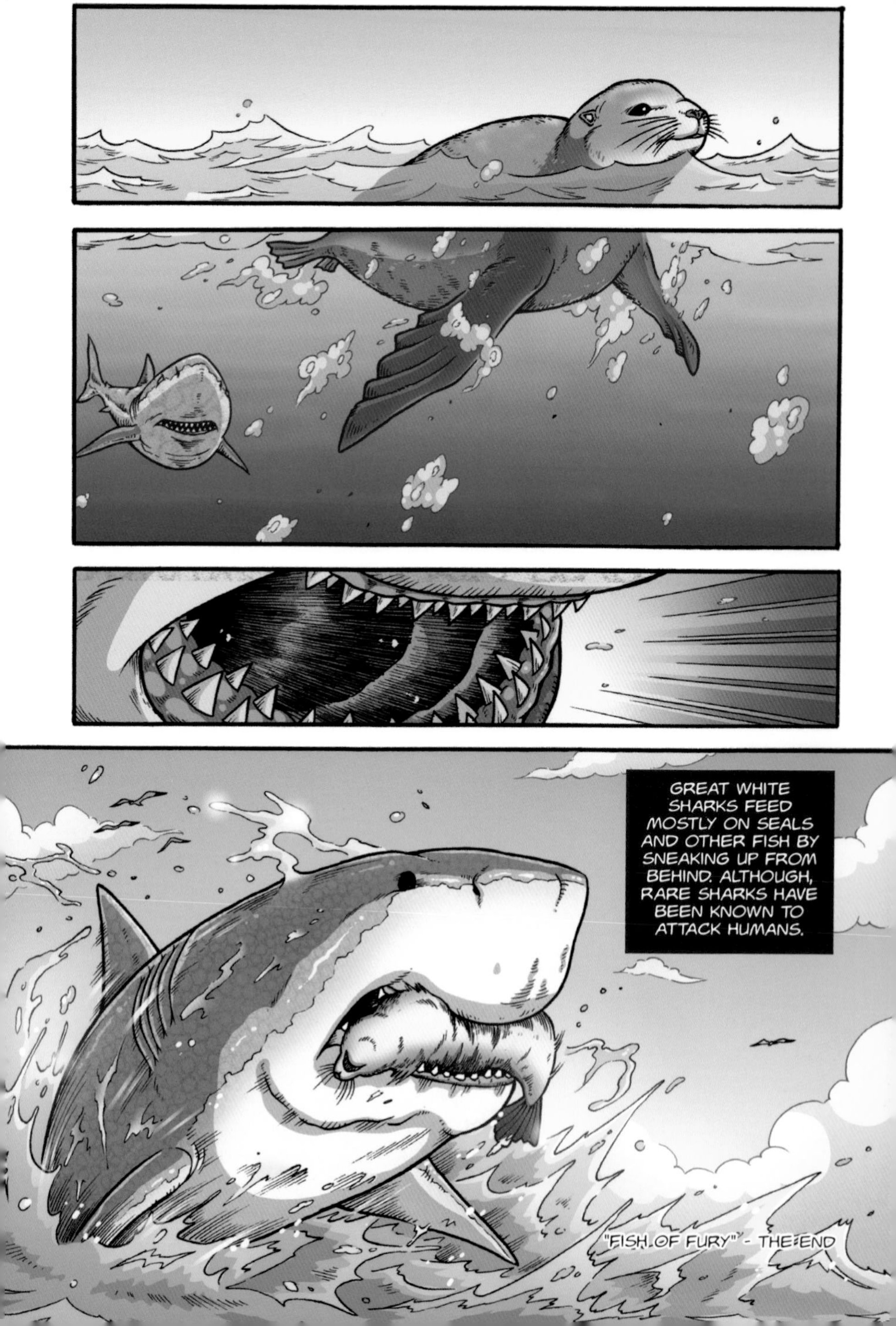
GREAT WHITE SHARKS FEED MOSTLY ON SEALS AND OTHER FISH BY SNEAKING UP FROM BEHIND. ALTHOUGH, RARE SHARKS HAVE BEEN KNOWN TO ATTACK HUMANS.
"FISH OF FURY" - THE END

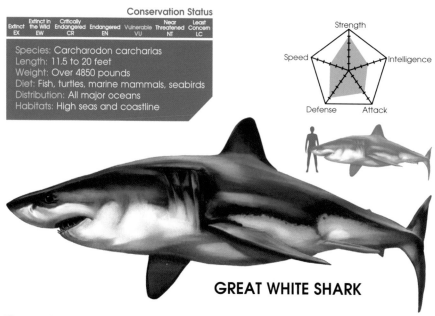

Conservation Status

Extinct EX	Extinct In the Wild EW	Critically Endangered CR	Endangered EN	Vulnerable VU	Near Threatened NT	Least Concern LC

Species: Carcharodon carcharias
Length: 11.5 to 20 feet
Weight: Over 4850 pounds
Diet: Fish, turtles, marine mammals, seabirds
Distribution: All major oceans
Habitats: High seas and coastline

Strength
Speed
Intelligence
Defense
Attack

GREAT WHITE SHARK

The great white shark is undoubtedly the most notorious and well known of all sharks, regularly labeled the culprit of intermittent attacks upon swimmers all over the world. This apex predator stalks its prey, possessing a keen sense of smell, good vision, and hearing, and armed with a formidable array of serrated razor-sharp teeth. Favoring stealth and obscurity, before launching a devastating strike, an experience that few of its victims ever survive. Its acute senses allow it to pinpoint subtle vibrations in the water, and the thinnest trace of blood, with special snout receptors able to detect minute disturbances to the aquatic electrical field caused by moving objects. A solitary animal, the great white invariably migrates thousands of miles as part of seasonal feeding or mating patterns. To remain active in chilly waters, it raises its body temperature around 25°F above that of the surrounding water.

How does the great white shark hunt?

Great whites normally hunt by sneaking up on its prey, maximizing the deadly effect of the first surprise attack. In the case of surface prey, great whites have been known to employ a tactic referred to as breaching, rising to the surface in a tremendous burst of velocity to seize unsuspecting prey in its terrible jaws.

Dorsal danger!

While on the prowl for prospective prey in the vicinity of the ocean surface, the telltale appearance of the shark's blade-shaped dorsal fin spells real and present danger, as anyone who has watched the movie "Jaws" will know. Preferring to take its prey unaware, the sudden disappearance of the dorsal fin can be read as a sign of imminent attack!

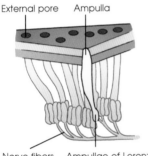

External pore   Ampulla

Nerve fibers   Ampullae of Lorenzini

Electromagnetic field detection

The great white and most other sharks have the ability to detect electromagnetic waves. It does this courtesy of the many external pores found upon its snout that are connected to special receptors called ampullae of Lorenzini, allowing it to pinpoint the location of prey by sensing the subtle fluctuations of localized aquatic electromagnetic fields as a result of movement.

Changing chompers

Due to the violent nature of catching prey and feeding, many of the shark's serrated teeth are often damaged or dislodged as a result. In order to retain their bite, sharks have many rows of teeth situated behind the front row, ready replacements in the case of damage or loss.

Do sharks attack humans?

The great white shark, like most sharks is curious by nature. To them, a swimmer represents prey just as much as any other marine creature would. Movement in the water, regardless of source, attracts a shark's interest. Struggling to free oneself from the jaws of death produces an instinctive reaction, biting, which, from jaws capable of producing a bite force of a whopping 4000 pounds per square inch, is almost always fatal!

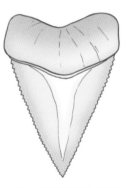

▲ Great White shark tooth

DID YOU KNOW?   The normally coastal great white sharks have been observed converging upon an area between Baja California and Hawaii dubbed the "White Shark Café" during winter and spring, possibly to mate.

TRAVEL BACK IN TIME WITH THE

DINOSAUR EXPLORERS™

Collect All The Action!

X-VENTURE XPLORERS™

DINOSAUR EXPLORERS #1
"PREHISTORIC PIONEERS"

DINOSAUR EXPLORERS #2
"PUTTERING IN THE PALEOZOIC"

DINOSAUR EXPLORERS #3
"PLAYING IN THE PERMIAN"

X-VENTURE XPLORERS #1
RAGE OF THE KINGS"

DINOSAUR EXPLORERS #4
"TRAPPED IN THE TRIASSIC"

DINOSAUR EXPLORERS #5
"LOST IN THE JURASSIC"

DINOSAUR EXPLORERS #6
"ESCAPING THE JURASSIC"

X-VENTURE XPLORERS #2
"CLASH OF THE TITANS"

DINOSAUR EXPLORERS #7
"CRETACEOUS CRAZINESS"

DINOSAUR EXPLORERS #8
"LORD OF THE SKIES"

DINOSAUR EXPLORERS #9
"KING OF THE SEAS"

X-VENTURE XPLORERS #3
"FISH OF FURY"

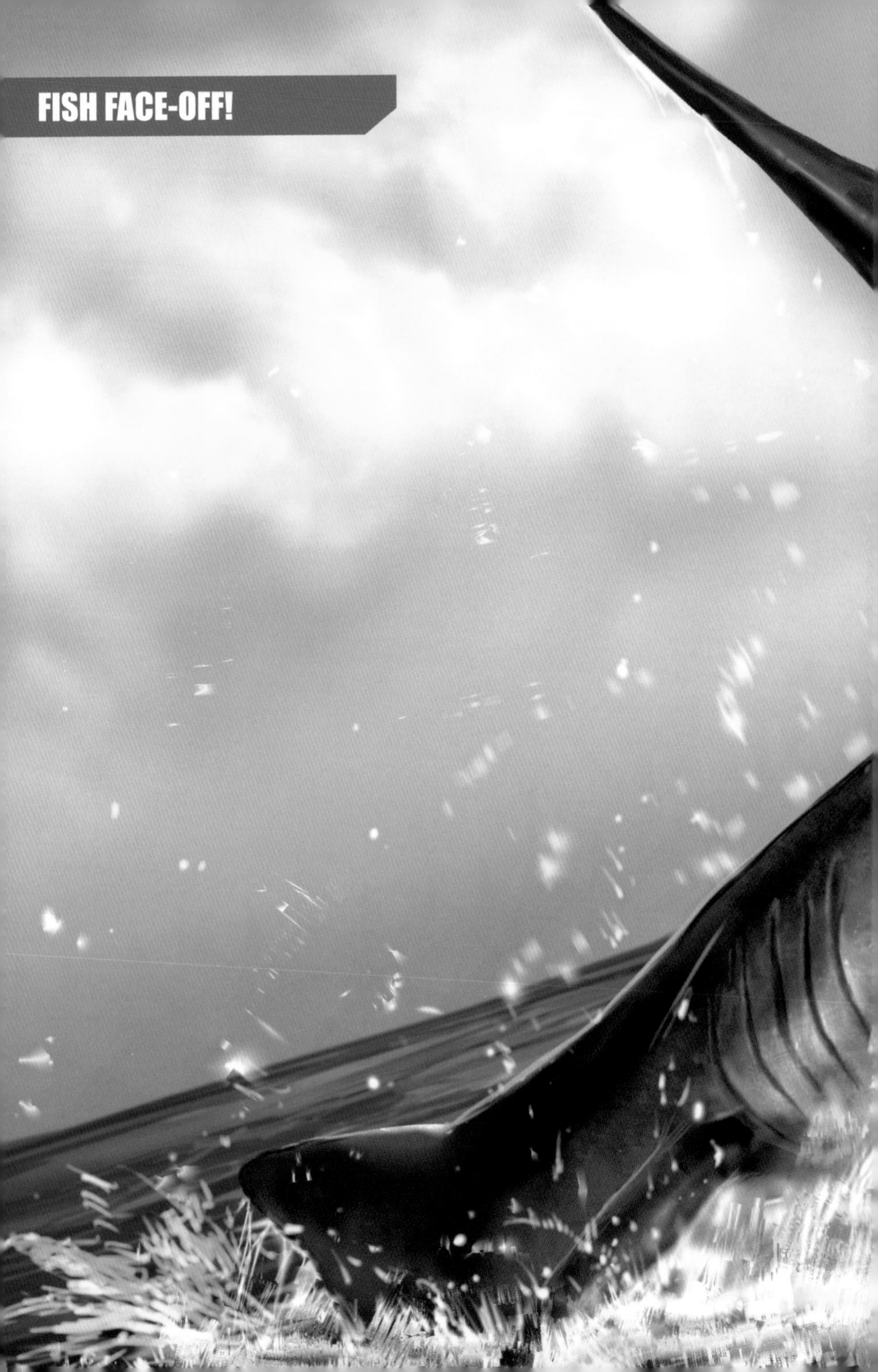

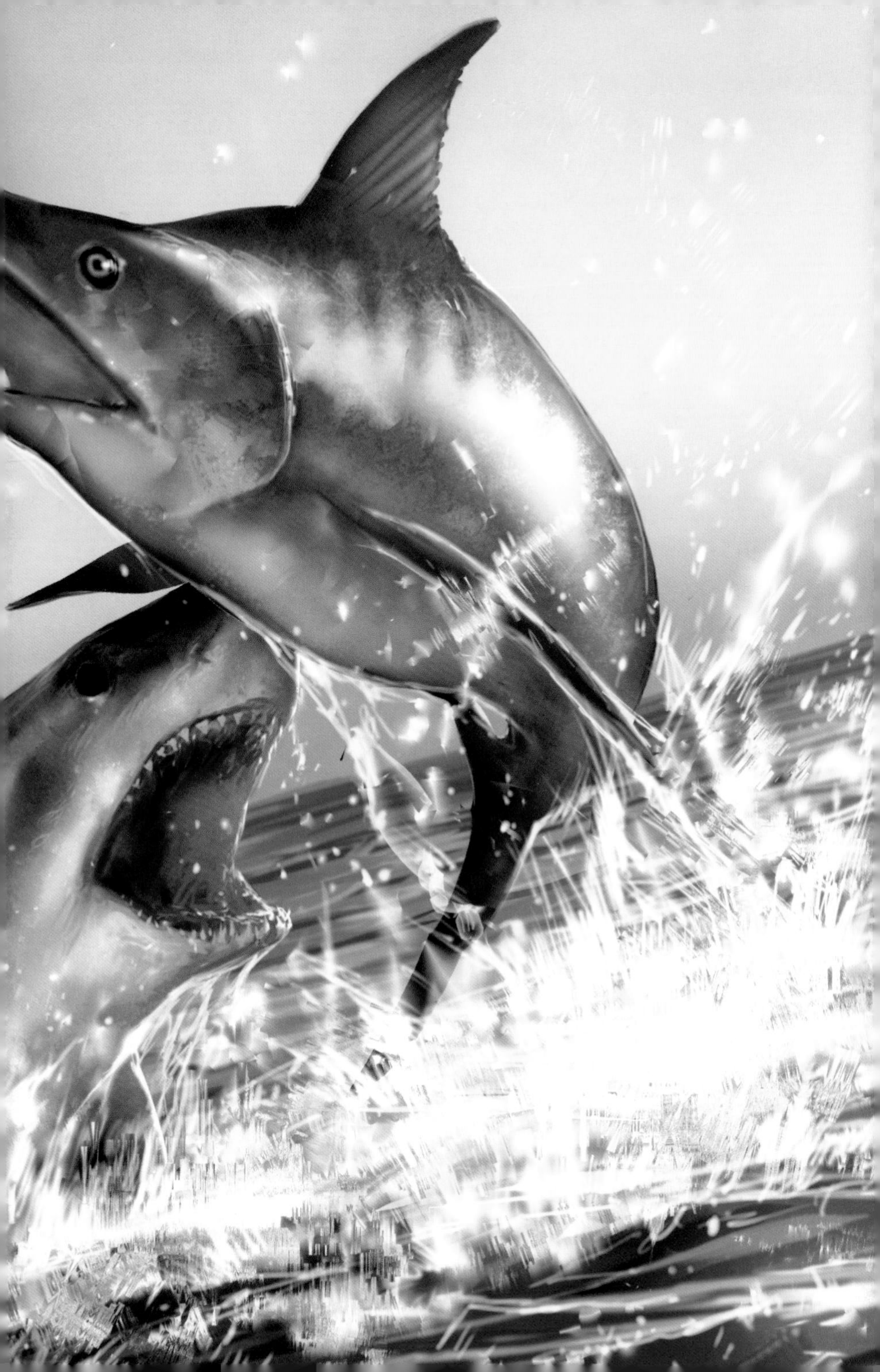

EXERCISE

01 **Which of the following creatures is not a fish?**

A. Sailfish **B.** Whale **C.** Shark

02 **Which of the following fish attaches itself to larger fish?**

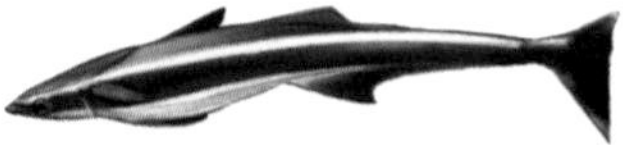

A. Live Sharksucker

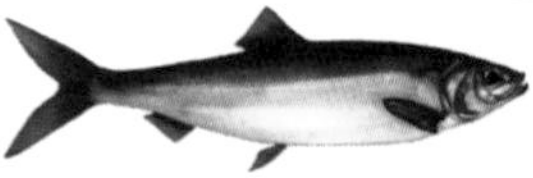

B. Atlantic herring

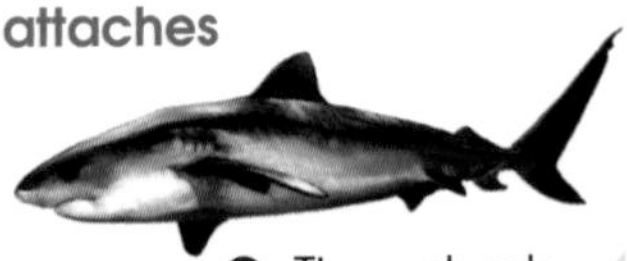

C. Tiger shark

03 **Other than skeletons, what differentiates bony fish from cartilaginous fish?**

A. Bony fish are omnivores; cartilaginous fish are carnivores

B. Bony fish have round, ctenoid or ganoid scales; cartilaginous fish have placoid scales

C. Bony fish prefer fresh water habitats; cartilaginous fish prefer salt water habitats

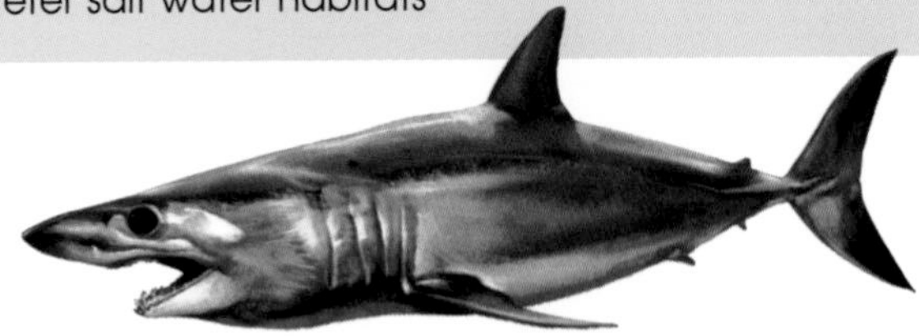

04 **The shortfin mako shark is a good swimmer that is able to reach speeds of up to ____ miles per hour.**

A. 40 **B.** 46 **C.** 52

05 **Why does a Cookiecutter shark swallow its old teeth?**

A. To provide it with extra nutrients

B. To recycle the calcium content for new teeth

C. To digest food

06 What is the function of the first dorsal fin (circled in red) of the Great White shark?

A. Attract prey   **B.** Attack prey   **C.** Maintain balance

07 When it locates prey, the Swordfish will likely _____.

A. Eat it immediately

B. Impale it with its bill and eat it

C. Injure it with its bill and eat it

08 Which of the following sharks has poisonous flesh?

C. Greenland shark

B. Oceanic Whitetip shark

A. Basking shark

09 How does the ampullae of Lorenzini help Great White sharks locate its prey?

A. By detecting the change in aquatic electromagnetic field produced by moving prey

B. By detecting the change of light produced by moving prey

C. By detecting the change of sound waves produced by moving prey

10 The largest and the second largest fish on earth are the _____ and the _____.

A. Whale shark; Basking shark

B. Whale shark; Great White shark

C. Great White shark; Basking shark

ANSWERS

HERE YOU GO...

01B 02A 03B 04B 05B
06C 07C 08C 09A 10A

PERFECT 10!

I'm not a born genius, it's just that I do a lot of reading in my free time!

SCORED 8 TO 9

To achieve my ambition, I must try harder!

SCORED 6 TO 7

Seeing animals in action in their natural habitat is much more interesting than researching sterile facts!

SCORED 4 TO 5

Sometimes I... find difficult... to speak what... I know, but... I will not give up!

SCORED 2 TO 3

Huh? B-but I love observing animals! This must change!

SCORED 0 TO 1

What?! Jake is smarter than me? No way!!

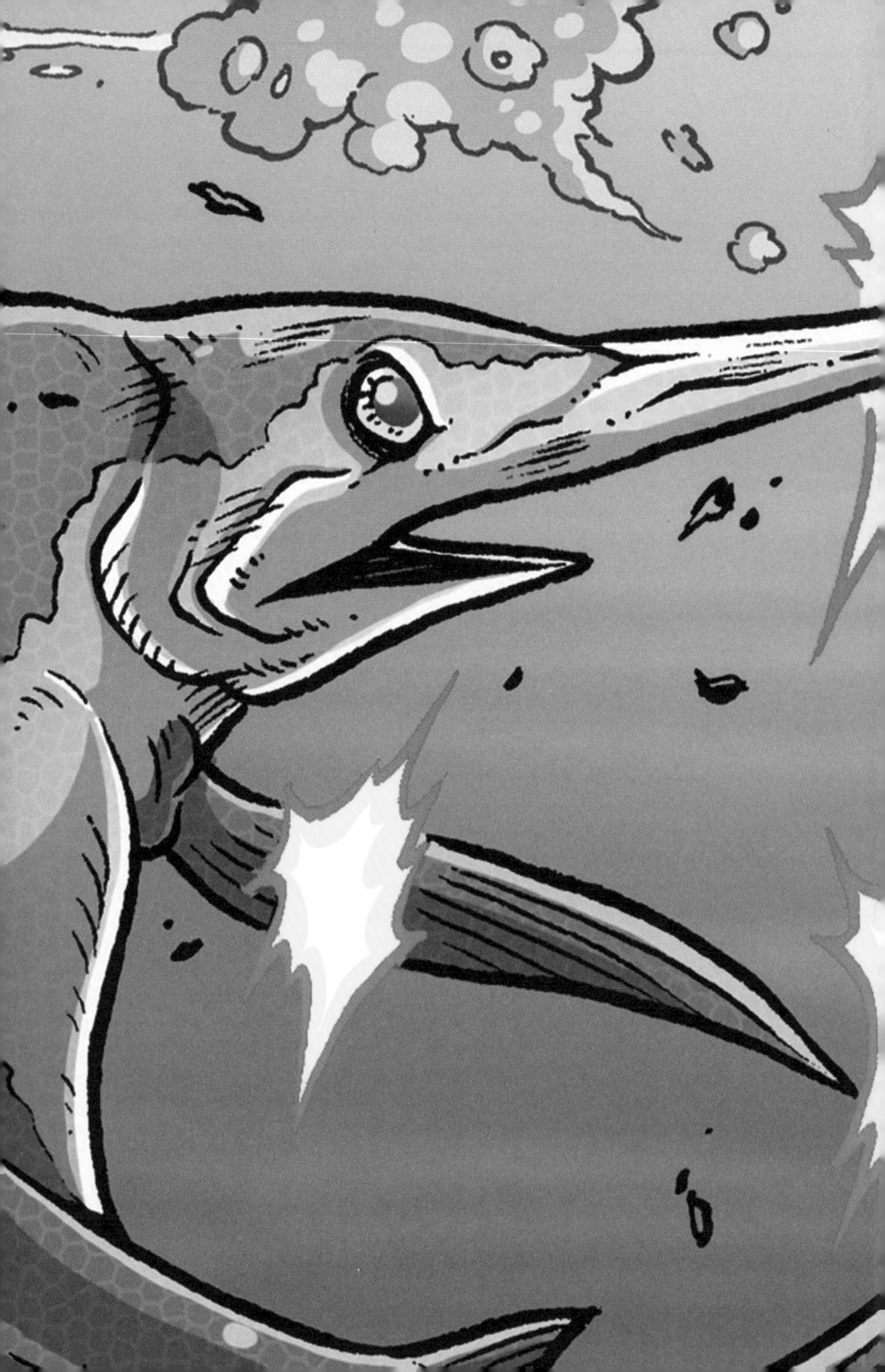